BY COMMAND OF THE KING;

OR,

𝔗𝔥𝔢 𝔇𝔞𝔶𝔰 𝔬𝔣 𝔱𝔥𝔢 𝔐𝔢𝔯𝔯𝔦𝔢 𝔐𝔬𝔫𝔞𝔯𝔠𝔥.

COMPLETE.

BEAUTIFULLY ILLUSTRATED.

LONDON:

"BOYS OF ENGLAND" OFFICE, 173, FLEET STREET, E.C.,

AND ALL BOOKSELLERS,

BY COMMAND OF THE KING;

OR,

THE DAYS OF THE MERRIE MONARCH.

"'COWARDS, RETURN MY CHILD—RETURN HIM, I SAY!' CRIED SIR HAROLD."

No. 1

BY COMMAND OF THE KING;

OR,

THE DAYS OF THE MERRIE MONARCH.

An Historical Romance.

By the Author of " Dark Deeds of Old London," " Traitors' Gate"
&c., &c., &c.

CHAPTER I.

AT THE SIGN OF THE " SILVER FLAGON."

WHAT had been a day of terrible storm was drawing to a close.

The streets of London, covered as they were with a thick layer of crisp white snow, were deserted, save for a few riotous gallants, who, defying the weather, went along arm-in-arm, singing any ribald songs they happened to think of, and disturbing the sleep of peaceful citizens.

The great and solemn-toned bell of Old St. Paul's had struck eleven, when a horseman rode slowly under Temple Bar into Fleet Street.

He was a big, burly, muscular man, with coarse vulgar features—features which at once proclaimed him to be a man much given to imbibing copious draughts of canary and the like.

He was well wrapped up, wearing as he did a long thick cloak and comforter, as well as a huge beaver hat, which he had drawn well over his eyes, as much to conceal his features as to keep out the piercing wind which pelted clouds of snow into his face, and caused him to utter more than one bitter curse, probably at his ill-luck in having to travel on such a night.

At length he reached the entrance to Whitefriars, and he was there suddenly confronted by a tall, bony man, who in an authoritative voice cried out—

"What ho, captain! Who art thou?"

"Mind thy business. thou lazy rascal," replied the horseman, "and let me pass."

"Lazy forsooth! Thou art indeed bold of speech, good lack! What art thou? A bailiff? And who is thy warrant for?"

"My warrant is for thee, Bodkin. And if thou dost not get out of the way I will deliver it upon thy thick skull."

And so saying, the horseman pushed his hat off his brow.

"By our Lady," quoth the man, "an I knew it was thee, I would not have stood in thy path, but would have craved a gold piece from your noble majesty."

This the man said in ironical tones, but they were unheeded by the horseman.

"Take thy gold piece," he said, as he flung the man a coin; "so now thou canst go and guzzle until thou art black in the face, or save it to buy a small mass for thy dirty soul. And now take thyself from my way."

This the man instantly did, diving after the coin with great eagerness, and pouring out his thanks with great profuseness.

The horseman, muttering his disgust

at the spareness of the man's body, resumed his journey, and before long stopped in front of a tavern, the rickety sign of which, swaying backwards and forwards with dismal groans, bore upon it the words: "The Silver Flagon," and underneath this intimation—

" Here's food for man, and food for beast,
    Here's plenty of meat and plenty of hay,
A jolly good bed—that's saying the least—
Good things by the load, and little to pay."

Here the horseman stopped, and in loud tones called for the host.

But in consequence of the terrific row caused by the revellers, he was not heard for some few moments, during which he heaped all sorts of imprecations upon the host and his brawling customers.

At last the horseman's voice—no mean one—reached the ears of the host, and he immediately came forth with many apologies if he had "kept his honour waiting long."

"Thou hast kept me waiting long," said the horseman, in angry tones. "Is thy pocket so full that thou canst afford to trifle with thy best customers?"

" Odd's life!" cried the landlord, with a start of surprise. "Colonel Blood!"

"Ay, Colonel Blood it is, thou varlet, and thou wilt feel the weight of this pistol-butt if thou dost not attend to me at once."

And Colonel Blood touched the butt-end of one of his pistols, which were stuck in a ready manner under his huge cloak.

"Is that lying knave of a Varney within?" asked Blood, as he swung himself off his horse and handed the reins to the host.

"Ay. He said that he expected thee, and, for what I know, is at this moment enjoying himself at thy expense."

"At my expense?"

"Ay, marry he is. He said thou didst owe him money for work done."

"By our Lady, he hath the impudence of the devil himself. But are there many within?"

"Ay, some two score. Good bloods, too, colonel, by my faith, as thou wilt see. There are some gallants whom you will recognise as belonging to Charles's court, and—"

"Speak not disrespectfully of his Majesty," said Blood, with affected sternness. "Knowest thou not that I am in his service?"

"Ay, that do I, and I crave thy pardon, worthy Master Blood," replied the host, humbly.

Then he muttered—

"Service of the king—zooks! Fine service, I trow me. Kidnapping, throat-cutting, and the like. The Lord defend us!"

"What art thou muttering about, thou over-fed fool?" growled Blood, as he fumbled under his saddle for some papers. "Take my horse to thy stable, and give him a good feed of thy boasted hay. Order thy man to clean him well, and to have him saddled and bridled again within two hours. Hast thou a spare horse?"

"Ay, good Master Blood, a fast stepper that was—"

"Stolen, no doubt."

"Nay, that was found astray," said the host, with a hideous grin on his bloated face.

"Strayed or stolen matters not to me," said Blood, "so that he is a fast-goer."

"He is that, I'll warrant me."

"Good. Then order him to be ready with mine."

And so saying, Blood strode majestically into the tavern, his huge spurs clanking merrily on the red bricks that paved the entrance.

At the time of our story, "The Silver Flagon" was one of the most notorious hostelries in Whitefriars, or Alsatia, as it was then called.

Here, night and day, congregated some of the biggest ruffians that ever trod the earth.

Men, and women too, who obtained money by every species of loathsome villainy, and then squandered it in riotous debauchery.

Their motto was, " Eat, drink, and be merry to-day, for to-morrow ye die."

And eat, drink, and be merry they did with a vengeance, much to the satisfaction of worthy—or unworthy—Tony Swill, the host, who was putting away many hundreds of golden pieces, which, if he were not careful, would one day be stolen by his customers.

The swashbucklers of Alsatia were

invariably joined in their riotous orgies by many court gallants of the highest rank, who, for the time being, put aside their court manners, and joined heart and soul in howling the choruses of indecent songs, and drinking until they made themselves more like devils than men.

It often occurred that a terrible quarrel took place, and then swords, daggers and pistols were brought into requisition with terrible effect.

Men's blood in those days was held very cheaply, and it rarely occurred that a murderer was brought to justice.

As Blood entered the principal room, in which were about forty or fifty men and women sitting in various attitudes, he was greeted with a shout of welcome, and a voice, made thick with deep potations of strong drink, called out—

"What ho, Blood! Right welcome, my gallant cut-throat, to this our den of right royal infamy!"

"Keep thy observations to thyself, Master Fool," growled Blood, as he threw off his hat and flung himself on a stool, which had been placed for his use by a young, pretty, albeit drunken woman near him, " or, mayhap, if I slit thy tongue thou wilt not prate so well."

At these words the man who had spoken burst into a loud laugh, in which he was not joined by the others present, who knew Blood's fearful temper too well to play with it.

"Art thou laughing at me?" asked Blood, who left his stool and walked deliberately up to the jester.

"Ay, marry am I! Methought there was but one Blood in the world, and a good Blood too—with the pistol or dagger in the dark, ha, ha!"

Blood stood erect, and glared fiercely into the face of the daring speaker.

Suddenly he started, and turned rather pale.

Then he said, in an undertone—

"I crave thy pardon, my lord. I recognised not thy voice."

"Nay? And yet mine is not so melodious, is it, good Blood? Not near so melodious as that of pretty Mistress Gwynne, eh?"

"Your lordship sayest right," replied Blood. "For, by my troth, it would puzzle the gentleman with the club-foot himself to discover a sweeter voice than Nell's. But I ask thee, my lord, not to rave out my name. It doeth me no good, and would lower me in the opinions of these present."

"Sayest thou so? Then I will call out thy name no more. But, good Master Blood, hast thou seen aught of pretty Nell?"

"Nay, not these two nights. But, prithee, hast thou seen aught of Varney?"

"Varney? I know him not."

"Not know him, my lord?" grinned Blood. "Seeing that he is one of my assistants, and that he hath lent me a helping hand when I have been on thy business, thou shouldst know him."

"Ah! by my faith, I now know the man. One of thy roaring blades, eh, Blood? Well, I wonder much that thou shouldst have overlooked him. Yonder he is."

And the speaker—none other than Lord Grafton, called in Alsatia "one of his Majesty's drunken ones," from the fact that he was continually in liquor—pointed to a long, low stool near the fireplace, along which lay the form of the man Blood sought, and who was known among his associates as Varney.

He was a man standing very near six feet in height, and although not very stout, he was a remarkably muscular man.

His face, if anything, was more hideous than Blood's; it was fearfully repulsive.

"The idiot is drunk, I'll warrant me," muttered Blood, as he walked towards him. "And if he be so, I have a splendid chance."

Taking one of the pistols from his belt, he took hold of the muzzle and dealt the sleeper a terrific clout with the butt-end on his chest.

This had a marvellous effect.

The sleeper started up like lightning, and his hand was instantly upon the hilt of his long sword.

All in the filthy den uttered cries of delight.

"Here's to thy health, Sir Snorer," cried one buxom wench, as she seized a ruffian's bowl of punch and held it aloft, "and may thou look as pretty in thy coffin as thou dost in thy sleep."

Varney took no notice of this.

Rubbing his eyes, he growled—

"May all the fiends incarnate seize upon thee for a lumbering dotard!"

"Silence!" cried Blood.

"Oh! it's Colonel Blood, is it?" cried Varney. "By my faith, I'm glad of it. My thirst drove me to sleep."

"As it will to hades," said Blood. "But it is good I found thee not drunk, or thou wouldst have fared badly. Come aside. I wouldst speak quietly with thee. Dost thou feel fit for business?"

"Ay, fit and fresh."

"Good. Let me whisper to thee."

And whisper Blood did, and for some considerable time.

And it was evident, from the amount of attention Varney paid to what he said, that it was something of vast importance.

"And what is to be my reward?" asked Varney, when Blood had concluded.

"A hundred crowns. Will that satisfy thee?"

"Right well, an I get some before starting."

"Thou shalt have half now."

And from his doublet Blood took out a leathern bag, which he handed to Varney, who immediately took out one of the pieces and shouted to the host to bring him a full bowl of his best.

For about two hours Blood and Varney stayed in the room, enjoying themselves in their own true style; but when the fun went down, and the revellers lay snoring in different parts of the room, they quietly left.

The host had brought round the horses, and impressing upon Blood the necessity of being careful of his horse and to return it safely, the two set out.

"The snow will hinder us to a great extent," said Blood, "but, the Virgin be thanked, it has ceased descending. I would the moon were not so bright, though."

"Nay, a bright moon is ill fitted for a dark night's work," said Varney.

CHAPTER II.

SIR HAROLD HARCOURT AND HIS SON—THE ROBBERY AND ABDUCTION, AND MURDER OF SIR HAROLD.

SIR HAROLD HARCOURT was one of the true specimens of the old English nobility.

He was a man who meddled but little with political affairs, preferring the seclusion of his own stately mansion in Bloomsbury, or his magnificent park near Epping Forest, to the riot and debauchery of Charles's court.

He was no lover of royalty, albeit he had taken the side of the Royalists against the Roundheads, and had been one of the principals in placing Charles II. upon the throne.

His riches were stated to be fabulous, and for that reason he could, had he so chosen, have been one of the most favoured of courtiers.

He married, at the age of forty, Edith, only daughter of Sir Wendle Barrett, but she died in giving birth to a son, the hero of this story, and who was christened after his father.

People said that his wife's death had caused Sir Harold to seclude himself, and no doubt, considering that Sir Harold loved his wife as never man loved a woman, there was some truth in it.

But it was not all true.

By no means.

The true reason was this.

Sir Harold had a cousin in the person of John Humphreys, and did he, Sir Harold, die childless, the title and estates would revert to his cousin.

Now Sir Harold was not on good terms with his cousin, not even on speaking terms.

Sir Harold knew too much of him to trust him in anything.

He knew him to be an unscrupulous villain, who would stop at nothing to gain his own ends.

It was only natural, therefore, that Sir Harold took good care to keep his son out of the clutches of John Humphreys.

He strongly suspected that, if he had the chance, Humphreys would seize upon the child, and no doubt make away with him.

He knew very well that his cousin was mixed up with plenty of ruffians, who, for a consideration, would be only too ready to assist him.

Sir Harold's servants had more than once hinted that John Humphreys was plotting to get possession of the child, and although he pooh-poohed the idea before their faces, he did not behind their backs.

He was quite certain that such was the case.

At the time we introduce Sir Harold to the notice of the reader, his son had just turned his fifth birthday, and, for his age, was a fine, tall, handsome child, bidding fair to become in all respects as strong and as fine a man as his father.

But we must now return to Colonel Blood and his villainous associate.

For some few minutes they rode along Whitefriars, and when before a tumble-down, singularly-constructed wooden house, which seemed to over-hang the river, Blood paused and uttered a low whistle.

"The Jew will be asleep," said Varney.

"Not he. It would fare ill with him did he keep me waiting here long," replied Blood. "Our attire is by this time ready to don."

In less than a minute the door of the house slowly opened, and the head of a man was cautiously thrust forth.

It was easy to see by his nose, which in shape resembled the beak of a vulture, that he was of the Jewish persuasion.

"All is ready, my gallants," he said, in harsh, grating tones, as he rubbed his hands and his rat-like eyes twinkled with glee, or more likely with greed.

Blood and Varney swung themselves on their horses and entered.

"Keep thy trap open," said Blood to the Jew, "lest some drunken brawler take a fancy to our steeds. Now, where are thy clothes?"

The Jew pointed to two elaborate suits on the sideboard.

"Goot suits, gentlemen," he said. "Everything there. Put 'em on, and ye'll then be gentlemen of the King's Guard at once."

Blood looked upon the suits, and examined them attentively.

"Where didst thou get these, Jew?" he asked.

"I bought them for a round sum of the officers to whom they—"

"Thou liest, Jew," said Blood, fiercely. "Thou art indeed a terrible liar. And mark ye well, one of these days thy lying tongue will get thee sent to Tyburn, so keep thine eyes open. If these suits were bought of the officers to whom they belonged, how comes it that new patches have been placed here and here"—and Blood took one of the jackets and held it under the Jew's nose—"where, I doubt not, blood has trickled down by murder."

Varney burst into laughter so loud that it caused the dirty little oil lamps to quiver.

"Ah! good Master Blood," whined the Jew, as he washed his hands in imaginary soap, "thine eyes require not spectacles. But it matters not to thee from whence they came, so that they fit well."

"Nay, for once thou speakest truth. But lie not to me, good Jew, or thou'll rue it."

In a few minutes Blood and Varney had donned the suits, and then they looked captains of the King's Guard.

"By our Lady!" quoth Varney, as he strutted along after the manner of a peacock. "Methinks I look every inch—"

"A bigger cut-throat than ever," interrupted Blood. "But come on, or morning will dawn ere we reach our destination."

"Hast thou far to go, colonel?" asked the Jew.

"Mind thine own business and our good clothes," replied Blood, "or thou'll be paid nought for thy trouble."

In a few more minutes Blood and Varney were again in the saddle, and putting spurs to their horses, they went along at a good pace in the direction of Bloomsbury.

They met with no obstruction, and arriving in front of Sir Harold Harcourt's stately residence, and which was called "Harcourt House," they stopped and dismounted.

Blood walked deliberately up the broad steps, which were covered with a thick layer of snow, and knocked gently at the massive door.

The wicket was drawn aside, and a voice said—

"What would ye, my masters? Dost thou know the house at which thou knockest? Away with ye! This is no house for drunken gallants."

"We well know it, companion," replied Blood. "This is the house belonging to Sir Harold Harcourt, whom we wish to see."

"Then if thou dost wish to see my master, prithee come in decent hours."

"We are here By Command of the King, so dally not, but open the door at once."

"By command of the king?" replied the servant. "And at this hour? Thou art jesting!"

"Officers of the King's Guard do not jest. Open in the king's name!"

The door was slowly thrown back, and before the servant, an elderly man, could utter another word, Varney was upon him.

Seizing him by the throat, he brought him to the ground, and Blood in an instant had gagged and bound him hand and foot.

"Attempt to free thyself," he said, "and thou art a dead man. Follow, Varney."

Blood and Varney each took a black mask from his pocket, and having adjusted them, Blood ascended the broad marble staircase, followed by Varney.

On the first floor Blood halted.

"I have been here but once," he whispered, "but methinks I know the room. On thy life make no noise."

"Fear not; I am as silent as the grave."

One door after another did Blood peer through, and at last he saw what he wanted.

"The child is here," he said, pointing to one of the rooms, "and both he and his nurse sleep soundly. Stay you here until I return."

Up the next flight went Blood, swiftly yet silently, and tried the handle of one of the doors.

But it yielded not.

It was fast locked.

"Now, may all fiends incarnate seize him!" muttered Blood. "An I get not the papers, methinks I shall fare but badly with John Humphreys. A light burns within. S'life! I trust he sleeps soundly; but it would be dangerous to try the door. Ha!" he exclaimed, in an undertone, as his eye fell upon a window by the side of the door.

It was just about large enough to admit of the passage of a man's body.

Blood caught hold of the small knob, pulled it cautiously, and the window flew open.

He then brought one of the small side tables, and placed it under the window.

Then he unbuckled his sword, for that would have prevented his admittance, and laying that upon it mounted the table and glided gently in.

"Master Humphreys said that he used to keep his papers in his bedroom, but, by our Lady! he may have placed them in another; or he may have handed them, for security's sake, to one of the goldsmiths," he thought.

But here his eyes fell upon the bed upon which lay Sir Harold, the expression upon his face denoting that he slept soundly.

Close by the bed was a small cabinet of curious and elaborate workmanship. To this went Blood. He examined it attentively, feeling about on all sides for some opening.

But none met his hands.

Directly in front was evidently the opening, however, and Blood, taking out his dagger, a powerful weapon, began to prise it open.

Of course, he had to go very carefully to work, for the slightest noise might awaken Sir Harold, and then everything would be lost.

All round the cabinet he went, and at length a slight, almost imperceptible "click" was heard, and the cabinet lay open.

With feverish haste Blood dipped his hands in, scattering the papers to the right and the left in dire confusion.

"A leathern case, bearing his name in gold letters," he thought. "I see it not. Gad's life! John Humphreys may be mistaken."

But although the leathern case Blood wanted so particularly did not come immediately to his hand, many other things did.

There was a small oaken box, bound with gold, and Blood knew, not only from its weight, but also by its appearance, that it was a jewel case.

To place this in his doublet was but the work of a moment.

" It all helps to swell thy purse, my gallant colonel," he chuckled. "But where is the case? Ha! we have it!"

And he brought forth a leathern case, upon which was the name, in gold letters—

"Sir Harold Harcourt, Baronet."

This he also pocketed, and leaving the other papers as they were, he returned to the window, wriggled his body through, and alighted in safety on the other side.

Buckling on his sword, he descended the stairs.

He found Varney still at his post, but evidently getting impatient.

" Hast thou tried the door?" asked Blood.

"Nay; thou didst not so direct me."

"Thou fool! Hast thou sold thy brains? Move thy ugly body aside."

Varney did so, and Blood gently turned the handle.

The door opened immediately, and Blood entered the room, followed by Varney.

A small wax taper was burning upon the mantelpiece in front of a small crucifix, and it threw sufficient light about the apartment to show Blood that the nurse slept soundly.

By the side of her bed was a little cot, its occupant being the son of Sir Harold Harcourt, and sole heir to all the vast Harcourt estates.

Blood looked round, and seeing a cloak hanging up, took it down, and motioned to Varney to hold it open.

Then he gently turned down the bedclothes, and raised the sleeping child in his arms.

But Blood's hands were not used to the handling of a child, and he nearly let it drop before he placed it under the cloak.

The rough usage caused the child to awake, and it immediately began to cry out—

"Nurse! nurse!"

"Hurry away with him, thou gaping idiot!" hissed Blood. "See you not that the nurse moves? Ha! she awakes. Away!"

Yes; the nurse did awake. For an instant she looked at the intruders in a stupefied, startled fashion; and then she jumped from her bed, and endeavoured to seize hold of Blood as he left the room.

But she was too late.

Blood pushed Varney, who had the child huddled closely to him, outside the door, and then pulled it to with a bang that caused the pictures on the walls and the armoured knights in the hall to tremble and send forth clouds of dust.

"Help!" shrieked the nurse. "Help! Mercy!"

And with her clenched fist she hammered at the door until her knuckles ran with blood.

Sir Harold heard these frantic cries, and he leapt from his bed.

Instantly his eyes fell upon the mass of papers which were scattered upon the floor.

Like a flash of lightning ran the thought through his mind—

"Thieves, maybe murderers were in the house. Was his son safe?"

To partially dress himself was but the work of a few seconds; then, seizing his sword, he tore it from its scabbard, and ran down the stairs like a madman.

By this time the nurse had contrived to pull the door open. But she was quite speechless.

As Sir Harold confronted her, she pointed helplessly at the hall door, which was wide open, allowing the snow to drift in.

His eyes fell upon his servant, lying bound hand and foot upon the threshold.

With a fierce rush, Sir Harold was at the door.

Blood was just in the act of assisting Varney to the saddle with the child, when he heard Sir Harold's hasty footsteps.

" By our Lady!" he cried, "the fool hath awoke, and would slay us."

"Cowards! murderers!" cried Sir Harold, as he caught sight of his son and heard his voice. "Return my child! return him, I say, or—"

"Stand back, fool!" cried Blood, as, with a swift flourish, he drew his sword, "or thy blood be upon thine own head!"

"My child, my child!" cried Sir Harold, making a wild lunge at Blood.

"Is safe in our custody," replied Blood, as he warded off the lunge.

"I see! 'Tis the work of John Humphreys, for which he shall pay dearly. His Majesty shall hear of it. My child! I say. My child, or I will have your life!"

And, worked up to a pitch of fury, Sir Harold made a furious onslaught upon Blood, who soon found that he had a skilful swordsman to deal with.

He would have drawn his pistol and have shot his assailant down, but Sir Harold's passes were so swift and furious that he had no chance.

"Draw, Varney," shouted Blood, "and hew the fool down!"

Varney required no second bidding. His sword instantly flew from its scabbard, and, with little Harold in his left arm, the coward advanced to the attack.

Poor little Harold! His screams were terrible as he saw his father fighting fiercely to get possession of him, and his little hands tugged at Varney's moustachios with such fury that the villain swore he would dash him to the ground if he were not quiet.

Suddenly Sir Harold made a feint, darted forward, and snatched the mask from Blood's face.

"Heavens," he cried; "the villain Blood!"

As he uttered these words he started back in astonishment, and, his foot knocking against the lower step, he stumbled.

"Thou art right," said Blood, who instantly took advantage of this, "and the knowledge has cost thee thy life."

Varney knocked Sir Harold's sword aside. Blood drew his arm back, and the next instant his sword had passed clean through Sir Harold's body.

"Thy will be done!" moaned Sir Harold, as he sank down across the steps amid the fearful shrieks of his child, his life's blood trickling down and making little red channels in the snow. "Heaven in its own good time will avenge me. Farewell, my son, farewell!" he moaned, as he saw his son placed before Varney on the horse. "Would that I could kiss and bless thee ere I die!"

"Now for Plumstead," cried Blood, as he mounted his horse. "Away for thy life!"

The nurse caught the name of Plumstead as she came forward; but it was forgotten for the moment as she saw her master lying upon the snow, his life fast ebbing away.

Throwing herself by his side, she burst into a passionate flood of tears.

"Weep not, nurse," gasped Sir Harold, "weep not. It is the will of heaven. Stoop—stoop—nearer—nearer—listen. Promise me that you will try to find my child—they may not kill him. I can—trust—you—promise!"

"I promise," sobbed the nurse; "I swear it!"

"I have no friends to whom thou canst fly for assistance—yet—yes, there is one—one whom thou didst nurse when he was sorely wounded. He will assist thee—he—"

Here Sir Harold paused.

"His name—his name—speak," cried the nurse.

"His name is—you know—he is— oh, heaven!—the light fades—my memory is— Oh! grant me one moment!"

"His name!" almost shrieked the nurse.

Sir Harold raised his head. The blood was oozing from his mouth, but, making a frantic effort, he cried—

"Claude Duval!"

As Sir Harold gasped out this name he fell back dead.

CHAPTER III.

AT THE "LOAD OF MISCHIEF"—THE NURSE'S VISIT AND DUVAL'S RESOLVE.

PLUMSTEAD is now a flourishing town, containing a population of about twenty-six thousand, but at the time of our story it was a straggling, marshy village, with not more than a couple of hundred inhabitants, whose means of subsistence was a mystery to all but themselves.

There were two or three inns which did a flourishing trade with travellers, but the "Load of Mischief" was the principal house, and did the most business.

Why it was called the "Load of Mischief" no one knew, but it is a certain fact that on more than one night in the week it held many loads of mischief.

Three days after the incidents we have described in the foregoing chapter, the kitchen of the "Load of Mischief," a fine, lofty apartment, with a fireplace large enough to admit of three or four men standing upright, was occupied by half-a-dozen men attired in what may be described as half-soldierly, half-courtier-like dresses.

The gold and silver braid upon their breasts, doublets and trunks was partially concealed by the heavy and splendid cloaks they wore, as were also the silver-mounted pistols they carried in their belts.

Each man was also armed with a long sword of powerful make, and not at all resembling the rapiers worn at Court, and which in nine cases out of ten would snap if brought into action.

Each man wore also long jack boots of French kid, which fitted perfectly, and the heels of which were ornamented with bright steel spurs, made for hard wear.

It was a terrible night, for it had been snowing for several days, and the roads and the fields, almost impassable, were covered with snow many inches in depth. The wind howled and shrieked, and shook the windows and doors of the old inn with terrific violence.

"By my faith!" said one of the men, as he dragged his stool nearer the blazing log, "this is no night for staying in

front of the fire. Ugh! 'tis cold even here. And the holy Virgin protect us! where is our good captain?"

"Mayhap not left London. Odd's life! I would not travel on such a night for a purse of— Hark!"

Every man started to his feet as the loud clanking of spurs was heard without, and a cheery voice shouted—

"Well, landlord, how fares it with thee and thy good dame? Are my men within? But I doubt it not— travellers are not on the road on such a night as this."

"The captain," cried the men, as if with one voice, "hurrah!"

Suddenly the door was pushed open, and a man, standing about six feet in height, and stout and muscular in proportion, entered.

He had thrown back his long cloak, revealing a fine black velvet doublet, white kerseymere breeches, trimmed with silver, and long jack boots. Upon his breast was a silver star of large size, artistically shaped, and having at its centre a single diamond of superb brilliancy.

His headgear consisted of a broad black hat with a single ostrich plume.

"Well, my young gallants," he cried, as he flung his hat upon the table and shook hands all round, "and how fares it with ye all?"

"Right well, gallant," answered one of the men, "and we see that it also fares well with thee, for thy smile is as good as when we parted with thee three days ago."

"Thou art right. Smiles make one grow fat and keep merry, and, by our Lady, it would take a lot to make Claude Duval look serious—or I should say, miserable. And yet, my friends, I have something on my mind which should make me serious if not melancholy, but it is naught that concerns you. Yet methinks ere long I may call upon you to do me a service, and I know that, did I ask you, all would be ready and willing to draw swords to defend the weak against the strong."

With a swift movement they drew their swords, and raising them aloft, surrounded their captain.

"Sheathe thy swords," said Duval, "and listen to me, for I have a melancholy story to tell you, but— Pah! no, I will not—the time will come for that. I am nervous, and unbidden tears well into mine eyes. Gentlemen, your very good healths, gold to our treasury, and confusion to all who oppress the poor and needy!

"Now, throw on more logs," he said, "and let us enjoy ourselves, for 'tis a night a dog should not be abroad."

They seated themselves round the fireplace, and as the host entered, Duval ordered several bottles of the best to be brought.

"And," he added, "if any stray traveller should give thee a call, pray conduct him hither, and we will make him welcome, and if he can sing us a good song, by our Lady! he shall have whate'er his heart thirsteth for."

The wine was brought, but one of the men had barely drawn the cork from the first when the landlord once more hastily entered, this time bearing traces of anxiety upon his face.

The captain turned to the landlord.

"Why, thy face glows, good host," said he. "Hast thou seen the Plumstead ghost?"

"Nay, good master," replied the host, "but there's an elderly female, who craves audience with thee."

"An elderly female?" asked Claude. "Thou must be mistaken. Now, hadst thou said a young and pretty one, I——"

"Nay, nay: she is elderly, with a grave face and tearful eyes, and she did beseech me in pitiable tones to say that she would crave a short speech with thee."

"Show her in, then, good host. If she be elderly as thou sayest, I shall not fear the hearts of these my young friends."

"Mayhap she may be one in distress," said one of the men.

"Then she shall not want for food or bread while I hath the wherewithal to provide them," replied the captain, as he touched his pocket.

In a few moments the female made her appearance.

She was attired in heavy and warm clothing, which almost concealed her face.

Claude rose and advanced to her.

The woman was evidently startled at his majestic appearance, and she drew slightly back.

Then she said, in trembling tones—

"Thou art Claude——?"

"At thy service, madam," interrupted the captain, bowing to her as he would have bowed to a duchess. "Prithee tell me thy business?"

"Thou dost not know me?"

"Nay," said Claude, looking at her with his large, dark eyes; "but that matters not. Tell me thy name."

The female dropped her cloak from off her face, saying—

"Dost thou know me now?"

"By Heaven!" exclaimed Claude, "I do. I know thee now as well as I should know my own mother were she alive. How could I ever forget thy kind, motherly face? How could I forget the woman who, when I lay sorely wounded and near death's door, nursed my weary head upon her breast, hushed me to sleep, soothed me when my poor brain seemed bursting, and prayed to heaven for my quick recovery?"

And overcome with his feelings, Claude sank into a chair, and buried his face in his hands.

It was a strange thing to see how affected were the men in that room.

It was strange indeed to see a tear creeping down the bronzed cheeks of more than one man who under Cromwell had stood unmoved on more than one sanguinary field of battle.

Well, we are all but poor human beings, each with a heart that can be touched.

Claude and his comrades were strong-nerved, determined men—men who would flinch at nothing, but once touch the gentle side of their natures, and they would weep like children.

"Look, comrades," cried Claude, leaping to his feet, "see this lady— whom may the Holy Virgin protect!— she is called Nurse Alice. It was she who nursed me when Sir Harold Harcourt saved me from the King's Guard when I was shot down. Ye can call that to mind?"

"Ay, ay," replied the men.

"I did only my duty," replied the nurse, gravely.

"And I said I would serve thee if I could. But thou didst say, 'Nay, sir, I trust I shall never need your services, and——'"

"I did say so then," interrupted the nurse, in a broken voice, "but I need thy services now, if thou wilt but offer them."

"Offer them? I offer thee or thy master my very life."

"Alas! I have now no master," said the nurse, as tears rained down her face.

"What?" cried Claude, "dost thou mean to say he is dead?"

"Dead? Ay, dead, indeed! And thou hast not heard the news which has rung through all England? Not heard that my poor master was foully murdered, and that his little son, the heir to the Harcourt estates, was taken away only to share the fate of his father?"

For some few moments Claude was so thunderstruck that he could not speak.

His face had turned very pale, and he had to grasp the table to keep himself firm.

Presently he said, in a hoarse whisper—

"Murdered? and by whom?"

"Heaven only knows. There were two men dressed as officers of the King's Guard. But listen, and I will tell thee all."

And the nurse told the story of the murder to Claude and his friends, who listened patiently and earnestly.

"And the child?" asked Claude.

"It is of the child I would speak. I went to Whitefriars two days ago to find thee, but no one knew where I should meet with thee. At last I met a young girl at the 'Silver Flagon,' a lovely girl, with golden tresses, who told me where I should find thee."

"It was Nell Gwynne, I'll warrant me," said Claude.

"Ay, that was her name. And she desired me to convey her respects and good wishes to thee. But now, Claude, let me tell thee that I want thee to recover the child who is more to me than my life, for I promised his mother,

who died soon after giving little Harold birth, to protect him."

"The son?"

"Ay; wilt thou do this for me?"

"With all my heart and soul. And my friends here will assist me if assistance be necessary."

"We will!" shouted the men, as they rose from their seats.

"But where is the child?"

"On the night of the murder I heard one of the murderers cry out—'Now for Plumstead!' But I have since ascertained that, owing to the wild night they did not go to Plumstead, but stayed in the Strand. I found the house, got friendly with the servant, and ascertained that the child would be taken to Plumstead this very night."

"This night?"

"Yes, and by coach."

"At what hour?"

"Midnight. It was to be a poor coach, so that it would not attract attention."

"Oh, indeed! By our Lady, it would be a strange coach that attracted not the attention of Claude. What say you, comrades? But in this case the coach will carry a right royal treasure in the person of the child. By its rescue from the hands of these villainous kidnappers I shall pay back to this good lady part of the great debt I owe her. And, good madam, thou knowest not who the leader of this foul murder be?"

"I know not by whom it was carried out, but that it was planned by Master Humphreys is plain enough."

"I know Master Humphreys, madam, and, by our Lady, I know nothing good of him. But we will talk over that and the welfare of the child anon. At midnight the coach will cross the common. Good! It is now within half-an-hour of the time. In a few more minutes the host will close his doors. Madam, you shall remain with the dame of the house. Pray follow me."

Claude whispered a few words to the host and his wife, and the latter immediately took the nurse under her protection, and accompanied her upstairs.

"Now, my men, to horse! And see that your arms are to hand, for if there be any large guard with the coach we may have a hard time of it."

CHAPTER IV.

RESCUE OF OUR HERO.

WHAT the nurse had said in reference to the coach being about to cross Plumstead Common on that night was quite correct.

On the night of the murder Blood found it impossible to proceed.

They could make no headway against the terrific wind and clouds of snow.

Blood therefore decided to wait awhile, but finding that the terrible weather continued he decided that to keep the child longer in London would be dangerous to his plans, for be it understood John Humphreys was under the impression that the child as well as the father were murdered.

All his plans he had confided to Blood, a man whom he knew to be a thorough villain and murderer, and he had not considered for a moment whether Blood would work a wheel within a wheel.

But more of this anon.

Early in the evening on which the journey to Plumstead was to be undertaken, Blood made his appearance at the house in the Strand where the child was confined.

Here he met Varney, whom he had commissioned to watch over the child.

"Art thou ready?" he asked.

"Ay, quite, and right glad shall I be to get the brat off my hands. But, by our Lady, I like not the idea of this journey."

"Of what art thou afraid, coward?"

"Of many things, though I am no coward. But look at the snow and hist ye to the howling of the wind."

"Bah! how will that affect thee? Art thou not going in a coach and four?"

"And art thou not going?"

"Have I not told thee, thou fool, that I am otherwise engaged? No, I shall not go, but shall send with thee two gallants from Whitefriars, who will guard thee and thy charge well. Thou will be in the coach while they will ride behind, well mounted and armed. But no one will stay thee."

"Thou dost not know that. Claude is about the neighbourhood, so I have heard, and no coach passes him without he inquires who be the occupants."

"Claude—may Tyburn claim him ere long, say I—is in London. Of that I have just heard. But even if he were not—even did he stay the coach, he would see that there were no valuables, nothing worth a gold piece except thou dost put that price on thy ugly carcase."

"Ugly carcase, Master Blood! Odd's life! what, then, is thine? An thou wert killed this moment, the medical students of the Fields would not bestow so much as a bottle of canary for thy ungainly body, which, as thou dost well know, frightens all the women folk, and often gets thee a———"

"Silence, thou thieving knave!" roared Blood. "Is this how thou dost talk to thy superiors? Thou sayest thou art ready. 'Tis well. See here—the coach has arrived. And look well at it. By our Lady, didst thou ever gaze on such a lumbering, dirty, foul-looking conveyance? If so be that Claude saw it, he would turn up his nose in contempt. Claude, mark you, would consider himself and also his companions too much above staying such a conveyance, which looks more like the cart for conveying plague-stricken patients than a gentleman's coach. Have the child ready, and away with thee. Observe that four powerful horses are harnessed to the coach—may our Lady pardon me, I meant the dirt-cart. And so thou wilt get over the snow at a good round pace. And mark thee well, stay not anywhere until thou hast delivered the child into the care of Mistress Ford. Take the child—ah! here he is—in thine arms and enter the coach at once. Farewell for the time. Forget not that I rely upon thee to give a good account of thy journey on thy return. Thou knowest where to find me. Stay; a gag for the child. It will prevent his cries being heard."

And the next instant the cowardly

Blood had placed a gag over little Harold's mouth.

Varney then took him, concealed him in several wraps, and entered the coach, which immediately drove off at a fairly good pace.

"All's well thus far," chuckled Blood, as he watched the coach out of sight. "And money will pour into my treasury ere long. John Humphreys, my good young gallant, thou wilt be my banker, and it will cost thee much if I am to keep my secret—and thine."

* * * *

"Where are we?" asked Varney, putting his head out of the window.

They had been travelling now some hours (although our young readers must bear in mind that Plumstead is only ten miles from St. Paul's Cathedral as the crow flies), and the horses were tired of dragging their load through the deep snow, and the two blackguards from Alsatia, who acted as guards at the back of the coach, looked fairly frozen.

They would have returned long ago, but they were too much afraid of Colonel Blood's vengeance.

"We are in sight of the common, good sir," replied the postilion.

"The common, are we?" replied Varney, the thoughts of Claude and his men still uppermost in his mind. "And what canst thou see?"

"See? I see naught but what we have seen all along—miles upon miles of snow. Not a bit of green to be seen."

"How dost thou know we are near the common?"

"I see the turnpike, and, moreover, I can see the 'Load of Mischief' there on our right."

"The load of what?"

"Of mischief. That is the principal inn."

"Then drive to it, and may the devil take Blood's orders! I'm frozen, and would partake of a bowl of hot punch."

"Alack! the house is fast closed."

"May the fiend take the landlord for a lazy varmint, then! Well, drive on as fast as you can. Ugh! it snows faster. Another hour, and we shall be buried in it. I say, my noble bloods," he cried to the frozen-looking guards,

"how fares it with thee? Hast thou thy weapons ready?"

"Ay," replied one of the guards; "but we shall not be called upon to use them, I'll warrant me. None but fools are out in weather such as this."

Once more the lumbering, snow-covered coach moved on at a slow pace.

The short, heavy whip the postilion used on the horses' haunches had no effect.

They were tired out, and the further towards the common they went, the deeper into the snow did they seem to get.

Once across the common, Varney knew they were safe, for the house at which he was to leave the child was within a stone's-throw of it.

They got to the edge of the common, and the postilion was making some of the safest cuts and trying to avoid the treacherous, snow-covered ditches, when a loud and commanding voice called out—

"Halt!"

Varney nearly dropped on his knees in affright.

Poking his head out of the window, he yelled—

"Who calls halt? Don't halt at all, driver, or, by my faith, thou shalt pay dearly for it. Go on!" he thundered, as he found that the coach had come to a standstill.

"Halt, driver!" again cried the voice, "or thy breast will hold a bullet, and thy bed will be the snow."

The next moment a tall, fine-looking fellow, mounted on really a superb-looking animal, stood in front of the door of the coach.

Varney snatched his pistol from his belt, and levelled it point-blank at the horseman.

But the horseman, by a swift movement, snatched the pistol from his hand and hurled it far over his shoulder.

"Thou art a fool," he said, "thou lean and lanky scoundrel. Dost know who I am?"

"An thou be not the hound Claude, I know thee not."

"My name is Claude, and I tell thee to get out of this lumbering cart. What hast thou in that bundle?"

And he pointed to the opposite seat.

"Only old clothes, thief, which thou

art welcome to, if so be thou dost require them."

"Yes, I will take them, friend. But descend from the coach, and at once, or, mark ye well, thou shall be dragged out!"

Varney crept out.

He was about to seize the bundle, but Claude dealt him such a stunning blow on the head with the butt-end of his pistol, that he drew back and cried out—

"Guards, draw!"

And like lightning he had drawn his sword.

But he soon lowered it, and as he looked his mouth opened wide in astonishment, for at the back of his coach, instead of the two guards he expected to see, and who had certainly, been at the back only a few minutes before, he saw half-a-dozen horsemen each having a drawn sword in his hand.

They looked like half-a-dozen statues, for they sat as motionless.

"Give me thy sword, good friend," said Claude calmly, "and do not gape about thee like that, or the snow may choke thee. Now list ye. Thou sayest that is a bundle of clothes?"

"Ay, good sir," replied Varney, now pretending to be very humble.

"Thou art a liar!" roared Claude; "it is a child, thou kidnapper. Bring it forth, or I will cleave thy skull in twain!"—

And he leapt from his saddle, and drawing his long sword stood over Varney as he brought forth the bundle.

Claude took it in his arms, his men approaching nearer and nearer to their chief, and they looked on with much curiosity.

Very gently did he undo the coverings of the bundle.

Suddenly he started back and uttered a loud cry.

His cry was echoed by his men.

It was a cry of horror.

Poor little Harold was in the centre of that bundle, his little mouth firmly fixed with the gag.

"Thou coward!" cried Claude, as he snatched the gag from the poor child's mouth. "Down on thy knees!"

"I did not do it, good sir; it was——"

"Who? Speak!"

"It was another."

"His name? Down on thy knees and tell me his name."

Varney saw the sword raised in a threatening manner before him, and he fell flop upon the snow.

"Good sir," he whined, "spare my life, I pray thee."

"I want not thy wretched life, thou coward. Tyburn will claim thee ere long, I'll warrant. Speak. I see thou art a servant. What is thy master's name? Methinks I have seen thee before, but I cannot call to mind where. What is thy master's name?"

"An it please thee, good sir, I cannot tell thee."

"It does not please me. Now mark well what I say," he said fiercely. "Didst thou ever hear that I ever broke my word? Nay! Now then, I tell thee that if thou dost not reveal thy master's name I call Heaven to witness that I will slay thee where thou art."

"Thou wilt not say who told thee?"

"Nay."

"His name is Colonel Blood, good sir."

"Blood!" cried Claude, aghast.

"Blood!" echoed his men.

"Rise. Here we will not discuss the scoundrel Blood. Dismount, driver," he added to the postilion, "and take out thy horses."

Then turning to one of the men he handed Harold to him, saying—

"Thou knowest where to take this child, heaven bless his pretty face. Bear him gently, good Brandon. I will join thee shortly. And now, thou varlet, what is thy name?"

"Varney, good sir."

"Varney. I will not forget that name. Stand where thou art for a moment. Hast thou taken out thy horses, driver?"

"Ay, good sir," replied the driver.

"'Tis well. To whom does this lumbering vehicle belong?"

"To my master."

"Who allows Colonel Blood to use his conveyances for the purpose of carrying stolen children? By our Lady, I tell thee he will not use this again!"

He took from his pocket a flask of brandy.

"'I WILL DO ANYTHING IF THOU WILT ONLY SPARE ME!' CRIED VARNEY."

No. 2

The contents of this he strewed over the interior of the coach, then he deliberately fired his pistol into it.

The result of this was to fire the spirits.

In an instant the interior of the coach was a mass of flame.

"Oh, good sir," howled the postilion, "I dare not return if thou dost burn my coach."

"Then thou mayest stay, good friend, and warm thy hands by the embers. But if thou shouldst return, tell thy master that it was I who destroyed it. And say that I will be willing to meet him any night that he may desire a journey this way. Thou wilt return without the coach, and with three horses less. I will give thee one horse only. That will carry thee to London. As for thee, good Varney, thou wilt come with us."

"Oh, sir," cried Varney, "I pray you let me at once return."

"Thou shalt not be long behind thy companion, trust me. Take thy horse, good driver, and haste thee away lest I change my mind."

These words he uttered in such fierce tones that the driver was only too glad to mount the horse, and with another glance at the coach, which was now burning with such fierceness that the reflection could have been seen for miles around, he dug his spurs into his horse and went off.

"By our Lady!" laughed Claude, "never has Plumstead Common been blest with such a beauteous fire! See, comrades, the ruddy glow! It maketh our faces look as cheery as children round the Christmas log. But yet look at this hang-dog face."

And he pointed to Varney, who stood wringing his hands in despair.

The men burst into a roar of laughter.

"Why dost thou not laugh? Art thou sorry because the fire burns in waste? Out on thee! But we will waste it not. Comrades, lend me a hand with this lank body, and we will give him a seat on the coach."

"Oh, I pray you, gentlemen, spare me!" cried Varney. "I will do anything thou mayest ask if thou wilt only spare me."

"Thou wilt do anything we may ask thee, knave, eh? Well, then, take you this dagger and pierce thy infamous heart."

This had again the effect of causing the men to laugh heartily.

And no one could have resisted a laugh at the figure Varney cut.

"Come, comrades, the fire burns out. Take the horses, while I lead this knave along."

In a short time they came to the stables of the "Load of Mischief," Claude speaking rapidly to his men in French as they went along, much to the agony of Varney, who could not imagine what was about to be done to him.

Arriving at the stables the men dismounted, and one of them lit a lantern and held it aloft.

They then surrounded Varney, took off his hat, and all his clothes, except his shirt and trunks.

"Now," said Claude, "stand thou firm. Move but one step or utter but one cry, and thou wilt never see thy master Colonel Blood again!"

Varney uttered a groan of despair.

He trembled in every limb, and his teeth chattered audibly.

He had heard only too much of Claude's determination and strange tricks.

What on earth was he about to do?

His mind was very soon set at rest.

In a remarkably short space of time and in a very business-like manner, Claude brought a razor to bear upon Varney's head, and in a moment his hair was cut so close as to remind one of short bristles placed round a billiard ball.

Then, holding Varney's nose, he shaved off one side of his long moustache.

Mark you—one side only.

Imagine now Varney's ludicrous appearance.

He himself knew what he must look like, but he thanked the Virgin that he was not to be killed.

"Now, good Varney," said Claude, gravely, "thou wilt be able to tell thy friends and good Blood that I am a fair barber, and that I charge nought for shaving, be it clean or half clean. Comrades, good Varney's clothes."

The clothes were handed to Varney,

who could not suppress a howl of horror and dismay as he looked at them.

They were torn to ribbons!

"Good sir," whined Varney, "thou dost not mean me to put these on?"

"What else hast thou to put on? And dost thou want to walk to London without clothes? Thou canst please thyself though."

Varney thought of the bitter cold, and tattered as they were he soon had the clothes on.

"Fare thee well, Varney. Soon maybe I shall see thee in Alsatia, where thou shalt drink my health. Go, kidnapper! and when thou dost steal another child, prithee think whether I will meet thee."

Varney crept out of the stable yard, and when in the open country took to his heels and ran for a long distance without pausing.

At last, however, he was compelled to stop, and he fell upon the snow from sheer exhaustion.

There for a long time he lay, till at length the gradual numbing of his long limbs warned him to move on.

At almost every house he tried to attract the attention of the inmates, but no one would pay any heed to him, and at last, just at the dawn of day, he crept exhausted, ragged and hatless into the "Silver Flagon."

CHAPTER V.

A LAPSE OF THIRTEEN YEARS—HAROLD LEARNS HIS HISTORY.

THE adventures of Colonel Blood for many years during the reign of Charles II. are well known to almost every reader, the doings of this notorious scoundrel and murderer often throwing London into a state of horror and consternation.

Blood's life would no doubt have been brief had it not been for the protection that the king afforded him.

Very often Blood had been taken red-handed and thrown into the Tower, whence the governor, acting under secret orders from the king, had often allowed him to escape, but if he hàd, for the say so of the thing, been eventually placed upon his trial at the Old Bailey, he was always acquitted by the infamous, blasphemous and depraved Judge Jeffries, whose son often made one of Blood's companions at the "Silver Flagon" in Alsatia and elsewhere.

In order to at once bring our hero and his strange and startling adventures before our readers' notice, we are compelled to skip thirteen years, for during that time nothing of very great importance occurred in which he had prominently figured.

He had been the whole of this time at school and under the charge of nurse Alice, who loved him as her own, and considered him a most sacred charge.

What would have become of poor Harold during all these years, however, if it had not been for Claude, there is no telling.

He had not a single relative in the wide world, and had grown to love Harold as passionately as had the nurse, and nothing delighted him so much as to visit him and have long chats with him respecting the country and its government, and Harold knew that Claude, or as he was known to Harold, "Master Roebuck," from his conversation, must have been well and personally acquainted with the king, the Court, and the state in general.

Claude, or as we shall now continue to call him, Roebuck, had sworn that one day he would see Harold righted and put in his proper place, but he knew well enough that this task would be difficult in the extreme.

John Humphreys, now "Sir John," reigned at Harcourt House and at the grand estate at Epping, and he was popular with the king.

Until Harold had almost reached his eighteenth birthday, both nurse Alice and Roebuck kept the secret of his birth from him.

Years had blotted out the memory

of the foul murder of his father, and he had never known any other name than Harold.

But from various hints let fall by Roebuck, Harold knew that there was a great secret attaching to him, and little by little visions of the past would rise before him.

The days of his childhood would haunt him, and sometimes at his bedside, the shadow of a tall, grave-looking gentleman would appear and look down upon him with sad, tearful eyes.

At last he became so restless to learn the true facts of his history, that "Master Roebuck" promised to make a special journey and tell him.

For that purpose he arrived late one evening at nurse Alice's house.

He was expected, and Harold met him at the door.

Roebuck was mounted on a splendid animal, and wore attire such as Harold had not seen him wear before.

"Thou hast a splendid horse, Master Roebuck," said Harold admiringly.

"Thou art right, lad; fleet as the wind, and with a foothold as sure as the goat on the Swiss mountains. Did they teach thee riding at thy school?"

"Yes, good sir. I ride, they say, right well."

"And shouldst thou like a steed like this, eh?"

"Ay, that should I. But, alack! it is impossible."

"Why sayest that?"

"Because I have not the wherewithal to buy or keep it. And even if I had, of what use would it be to me?"

"True—true," said Roebuck.

Then he thought—

"Mayhap bring thee into no end of trouble."

"And thou hast noble pistols," said Harold, as his keen eyes rested upon the pistol butts peeping from the holsters. "Good Master Roebuck, why dost thou need pistols on thy journey?"

"To keep off evil-doers, Master Harold. But let us enter."

Harold saw "Master Roebuck" was not in the humour to explain much, so he followed him indoors.

There, without further preface, Roebuck made Harold acquainted with his father's history and murder, and of his (Harold's) abduction, and rescue.

"Then it is to thee, good sir, that I owe my education—nay, my life."

"Nay, but to good nurse Alice there, who for so many years has watched over thy life. It is she who deserves all thy gratitude and love."

"She has it," said Harold, as he pressed a kiss upon nurse Alice's cheek. "But, sir, according to you, this Colonel Blood believes me dead?"

"Yes; the scoundrel from whom Roebuck rescued you swore to Blood that a great fight had occurred on Plumstead Common, and that the child — you — had been accidentally shot dead, and that he then threw you into a well."

"I see, I see! Oh Heaven! into what hands had my father and I fallen!"

"Ay, into what hands indeed! But as I have told thee, John Humphreys it was who was at the bottom of it all."

"But, alas! from what thou sayest I am powerless to touch him."

"At present, because——"

Roebuck paused.

"Why dost thou pause?"

"John Humphreys, dear Harold, is a favourite of the king."

"Indeed! But cannot we make this Colonel Blood confess to the foul crime?"

Roebuck could not resist a laugh.

"Nay," he said, "I know Colonel Blood well enough, and by our good Lady! he hath cause enough to know me. Nay, Colonel Blood would confess to nothing. He would not even take a bribe to confess to anything, and by the Holy Virgin! even did he make a confession, everyone would laugh at him for a lying knave."

"They would not believe him!"

"Nay, and nay a thousand times."

"But if he were dying!"

"Ah, that I cannot say, but I should think not. But, mark ye, thou wilt not find Colonel Blood dying yet, I'll warrant me."

Roebuck did not notice the fierce look which for a moment rested upon Harold's face; but Alice did, and she trembled violently.

Pressing his friend's hand, Harold said—

"I cannot sufficiently thank thee, good Master Roebuck, for thy great attention to me. Thou hast told me my father once saved thy life, and that therefore thou art indebted to me. But that debt, if debt it be, was long since repaid. My education is now complete, and I must go forth into the world to try and earn my bread."

" Tut, tut, wait awhile, Harold, and I will see what I can do for thee," said Roebuck.

"Maybe I can assist thee in thy affairs," suggested Harold.

"Nay, nay!" replied Roebuck, hastily. "I am an independent gentleman, with plenty of money, my son, and with naught to trouble me but thyself and good Alice. But until the time comes for thee to try to regain thy rights, thou must move in the world to see how men battle with fortune. I will at once see what can be done. How wouldst thou like to be of the King's Guard!"

"Right well," cried Harold, joyfully.

"No, no," cried Alice, "not that, my boy, not that! Danger would surround thee every hour of thy life! If thou didst leave me but for a day, my heart would beat with apprehension for thy safety."

"Wouldst thou have the boy a coward, Alice?" asked Roebuck, reproachfully. "Dost thou think that if he lead the life of a milksop, he will be in the possession of courage to attempt to regain his rights?"

"Thou knowest best, good Master Roebuck," replied the nurse, sorrowfully. "I will not again interfere, yet I cannot but remember his father's sacred trust."

"Be easy in thy mind. Thou knowest my influence is good. Leave all to me. Harold, I will now bid thee farewell until the morrow, when I shall have some news for thee. See, darkness is coming on, and I must away."

He embraced Harold, pressed nurse Alice's hand, in which he left a full leathern purse, and leaving the house, sprang into his saddle and soon disappeared from sight.

Harold then turned sadly to Alice, who saw that tears stood in his eyes.

"Thou must not give way to thy feelings thus, dear Harold," said Alice. " Leave all to good Master Roebuck and to Heaven, and one day all will be well with thee."

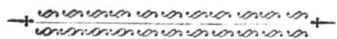

CHAPTER VI.

IN WHICH HAROLD MAKES A WONDERFUL DISCOVERY, LEAVES HIS HOUSE IN A SOMEWHAT STRANGE MANNER, AND IN PURCHASING A WEAPON ENCOUNTERS THE SON OF A NOTORIOUS PERSON.

NURSE ALICE always retired to rest somewhat early, and on the night of Roebuck's visit the hour of ten had not struck ere she bid an affectionate good-night to our hero and went to her room.

Harold's room was situated on the third story at the back of the house.

Now this room, though small, was of singular construction.

It possessed a lofty ceiling for a third floor, and the walls, which were of richly-carved oak, abounded with curious niches.

The bedstead was a marvel of ingenuity.

It was of massive Spanish mahogany, and was hung with large, gilt, damask curtains.

Round the sides of the lower part of the bed ran some oaken panels.

Harold had always been under the impression that these panels were part and parcel of the bedstead.

After bidding good-night to Alice, Harold ascended to his room, placed his lamp upon a chair, and flung himself with a low moan upon the bed.

Now, it so happened that his feet came sharply in contact with the corner of one of the posts, and instantly there rang out a sharp click, then a kind of rumbling, hissing noise.

He leapt to his feet and gazed in wonder, not to say awe, at the lower part of the bed.

What wonder was it ?

The panel at the lower part had

slid over, and from under it was emerging a broad, long drawer.

Harold's feet had touched a secret spring.

Slowly, and almost imperceptibly, the drawer came out before Harold's astonished eyes, then suddenly it stopped with another sharp click.

Upon the top of it, and the whole length, was a dark cloth, neatly and carefully arranged.

What did it contain?

Was there some horrible history attached to the house, and was it possible that this drawer might contain skeletons of the men whose lives had been brought to an abrupt termination?

These thoughts ran like the lightning's flash through Harold's mind, for he knew that Master Roebuck had taken the house as it stood, for himself and nurse Alice.

It was fortunate that he was possessed of a bold heart, and was imbued with the spirit of curiosity.

Starting forward, he snatched the cloth from the drawer, and simultaneously a great cry of astonishment escaped his lips.

What did the drawer contain?

Well, it contained a collection of articles of a most extraordinary, albeit valuable description.

Very carefully did Harold turn these over, wondering how on earth such things came to be there.

But another surprise was in store for him.

At the bottom was a piece of paper containing an entry of everything in the drawer, and then came the words, written in a large, singularly bold hand—

"Claude, his property."

"That name seems to be associated with my life! 'His property!' Gracious Heaven! how on earth did they come to be here? Why, of course, that is the man Master Roebuck was so careful in telling me saved my life! I will tell nurse Alice of this. But, Heaven be thanked, I have found something I shall require for the journey upon which I am fully resolved. I will but borrow it, and replace it upon my return."

Thereupon Harold brought forth several of the swords, withdrew them from their sheaths, and tried their strength by bending them across his knee.

Having selected one he buckled it round his waist and endeavoured to close the drawer.

But in this he failed.

Despite his narrow inspection he was unable to discover the secret spring, so he left it as it was.

Blowing out the lamp he opened the door of the room and went forth.

What was his astonishment to find that the door on the landing was fast locked!

What could it mean?

The real reason was that nurse Alice was under the impression that Harold one night would venture forth after she had retired and probably get into trouble, and therefore she had latterly taken the precaution to lock the door.

Entering his bedroom once more, he opened the shutters and admitted the rays of the moon, which was at its full.

Then he mounted a stool, and undoing the bed curtains all round, took out the long silken ropes.

The strength of these he tried by tugging at them with all his might.

He was quite satisfied as to their safety.

Having securely knotted the ropes and tied them firmly together, he opened the windows, tied one end of the rope to a large ring outside, got upon the window-sill, took the rope in his hand and lowered himself slowly down.

He landed safely on the low wall that surrounded the back part of the house, and then the thought struck him—

"Suppose anyone saw the rope? An alarm would surely be given. Or someone might have the audacity to ascend and steal the jewels. I must break it," he thought.

Looking about the yard, he found a small, thick piece of wood.

Around this he tied the end of the rope, and using the wood as a lever he soon had the satisfaction of seeing the rope snap almost at the top.

Placing it out of sight, he once more mounted the wall, and dropped over on the other side, when he struck out for the place he had made up his mind to visit.

And where was that?

No less a place than Alsatia, and the man he wanted to see was the mighty and dreaded Colonel Blood.

Harold proceeded through the streets, and at last he came to a large shop at Holborn Bars, in appearance very much like those which at this present day stand by the side of the entrance to Staple Inn, and by its sign he knew it to be a fashionable gunsmith's.

"I shall feel safer if I am in possession of a pistol," he thought.

Although it was late and the shutters were up, the gunsmith was still transacting business.

Harold did not pause to see who was within.

He at once pushed open the door and entered.

He found himself in the presence of half-a-dozen gallants of the boisterous order, who were laughing and chaffing with the gunsmith's daughter.

As Harold entered, the gunsmith darted forward, and with many curious grins and back bendings, inquired—

"What d'ye lack, friend? What d'ye lack?"

Harold soon made him acquainted with the object of his visit, and the gunsmith having shown him several cases of instruments, Harold selected one, and some ammunition, and loading the pistol, placed it in his doublet.

"Now by our good Lady," sneered one of the gallants, an ill-looking youth of perhaps twenty, "didst thou ever know a boy require powder and shot before? Odd's life! No doubt he is about to follow in the footsteps of some we know of."

"An he does," said the gunsmith's daughter, "he hath his good looks to help him, Master Jeffries, which is more than thou hast."

Harold was about to pass out, when the insolent gallant had the audacity to place himself directly in front of him.

"Didst hear what I said, boy?" he asked.

"Ay, boy!" replied Harold, pushing him gently away; "take thy ugly face from mine. Thou hast been drinking, and I would advise thee to seek thy mother."

A great roar of laughter followed this speech.

Even over the bloated face of the gunsmith there crept a broad grin, and as for his daughter, she laughed and clapped her hands with glee.

Once more did Harold attempt to pass, but the insolent youth again barred his passage.

"Get out of my road, fool!" cried Harold, who soon became impatient.

"I will, boy, an thou wilt apologise," and again the half-drunken and foolish youth pushed his nose into Harold's face.

Without further ceremony, Harold gave him such a terrific push, that he went flying through the doorway into the street, where he fell with a crash.

"It is but thy deserts," said Harold, "and will teach thee better manners in the future."

Assisted by his companions, the fallen and enraged gallant was soon upon his feet.

He thrust off his companions, and with a swaggering flourish drew his rapier.

"I fight with none but gentlemen," he shouted, "but I cannot be assaulted by a boy. I see thou hast a sword. Draw and defend thyself, or I will chop thee down as thou standest!"

"Chop away then, friend," replied Harold, calmly, as he folded his arms across his chest; "thou hast allowed the liquor to get the upper-hand of thee; an I fought with thee thus, and did thee injury, I should be called coward."

"Draw!" shouted the gallant, as he pushed slightly forward, waving back his companions who would have interfered.

It was a certainty that the half-drunken fool would have done Harold some injury had he not attempted to defend himself.

He therefore drew his sword.

"If you will fight," cried Harold, "then have your will."

In a second their swords crossed with a loud and startling clash—a clash which caused the gunsmith and his daughter to utter a loud "Oh!" and clasp their hands in horror.

In a few moments the fight became fast and furious.

Several times Harold could have taken the life of his opponent had he felt so disposed.

But he was not.

Suddenly, Harold, by a swift and skilful movement, twisted his sword near to the hilt of his opponent's weapon.

The next instant it was lying snapped in twain upon the ground, and several voices shouted out—

"The watch! the watch!" and Harold, glancing ahead, saw several lanterns moving swiftly along.

"Fly," whispered a voice in his ear, "fly while there is time. Thou hast been fighting with Hugh Jeffries, the son of the infamous judge. Fly, for the watch know him well and would harm him not, but thy life might be forfeited at Tyburn."

Harold turned, and saw that the speaker was the gunsmith's daughter.

He felt persuaded that her advice was good, and therefore, while the gallants were trying to soothe their crestfallen companion, he slipped away and was soon lost in the darkness.

But fate decided that he was once more to stand face to face with the son of the blasphemous Judge Jeffries, and before two hours had passed.

CHAPTER VII.

HAROLD'S FIRST VISIT TO ALSATIA—HE CHALLENGES COLONEL BLOOD TO MORTAL COMBAT—HE IS SURROUNDED, SORELY WOUNDED, AND FALLS INTO THE HANDS OF JEFFRIES.

HAROLD'S knowledge of Whitefriars had been gained from hearsay.

He recollected that Master Roebuck had often told him what a place it was, and what a terrible crew the inhabitants were.

No sooner did he enter the precincts of Alsatia, than he was challenged by one of the guards called a "friar," who would give an alarm in case of surprise.

"Well, my young master," said the friar, as he sailed up to Harold with all the assurance in the world, "and who dost thou want?"

"I am here to meet someone."

"Eh? Ah! and who, my young master?"

"A friend."

"His name?"

"Bob."

"Bob?" said the friar, slowly. "I know him not. By our Lady, there are many here, but not of the name of Bob, methinks. What is he like, young master?"

"Long and lank, with the braggart of the devil; much after thyself. And I have come to give him some gold pieces borrowed—one of them I give thee."

And Harold flung him a piece, which the friar, with much dexterity, caught on the crown of his hat.

Then he said—

"Long and lank, good master, is the description of many among these our royal palaces," and he pointed to the filthy dens on all sides; "so pass on, young sir, and pick thee out one."

"Dost thou know the 'Silver Flagon?'" asked Harold.

"Right well, young sir; it is there on thy left. Walk thee straight on, and thou canst not mistake it, for thou wilt see the finger-marks of the devil on the outside. An I could leave here, I would drink thy health at thy expense."

"I will leave thee a cup, if thou wilt but tell me thy name."

"My name, young sir, is Varney, and I am friar here for the time being. Pass on, and the Virgin guard thee until thou dost leave me a good bowl of red punch, for I am faint and athirst."

"I will not fail," replied Harold, as he passed on, while Varney turned to embrace a buxom wench, who came up and handed him a plate of food.

When Harold reached the "Silver Flagon," he saw a sight which filled his heart with horror.

Outside the house were a couple of women, in a semi-drunken state, standing up and fighting like men.

On the steps of the "Silver Flagon," and, indeed, on all sides, were men and women of all ages and sizes.

And they were attired in dresses of almost every conceivable description.

All were more or less in a state of intoxication.

Some leaned up against the wall, others lay full length upon the ground, with their mugs of home-brewed near them, but all were thoroughly enjoying themselves in watching the progress of the fight, and were shouting to one or other of the combatants.

As Harold approached closer to them, he saw that both bore severe marks of violence, and that blood was saturating what little upper linen they were wearing.

"By the Holy Virgin," he muttered, "in good truth Master Roebuck said well. An that is a fair specimen, I trust it is but little I shall have to do with Alsatia."

He was about to turn from the horrible scene in disgust and enter the "Silver Flagon," when a powerful voice called out—

"How now, ye witches of Beelzebub! is this thy conduct in a Christian country? Out on ye for drunken brawlers! Make way and let gentlemen pass!"

Instantly the women ceased their fighting and stood aside.

The men, too, leapt to their feet as though an elephant was about to trample upon them.

"All's well, noble captain," said one of the men, as he scraped and bowed until his body seemed about to break in twain; "we are but idling the long hours. What ho, there, companions! make way for Colonel Blood and the good gentlemen."

Harold stood aside and looked hard at the first comer.

He saw before him a man of about forty-five years of age, somewhat tall, but not stout, with a face of savage fierceness.

He was handsomely attired, and wore upon his fingers huge rings, studded with precious stones.

It did not take Harold long to recognise this man.

Master Roebuck's description of Colonel Blood had been marvellously accurate.

Blood was followed by four gentlemen, neither of whom was anything near the prime of life.

Little did Harold dream that these men were lords, who had not long left Charles's Court.

Each wore a long cloak, the collar of which was turned up to conceal the features.

"This way, gentlemen," whispered Blood, "and do not pause. Our room is all prepared."

In another moment they had entered the "Silver Flagon."

Harold followed, by no manner of means daunted by the haughty and swaggering appearance of Blood and his "gentlemen."

Blood went through the crowd of dissipated brawlers in the tavern, and with his companions ascended a narrow flight of stairs.

Harold was about to follow, when he was confronted by the host.

"Halloa, young sir!" he said, "what is thy business? Art thou Colonel Blood's servant?"

"Servant!" replied Harold. "Do I look like a servant?"

"Nay, in good truth, thou dost not. But then, my young master, our good colonel knoweth well how to attire his servants, and he ofttimes clothes them in apparel befitting a Court gallant."

"I suppose he does," replied Harold, "when he wishes to gain his own ends thereby."

"Ay, true, young sir. But prithee tell me thy business. Thou must not follow up these stairs, mark thee, for it leads to the banquetting-room, which thou must know, if so be thou hast favoured us with thy presence before, and it is private."

"I know it quite well," replied Harold, who knew that it would not do to say that he had not been there before, "but I would speak to Colonel Blood."

"Odd's life, young sir," replied the host, "he would see no one, for business of a private nature commandeth his attention. But, an thou wilt wait, I will send up thy name."

"Nay, I thank thee," replied Harold. "It is on a matter of but little moment, and will do on the morrow. Prithee give me a bottle of thy best."

And unconcernedly Harold seated himself, while the host went off to his business, in which he was soon deeply engaged.

Harold pretended to be deep in the enjoyment of his wine, and soon the host forgot all about him.

Soon the place became crammed, and Harold, watching his opportunity, crept up the stairs.

At the top he heard loud shouts and the clinking of glasses.

Approaching the door whence came the sounds, he took out his pistol, and with the butt-end hammered loudly upon the panel.

There was a pause for a moment, and then a loud voice, which Harold recognised as that of Blood, shouted in angry tones—

"Enter, thou noisy fool!"

Blood was evidently under the impression that it was the landlord entering with something which had been ordered.

Imagine his and his companions' astonishment when Harold, firm and erect, entered the room.

For some seconds the gallants looked hard at Harold's young-looking face and graceful form, as much as to say—

"What manner of person is this, and what is his business?"

Blood laid down his glass of wine, and stretching his legs out at full length, he asked—

' Thy business, young sir? What dost thou mean by entering this, our private chamber?"

"Because thou didst invite me," replied Harold, keeping his eyes fixed upon Blood's fierce-looking face.

"Hum! and since thou hast accepted the invitation, prithee tell us thy business."

"I would speak with thee."

"Speak on, then, young sir."

"It may be better an thou dost hear what I have to say in private."

"Hum! who sent thee here?"

"No one. I came of my own inclination."

"Good! A liberty for one so young, by our Lady. But say on, youth. These gentlemen are particular friends of mine, and if they hear anything of an important or private character, which does not concern them, it goes in at one ear and comes out at the other."

"Thou wouldst say that they are assassins like thyself," said Harold, calmly.

At this bold speech, Blood and his associates became speechless with astonishment.

But presently one, a somewhat tall and fine-looking man, started from his seat, upsetting as he did so several glasses, which fell upon the oaken floor and were smashed.

Rushing forward, he drew his sword, and, in loud tones, cried—

"By heaven's mercy, canst thou sit there and be insulted in this wise?"

Blood chuckled.

Carefully refilling his glass, he said—

"Sit thee still. This youth hath but appeared to amuse us, for which we should thank, rather than show hostility towards him."

"He will have to withdraw those words, or he leaves not the ' Silver Flagon ' alive!" shouted the gallant.

One of the others approached him, and bending over his shoulder, whispered in his ear—

"Take thy seat. People talk of thy coolness and indifference, and yet thou dost allow a few words from the mouth of a demented lad to undo thee. It is a strange exhibition of thy true temper."

This, although delivered in a whisper, caught the ears of Harold, who smiled faintly as he saw both gallants resume their seats.

"Now, youth," resumed Blood, as he carelessly crossed one leg over the other, and surveyed Harold with an insolent stare, " say thy say! but speak slowly, mark thee, or mayhap we shall not catch thy words. But first tell me and these good gentlemen from what playhouse thou dost appear ; and pray let us know whether thou dost recite the writings of learned Will Shakespeare, or hast thou a young damsel with thee to assist thee in parts from one Phil Brockley?"

"I am no player," said Harold, sternly, as he returned Blood's stare ; " but since thou dost wish me to speak in the presence of these persons, I will do so. Ay, thou màyst look curiously at me, for thou hast cause to. Look closer."

And Harold, advancing a few paces nearer to Blood, flung his hat upon the floor, saying—

"Dost thou recognise me?"

"Recognise thee? In the name of the Virgin, how dost thou think I am to recognise every fool who thinks proper to present himself to me? And yet, now that I look fully at thee, methinks I remember a face like thine. Who art thou?"

"The son of he whom thou years ago foully murdered. I am Harold Harcourt."

"Thou art Harold Harcourt?" said Blood, slowly. "Pah!"

"Ay, I am."

"Or a foolish pretender?"

"Nay, I am no pretender. I tell thee I am Harold Harcourt."

Blood burst into a loud roar of laughter, in which he was joined by his companions.

But although a hot flush rested for a moment upon Harold's face, and his breath came in short, quick gasps, which showed the fire raging within his breast, he waited patiently.

"From what asylum hast thou escaped, young sir?" asked the gallant, who but a short time before had leaped from his seat and drawn his sword.

Harold, however, heeded him not, yet he marked well his features.

Little did Harold think, as he stood there at that moment, that he was confronting such favourites of the king as Buckingham, Clifford, Arlington, Ashley, Lauderdale, and another of equally high rank.

"Thou mayest laugh, Colonel Blood," said Harold, "but be careful. I tell thee I am Harold Harcourt, and I can, if need be, produce witnesses to prove it."

"Then go and tell thy tale to Sir John Humphreys, good youth," replied Blood, who really began to think that Harold was some youth whose brain was turned.

"At the present time such a thing is useless," replied Harold. "You are in his pay, and in murdering my father, you acted under his instructions."

Blood turned slightly pale.

"This youth must be someone knowing all about it," he thought; "but of a surety he is not the child of Sir Harold, for was he not accidentally killed, and thrown into a well by Varney? Pshaw! who, I wonder, has been instructing the boy to frighten me?"

Aloud he said—

"Look you, boy, you try our patience with your foolery. Go, leave us."

And Blood pointed to the door.

"List ye, Colonel Blood, prince of assassins!" cried Harold. "I am tempted to strike thee dead as thou sittest, but that would be cowardice. I am here to challenge thee to mortal combat. Draw, therefore, and defend thyself."

And like a sudden blaze of light, Harold's sword flashed before Blood's eyes.

Every man jumped to his feet, but surprise at the lad's daring held them speechless.

Presently Blood said—

"As I live, gentlemen, we have here a dangerous lunatic."

Blood's companions now found their tongues.

"Cut him down, then," cried one.

"Nay," said another, "that would hardly be fair, seeing that he is but a child."

"Ay," said Blood, "thou art right. He is but a child with a dangerous weapon in his possession, and it will be but right to disarm him, so that he injures not himself nor anyone else."

And taking a stride forward, Blood suddenly seized the weapon Harold held.

He little dreamt of what great strength Harold was possessed.

Blood held the weapon in his left hand for an instant; the next, a howl of rage escaped his lips.

Harold, by a swift and powerful wrench, had drawn the weapon through Blood's fingers, with the result that they were severely cut.

Instantly Blood's sword left its scabbard.

"By the Holy Virgin!" he shouted, "thou hast forfeited thy life, thou imp!"

"Not so," replied Harold, calmly placing his left arm round his back, and with his sword warding off Blood's furious onslaught. "Thou wilt see that thou hast neither fool nor child to play with."

For a few minutes Blood fought fairly well, but all attempts at taking Harold off his guard failed completely, much to the astonishment of the on-lookers, who were aware of Blood's reputation as a skilful swordsman.

Blood now became more furious than ever, especially when once Harold's sword came very near his heart.

He gnashed his teeth and great drops of perspiration poured down his ugly face.

In a few more minutes his cowardly nature asserted itself, and pressing Harold more closely, he cried—

"Let this farce be ended, gentlemen. Pray drive thy swords through the cub's back."

Their swords were at once with-drawn, and there is no doubt this story would have come to a sudden termination had not a strange incident occurred.

Two enormous curtains on the opposite side of the room were suddenly withdrawn, and a lady of most beautiful features and of very graceful person rushed into the room.

Flinging herself before the combatants, she cried, in excited, albeit silvery tones—

"How now, gentlemen—or shall I say cowards? What, four to one? Out on ye! Blood the brave calling out to proud English nobles to slay a youth who is doing his best to defend himself? Shame upon thee! shame upon thee! 'Sdeath! an I told this to his majesty, the Court in less than an hour would repeat, and loudly too, my cry of shame! Lauderdale, replace thy sword for fear of incurring my displeasure. I have heard it said that thou art good at thy pen, but, by our Lady! if thou art as cowardly with thy pen as thy sword, Heaven help thee; for the block will in course of time answer for thy head. And thou too, Buckingham! Of thee I am more than surprised. Until this moment I ne'er deemed thee a coward."

Buckingham smiled faintly as he sheathed his sword, and crossing over to the lady, said—

"We are but rehearsing, pretty Nell. Prithee change thy frown into smiles, for which thy face is only fitted."

"Nay, nay, Buckingham; thou canst not deceive me. I cannot smile at murder, my lord, which but for my timely intervention might have been committed," replied the lady, who proved to be none other than pretty golden haired, albeit eccentric, Nell Gwynne.

Turning to Harold, she said—

"Sheathe thy sword, good youth, for a lady's eye doth not like to dwell upon naked weapons. Sheathe it, and go thy way. What is thy name?"

"Harold Harcourt, an it please thee, madam," replied Harold, bowing gravely.

"Harcourt — Harcourt!" repeated Nell, slowly. "Methinks that name sounds familiar to my ears. But go thy way, good youth, whatever thy quarrel with these gentlemen might have been. I see that thou art not accustomed to Alsatia, and if thou wilt but take my advice, thou wilt not return here again. Fare thee well."

Harold bowed and walked to the door.

Turning, he fixed his eyes upon Blood and said—

"Mark thee well, thou murderer. A day of reckoning will come. Thou didst murder my father, and by my hand shalt thou fall. Thy friends may be powerful, but they will avail thee nought when the hour of vengeance has come."

With a defiant look at the Colonel, Harold passed down the stairs.

Passing through the house into the street, he was walking rapidly in the direction whence he came, when suddenly a group of young gallants turned the corner.

He was about to avoid them, when a voice, which he instantly recognised as belonging to the insolent Hugh Jeffries, cried out—

"By our good Lady! as I live here is the very youth about whom I have spoken to thee. Seize him!"

Before Harold could recover from his surprise, half-a-dozen hands were laid upon him.

By a mighty effort he threw them off, and drawing his sword and placing his back against a wall, he shouted—

"Back, cowards! or I swear that the lives of some of thee shall answer for this outrage."

A loud laugh was the response, and the next instant a stone thrown with great violence struck Harold on the breast.

This roused his temper.

Snatching his pistol from his doublet, he took aim at the youth who threw it, and fired with effect, for the youth, uttering a howl of agony, fell among his comrades.

"Seize him! to the lock-up with him!" cried Hugh Jeffries; "he is a conspirator!"

The rapier of each gallant was at once brought to bear upon Harold, but one after the other he snapped the slender weapons, and there is hardly a doubt but that he would have come off victorious, had it not been for the cowardly conduct of Hugh Jeffries.

This youth, unseen by Harold, fell upon his knees, crawled to Harold's side, and pierced his thigh with his rapier.

Still for some moments longer Harold gallantly continued the fight, but loss of blood told upon him, and he suddenly fell senseless to the earth.

"Now seize him!" cried Hugh Jeffries, with an exultant laugh, "and haul him off to the Fleet watch-house. By the Holy Virgin! trust me to concoct fine evidence against him! And I shall have the satisfaction of hearing my good and righteous father —from whom may his highness of the cloven hoof keep aloof!—sentence him to be hanged by the neck at Tyburn, and thus shall have the insult I have received washed out!"

The gallants ranged themselves on either side, and seizing his arms and legs, they partly dragged poor insensible bleeding Harold to the foul and filthy Fleet watch-house, which stood close against Temple Bar.

CHAPTER VIII.

IN WHICH "MASTER ROEBUCK" VISITS HIS GIGANTIC FRIEND, ROBIN RENARD—HE HEARS BY CHANCE OF HAROLD'S ARREST, AND SETS OUT WITH ROBIN, DETERMINED TO RESCUE HIM AT ALL HAZARDS.

"MASTER ROEBUCK," as Claude was pleased to call himself, was a man much given to the enjoyment of the good things of this life.

He was as fond of a flagon of canary as of a sack posset, and as fond of good company as he was of a pretty damsel.

He was liked wherever he went for his polite and gentlemanly behavior, and he was beloved by the damsels as well for his gallantry as for his expertness in the dance.

As simple "Master Roebuck" he was beloved by the poorer classes, to whom he was remarkably considerate and kind, often relieving them in their distress.

Many persons, of course, knew him to be none other than the daring Claude, and that a price was set upon his capture.

There is one thing that always stood to this man's credit, and that was, he never slew a man except in fair fight.

But to proceed with this our story.

When "Master Roebuck" (as with the permission of our readers we will so continue to call him for the time) left the house of nurse Alice, he rode along towards Holborn at a walking pace, for he was somewhat thoughtful.

He began to consider how it was possible to obtain for Harold a position in the King's Guard.

"If money were needed to obtain it," he thought, "I have it ready. Hem! Well, I will enjoy myself to-night, and devote my attention to it on the morrow. I shall see a way to do it beyond question."

Thereupon he put spurs to his horse, and rode on at a good pace until he came to Little Britain, when he slackened speed, the better to thread the narrow and intricate turnings of that ancient, and at that time, despite its narrowness, picturesque thoroughfare.

At the time of the plague, Little Britain was one of, if not the most crowded thoroughfares in the city, and it was there that the plague raged in the most appalling manner.

There was not a house in the whole place but that, long before the plague, by Heaven's mercy, finally ceased, was quite empty.

Every shutter was nailed up, and every door, upon which was painted the red cross, and over it the piteous words, "Lord have mercy upon us!" was closed.

Grass sprang up in the roads and footpaths, and for weeks and weeks no sound was heard but the melancholy crowing of a few starved cocks who found it difficult to exist.

In about the centre of Little Britain, and seeming as if it had been dropped from the very skies into the roadway, stood a small but yet pretty house, over the front of which a vine of a sturdy nature had spread itself.

At its side was a shed of about twelve feet in height, with a slanting roof of red tile.

As Master Roebuck reached this, there issued from the shed the sound of a heavy hammer striking an anvil, and as if for an accompaniment to its noisy, albeit somewhat musical sounds, a loud voice was chanting the chorus of a hunting song.

For a few moments Master Roebuck listened to this with a pleased expression of countenance.

The sounds were evidently neither new to him nor his horse, who nodded his handsome head as the hammer struck the anvil, and neighed right joyfully.

Raising his voice, Master Roebuck shouted—

"What ho, within!"

Instantly the huge oaken door was swung open, and there issued forth the most extraordinary man that could have been found in all London.

In height he was close upon eight feet—mark well that, eight feet—and he was stout and muscular in proportion.

He was possessed of a fine, handsome, and most intelligent face, and his blue eyes sparkled with merriment.

This was Robin Renard, the smith, known among his friends as the "Giant of Little Britain."

In his right hand he carried one of his hammers, with which gigantic instrument he could crack a stone of a hundredweight at a single blow, or the smallest nut without crushing the kernel.

About his waist he wore a leathern apron, which was of sufficient size to cover an ordinary person's bed.

In the waistband of this was stuck several of the smaller instruments used in his business.

"Well, friend," he said, in cheery tones, "was it thee who cried, 'What ho, within?' An it was, pray tell me thy business, for, as thou seest, I am now without."

"Then use thy eyes, good Robin, and recognise thy friend."

"What, Master Roebuck!" cried Robin. "By our good Lady, I am right glad to see thee. How dost thou do, friend Roebuck?"

And his huge fist shook Master Roebuck's somewhat slender hand with such force that his fingers felt crushed.

"I feel in pain, friend Robin. Gad's life! thy huge paw is like unto the detested Boot."*

"By Heaven's precious mercy!" replied Robin, as he crossed himself, "let us trust that neither of us will feel that. But, friend Roebuck, why didst thou not let me know thou wast coming?"

"Because I knew it not myself, Robin. But to-night I have a fit of the blues, and so I have come to thee, knowing that thy company suits me right well. Dost thou expect any company?"

"Ay, but one only, and thou knowest him an I mistake not."

"His name?"

"Oates."

"What, Titus the black?"

"Ay. His company is not to my liking, but as thou knowest, my wife is fond of what she is pleased to term spiritual comfort."

"I know Titus Oates," said Master Roebuck, "and it strikes me that he knows me. Well, he will not be in my way, Robin. Summon thy com-

* A dreadful instrument of torture used in the Tower of London.

panions and we will enjoy ourselves."

Thereupon Master Roebuck dismounted, and Robin took his horse inside the shed, where there was fodder in plenty, escorted Master Roebuck to the principal room in the house, and then left him to call his companions, who in a short time arrived—and jolly companions they were.

Some two hours later, Mistress Renard announced that supper was ready, and Robin directed her to serve it at once.

This was done, and soon the table groaned beneath the viands of all descriptions.

Robin filled the platters of his guests, and then helped himself to a lordly-looking baron of beef.

With this he soon filled his platter, the largest of the lot, but all the huge slices disappeared down his capacious throat as if by magic, and his platter was empty long before those of his guests.

He was a tremendous eater, but the presence of Master Roebuck deterred him from eating as he liked.

But he got sick of eating from what he termed "a child's plaything," and so, ascertaining that his guests were well supplied, and craving their pardon, he pulled the huge dish with the beef before him, and taking the carving knife and fork, commenced to eat in a manner more suited to his enormous stomach.

At this moment there came a rap on the door.

"It is our reverend guest," said Mistress Renard.

"Come in!" cried Robin, as well as he was able, his mouth being full of juicy beef at the time.

The door opened, and in walked a man in a semi-clerical garb.

He had evidently passed the prime of life, but his bulky body, his bloated cheeks and mulberry nose showed that he was well acquainted with the good things of this life.

"I bid you all a good-evening, gentlemen," he said, bowing and grinning profusely, "and I trust thy mind is easy, Mistress Renard, and thine also, good Robin."

"Ay," replied Robin, "my mind is easy enough, a lot easier than thine, I'll warrant me."

"Nay, nay, not so, good Robin. How can thy mind be easier than mine?"

"How? Have I any heads to answer for?"

"But it was all in the service of his most gracious majesty."

"Pah! Well, well, Master Oates, sit thee down and eat what thou canst find, which, I fear me, is but little, since, knowing you were coming, we have hastened to devour as much as possible."

Saying which, Robin seized a veal and ham pie of goodly dimensions, which he demolished in such a marvellously rapid manner as to elicit expressions of astonishment from all who beheld him.

Master Oates looked around him in dismay, for in good truth the viands had all but disappeared.

He was a fair trencherman, and it was no wonder that his bloated face assumed a woeful expression, for, although his visits to Mistress Renard were ostensibly to administer "spiritual comforts" to her, in reality they were to administer to himself as many "creature comforts" as he possibly could.

"Well, friend Renard," he said, as he made frantic but fruitless endeavours to assume a cheerful demeanour, "I know when once thou sittest at thy table it is little that remains upon it when thou dost rise. As thou sayest, I perceive thou hast nearly cleared the board, but mayhap there remains enough to satisfy my small appetite."

"Ay, marry, is there, Master Oates. An there be not enough, I will e'en go to the shed, and bring thee a large platter of what should be most suited to thee."

"And that, good Robin?"

"Hay and Oats."

Master Oates relished not this jest, mayhap he did not see it; neither did he relish the laughter which followed.

He sat himself at the table, and being supplied with what little remained by Mistress Renard, who did not dare to seek for more for fear of offending her husband, commenced operations.

MURDER OF PRINCE ARTHUR BY KING JOHN AT ROUEN.

"'I AM RIGHT GLAD TO SEE THEE!' CRIED ROBIN RENARD."

No. 3

During his meal the wine flowed freely, and jests and songs became the order of the evening.

Several songs did Master Roebuck sing, in a voice of good quality, much to the infinite diversion of the guests, who applauded vociferously.

Titus Oates frequently looked long and curiously at Master Roebuck, who was not slow in noting it.

He saw plainly enough that he was trying to recollect where he had met with him before.

Towards the close of the evening the subject of the many and various plots against the crown, and in which all present knew that Titus Oates was most intimately connected, became the topic of conversation.

Master Roebuck affected to take but scant interest in this discussion—in which ere long Master Oates waxed exceedingly warm, denouncing every one and everything he could call to mind—yet in reality he took a great interest, for he did not forget that a certain Sir John Humphreys (wrongfully so-called) took a great share in the plots.

Presently Robin said—

"And who is thy latest victim, Master Oates, an it be a fair question?"

"Not my victim, Robin. Thou shouldst say the State's, of which I am but an humble servant. But the latest capture, from a paper which I have not long since received from Hugh Jeffries, the son of the eminent and learned judge of that name——"

"Whom may Heaven confound!" roared Robin, as he dashed his huge fist upon the table with the force of a sledge-hammer.

"Say not so, Robin," continued Oates; "he is a most impartial judge, and deserves the respect of all right-thinking men."

"Pah! it is to thy interest to say so, Master Oates. By Heaven's gracious mercy! ere long the eyes of the people will be opened to his infamous practices, and they will tear him in pieces.* Would that he were sent to the block or to Tyburn as he hath sent many hundred innocent men and women. Oh, would that I had the wielding of

the axe for him! 'Fore heaven, I would hack him in pieces, and nail his foul remains to the back of the judges' seat as a warning to them."

"Well, to proceed," continued Oates; "I have received a paper from Hugh Jeffries—here it is," taking it from his pocket—"in which he says: 'In the morning meet me without fail at Temple Bar. I have information for thee. A youth who gives his name as Harold Harcourt——'"

"What!" thundered Master Roebuck, as he leapt from his seat, and stretching forth his hand snatched the paper from Oates. "What name?"

"Harold Harcourt; dost thou know him, good sir?"

Master Roebuck, with trembling hands, perused the document, which he then placed in his doublet.

His face had turned deadly pale, a fact not unnoticed by Oates.

"Ay, I do know him," replied Master Roebuck, in faltering tones, "but it says in this note that he is connected with some plot against his Majesty, and for that reason has been arrested, although it does not say where he has been taken."

"If Master Jeffries says he is connected with a plot, it must be so."

"Thou art a liar!" shouted Master Roebuck.

"Well, friend, what he says will surely be believed by his father if this person be brought before him, and a rope at Tyburn will be his doom."

"Silence, fool! A rope at Tyburn should have been thy doom years ago. Robin, attend me, I pray you."

Oates waited until the door had closed upon them, then he turned to Mistress Renard, and fixing his rat-like eyes upon her, said—

"Who is thy friend, Mistress Renard?"

"Didst thou not hear his name? It is Master Roebuck. A very——"

"By the blessed Virgin!" interrupted Oates, as he left his seat, "if he is not that incarnate master of dare-devils, Claude, my name is not Titus Oates! Ha, his life is in my hands!"

*　　*　　*　　*

"What ails thee, Master Roebuck?" asked Robin, with great concern, as they reached the shed.

---

* This really did occur.

"My heart is well-nigh broken, good Robin," replied Master Roebuck.

"Eh? God wot! I trust not. Prithee tell me what hath so affected thee? Dost thou really know this person who has been arrested?"

"Ay, Robin: it is the boy of whom I have so often spoken to thee, the only one I love."

Robin became very grave.

"This is indeed bad news," he said, "but how dost thou know it is the same?"

"It must be the same. There is but one Harold Harcourt, Robin. How he came to leave his house in which, not many hours ago, I left him, I know not. But it is evident that he has done so, and has somehow incurred the displeasure of the villain, Hugh Jeffries. Robin, he must be rescued."

"By Heaven, he must!"

"And I can rely upon thy assistance?"

"With all my heart," replied Robin, as he grasped the hand of Master Roebuck in a vice-like grip. "Only tell me what to do, and I am with thee, heart and soul."

"Listen, then, for walls have ears, and I verily believe that that perjured scoundrel Oates suspects who I am."

"An I thought he did and intended to injure thee I would place him on top of my forge and consume his blasphemous carcase."

"List ye, Robin, and all may be well with my boy."

And, taking Robin on one side in the shed, he for some time whispered in his ear.

When the guests had departed, and Mistress Renard came to look for the missing couple, she found both gone as well as the horse, and happening to glance over the forge she saw that the two pistols, and the gigantic sword belonging to her husband had also disappeared.

"Heaven's mercy upon us!" she muttered, "for surely some desperate deed is about to be done."

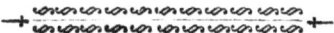

CHAPTER IX.

IN WHICH HAROLD IS CONVEYED FROM THE WATCH-HOUSE TO THE OLD BAILEY—BY THE COMMANDS OF HUGH JEFFRIES HE IS TAKEN TO ONE OF THE TORTURE CHAMBERS, AND CHAINED TO THE WALL.

IN a short time the gallants, led by Hugh Jeffries, arrived at the watch-house at the side of Temple Bar, now removed.

Of the room over this, and which many of our readers may remember, Hugh Jeffries had the key.

At that time the room contained volumes of curious records and numberless horrible instruments of torture used in the Tower and the press-room of the Old Bailey, many of which may still be seen in the Tower.

By the side of the watch-house sat a watchman fast asleep, and his halbert lying upon the ground.

Upon his face, by no means remarkable for its beauty, Hugh Jeffries delivered a stunning smack, which had the effect of causing the man to start to his feet, and deliver a string of terrible oaths, but discovering who his assailant was, he wound up by muttering an apology.

"Whom hast thou there?" he asked, pointing to Harold, who was still insensible.

"One of the leaders of a conspiracy against his Majesty," replied Hugh, "whom we captured at the risk of our lives. Open the door of the stone cell, good Collette."

The watchman produced a bunch of heavy keys and opened a massive door.

It disclosed a small and filthy stone cell.

"Now, companions," cried Hugh, with an exultant laugh, "in with him."

The gallants drew back a pace, and having swung Harold backwards and forwards for a few moments, launched him into the cell, where he fell with a crash, amid the loud laughter of the gallants.

"Now close the door, Collette," said Hugh, "and doubly lock it, mark you, and do not open it without my permission."

"Be assured that I will not, good Master Hugh," replied the watchman, as he pulled the heavy door to with a crash, "but must I not supply him with water?"

"Dolt!" cried Hugh, stamping his foot with rage. "Supply him with nothing, or by the holy Virgin, thou shalt have the cell next him."

"But, good Master Hugh," persisted the watchman, who was really a good-hearted fellow; "he may die ere morning dawns."

"Well, let him die. What will it matter? If the infamous plotter dies it will but save my good father the trouble of trying him. Come, companions, let's enjoy ourselves and leave him to die!"

And Hugh, followed by his companions, strode off and entered the Bar, in the room of which they intended to pass the night.

"The trouble of trying him," muttered the watchman as he resumed his seat. "Heaven's mercy! I pray I may never be tried, as they call it, by Bloody Judge Jeffries, for of a surety, though I did nothing, I should swing at Tyburn. But is this youth, for he is no more, really a plotter against his debauched Majesty? Or is it some new freak of Hugh Jeffries and his drunken companions? 'S life, I would wager my life that it is the latter. Albeit, I have sons of my own, and will not see this youth craving for a drink of water, despite the commands of Hugh Jeffries, whose throat I would like to squeeze until the breath left his ugly carcase! I will look at the youth."

So saying, the watchman brought forth his lantern, took the keys from his girdle, and opened the door, which sudden movement caused a number of hungry rats to scamper across the stone floor.

Holding aloft the lantern the watchman examined Harold, who lay in the position he had been thrown.

"I pray heaven I am not too late," muttered the watchman, as he knelt down and raised the lantern over Harold's head. "Of a surety he is in a bad state, and—holy Father!—he has been bleeding like an ox! Brandy will be of more service to him than water."

The watchman brought forth a flask, and poured some of its contents down Harold's throat.

The effect was instantaneous.

Harold breathed more freely, and uttering a deep sigh, opened his eyes, which, being of a very handsome description, caused the watchman, the father of a numerous family, to utter an exclamation of astonishment.

"Where am I?" asked Harold, in a voice made weak from exhaustion, consequent upon loss of blood.

"Thou art in the Fleet watch-house, young sir," replied the watchman. "Thou wert brought here by Master Hugh Jeffries on a charge of conspiracy."

"A charge of conspiracy?" said Harold, slowly. "Of what nature is the conspiracy?"

"Against the life of his sovereign Majesty Charles."

"Now, by the blessed Virgin, that is an infamous lie!" replied Harold, "and has been concocted by this Hugh Jeffries to do me an injury."

"May the Lord have mercy upon thee, young sir, if thou art brought to trial! Conspiracy or no conspiracy, I would not stand in thy shoes for a handful of diamonds from the royal crown. Judge Jeffries will believe his son, and will curse and bully a jury till he is black in the face, and they return a verdict of guilty."

"I have heard of him, but I fear him not."

"Alas! Thou hast not had sufficient experience, young sir. But hast thou any friends?"

"Alas, none!"

"No mother?"

"Nay."

"No father?"

"Nay. Would to heaven I had."

"Amen, say I. Thou art indeed then a friendless orphan, and thou art surely doomed to die the death of a dog at Tyburn. These are strange times in which we live, young sir. Heaven wot! strange times indeed, for a man hardly dare say his soul is his own. But drink some more brandy, and I will bind up thy wounds for thee, and will give thee water to wash thy face. But thou must swear thou wilt not attempt to escape."

"I swear it."

"Because if thou didst do so my life would not be worth a moment's thought. I believe thou art not a plotter against our royal sire, and would liberate thee, but that I am powerless so to do."

"I know it, friend, and thank thee most kindly. Mayhap a day may come when I can reward thee."

"Speak not of reward. I am a father and know my duty."

In a short time Harold's wounds were dressed and his face washed, and the good-natured watchman gave him a pallet of straw to lie upon, and after telling him that, when the morning advanced he would be conveyed to the Old Bailey, he bade him good-night and departed.

For some time Harold sat upon the straw heedless of the rats, whose movements he could plainly hear, but at last nature got the upper-hand of him, and stretching his numbed limbs upon the pallet, he fell asleep.

How long he slept he knew not, but he was awakened by the sound of loud voices in, as it appeared to him, angry conversation.

Then he heard the rattling of keys, and soon one was inserted in his door, which at once swung open.

There being no grating to admit of the least particle of daylight, nothing could be seen of Harold nor of his pallet, which was given him by the good-hearted watchman.

"Now come forth, thou prince of conspirators!" shouted a voice, which Harold at once recognised as belonging to Hugh Jeffries, "and let us have a fair look at thee."

Harold folded his arms proudly across his chest and came from the cell into the passage, where he found a large number of persons assembled.

In the centre of them stood Hugh Jeffries, and by his side a man clad in a semi-clerical garb, and wearing a hat of extraordinary dimensions.

Our readers are acquainted with this individual.

He was no less a personage than Titus Oates.

"There he is," said Hugh, pointing to Harold; "behold the traitor!"

"Heaven's grace defend us!" cried Titus Oates, as he raised his hands in what he intended to be meant for pious horror. "Who would have thought that one so young would have conceived such a diabolical plot against his gracious Majesty! Odd's life, Master Jeffries! to your strong desire to faithfully serve our royal master is due this youth's timely arrest. We must at once prepare the depositions, so as to bring this misguided youth to a speedy trial."

"On whose information am I to be committed to the Old Bailey?" asked Harold, fixing his keen, black eyes upon the bloated countenance of Titus Oates.

"On whose information?" said Hugh Jeffries, with a hideous grin. "On mine."

"Thou dost wish then to swear my life away?"

"Nay, I wish to bring thee to a fair trial," replied Hugh, with another grin.

"An I be brought to a fair trial," said Harold, "I shall appear before twelve of my countrymen, who will soon see that thou dost possess a lying tongue, and the brutality of thy father—on whose head may heaven's vengeance speedily fall!"

"Dost hear the prating of the insolent boy?" yelled Hugh. "Away with him! The cart waits."

"Stay but a moment, and I am ready," said Harold. "Who are thy witnesses?"

"They are here," replied Hugh, pointing to the gallants about him, many of whom looked somewhat ill from their night's debauch. "And they are ready to swear that they saw thee with divers persons at present unknown, writing out instructions for the king's assassination."

"May heaven pardon thee and them!" said Harold, solemnly. "I see it is a plot against me to appease thy vengeance. I must, however, submit, for I am powerless to prevent it. Lead on, I follow."

"Nay," replied Hugh, with a sneer. "Do thou go on, and we will follow."

"As you please," said Harold, who then walked to the street, where a cart, surrounded by watchmen, stood ready to receive him.

This he mounted, the signal was given, and the cart moved off down Fleet Street.

Hugh Jeffries, his numerous friends, and Titus Oates, who hobbled along with closed hands and meditative attitude, which he thought became him exceedingly, were at his side.

For some time Harold was silent.

He gazed listlessly at the crowd of citizens who followed the vehicle.

Presently he roused himself, and leaning forward, said—

"Mark thee well, Hugh Jeffries, if by heaven's grace I escape, look to thyself."

"Escape!" yelled Hugh. "Escape, fool! Dost thou think I will allow thee to eacape? No! by all the fiends incarnate, I will have thee chained to the walls of Newgate, with the heaviest chains that can be found, and bread and water shalt thou have until thou art brought to trial."

"Well, I will not argue with thee now, thou infamous liar, but I again call upon thee to mark well what I have said."

In a short time the cart halted before the doors of the Old Bailey.

Harold was handed down, and escorted inside the gaol, where he soon found himself before the governor.

That individual, being satisfied with the papers shown him, and much more so by Hugh's explanation, Harold was handed over to the care of two stalwart warders, in whose ears Hugh had been whispering for some moments.

Having told his friends where he would meet them in the evening, Hugh Jeffries gave the word, torches were procured and held aloft, and with the warders on either side, and Hugh and Titus Oates following, Harold was marched off.

During the journey from the watch-house to the Old Bailey, Harold, as a matter of course, had been thinking of the chances of escape ; but as he was marched through one long stone corridor and then another, through innumerable passages and many curious doorways, his heart sank within him.

"Heaven help me," he thought, " for here I am lost! There are no chances of escape. What will dear, kind Alice, and good Master Roebuck think of me ! I have heard of people being brought here, as at the Tower, and mysteriously done away with without even being brought to trial, and I think it will be so with me."

Not much was said during the journey through the vaulted passages, but suddenly Hugh cried out in a loud, commanding tone—

"Halt!"

The party stopped.

Harold looked in front of him, and as he looked, utter despair seemed to take possession of him.

Huge drops of perspiration ran down his face.

He saw that they had paused before a row of cells, which he had heard called torture chambers.

The entrance to all of them was through a small, narrow, but massive oaken door, which was studded with gigantic bolts and nails, and presented a most forbidding aspect.

"Am I to remain here ? " asked Harold.

"Silence ! " cried Hugh. "Thou art a prisoner here, and prisoners are not allowed the use of of their tongues."

"I would to heaven I had the free use of my limbs upon thee, thou caitiff ! " cried Harold, bitterly. "Thy ugly carcase should not go hence until it was bereft of breath."

Titus Oates raised his eyes and hands in pretended horror.

"In heaven's name," he said, "didst thou ever hear the like ? Truly this is a most depraved youth."

"Not so depraved as thou art," replied Harold. "Thy blasphemy is well known, an thou be really the blackguard Oates. I have heard much of thee, and my great wonder is that heaven's lightnings have not ere now stricken thee dead ! "

"Silence ! " roared Hugh. " In with him, turnkeys."

One of the warders applied his key to one of the doors, and flung it open.

Instantly there was heard a howl, which sounded like a howl of joy, and a man half-nude, and whose emaciated body was chained to the wall, darted forward.

Falling upon his knees, he raised his

hands in supplication, and in loud tones, cried—

"Art thou come to release me? I see thou art satisfied of my innocence. I thank thee, good gentleman. Pray take the chain from my poor body, and let me return to my wife and children, that I may press them to my heart and bless them ere I die!"

Truly and indeed this man looked a terrible picture as he knelt thus, his long beard reaching nearly to his knees.

His piteous entreaty caused Hugh Jeffries and the turnkeys to utter a loud laugh, while it filled Harold's eyes with tears.

"A prisoner," he thought; "no doubt been here for years, chained like a wild beast to the wall, and never to be released until kind heaven releases him from his horrible sufferings."

"Get thee in, Snowdrop," said Hugh, as he delivered a brutal kick upon the poor man's side. "We thought this was an empty cell."

The poor man rose to his feet, and fixed his eyes upon Harold.

He at once saw that it was a new prisoner brought in.

Raising his long, bony hands, he cried, in awful tones—

"Another youthful prisoner. Pray to heaven, good youth, pray night and day that heaven will release thee by death. I have been here for many years. When I entered here my beard was black, but now it is grey. For years—how many I know not—I have had no bed upon which to lay my aching limbs but a miserable pallet of straw. For years have I prayed heaven to close my life, or convert me into a lunatic, and so dull my senses to all misery."

"We have allowed thee to talk too long, Father Snowdrop," cried Hugh. "Get hence."

"My name is not Snowdrop," cried the old man, passionately; "it is Sir Vane Stanhope, and thou knowest it well. I advanced all my money to the king, and because I asked for it I was thrown in here, and—"

Hugh Jeffries, with a sudden push, sent the old man with a crash on to the floor of his cell, and closing the door with a bang, said—

"And thou art not likely to be thrown out!"

The door of the next cell was opened, and into this Harold was placed.

No sooner did he stand under its low roof than he shuddered visibly.

It was a cell in every respect like that in which the old man was confined.

Floor, walls and ceiling were of solid stone, and, there being no window, total darkness prevailed day and night.

Against the wall on the left, and about a foot from the ground, was a massive chain, each link being at least four inches in diameter.

One end was firmly fixed in the stone wall, and the other end of the chain held a steel band for placing about the person of the prisoner.

It was made of steel, so that in the event of a prisoner having a file secreted about him, or of having one smuggled in by a bribed turnkey, it would be impossible to sever the band.

Besides the chain, there was a stone jug, sadly disfigured by repeated falls, and a pallet of dirty straw.

"For what length of time am I to remain here?" asked Harold.

"For what length of time?" replied Hugh. "Until I think proper to release thee."

"Indeed? Art thou governor here?"

"Nay, but I am more. Thou wilt remain here until the depositions are made out for thy trial."

"Which will not be long," said Oates. "But we would give thee time for reflection, young sir, and for repentance ere Tyburn claims thee."

"Thank thee for nothing, thou blasphemous scoundrel!" cried Harold. "An I am to remain here, go thy way, and leave me in peace."

"We will speedily leave thee of a surety," said Hugh, with a chuckle. "Turnkeys," he added, with an air of command, "the barrel key."

What this order meant Harold knew not, but he was soon made acquainted with it.

One of the turnkeys took the bunch of keys from his girdle, and selected one of a peculiar pattern, much resembling the barrel of a pistol, and nearly of the same size.

This he inserted in the belt of the chain above referred to, and motioned Harold to place himself within it.

"Great heaven!" cried Harold, "thou dost not really mean to chain me down?"

"That do I, then," replied Hugh. "Seize him, jailors, and do my bidding."

But the jailors found no difficulty in placing Harold within the belt and locking it.

"It is useless to struggle against armed men while I myself am defenceless," thought Harold.

When he was securely fastened, Hugh gave the word, and the turnkeys went forth with their torches.

"Thou wilt have plenty of time to pray, young sir," said Oates, "and that without interruption. And thou mayest pray as loud as thou dost like, for no one will hear thee but the rats."

"An I do pray," replied Harold, "I will not forget to pray on thy behalf, and my prayer for thee shall be that ere long a rope will be thy portion."

"I will visit thee anon," said Hugh, with a grin, and stepping forth, he pulled the door behind him.

It closed with an appalling bang, and Harold was alone, in total darkness and the silence of the tomb.

CHAPTER X.

IN WHICH IT IS SEEN THAT "MASTER ROEBUCK" AND THE GIGANTIC ROBIN ARE AT FAULT, BUT BY A MERE CHANCE THEY LEARN WHERE HAROLD WAS TAKEN, AND "MASTER ROEBUCK" SUMMONSES THIRTY MYSTERIOUS INDIVIDUALS FROM THE NEIGHBOURHOOD OF PLUMSTEAD, AND A PLAN TO ATTACK THE OLD BAILEY IS FORMED.

IT will be remembered that we left "Master Roebuck" (our readers will be pleased to keep in mind his real name—that is to say, Claude) and his gigantic friend, Robin Renard, in earnest conversation in the shed, and will also remember that when Robin's wife came to look for him she found that he and his arms had vanished.

While the good lady was praying for her husband's safe keeping, Master Roebuck and Robin were speeding along towards Whitefriars.

They made inquiries at every watch-house on the road, but no one answering Harold's description was lodged at any of them.

"I cannot understand what could have caused the youth to leave his home," said Master Roebuck.

"The spirit of adventure, I'll warrant me," replied Robin.

"Maybe, maybe; and yet I often warned the boy not to stir abroad alone, especially at night."

Watch house after watch-house was called at, but singularly enough Temple Bar was omitted.

"We are at fault, good Robin," said Master Roebuck, gravely, as he drew rein in about the centre of Fleet Street.

"Truly so," replied Robin, as he thoughtfully picked his enormous teeth with his dagger.

"There is no telling," replied Master Roebuck: "the lad, who has the strength and courage of a lion, may have escaped, and if that were so, of course the watch would not say that any such person had been taken."

"Right," cried Robin; "I thought not of that."

"And in the event of his escaping, he would return home. I therefore propose that we go there."

"I agree with thee, and since it is fitting we go, I propose I do get a horse, so as not to over-exert my poor limbs."

Master Roebuck could not resist a hearty laugh as he looked at Robin's enormous limbs.

"Odd's life, man!" he said, "where canst thou find a horse that will carry thee?"

"Leave me alone for that. Dost thou not know that besides being smith I am farrier, and that besides farrier I am a veterinary? So, so, Master Roebuck, for some time I kept mine eyes open, and at last I found a fine brave horse, sound everywhere, of great height, a fine stepper, and who carries his head far above his fellows."

"Thou wast lucky, then, Robin; but, prithee, where dost thou keep him?"

"At the house of one Croft, a horse-dealer by Blackfriars, so that he attends to him when I have no time. Come along, and we will get him."

But when they arrived at the horse-dealer's house they found it closed, it being midnight, so also was the stable, upon the door of which a massive pad-lock was placed.

Robin's countenance fell as he beheld this.

"Croft must be asleep," he said, "but since I must have the horse, I must awake him."

Thereupon he hammered at the door.

In a few moments a female, whose head was adorned with a nightcap, of a pattern which would have caused a saint to laugh, opened the window, and in anything but pleased tones, cried out sharply—

"What do ye want, ye disturbers of the sleep of peaceful citizens? Oh, is it thou, Robin, thou ungainly lump of humanity?"

"Ungainly, good Mistress Croft? Thou didst not call me ungainly when thou didst ask me to kiss thee only yesterday."

'Oh, fie, fie, Robin!" replied Mistress Croft, now in sweet tones. "But what dost thou want?"

"My horse."

"Thy horse? By our good Lady, then thou canst not have him, good Robin, for see, the stable door is fast locked."

"I observe it, but tell thy good man to throw down the keys."

"Alas! my good man hath not yet returned from his drunken bout in Alsatia, upon which foul den may heaven send another plague!"

"Hush, hush!" good Mistress Croft," said Robin. "Let not thy sweet lips utter such terrible words, lest thou shouldst offend the Almighty, and He strike thee first. But I am right sorry thy husband gives way to drinking, which, of a surety, if he doth continue

it, will ruin him in pocket, mind, and body. But dost thou mean to say that he hast the keys with him?"

"Ay, good Robin, more's the pity, for if he should be robbed of them the thieves will come here and steal his property."

"Thou art right, and they might steal thee too, which would e'en cause me to weep, for of a surety I like a kiss from thee now and again."

So coolly and unconcernedly did Robin say this, and it was so evidently to Mistress Croft's satisfaction, that Master Roebuck could not resist a hearty laugh.

"I am so sorry for thee," said Mistress Croft, "but thou wilt have to go away horseless."

"That would be impossible, dear Mistress Croft. An thou hast not the keys, I must open the door without them."

"Odd's life! how wilt thou do that?"

"I will show thee in a moment," replied Robin, looking about him.

"Dost thou mean by breaking open the door?"

"Ay."

"That thou wilt never do. It is of solid oak, and hath huge bars of iron within."

"I care not for all the bars ever made," said Robin. "An I do break it open, lay all the blame on me, and say that I will come with my tools and mend it."

Robin's eye now lighted on a great stone of fully three hundred pounds in weight, and which stood at the corner of the road, so that vehicles in turning should not get upon the footway.

Up to this he went, and by the exertion of all his immense strength, he, to Master Roebuck's and Mistress Croft's intense astonishment, drew it from its position and carried it in his hands as easily as a child would carry a kitten.

Approaching the door, he raised the huge stone fair over his head, and hurled it at the door, and near to the padlock.

The force of the collision was of a nature that defies description.

Truly it seemed for a moment as if the whole house would topple down

The ironwork of the padlock and no small portion of the door was crushed into pieces, and flew open amid the neighing of the terrified animals within, who, had they been gifted with the power of thought, must have imagined that a bombardment of their quarters had commenced.

Master Roebuck had seen many strange things in his life, but this was certainly something more than marvellous.

"Truly," he thought, "Robin has the strength of six men."

In another moment Robin led forth his horse, which he had somewhat pacified by caresses, and Master Roebuck could not resist an exclamation of astonishment, not unmixed with wonder.

The animal was of tremendous height, and, beyond the shadow of a doubt, of terrific strength, and, moreover, he carried himself bravely, as Robin had said, and not with drooping head.

He seemed to be quite conscious of the fact that he was a wonderful horse.

He was saddled and bridled, and into the holsters Robin placed his pistols, and securing the stable door in the best fashion he was able, Robin mounted.

"A fair night's rest to thee, dear Mistress Croft," said Robin. "I am sorry to leave thee so soon. Would that I could give thee just one kiss to show there was no ill-feeling existing between us. But stay," he added, as he drew his horse under the window. "Prithee, good Master Roebuck, hold his head one moment. I know thou art of a quiet disposition, but love a kiss as well as thy fellows."

Master Roebuck held the horse as desired, and before he could understand what Robin was about to do, that worthy had placed his feet on the saddle bow, and so, standing erect, he was on a level with the window, at which stood Mistress Croft.

"Prithee, take off thy hideous headgear, dear Mistress Croft," said Robin, "for of a surety thou dost make thy face somewhat ugly with it. Mark thee well, Master Roebuck," he said, as Mistress Croft threw off her night-cap, "didst thou ever see such raven tresses and lovely eyes? I pray thee not to envy me this one kiss."

And with this the bold Robin delivered at the very least a dozen kisses upon Mistress Croft's lips, and if bright smiles would show an approval, then certainly they rested upon Mistress Croft's dimpled and pretty face.

Mistress Croft, be assured, did not forget to return them, albeit her kisses were of a more refined and quiet character than were Robin's.

"Now go," she said, "or Croft may return, and a quarrel may ensue. Fare thee well, Robin, and heaven guard thee, for I see by the way thou art armed that thou art upon some expedition not suited to thy calling, yet thou art big enough to defend thyself."

Robin resumed his seat, raised his hat, and with Master Roebuck rode off.

When not a hundred yards from Croft's house, Robin paused and directed Master Croft's attention to a man of somewhat diminutive stature, who was howling out the chorus of some ditty of the times, and reeling against everything he came to.

"There," said Robin, "that is Croft."

"Is it? Then heaven have mercy upon him, say I, for see, the drink hath stolen his brains, and ere long the bravos of Alsatia will steal his money. But haste thee now, good Robin, for I am getting anxious."

*   *   *   *

It is needless to give a full account of Master Roebuck's interview with nurse Alice.

It was early morning before he and Robin arrived, and startled indeed were they to behold nurse Alice standing upon the steps of the house, surrounded by neighbours and the watch, and bewailing in heart-broken tones the strange disappearance of Harold.

Dismounting and directing a man to mind their horses, Master Roebuck and Robin — whose gigantic proportions caused everyone present to utter an exclamation of intense astonishment— entered the house, and were informed that Alice had learned of Harold's mysterious departure through the watch, who, on going their rounds, had discovered the window open and a small piece of rope dangling from it.

That they then roused Alice, who

proceeded to Harold's bedroom, which she found in the state we have described in a previous chapter.

"It is passing strange," said Master Roebuck, gravely, "that he should have so made his exit. What on earth could have caused him so to do?"

"Alas!" said Alice, "didst thou not say that Colonel Blood had to do with the murder of his father?"

"Ay, that did I. Ha! I see, I see. Fool that I was! But cheer up, Alice; trust me to find him."

It will be observed that Master Roebuck did not inform her of what he had heard.

He knew that did he do so, Alice would become distracted, and so that she should not question him, he set out.

"One moment," said Alice; "I had forgotten to tell thee that thy drawer was wide open, and that when I counted one sword was missing."

Master Roebuck became grave indeed at this intelligence.

"Didst thou show him the spring, Alice?" he asked, sternly.

"Nay, nay: on my knees I swear it!"

"I believe thee, Alice. Rise, rise! Kneel not to me. Kneel not at all, but to heaven and thy king, who, by the Virgin, would not be fit to have thy pure services. Wait patiently, dear Alice. Thou knowest my life is devoted to the boy, whom I will find at the risk of my life. Good Robin, I pray thee remount."

Robin was instantly in the saddle, being closely eyed by the persons present, who appeared to be under the full impression that he was at least a descendant from Goliath, and he was met by such exclamations as—

"Gad's life, what limbs!"

"By the blessed Virgin! of what a stature!"

"Thunder and lightning! a royal baron of beef would be but food for his reflection!"

"Snakes! his brawny fist on our poor pates would dispose of us most effectually!"

To all this Robin made no remark, but smiled good-humoredly, as was his wont.

Master Roebuck was soon in the saddle, and putting spurs to his horse, soon found himself and Robin once more in Fleet Street.

Having made more inquiries, and meeting with no success, they retired for a few hours' rest.

The morning was somewhat well advanced ere they were again in the saddle, and they now turned their horses' heads to the house of a drawer (publican) in Fleet Street, and which was then called the "Dragon's Head."

Here they called for refreshment, which being supplied, they both sat down to partake of.

They had not been seated five minutes, however, before a watchman entered, and having greeted his companions, a number of whom were in the house, he said—

"Didst thou see the boy taken away?"

"Nay; what boy was it?" asked many of them.

"One Harold Harcourt, who was charged with a——"

Master Roebuck, who had been paying attention to Robin, whose appetite there seemed to be no chance of appeasing, for a veal pie and venison pasty had followed each other with lightning-like rapidity, started up with such haste as to upset a number of platters and glasses, and springing at the man's throat, he shouted—

"Charged with what, thou liar! Speak! Quick! or thy life is not worth one straw!"

As a matter of course the watchman's companions moved forward to assist their comrade, but they were met by Robin, who, placing his immense body beside Master Roebuck, swore that he would make "cinder bags" of the first who moved a peg, and the men, seeing that the threat was no idle one, stopped short.

"For the love of heaven!" gasped the watchman, "release my throat. What have I done that I should be thus treated?"

"I crave thy pardon, good watchman," said Master Roebuck, releasing him, "but the youth of whom thou didst speak is very dear to me. I am even now endeavouring to trace his whereabouts, and the mention of his name excited me. Thy pardon again, friend; I meant thee no harm, I swear it."

"If the youth is a friend of thine I must perforce forgive thee, master; but let me tell thee thy fingers are like unto the talons of a vulture. Heaven wot! another moment, and Temple Bar would have had one watchman the less."

"Since thou hast forgiven my hasty conduct, thou and thy companions may order whatever thou dost see fit, and then thou canst tell me all about this youth and as to the manner of his capture."

Thus invited, the watchman and his companions ordered several bottles of canary, and were soon in high spirits.

They offered a glass to Robin, who shook his head in a most melancholy manner.

They did not understand, but Master Roebuck did, and he ordered a small cask of ale.

This was placed before Robin, together with a large glass, but he heeded it not.

He deliberately removed the head, and raising the cask to his lips, almost drained it at one draught, to the infinite astonishment of all who beheld him.

The watchman now told Master Roebuck all the particulars, with which our readers are well acquainted.

It is needless to say Master Roebuck became very grave, and so also did Robin, who swore that if he happened to lay hold of Hugh Jeffries, he would surely make mincemeat of him.

This was much to the delight of the watchmen, none of whom had any good feeling towards the son of the judge.

"Well, friend Collette," said Master Roebuck, "since thou hast been kind to the youth, I thank thee heartily, and assure thee that what Hugh Jeffries has said is a parcel of lies. I will say 'good-day' to thee, and will beg thee to accept this in token of my gratitude."

And with this Master Roebuck handed a purse to the watchman, and then with Robin (who, seeing a man before him much the worse for the fluids of which he had partaken, coolly lifted him with one hand upon the drawer's counter, amid the great laughter of every one present, who marvelled much at his tremendous strength) left the house.

The watchman opened the purse under the eyes of his comrades, and when he poured out the contents, an exclamation escaped the lips of all present.

It was no wonder.

The purse contained gold pieces to the number of fifty.

"Truly he must be a rich man," said several.

"My blessings on him!" cried Collette, excitedly. "For a whole year have I promised my eldest daughter something on her wedding day, which is not far hence, and of a truth it was only a promise, but now I can do so."

"We will drink to his good health," said one of the men, "and to his companion, Goliath, from whose fist heaven send we may never receive a blow!"

"We will," said Collette, "and at once."

*   *   *   *

"Whither now?" asked Robin, as he vaulted into the saddle.

"Plumstead, Robin; and if you value me as a friend lag not behind."

"If I do, Master Roebuck, may I never wield a hammer again!"

With that both started down Fleet Street at a swift pace.

They had just rounded Ludgate Hill, when they saw several persons coming from the direction of the Old Bailey, and suddenly a voice cried—

"What ho! Arrest him! Arrest him! A thousand crowns for him! It is Claude!"

And a young man drawing his sword dashed at Master Roebuck's horse, being followed by many others.

"Thou art right!" cried Master Roebuck, as he raised his riding-whip over his shoulder, "and thou art Hugh Jeffries, who now receives the butt-end of my whip upon thy thick skull!"

And raising his heavy whip, he brought the butt-end fair upon Hugh Jeffries' head, and with such force that it sent him like a log to the earth.

Then pushing through those who attempted to oppose him, Master Roebuck and Robin once more dashed off on their journey.

"I saw Titus Oates **among them**," said Robin. "An he speaks one word of me, I will grind his carcase to dust!"

"Nay, do not do that, Robin," replied Master Roebuck; "for in that case thou wouldst spare the hangman of a job, which would be wrong, seeing that the rope to hang the blasphemous and treacherous scoundrel must have been woven."

Nothing of any further importance occurred, and the pair reached Plumstead about mid-day.

Just before they came to the "Load of Mischief" they were met by a man attired in the dress of a farm-labourer.

Walking straight up to them, he, without a word, took the horses by the bridles, much to Robin's astonishment.

"Take thy hands off, fool!" exclaimed Robin, in loud and angry tones; "and get thee to the trough yonder, and wash thy dirty face, which thou must have been rubbing in soot."

Master Roebuck burst into a roar of laughter, and the presumed farm-labourer grinned from ear to ear.

"All is well, Robin," said Master Roebuck; "he is my ostler. Dismount, and follow me."

"Thy ostler is he? Then, see here, thou black ostler, before thou dost feed my horse—of whose hoofs beware!—wash thy hands, for I am somewhat particular."

The man made no reply to this, for, as Robin dismounted and he saw his size, he appeared dumb with astonishment.

"Odd's fish!" he ejaculated, as he looked fearfully after Robin, "what a mountain of muscle and bone! Truly he would make a fine headsman, and, by heaven, one of his blows would chop off the heads of six men at once!"

Master Roebuck, followed by Robin, entered the "Load of Mischief" by a secret door in the wall at the back, and proceeded upstairs to one of the rooms, of which he had the key.

Here by the fireplace was a bell-shaped mouthpiece, and down this Master Roebuck directed a huge puff of wind, which caused the sound of a whistle to be heard in the distance, much to Robin's surprise, for he had never seen such a thing before.

In a few moments there came the sound as of a chain being removed in the flooring, and the next instant a round piece of wood was removed, and there crept into the room such a mite of humanity that Robin dropped into the nearest chair in amazement, greatly to the landlord's surprise, for Robin's weight broke the legs of the chair completely off.

The person who had crept through the aperture in the floor was a little fellow of about three feet in height, or maybe a little under, yet he was at least twenty or more years of age.

He was attired in a dress of black velvet and gold, and carried both sword and dagger, which were of infinite smallness.

It may be supposed that he was of ungainly person, but he was not.

No, he was well made, and carried himself somewhat haughtily, much to the amusement of Robin, who asked Master Roebuck whether he had a pair of spectacles the better to command a good view of him.

This had the effect of causing the little fellow to turn upon Robin very sharply.

Placing his little hands upon his hips, he looked up and down Robin with the utmost contempt.

Then he said, in somewhat silvery tones, albeit they were intended to be angry—

"Who art thou that dares to offer me an insult? Were I not assured that my blade would be polluted with the blood of one lower than myself, I would this moment challenge thee to mortal combat."

And he tapped the hilt of his tooth-pick sword in a significant manner.

"Odd's life!" roared Robin; "one *lower* than thyself, didst thou say? How can that be seeing that I am many feet *higher* than thyself? But come here, little master, and let us shake hands and be friends. On my life, I like thee right well, for I can see thou art little and good. Come, and tell me thy name."

The dwarf at once forgot his anger, and coming forward placed his hand in that of Robin, where of course it was utterly lost.

"My name, good giant," he said, "is Pipkin, and I am secretary to this good gentleman," pointing to Master Roebuck, who nodded smilingly.

"Pipkin, eh? Secretary, eh? By our Lady! and a good secretary too, I wot not. Well, we shall drain a bottle of sack together, good Pipkin, and when I have any love-letters to send off thou wilt write them for me, eh?"

"That I will. And now, what is *thy* name?"

"Robin."

"Robin? A good name too. But is that all? Or is thy full name Robin Redbreast?"

"Ay, 'tis so. Thou hast guessed aright."

"No more fooling, Pipkin," said Master Roebuck, sternly. "Pens and paper, and list to what I say."

Pipkin procured pens and paper, and seated himself on a high stool.

Master Roebuck then dictated, in a low tone, a few strange and mysterious words.

The strange words were copied out thirty times, doubled up, and marked with a secret sign, and then Pipkin, placing them in his doublet, disappeared down the hole in the floor as rapidly as a clown down a stage-trap.

"What is all this writing for, good Master Roebuck?" asked Robin.

"Thou wilt see ere darkness gathers over the country, Robin, and till then we will amuse ourselves by eating and drinking," said Roebuck.

It is needless to say that to this proposal Robin readily agreed.

*   *   *   *

It was just dusk when Master Roebuck and Robin descended the stairs and vaulted into their saddles.

No sooner had they done so than a horseman, wearing a very broad-brimmed hat, which was pulled over his brows, and a long cloak, glided silently by Master Roebuck's side.

Not a word was spoken.

In a few moments another horseman, attired exactly like the first, glided up. Then another and another, till at last there were thirty men.

And fine powerful fellows they were, too.

Master Roebuck now rose in his stirrups, and said—

"Gentlemen, for your kind attention I thank you, and will not fail in my reward. You are well acquainted with our place in Smithfield! Ride there as hard as you can, but in different directions, and I will meet you and give you further instructions. At this moment I need only tell you that my intention is to attack and enter the Old Bailey, and rescue my beloved boy. On, gentlemen."

None of the men made any remark, but putting spurs to their horses, they shot off in various directions, and soon disappeared from sight.

"By heaven's mercy!" cried Robin, who had watched the scene with much curiosity, "these men look determined enough."

"They are, Robin, as you will see ere long. But now let us hasten to London."

In order that our readers may be prepared for what is about to transpire, we must precede Master Roebuck and his somewhat mysterious followers by some little time.

CHAPTER XI.

IN WHICH TITUS OATES AND HUGH JEFFRIES PAY A VISIT TO THE GOVERNOR—HUGH VISITS HAROLD AND TORMENTS HIM—THE TABLES ARE TURNED, AND HUGH FINDS HIMSELF A PRISONER IN HAROLD'S PLACE—HAROLD'S MARVELLOUS ESCAPE.

WHEN darkness had gathered over the City, Hugh Jeffries and Titus Oates emerged from Temple Bar and made for the City.

Before long they arrived at the gaol, and were at once admitted.

"Do thou make for the governor's room, Oates," said Jeffries, "and I will visit my prisoner."

"And take care no ill befalls thee, good Hugh," returned Oates. "From what I can see of him, he is a desperate and determined youth, and may do thee injury."

"Fear not," laughed Hugh; "he is chained down. Ha, ha! like the lions in the Tower."

Procuring the keys and taking a lantern, he went off to the torture-chamber, chuckling with glee at what he was about to do.

*   *   *   *

Poor unfortunate Harold!

How long the time had seemed to him!

His sufferings were really and truly fearful!

Throughout the whole day total darkness had prevailed, and, except when the wicket in the door was pulled aside and a piece of dry bread thrust through, so also had silence.

The walls were of such tremendous thickness, that although he had shouted as loud as his lungs would permit him, he was not heard by his fellow prisoners.

Time after time he had thrown himself on his wretched pallet and had tried to court sleep, but now sleep was very far indeed from his eyes.

For the twentieth time had he laid himself down as well as his heavy chains would permit, when he heard a key placed in the lock.

The door was flung back, and Hugh Jeffries, whom he now looked upon as his most bitter enemy, appeared before him.

"Ha, ha!" chuckled Jeffries, entering the cell and holding the lantern aloft, so that its rays fell upon Harold's face. "And how dost thou like thy new quarters, eh? I see by the terrified expression upon thy face that thou dost not like them."

"Thou art a liar!" replied Harold, folding his arms. "I am not terrified. Nothing *thou* canst do would terrify me, thou prince of cowards!"

"Sayest thou so? Ere long we shall see! Thou art a conspirator against his Majesty, and the 'rack and the thumbscrew shall terrify thee, I'll warrant me?"

"Thou art a worthy follower in thy father's evil footsteps," rejoined Harold with disgust; "and thy end will be as sudden as will his."

Hugh burst into a loud laugh, but before it had subsided, Harold seized the water-jug, and before he had time to recede, he dealt Hugh a stunning blow upon the head, which sent him senseless to the stone floor.

It follows, as a matter of course, that the crash of the jug upon the flags created a great amount of noise, but it was not heard beyond the threshold of the door.

Harold pulled Hugh towards him by the leg, seized the bunch of keys, and by the aid of the lantern, which, fortunately, had not gone out, he found the "barrel key," inserted it in his steel belt, and with unutterable joy found that it easily opened, and that so far as that was concerned he was free.

With great rapidity he fastened the belt around Hugh's waist and locked it.

Then he disarmed him, and fastening the sword about his own waist, took the lantern and left the cell.

For a few moments he tried to find the key to lock it, but he was unable, so he contented himself by pulling the door to.

Holding the light before him, he proceeded along the passage, which he thought looked like the one by which he had entered.

Suddenly he saw a light advancing towards him, and fearful that it was the turnkey's, he blew his own out, and squeezing himself into a recess, laid his hand upon the hilt of his sword, which had been Hugh's so recently.

Nearer and nearer came the light, but it being held by the side of the person who carried it, Harold was unable to make out who could be advancing.

But he soon found out.

The person carrying the lantern paused exactly opposite Harold, who had to hold his breath, and he saw that it was none other than Titus Oates.

"Hugh!" he cried, "where art thou? Odd's life! I am lost here; speak!"

The last word had barely left his lips ere Harold raised aloft his lantern, and brought it down with such force on Oates' head, that he fell to the ground, stunned.

Another Picture is Given Away with this Number.

"'SPEAK! QUICK! OR THY LIFE IS NOT WORTH ONE STRAW!' CRIED ROEBUCK."

No. 4

"It would be well for hundreds did I drive this sword through thy infamous heart this moment," muttered Harold ; "but I am no murderer like thee and thy blasphemous companions."

Snatching Oates' lantern from his hand, he again hurried along.

But where the narrow and intricate passage led to he knew not.

He darkened the lantern in order to see if there was a light ahead, but no, all was profound darkness.

"If Oates recovers and gives an alarm, I am lost," he thought.

Suddenly he came upon a stone staircase, and of so narrow a description that certainly only men of an ordinary stature could have passed up it.

About half-a-dozen steps up he came upon an iron door, which was partially open, emitting rays of light and smoke as from a torch.

In the lock of the door was a huge key.

As Harold crept cautiously up, he heard sounds of loud laughter, accompanied by deep groans, and looking in saw a sight that almost froze the marrow in his bones.

Three turnkeys were amusing themselves by torturing with some horrible instrument an old man who cried aloud to them to show him a little mercy or take away his life at once.

Harold felt that he would have liked to have stricken the villains dead, but, alas ! he could render the old man no assistance.

He, however, took hold of the ring in the door, and, exerting all his strength, pulled it to with a crash, and locked it amid the yells and curses of the turnkeys.

Now Harold went straight up the stairs, which verily seemed to have no end.

Round and round, round and round he went, and at last he came to a sudden halt, for before him, and barring his further progress, was another door.

A cold sweat broke out all over Harold's body as he came to the door, for on trying it he found it fast locked.

He still had Hugh's bunch of keys with him, and with trembling hands he tried first one and then the other, but with no success.

His hands became quite sore from the great exertions he made, and he was about to give up in despair, when he espied some distance from the lock a small steel knob.

He at once saw what this was, and saw too that there was no lock at all, but that the keyhole was placed there simply as a blind.

Pressing the knob with all his force, his astonishment was increased when he heard a sharp "click," and observed that the door did not fall back, but that it began to descend gently, and without the least sound *into the stairs!*

He, however, did not trouble himself about this extraordinary circumstance, but before it had quite descended he leapt over it, and to his great joy found he was in the open air.

He saw that it was night, and a profoundly dark one too, but what the hour was he, of course, could not guess.

Looking about he soon found out that he was on the roof of the gaol.

And now a fear took possession of him.

How was he to get down ?

He had no rope.

He crept to the parapet and looked over.

"Gracious heaven ! " he muttered, "it is indeed a great height. What shall I do ? Ah ! as I live, here is my chance. By heaven's grace, I shall yet escape. Heaven send it may approach beneath the walls ! "

A waggon, drawn by a team of four horses, and laden with hay and straw, was coming slowly up Newgate Street (then called Middle Row).

The driver, who seemed lost in thought, was walking at the head of the animals, and did not appear to heed the path they were taking.

To Harold's intense delight, they came within two feet of the walls.

Placing the lantern on the parapet, and in his excitement forgetting to blow it out, he stood on the narrow ledge, and, as the waggon came beneath him, he took a mighty spring and landed safely on the top.

Very little noise he made, and he might have lain there in safety for awhile, but, as we have said before, in his excitement he forgot to put out the light in the lantern.

And as he stood on the parapet of the gaol in the act of springing down, he was observed by a watchman on the opposite side, who, as soon as Harold leapt, raised a cry of—

"An escape! an escape! after him!"

And forthwith he ran to the gaol gates and roused the turnkeys, who ran out in a body.

They were just in time to see Harold scrambling down from the waggon, and, raising loud cries of "Stop him in the king's name!" ran after him as fast as they were able, and with drawn swords.

It soon became an exciting chase, and was taken up by many persons, including a number of mounted men, until it became a crowd of a most motley character.

Away up Holborn ran Harold at a tremendous pace, and, with the turnkeys and the crowd after him, like hounds after a hare, we will leave him for awhile.

CHAPTER XII.

IN WHICH TITUS OATES AND HUGH JEFFRIES, BEING RELEASED, JOIN IN THE CHASE—HAROLD IS RECAPTURED, BUT IS RESCUED BY MASTER ROEBUCK AND THE GIGANTIC ROBIN AT THE HEAD OF THIRTY HORSE- MEN—ROBIN LETS HUGH JEFFRIES AND TITUS OATES FEEL THE WEIGHT OF HIS SLEDGE-HAMMER FIST.

THE first thing Titus Oates did when he recovered his senses was to utter a howl for mercy.

"Oh, Lord, Lord!" he groaned. "I am dying, going fast."

Finding that no one replied to him he got upon his feet.

Then it was that he found his face covered with blood, and another howl left his lips.

Who it was that dealt him the blow, of course he could not imagine.

While he was pausing to consider how it had come about, he heard foot-steps rushing along the passages.

This was the turnkeys turning out at the cry of "An escape!" and Oates at once ran in the direction of the sounds, banging himself repeatedly against the buttresses as he went.

At last he came to the entrance gateway where stood the governor and a few of the higher officials, directing the men.

The appearance of Oates caused them no little astonishment.

They looked at him in wonder for a moment, and then every man burst into a loud laugh.

Well they might, for the expression upon Oates' face was comical in the extreme.

"Heaven's mercy, gentlemen!" cried Oates, "do not laugh. Something serious, I much fear me, hath occurred, and——"

"Serious!" cried the governor; "serious enough! Thy conspirator hath escaped!"

"Escaped? Marry come up, I thought so. And it must have been he who struck me."

"No doubt of it. He is a desperate and daring youth."

"He is, he is!" cried Oates. "But where, then, is Hugh Jeffries?"

"We have not seen him."

"Holy Virgin! he may have been killed! Come, gentlemen, and let us search for him."

Headed by the governor, the turn-keys commenced to search the passages for Hugh, during which Oates bewailed him as dead.

At last they came to the cell from which Harold had escaped.

What a sight met their eyes when they pushed the door open!

Hugh had regained his senses, and he was dancing about, as far as his chain permitted, like a madman, foam-ing at the mouth, and uttering curses of a most appalling character.

His face and doublet were covered with blood, and the floor of the cell was strewn with water, blood, and pieces of the jug.

He was soon released, and being

taken to the governor's room, his wound was dressed and his face washed.

He had lost a lot of blood, and was now deadly pale.

Hugh borrowed a sword, and the landlord of the " Bell Tavern," opposite the gaol, having lent two horses, Titus Oates and Hugh dashed off in the direction of the chase.

When they reached Holborn Bars, they found a mob of quite two thousand persons collected, and in the centre, surrounded by turnkeys, they saw Harold.

No sooner did Hugh's eyes rest upon him, than he uttered an exclamation of delight.

" Make way, make way ! " he shouted, as he urged his horse through the crowd.

The people drew aside, marvelling much at his death-like paleness.

" So thou art caught once more ! " cried Hugh, shaking his fist at Harold and striking him in the face. " No more chances of escape shalt thou have. By the Holy Virgin, I will be even with thee before many hours have passed. No trial shalt thou have now. The Press-room* awaits thee, and, by heaven, thou shalt feel the torture at once ! "

Harold smiled contemptuously at him.

" Away with him ! " shrieked Hugh, almost bursting with rage.

" In one moment, good Master Jeffries," said one of the turnkeys. " We are waiting for the cart. Ah ! here it is. Stand aside, in the king's name, good people ! "

The cart was drawn up, and Harold, having been bound hand and foot, was placed in it, but in such a position that he could be seen by the people.

" Look, citizens ! " shrieked Oates ; " behold one of the principal plotters against the king ! Young in years he is, in good truth, but old in crime ! "

The people knew not otherwise, and they responded with groans for Harold, and followed the cart as it moved off in the direction of Newgate.

* * * *

* A torture-room in Newgate, in which a horrible instrument called the Press was used. It consisted of a tremendous iron weight, which gradually but surely crushed its victim to death.

In one corner of Smithfield there stood at the time of our story a somewhat large house of a peculiar pattern, having more the appearance of a " round-house " than anything else.

The proprietor of this was a Jew of the name of Phillips, and his business was ostensibly that of a dealer in old apparel and such like, but in reality he was a money-lender and a purchaser of all sorts of valuable property.

At the back of this house was an immense courtyard, surrounded by a high wall, the top of which bristled with powerful spikes, which at a distance had the appearance of the bayonets of a regiment of soldiers.

It was, of course, quite dark ere Master Roebuck and Robin—who had often viewed the wall of this house with much curiosity—arrived.

Master Roebuck went to the back of the house, having just taken a careful look to see that no one was watching his movements. " By our Lady ! " muttered Robin, " if thou art going into this place, why not enter by the door ? "

" That is what I am about to do, good Robin," replied Master Roebuck, as he smiled at the curious look on Robin's face.

At that moment he halted, and whistled in a prolonged and peculiar manner.

It was a whistle that could not have been well imitated.

Almost before the sound of it had ceased a portion of the wall, and of sufficient space to allow of the passage of a horse and man, moved slowly and noiselessly back.

Master Roebuck entered, and being followed by Robin, the wall resumed its former appearance.

For some few moments Robin could not make out where he was.

Total darkness prevailed, and yet he fancied he could hear the champing of horses' bits.

The whistle was again repeated, and as if by magic a brilliant light burst upon the scene.

And now, indeed, Robin could not suppress an exclamation of intense surprise.

Before him, in the form of a half-circle, were the thirty men he had seen at Plumstead, but now each man wore a pink mask.

No sooner had Master Roebuck entered, than Pipkin, who was mounted on a small pony, rushed up to him and in hurried tones informed him of Harold's escape.

"And," he concluded, "but a little while ago the chase after him commenced."

"Then by all the saints!" cried Master Roebuck, "ere now he may be captured. I am——"

"Hist, hist!" cried a voice in husky, cracked tones.

And a man, one of the most ugly ever beheld, with a vulture-like nose, and tiny, glittering eyes, made his appearance.

"What do you know, Phillips?" asked Master Roebuck.

"Hist! The youth of whom thou art in search has been recaptured, and is this moment being conveyed to Newgate in the gaol-cart. Heaven wot! thy efforts will be useless, good captain. I see from the turret of my house a crowd of more than two thousand people. See, see," and he pointed to the heavens, "the moon hath burst through the clouds, and its rays rest upon a forest of naked weapons. Let me counsel thee—stay where thou art. If thou and thy followers attempt his rescue, oh, misery, misery! Holborn will run with blood, and there will be wailing and gnashing of teeth."

And Phillips, who was known as "The Maniac Jew," tore his hair in agony.

"Get hence!" cried Master Roebuck in angry tones. "Go tend Nelly and guard thy premises. Robin!"

"Ay, ay. I am here," replied Robin.

"Art thou ready?"

"Ay, quite."

"Good! Gentlemen, are you all ready?"

A murmur of assent ran round the half-circle.

"Pipkin," continued Master Roebuck, "the door! and mark thee well, when we are gone haste thee to Plumstead. Robin, thy arm I rely upon. To thee I leave the actual rescue of Harold Harcourt. When thou hast got him, ride for thy life to Plumstead. We shall follow. Dost thou understand?"

"Right well."

"Good. Now, gentlemen—draw!"

Thirty swords flashed in the moonlight, which now flooded the courtyard.

Master Roebuck turned his horse's head, being followed by Robin.

Pipkin pressed a knob which caused the wall to re-open, and the whole party sallied forth.

"Quick, gentlemen," cried Master Roebuck, putting spurs to his horse. "See, the crowd advances. Hark to the shouts."

The men followed the action of their leader, and in a few seconds the whole of the men bore down in the direction of the cart, after the manner of a whirlwind.

Hugh Jeffries saw the advance, and wildly waving his sword, he shouted—

"A rescue! a rescue! Citizens, defend our prisoner, in the king's name!"

The turnkeys, with drawn swords, surrounded the cart, and so also did every citizen who had a weapon; but the effort to protect the cart was useless.

Dozens were trampled under the hoofs of the horses of the masked and determined men.

Robin urged his gigantic horse up to the cart, the driver of which he seized with one hand and hurled him among the crowd, which was now fast becoming panic-stricken.

Then with his sword he cut the cords which bound Harold, and dragged him on to the saddle of his horse.

Hugh, frantic at the idea of his prisoner again escaping, made desperate attempts to get near the cart; but he was kept at bay by Master Roebuck, who treated his plunges with a smile of contempt.

Many times he could have cut him down; but he did not wish to do so if he could possibly help it.

Robin, with Harold clinging to him, endeavoured to get clear away from the cart, and in this he was assisted by the horsemen who covered, as best they could, his movements.

Suddenly Oates confronted him.

"By our Lady," roared the blasphemous scoundrel, "as I live it is Robin Renard, who lends his services to these assassins. Keep back, or I will strike thee a blow with this!"

And he brandished aloft a huge oaken staff.

Robin calmly placed his sword in his left hand, and, getting close to Oates, he raised his huge fist and brought it down with terrific force fair on Oates' pate.

"Oh, Lord! oh, Lord!" groaned Oates, "I am killed."

Robin, seizing Oates by the collar, dragged him fair off his horse and dashed him to the ground.

Then once more he attempted to push on.

"Give me thy sword," cried Harold.

"Nay, nay! Thou couldst not use it, for it is far too weighty; and besides, we do not wish to take lives if we can help it."

"True, true; but look—quick!"

Robin turned his head hastily, and saw Hugh Jeffries in the act of plunging his sword into his side.

Before it could descend Harold again raised his fist, and struck Hugh such a terrible blow in the chest that, with a howl of agony, he fell from his saddle into the road to be trodden on by Master Roebuck's horsemen, who now began to make good headway.

Of course, during all this time Master Roebuck had been trying to keep the crowd off the cart, and when he saw Robin take Harold on his saddle he heaved a sigh of relief.

Just when Robin felled Hugh Jeffries to the ground, Master Roebuck saw a body of men advancing up the hill, and by the cut of their clothes and the glitter of their weapons, he recognised them as belonging to the Tower Guard.

Getting again close to Robin, he shouted—

"Ride, Robin, ride! The guard is advancing."

Hugh Jeffries heard these words, and extricating himself as well as he was able, he endeavoured to rally the people and the exhausted turnkeys.

"Seize him, good citizens!" he cried, pointing to Master Roebuck; "he is the leader. Seize him! A thousand crowns for him, dead or alive!"

Robin, by a great effort, got his horse through the crowd and dashed off.

"I heard a voice call to thee," said Harold; "and methinks the voice sounded familiar to mine ears."

"Ay, ay! No doubt, no doubt. But hist ye, good Harold, for ye know not who may be lurking by the roadside."

"But one moment, and I have done. For what part are we bound?"

"Plumstead Common."

"That name sounds familiar to mine ears."

"No doubt, no doubt!" replied Robin, and from the tone of his voice Harold concluded, and rightly too, that all further conversation for the time being must cease.

Along the quiet country roads—for they were so at the time of which we write, good reader, and the houses were few and far between, and in those days, when a man was a mile from St. Paul's, he breathed the pure air of heaven; but, alas! at the present day for miles from St. Paul's nothing can be breathed but the foul odours from numberless factories—went Robin, his horse's hoofs striking the ground with such force that the sound could be heard at a tremendous distance off.

On and on he went, the animal increasing his pace as he warmed to his work.

Harold for the moment forgot the danger through which he had passed, and he devoted his whole thoughts to the strength of the horse and the man before him.

He began to think that the horse and Robin were possessed of more than wonderful strength.

This was the first time that Robin had actually tried the going power of his giant horse, and Harold heard him repeatedly exclaim in delighted tones—

"Sound, by the Virgin! Sound as a bell! Bravo, Charley! Bravo, brave horse!"

At last the trees on Plumstead Common came in sight, and Robin was rounding a hedge, when he suddenly felt his foot grasped.

He was about to seize his sword, when a small voice, which he instantly recognised, said—

"Hist, good giant, follow me!"

And Pipkin darted forward.

"Stay!" replied Robin; "since I cannot see thee, good Pipkin, pray how is it possible that I can follow thee ! ”

“ Ah, true. I had forgotten. But hand me thy reins, and I will lead thy horse.”

Robin did as desired, and once again they moved forward.

In a short time they were at the secret door at the back of the “ Load of Mischief,” and the ostler took the horse’s head, while Harold and Robin dismounted.

“ Follow, gentlemen ! ” said Pipkin, in such authoritative tones that both Robin and Harold were compelled to laugh, “ and I will see that refreshments are placed before thee immediately.”

“ I thank thee, little Pipkin,” replied Robin, with a mock bow, “ and prithee order me something of a substantial character, for in good truth I am empty. But thou dost not ask me whether all is well.”

“ I see that the captain hath rescued the youth, for here he is.”

“ That I know.”

“ Good. Then if he hath successfully accomplished that, he is safe himself, and is on the road back. But I am now awaiting his message with much anxiety.”

“ Who will bring it ? ”

“ Thou shalt see ere long. Pray enter this room, and the host will provide for thee. Thy name, sir, is——? ”

And he placed himself before Harold, his hands on his hips, and his little legs stretched apart.

“ Harold Harcourt, good sir,” replied Harold, doffing his hat and making a profound bow.

“ Harold ! And a right good name, too. I like thee, Harold Harcourt, and I like thy honest face and good manners, which, of a truth, are far different to thy friend Cock Robin here. Thou shalt have a very fine bottle of sack. As for thee, master giant, thy fare will be ale.”

“ Very well, good Pipkin. I care not so that thou dost send me plenty of it, and at once.”

“ Fear not, good giant. A full barrel of ale shalt thou have, and an abundance of food.”

Thus assured, Robin seated himself very carefully on the strongest table, while Harold seated himself in the most comfortable chair.

“ For whom are we waiting, good sir ? ” asked Harold, after he had indulged in a quiet laugh concerning the infinite smallness of Pipkin.

“ For whom ? Ah, did I not tell thee ? ”

“ Nay.”

“ Hum ! We are waiting for Master Roebuck.”

“ Impossible ! ”

“ Nay, there is no impossibility about it. If no accident hath happened to him he will be here anon.”

“ Art thou one of his companions ? ”

“ What dost thou mean ? ”

“ Well, art thou a follower of his ? ”

“ Nay, nay ! I am a simple blacksmith, young sir.”

“ Then, pardon my asking, how comes it that thou didst rescue me in company with Master Roebuck ? ”

“ Well, dost thou see, Master Roebuck hath ofttimes rendered me a service, and I could not well refuse him one in return.”

“ It is certainly a most singular thing that Master Roebuck takes so great an interest in me. It has been told me that it was he who had to do with my——”

“ Hist ! here is Pipkin ! ” interrupted Robin, who had received his full instructions from Master Roebuck.

The door was thrust open, and Pipkin, who had placed on a white apron in front of him, and who was carrying a huge carving knife and fork, entered, and then standing aside, he allowed the host and two female servants to advance with their huge trays, each of which was loaded with both flesh and fowl, and of such a quantity that Robin’s mouth fairly watered.

“ Gad’s life ! ” he cried, as he seized the tray the host carried, and which contained a right royal baron of beef, “ let me have this, friend host of the round belly.”

And Robin placed the beef on one side and told the host to hasten off for the bread.

Then he took the tray from the two servants who stood looking at his immense figure in great astonishment.

Robin laughed, and rubbed his hands, saying—

"That's right, my pretty damsels, all is now ready. Stay, I am not a married man, and will pay thee thy dues."

Thereupon he took the girls in his arms and delivered upon their ripe lips several sound kisses, at which they seemed mightily pleased, and when released, ran laughingly from the room, just as the landlord entered with a basket of bread.

They met him full butt, and the consequence was that the worthy and full-bellied host went sprawling on the floor, the girls on top of him, to the infinite amusement of Harold and Robin, the latter laughing so heartily that he had to hold his sides.

"Well done," my pretty dears," said Robin, as soon as he could get breath. "Get up, good host," he added, and stepping up to the host, who was groaning miserably, he seized him with one hand and stood him upon his feet.

"Don't stand gaping there with thy great mouth," continued Robin ; "but pick up thy bread and let me and my friend eat. Hi, Pipkin, Pipkin ! where art thou ?"

Looking about the room, he saw Pipkin under the table, so convulsed with laughter that he was actually rolling about like a nine-pin.

"Get out, my little Pipkin," said Robin, "and have thy supper with us. I will pick thee out the choicest tit-bits, mark thee."

Pipkin got out, but there not being a chair upon which he could sit to reach the table, Robin took him upon his knee, which delighted Pipkin to no small degree.

It was indeed a real treat to see how carefully Robin sliced off the choicest pieces of the beef and gave them to Pipkin.

The little man declared he had never enjoyed a meal so much in all his life.

Harold had lapsed into a thoughtful mood, and partook of but little.

Just as Robin was raising the last bottle of wine to his lips—for he scorned the use of glasses, they were so small —there came a slight noise at the window.

Pipkin scrambled down, and seizing a cord, pulled the top part of the window down, and in fluttered a pigeon.

"Odd's fish !" exclaimed Robin, " I did not know this was a bird's nest."

"Neither is it," replied Pipkin, as he caught hold of the bird. "A while ago thou didst want to know who would bring a message from Master Roebuck —behold the messenger."

And Pipkin pointed to the pigeon.

"Eh !" said Robin, gravely, laying down his knife and fork, "dost thou think I am such a fool as to believe that that bird can speak ? "

"Nay, but *look !*"

And turning up the bird, Pipkin showed the astonished Robin a small piece of paper tied to its breast.

"Of a truth, this is a wonderful age, good Master Harold," said Robin, whose surprise was such that he had forgotten his meat.

"Truly so," repled Harold.

"Listen," said Pipkin, as he untied the paper and spread it out, "listen to what he says."

CHAPTER XIII.

THE DISCLOSURE—HAROLD'S RETURN HOME.

" 'ALL is well. Few of our men slightly injured, but many turnkeys and citizens killed. On the road. Tell Robin to detain Harold.' There, there," said Pipkin, " I knew he was safe."

" True," said Robin ; " and I thank heaven for it."

" Why am I to be detained ? " asked Harold.

" I suppose Master Roebuck would speak with thee."

"Very well ; I can then thank him for rescuing me."

"Of course," replied Robin ; " and now let us enjoy ourselves until he return."

And enjoy themselves they did.

Robin persuaded the host to send up

the two servants, who proved capital girls for fun.

There was only one thing Robin regretted, and that was that a flute, and somebody to play it, was not handy, so that they might dance.

But had he danced, it was likely enough that he would have brought the house down.

Until past midnight the fun waxed fast and furious.

Then it came to a sudden termination.

Pipkin announced the return of Master Roebuck, and the girls vanished.

Presently the door opened, and Master Roebuck entered.

Harold started.

Master Roebuck's features were concealed by a pink mask.

"By heaven's mercy," cried Robin, as he seized him by the hand and shook it with terrific force, " I am indeed glad to behold thee safe and sound. Truly, Master Roebuck, thou dost seem to have a charmed life."

Master Roebuck!

Yes, there was no doubt of it.

Harold stood as if dumb with astonishment.

Then starting forward, he said, in ringing tones—

"What means this mystery, Master Roebuck? Who and what are you? Speak, speak, thou man of mystery!"

And he placed himself before Roebuck.

"I am thy true friend—Master Roebuck—but I am known also as—"

Here he whispered in Harold's ear, and took the mask from his face.

Harold sank into the nearest chair and covered his face with his hands.

For some few moments Master Roebuck looked at him sadly, albeit anxiously, and Robin saw that a tear glistened in his fine eyes.

Presently he took two or three rapid turns up and down the room, then, pausing before Harold, he said, in a voice full of emotion—

"Harold, my lad, I knew that ere long thou wouldst find out that Master Roebuck was some mysterious character, and so I thought it better to tell thee myself. Do not hide thy face from me, Harold, for I cannot bear it. Only heaven above knows how I love thee, my boy, how I have watched over thee. Think not of what I am— and after all I am no worse than other men —but look upon me as a man who has only thyself to love in all the wide world."

Harold rose and placed his hands in Roebuck's.

"I forgive thee thy deception," he said. "To thee I owe my life, and I love thee as well as thou dost love me. Thou hast been a father to me, and I will still do as thou dost direct me. Believe me, the fact of thy mysterious movements will have no weight with me. I am truly startled to learn about it, but it cannot be helped. Yet I wonder much that Alice did not inform me."

"She had instructions not to do so, Harold," replied Roebuck, as he pressed him to his breast. " I feared the revelation, until thou didst reach near manhood's estate, would shock thy sensitive nerves."

"All is well now," said Harold, gaily; "I have recovered from my great and not-to-be-wondered-at astonishment, and now I propose we drink each other's healths."

"Agreed," cried Robin, " agreed! Pipkin, thou pretty gentleman, pour out the wine."

And Robin scrambled up half-a-dozen bottles at once in his huge fists. but discovering their emptiness, he let them fall again.

"Out on thee for a guzzler!" cried Pipkin. "Six bottles of wine and a cask of ale hast thou put down thy tunnel throat. Odd's life! dost thou see how his huge paunch hath swelled?"

And Pipkin pointed in disgust to Robin's huge belly.

"Marry come up!" said Robin, "did I not give thee a share? They were but thimblefuls, truly, but enough were they for thee, for it excited thee to kiss both the girls. But, by our good Lady, Master Roebuck, thou wilt see I have no money wherewith to pay for more wine."

And Robin ruefully turned out his pockets, and there dropped on the floor two articles, namely, a large horse-shoe nail, and a piece of tobacco.

Pipkin came forward, and standing

before Robin, looked up at him contemptuously.

"Look thee, sirrah," he said, "thou didst not pay for thy *supper !* "

"Eh ? Well, didst thou not invite me ? But it matters not. I will *owe* mine host the money till I come this way again. Tell him so, good Pipkin, and for ever shalt thou rank as my good friend."

"I will pay for it, good Robin," said Pipkin, "and do thou owe me the money. I will now order wine for Roebuck and Master Harold, and a cask of ale for thee."

"Thou wilt ?" said Robin. "Odd's life! thou art indeed small and good. Come along, then, Pipkin, and I will carry the cask."

Robin knelt upon the floor, and amidst the laughter of Roebuck and Harold, Pipkin mounted upon his shoulder, and thus Robin marched off.

"And now," said Roebuck, "the best thing to be done is for you to go home. I have despatched a message to Alice, who is now expecting you. But you had better rest here until the morning has advanced. You are tired, and so also are I and Robin. We must go disguised. I will see to all that. You will be safe when you get to Alice, for thine enemies know not where thou dost reside. It will not be long ere I get thee an appointment in the King's Guard. I have a plan to do so now. Leave all to me, and a commission shall be thine ere long."

Before many minutes had passed, Robin and Pipkin returned, carrying ale and wine, and the host having placed supper before Master Roebuck, a merry hour was passed, when all retired to rest.

But that night was a mysterious one to the host.

He, forgetting all about Robin's height and bulk, had directed the servant to show him into one of the ordinary rooms.

This was done, and Robin waited until the servant had gone, when he examined the bedstead.

It was only about six feet long, and Robin shrugged his shoulders in disgust.

Then he sat down and thought of how he was to get to rest that night.

He soon saw a way out of the difficulty.

Opening his door, he passed down the next flight of stairs.

Seeing a door before him, he pushed it open and entered a fine lofty room, which was full of handsome furniture.

This was the host's room, but Robin did not pause to consider whose it was.

Walking deliberately up to the bedstead, which he could indistinctly see, he, without thinking whether anyone might be in it or not, stripped it of all its bedclothes and bedding, and taking them in his arms, returned to his own room.

There he threw the things on the floor, added to them the bed and clothes from the bedstead in the room, arranged them to his satisfaction, and composed himself to sleep.

When the host and hostess entered their room, they were, of course, thunderstruck, for not a vestige of bedclothes was to be seen.

* * * *

At about nine in the morning Master Roebuck descended to the breakfastroom, where he found that Robin was already up and anxiously awaiting the breakfast.

Harold soon afterwards came down, and the meal was thereupon placed upon the table.

Neither Roebuck nor Harold felt inclined to eat ; but Robin did, and in a very short time he had disposed of a whole string of sausages, besides a dish of eggs and other sundries.

"Not that I am particularly hungry, Master Roebuck," he said, "but it will save the trouble of taking it back."

Roebuck now gave Pipkin some instructions in writing, and before long a large bundle of clothes was brought upstairs.

This, on being opened, proved to be several countrymen's suits.

Master Roebuck selected a suit for himself and one for Harold.

"As for thee, Robin," he said, "I know not what to do ; but here, take this. This suit must have fitted a man fully six feet. Take it, and make thyself look as respectable as it is possible."

Robin did as desired, and truly he looked a very scarecrow in it.

"No matter, Robin," said Roebuck ;

"no one will see much of thee on the road to London."

Soon the three descended to the yard, where they found a waggon ready to start.

Into this they got, and the ostler, giving the horses the word, they started for London.

"But is not Pipkin coming?" asked Robin.

"Nay; he will await my instructions," replied Roebuck.

Nothing of any importance occurred on the road, and in due time the waggon arrived in Holborn, where they saw numerous little crowds of people collected, discussing the events of the previous night.

Before long the waggon reached St. Giles', and Harold was soon clasped in the arms of nurse Alice, who shed tears of joy over him.

Master Roebuck stopped several hours in earnest conversation, and when he rose to depart, he placed his hand upon Harold's shoulder, and said—

"Be assured, Harold, that ere long a commission in the King's Guard shall be thine. I have to repeat what I said last night, and that is that I have a plan for getting thee a commission. Trust all to me, and give me thy promise that thou wilt not cross the threshold of this house until thou dost hear from me."

"I promise."

"Good. for the time, then, farewell. Come, Robin!"

"Fare thee well, Harold," said Robin, taking Harold's hand within his own. "If thou dost want a friend, come to Robin Renard in Little Britain, and he shall be at thy service."

"I thank thee," said Harold, warmly; "for the time, then, farewell."

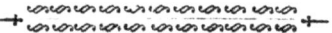

CHAPTER XIV.

IN WHICH MASTER ROEBUCK MEETS KING CHARLES AT HOUNSLOW, AND COMPELS HIM AND HIS MISTRESSES TO EXECUTE A DANCE—IN RETURN FOR THE COFFER OF GOLD HE OBTAINS THE KING'S PROMISE OF AN APPOINTMENT FOR HAROLD.

IT is well known to every student of history that King Charles II., *alias* "The Merrie Monarch," and with a score of other *aliases*, was a man much given to pleasure.

He and his courtiers were continually devising some new scheme for the gratification of their pleasures.

His Majesty was not a particular man, and he never enjoyed himself so much as when mixing with the men of Alsatia, or planning with notorious women for pleasure.

On the same day as our hero arrived home, Charles was at Barnes, on a visit to Lord Stanley, a man much after his own stamp.

He had with him two of his ladies — both women of striking beauty.

One was a Welsh lady, of the name of Minnie Thomas, and the other was Nell Gwynne.

With him was also a number of attendants, including a man our readers have by no means forgotten—that is to say, Sir John Humphreys.

His Majesty had been at Barnes for six days, and during that time had indulged in riot to his heart's content.

But suddenly a messenger was sent from Whitehall with despatches for him, and they were handed to his Majesty by Sir John Humphreys.

They set forth that the presence of his Majesty was urgently requested in the council chamber.

"Odd's fish!" cried Charles, impatiently, "then we must leave at once; and that is a great pity, Sir John, seeing that we have but just commenced to enjoy ourselves, eh?"

"True, your Majesty, but business before pleasure, they say."

"Yes, yes—true, true. Odd's fish! but I would rather stay here. Our presence is required early on the morrow, eh? *Morrow,* eh? S'death! then we must travel to-night, Sir John."

"That is so, your Majesty."

"Then, prithee, see that all is in readiness. After dinner we start."

Sir John Humphreys departed to carry out the royal commands.

Our readers only know Sir John Humphreys by name, so we may as well tell them that he was a man of about forty years of age, rather tall, and remarkably thin.

He was a great favourite with the king, for that he had purchased.

How?

Well, he had advanced the king large sums of money—money which our readers know well enough was not rightly his own.

After dinner the king and his train set out.

When the king saw his attendants, he stopped short.

"Sir John, Sir John," he cried, "how is this? Here we have not more than a dozen men to attend us. Odd's fish, suppose we should chance to meet with that Master — Master — er — Buck, I think his name is, Sir John? Is it not Buck, who thinks proper to promenade the heath?"

"Roebuck, your Majesty."

"Ah! Roebuck—yes, yes. Well, suppose we meet with him, Sir John?"

"It is not likely, your Majesty. If we did, we are more than a match for him. But his operations are carried on at Plumstead, and not anywhere near here."

"Eh! sayest thou so? Stanley, Stanley!"

"Here, my liege!" replied that worthy.

"Didst thou not say that this Master Roebuck actually stopped thee at Hampton?"

"He did, sire, and took from me, among other things, the gold snuff-box your Majesty was pleased to present to me."

"Odd's fish! he is a very daredevil, my lord. And—and when he took thy snuff-box, he was evidently up to snuff, my lord, eh?"

And his Majesty chuckled at what he considered was a huge joke.

The ladies now made their appearance, and both were handed into the royal carriage by the king himself.

When all was ready the word was given, and away dashed the train.

It was a bright moonlight night, and the carriage and train looked fine indeed.

The six horses in the king's coach, which were driven by three postilions in gay livery, were thoroughbred animals, and they went along at a spanking pace.

The king passed the time merrily enough.

His voice and the laughter of Nell Gwynne and pretty Minnie Thomas was heard high above the tramp of the horses.

Occasionally the king put his head out of the coach to chaff Sir John and Lord Stanley, to the infinite amusement of the servants.

Suddenly the king became aware of the fact that they were going along at an unusual pace, and he asked Sir John, who rode by the carriage door, the reason of it.

"We are now crossing Hounslow Heath," replied Sir John, "and travellers generally go faster there."

"Eh? Oh! is that so? Hem! Thou seest, Mistress Nell, that we are afraid of this daredevil of a fellow called Roebuck. Hast ever seen him?"

"Ay, my liege," replied Nell.

"Pray heaven I never shall," returned Charles. "Tell them to urge the animals on to their fullest speed."

The words had barely left his lips before a powerful voice cried out—

"Halt!"

Instantaneously the coach came to a standstill.

The king turned very pale.

He did not notice the smile which, for a moment, rested upon the beautiful face of Nell Gwynne.

"No, no," cried the king, but in low tones, "do not stop! Gad's life! we shall be all killed."

"Forward," roared Sir John, drawing his sword, "forward, and stop again at at your peril!"

"Silence thy prating tongue, Sir John Humphreys," said a stern voice, "or thou mayest find it slit ere long. And put by thy pistol, my Lord Stanley. I see thou hast thought proper to level it at my breast, but thy body is covered by a dozen pistols at this moment."

Lord Stanley lowered his pistol and said—

"Dost thou know whose carriage thou hast stopped this time?"

"Right well. It is that of his Majesty, Charles the Second."

"Eh?" said the king, putting his head cautiously out of the window. "And, pray, who art thou who dares to stop us?"

"Master Roebuck, sire, at your service!"

And Master Roebuck, masked, and attired as we have seen him before, and mounted on the black horse, advanced to the window in the most fearless manner, bowed politely and raised his hat to the ladies.

"Gad's life!" cried the king. "Didst ever see such a fellow? Of a truth he hath the breeding and impudence of a courtier, Stanley, eh?"

"He has, my liege. And I have no doubt he has my snuffbox in his pocket."

Roebuck laughed softly, then he said—

"Your Majesty has turned pale. I therefore propose we drain a flask of brandy together."

This he said in the coolest manner imaginable, and producing a flask, the top of which did duty for a glass, he deliberately poured out some of the spirit and handed it to the king, who was so thoroughly thunderstruck at his cool impudence that he could not speak for several seconds.

It must be borne in mind that the king was not a man in possession of very strong nerves, and he thought it would be better to comply with Roebuck's request.

His trembling hand took the brandy, but before he raised it to his lips, he said—

"But one moment, Master Roebuck, how am I to know that this is not poisoned!"

"Take my word as a gentleman, and a man of honour, that it is not."

Sir John Humphreys laughed contemptuously.

"Laugh not, Sir John!" said Roebuck, in fierce tones; "if thou dost laugh at me again, thou wilt forfeit thine ears."

"By heaven's gracious mercy!" cried Sir John. "Are we to stand here and be insulted by this man, your Majesty? What ho! surround this scoundrel!"

Roebuck whistled in a peculiar manner, and then he said—

"Look ahead, Sir John. Art thou not sufficiently surrounded?"

Sir John almost dropped from his saddle in astonishment.

From, as it appeared to him, out of the very heart of the trees a body of horsemen had come and had arranged themselves round the coach and the servants, who were surveying the scene with anything but easy minds.

Our readers have seen these mysterious individuals before.

"Have no fear, your Majesty," said Roebuck, politely; "they will not injure thee nor thy servants except at my command. Prithee let me drink the brandy first, since thou dost fear foul play."

And he drank the brandy he had offered to the king, for whom he poured out a fresh lot.

"'Fore heaven, Master Roebuck!" said the king; "wert thou not a good-for-naught, I would make thee my taster. Mistress Nell," he added, as he raised the brandy aloft, "here's to thy good health and better prosperity, and—"

"Rather say to the prosperity of Master Roebuck, who I fear me will now dub himself the king's own stopper," interrupted Nell, with a merry laugh, in which she was joined by pretty Minnie.

The king swallowed the brandy at one draught, to the disgust of Sir John Humphreys, and returning the top of the flask to Roebuck, he said—

"Since we have done thy bidding, thou wilt now permit us to resume our journey."

"Nay, nay," replied Roebuck, with a laugh and a wink at Nell, which it is needless to say she understood; "it is not often I am honoured with the king's company, nor with the presence of two such pretty ladies" (again raising his hat). "See, your Majesty, what a beautiful moonlight night it is.

Your Majesty does not often partake of such a treat as I now offer you."

"And that is?" asked the king uneasily.

"A dance on the green sward. I have my piper with me, and we can dance a minuet right merrily, and I am sure mistress moon will never have looked upon a more beautiful scene."

"Gad's blood, Mistress Nell! Didst thou ever hear of such a proposal to us? Of a truth this Master Roebuck is the very essence of politeness. But," he added, quietly, "we can never consent to such a proposal. On our lives! the news will spread all over the kingdom like wildfire."

"Better not offend him, my liege," whispered Nell, who was only too ready to start the fun.

The king considered for a moment.

Then he said—

"Well, be it so, Master Roebuck, we will dance a minuet. But, mark thee, if at any time thou art captured, expect no mercy from me, for thou shalt swing at Tyburn for thy impudence, I'll warrant me."

Roebuck again bowed.

"I will bear thy words in mind, sire," he said, "and all I shall ask is that thou will be the one to hand me the last cup of wine on my last journey."

The king could not help smiling at this, for he saw that Roebuck was quite as good a hand at *repartee* as himself.

Master Roebuck again whistled, and dismounting, a horseman came forward and took his horse.

The king stepped from the coach and handed Nell and Minnie out.

Then he directed Sir John Humphreys, Lord Stanley and the servants on to the right side.

The coach was allowed to remain on the left, where it was surrounded by Roebuck's companions, "to protect it," he told the king.

Another horseman came forward, and pausing in front of the king's servants produced a pipe, and soon the merrie strains of a minuet burst upon the air.

The king took as his partner Minnie, while Roebuck took Nell, and soon the quartette were footing it right merrily.

Before ten minutes had passed the king forgot all about where he was, and entered into the dance with all his heart and soul.

"What is the meaning of this, Roebuck?" asked Nell, quietly. "Art thou going to rob the king?"

"Nay, nay, pretty Nell," replied Roebuck. "An I robbed the king it would be to thy disadvantage."

"I fear me thou art telling me a falsehood!"

"Eh! What makes thee think so?"

"My eyes are sharp, and this moment I saw one of thy men crawl to the door of the coach and steal the coffer."

"Ay, but it will be returned. It is but part of a plan to get a promise from his Majesty. I never yet told thee a falsehood, Nell."

"I trust to thee, then. Rob the king, and thou wilt rob me, and if thou didst that my forgiveness thou shouldst never have."

The dancing of this minuet on Hounslow Heath was really a most beautiful sight.

The moon, which was at the full, revealed the gorgeous dresses of the king and his servants, and the handsome trailing dresses of the ladies to perfection, and caused the gold work of the coach to glitter like streaks of fire.

The tall, graceful figure of Roebuck was likewise shown to advantage.

Although the king did not openly say so, he inwardly vowed that he had never beheld such a beautiful picture in all his life.

At last the dance came to a conclusion, and the king said—

"I trust that thou art now satisfied, Sir Roebuck."

"In good truth, yes," replied Master Roebuck. "I thank your Majesty for thy attention. Ladies, accept, I pray you, my most hearty thanks, for I do swear that I never enjoyed a dance so much in all my life."

"Nor I such a novel one," said the king. "Ladies, to your seats. Sir

John, I pray thee prepare to resume our journey."

So saying, the king entered the coach and took his seat, and when he thought no one was looking, he placed his hand beneath it.

But he instantly withdrew it.

He could not have been quicker had his hand touched a bar of red-hot iron.

A deep groan escaped his lips, and he covered his face with his hands.

"What ails thee, my liege?" cried Minnie, starting up. "Speak, I pray thee!"

"Heaven's mercy," replied the king, in a broken voice, "we are ruined! Our coffer of gold, which was nearly full, has gone."

"Gone!" cried Minnie, clasping her hands.

"Ay, gone!" said the king, bitterly. Then, rising and placing his head out of the window, he whispered—

"Roebuck!"

"Here, sire!" replied Roebuck, coming close to him.

"Thou hast betrayed our confidence. While we have been dancing with thee, thy companions have stolen our coffer of gold."

"Is that indeed so?" replied Master Roebuck, pretending utter ignorance of it. "Well, what will your Majesty give for its recovery?"

"Anything—except thy free pardon."

"'Tis well, sire. I will restore thy coffer if thou wilt grant me a favour."

"Name it."

"A youth in whom I take a great interest wishes to join the Guards. He is but very young; yet he hath received a good education, and is as brave as a lion."

"He is not thy son?"

"Nay."

"Swear it."

"I swear it."

"Is that all thou wouldst ask?"

"All, sire."

"I will grant it. Take this ring, and when the youth is ready, send it with him to Whitehall, when I will see and speak with him."

And taking a signet-ring from his finger, the king gave it to Master Roebuck, who, bowing, and kissing the royal hand, retired.

In another moment the coffer was returned to its place, the king gave the word, and, with Lord Stanley at the head, the train moved off towards London.

Sir John Humphreys was about to follow the train, when a heavy hand descended upon his shoulder, and a voice said—

"Stand still! Move a step and thou art a dead man!"

Turning, he saw that the hand that had arrested him belonged to Master Roebuck.

For some few seconds he could not speak.

He turned as pale as death, and trembled in every limb.

Recovering himself by a great effort, he said—

"Why do you wish to detain me?"

"You will see anon," replied Roebuck, sternly. "I have much to say to thee, and what I *shall* say will no doubt surprise you."

In a few moments the royal train had disappeared from sight.

Then Roebuck said—

"Come, my men, let us get on. But first, Sir John Humphreys, thy arms."

Sir John had no alternative, so he at once delivered up to Roebuck his sword and pistols.

Master Roebuck handed them to one of the men, and said to another—

"Blindfold him!"

And, to Sir John's horror, his hands were tied behind him, and he was blindfolded.

Master Roebuck then gave the word, and the whole party moved silently off.

"HUGH WAS DANCING ABOUT, AS FAR AS THE CHAIN PERMITTED, LIKE A MADMAN."

CHAPTER XV.

THE STRANGE PLIGHT IN WHICH SIR JOHN HUMPHREYS REACHED WHITEHALL.

ON the following evening the king was in his throne-room surrounded by his lords and ladies.

He was uneasy, and gave vent to his uneasiness in many exclamations which cannot be repeated here.

At last he said—

" Clifford, hast thou yet heard aught of Sir John Humphreys ?"

" Nay, sire," replied Lord Clifford, coming forward ; " I have caused enquiries to be made everywhere, but with no success."

" By heaven's mercy !" cried the king, stamping his foot ; " I cannot understand it. Yet I think there can be no doubt but that he was detained by this daring Master Roebuck. What dost thou think, Mistress Gwynne ?"

" Alas, my liege, I know not what to think. What object could this Master Roebuck have in detaining him ?"

" Hem ! true, true. If we do not hear aught of him soon, Clifford, the whole country, from here to Barnes, must be searched, and do thou take command of the party."

Clifford bowed and retired, while the king again commenced to pace the room.

Suddenly the young Duke of Buckingham entered the room, advanced to the king, and bent his knee.

" Rise, Buckingham," said the king ; " thou hast news for me—eh ?"

" Aye, sire. May it please your Majesty, but ten minutes ago a waggon drawn by four horses arrived here with a long box, strongly corded, and covered with green baize.

" Well, well !"

" It has a paper affixed," continued Buckingham, " which says, ' A Present to His Most Gracious Majesty, King Charles the Second, from a loyal and loving subject.' "

" Eh—a present ? Order it to be sent here, good Buckingham, that we may examine it. Was there no name attached ?"

" None, sire !"

" Gad's life ! It is from an eccentric citizen, I wot not. Well, have it sent hither !"

" But, may it please your Majesty, it is of great size, and I had forgotten to say that at the bottom of the paper are the words ' To be opened carefully.' "

" The saints preserve us ! What can it contain ?"

" Fruit, I doubt not," said Nell Gwynne.

" Fruit ?" replied the king. " Ay, I doubt not it is. Our citizens, the merchants, are well aware of our liking for good fruit. Where is the box, Buckingham ?"

" In the blue-room, sire."

" Lead the way then, and we will have it opened. Gentlemen, pray attend us."

The whole of the assembled nobles followed his Majesty to the blue-room.

Upon the massive oaken table lay the box, which, as Buckingham had said, was covered with green baize.

It was quite six feet in length, and about two and a half in breadth.

" Odd's fish !" exclaimed the king, when he beheld it, " what manner of fruit can this contain ? Of a truth, if it be fruit, there is enough for our tables for a week. Clifford, prithee, order the men to open it."

In a few moments two men appeared with the necessary tools, and they were first ordered to take off the baize covering.

An exclamation of wonder escaped the king and every one present, when this was done.

The box was a dull black, and at the top were about two dozen small holes.

" Heaven's gracious mercy !" cried the king, starting back, " this is no fruit, Buckingham. By heaven! it is some infernal machine sent here by some infamous traitor. Of a truth, if it be so and I discover the sender, the block of Tyburn shall answer for him in less than two days."

At the mention of "infernal machine," the men took to flight, and despite the most terrible threats they could not be persuaded to return.

There were present many nobles well known for their bravery, but for some moments none offered to reveal the contents of this mysterious present.

Suddenly, while all were anxiously conversing as to the best course to pursue, a deep groan was heard.

"Holy Father," muttered one of the courtiers, "here is mystery enough."

The king was unable to speak. He stood looking at the box as if he were fascinated.

While thus they were joined by Nell Gwynne and Minnie Thomas.

"Well, my lords," said Nell, with a little laugh, "is a serpent within the room? By our Lady, it would seem so by the way you stare. Prithee what has happened?"

The king pointed to the box.

"It is not fruit, Nell," he said, "but an infernal machine, some one has been pleased to send us."

"Indeed," replied Nell, approaching the box, and looking curiously at it. "And these holes, my leige, what are they for? Ah!"

Nell suddenly started back as if shot.

"What is it?" asked the king.

"I heard a sound of a man's breathing," said Nell, excitedly.

The young and powerful Lord Travers seized the tools.

"Infernal machine or not," he cried, "I intend to fathom the mystery."

In another moment the hammer and chisel were at work, and in less than three minutes the lower part of the box was prised up.

By this time the king had somewhat recovered his self-possession, and with his own hands he helped to raise the lid.

In a very short time it came completely off, and revealed another baize cloth.

Travers snatched this off, and then a regular loud shout of horror ran round the room.

It was no wonder either.

There in the box lay Sir John Humphreys. He was bound hand and foot, gagged, and his face and head completely shaved.

Not a solitary hair was left.

His face was deathly pale, and the look of his eyes showed that he had been suffering for some time from the greatest terror and uncertainty.

"Mercy!" said the king, "what can be the meaning of this? Who can have done this deed? Release him at once, my lords, and hand me that piece of paper which I see is tied to his breast."

Sir John's release was soon effected, and they sat him in a chair, and applied restoratives to him.

As the king read the paper he became paler than ever, and his courtiers noticed that his hand trembled violently.

If they expected that the king would read the paper to them, they were disappointed.

When his Majesty had read it, he crushed it in his hand and paced the room in the most agitated manner.

But we must let our readers know the contents of this document.

It was written in a fine, bold hand, and ran as follows—

"TO ALL WHOM IT MAY CONCERN. GREETING—

"Know that Sir John Humphreys (wrongfully so called) was the man who signed the paper which commanded Colonel Blood and a villainous associate to murder Sir Harold Harcourt, of illustrious fame.

"And know also that the son, reported dead, is alive and under my care and protection. And know that the man who dares to raise a finger against him will forfeit his life!

"Sir John Humphreys is sent thus to Court as a warning to others, and to appear disgraced in the eyes of his fellow-men.

"One day the title will be wrested from his avaricious grasp, and the rightful heir to the Harcourt estates put in his place, for the papers will one day be discovered and Blood made to confess. So beware!

"And mark well these words, and mark well what it is to offend the writer of this, who signs himself

"RODERICK ROEBUCK."

"The son alive!" muttered the king. "I had heard to the contrary. Phew! it cannot be. And yet, and yet—hem!—I will question Sir John anon. Would to heaven he had not advanced me any of the money. But I will have no more—no more, or this Roebuck may waylay and murder me. Truly, truly, he is a man much to be feared."

In a few moments Sir John recovered sufficiently to be able to speak.

"Who did this deed, Sir John?" asked Buckingham.

Sir John was about to speak, but a look from the king checked him.

"Question him not," said the king—"at least, not at present. Call the attendants, and have him removed to my chamber. Sir John, give no information nor answer any questions as to this. We will investigate the affair privately."

And the king turned away in the most agitated manner, waving off Nell and Minnie, who attempted to follow him.

CHAPTER XVI.

SEES THE DESTRUCTION OF THE "TOAD IN THE HOLE," IN WHAT MANNER VARNEY MEETS WITH HIS DEATH, AND HOW TITUS OATES AND HUGH JEFFRIES ARE TARRED AND FEATHERED.

OUR readers have seen how Master Roebuck returned Sir John Humphreys to London, but we may now mention that directly he had sent the waggon off, he made a fresh appointment with his men, and at once rode away.

Arrived on the outskirts of London, he took his way to a small farmhouse.

Here he dismounted and knocked at the door.

It was instantly opened, and Master Roebuck and his horse entered.

This house was his "place of call" when that way. Here he rested a few hours, when, being much refreshed, he again set out, first, however, changing his clothes for those of a gentleman farmer.

Putting spurs to his horse he rode to St. Giles', only pausing once, and that was to throw a poor beggar (who, seated upon "Mary's Stile," at the commencement of Marylebone Fields, now known as Regent's Park, was munching a dirty piece of bread), a gold piece, for which the beggar, casting himself on his knees, and raising his hands aloft, called down heaven's choicest blessings upon him.

Stopping at nurse Alice's house, he entered and found Harold impatiently pacing the various rooms, and waiting for some news from him.

Roebuck at once entered into conversation with him.

He told Harold how he had served Sir John Humphreys, at which Harold could not resist a hearty laugh.

Then he informed him of his conversation with the king, and handing Harold the ring, told him exactly what he was to do.

"And when am I to present myself?" asked Harold.

"To-morrow will be soon enough. Send up thy name and this ring, and thou wilt be at once admitted to an audience with his Majesty."

"I thank thee sincerely for the interest thou dost take in my behalf," said Harold, warmly.

"No thanks are due, dear Harold. But now do not forget, for I shall be absent from London for awhile. I will not forbid thee to go out, but I pray thee get into no trouble."

"I will be careful."

"To-morrow night I will call again, if possible, and learn the result of the mission to the king. Yet that will be all right, I warrant me. His Majesty is a singular being, heaven wot, and not fit to hold the sceptre of this or any other country. His promises are frequently broken, but I will swear that he keep this one. Now do not forget, Harold, to stand clear of trouble. Go not near Alsatia."

"I will not. And that reminds me. What was the name of the man who assisted Blood to steal me, and murder my father?"

"His name? Well, let me see. Oh, his name was Varney—that was all. He was simply some Alsatian assassin, and as I have not seen him for some time, there is no doubt he is dead."

Bidding Harold and Alice an affectionate good-bye for the time, Master Roebuck departed.

"Varney," muttered Harold, "Varney. That was the very man who stopped me when I went to the 'Silver Flagon.' It must be. Well, well, I must keep my promise, and not go to Alsatia. But if I happen to come across him, let him look to himself."

*　　*　　*　　*

When evening came round Harold determined to go for a short walk. But in what direction to go he knew not, for he had no friends to call upon.

At last, however, he bethought him of Robin.

"I will go to Little Britain," he thought.

No sooner thought of than he set out.

By the time he reached Little Britain the evening had well advanced, and almost total darkness prevailed everywhere.

Not having been to the place before, he had some difficulty in discovering Robin's residence.

Many houses he called at with no success, and he was about to give up the search in despair, when a fine powerful voice commenced singing a hunting song, and from the sound he ascertained that the singer was accompanying himself with a hammer and anvil.

Harold now crept up to the house whence the sound proceeded, and to his intense delight beheld Robin Renard.

His immense form was enveloped in a huge leathern apron, his shirt-sleeves were tucked well up, and from his black hands and face it was evident that he had been hard at work.

Suddenly Robin finished his song, and then came a slight clapping of hands, and a little voice cried out—

"Bravo, giant, bravo! well done, on my soul! I will stand thee a good

bottle of sack ere the night hath passed."

Casting his eyes about the place, for he thought he recognised the voice, lo! he saw, seated on the handle of the forge, the small yet graceful figure of —who?

Pipkin!

Yes, it was Pipkin, sure enough, and he was enjoying himself by smoking a pipe of tobacco, a practice not generally followed in those days.

"Bravo, say I!" cried Harold, appearing in the doorway.

"Eh?" said Renard, throwing his gigantic hammer over his shoulder. "Who speaks?"

"It is I, Harold Harcourt."

Robin instantly flung his hammer to the ground, and seizing Harold by both hands shook them heartily.

In this he was followed by Pipkin, who with lightning-like rapidity, scrambled down from his perch.

"In good truth," said Robin, "I am right glad to see thee, Master Harold. Yet, by our good Lady! I do declare that one would think thou didst drop from the skies—eh, Pipkin?"

"Thou art right," replied Pipkin, "and yet, methinks, had he really dropped from the skies his bones would be somewhat sore. But now, Robin, since there is a party of us, I propose that we go to the place thou didst not long since inform me about."

"Agreed," replied Robin. "Wilt thou go, Harold?"

"Where to?"

"Close by, at Bishopsgate. There we shall meet with some of my friends, right good fellows, who enjoy a bottle of sack and a song."

"I am ready," replied Harold, "if so be that strangers are welcome."

"Marry come up! All are welcome. I will not wait to wash myself, for that matters not, but will put on my things and be ready."

Throwing on his clothes in the most careless manner it was possible, Robin went off, accompanied by Harold and Pipkin, who—our readers must be made acquainted with the fact—was on a visit to London without leave.

Through several narrow and curious turnings went Robin, and at such a pace that our hero and Pipkin had enough to do to keep up with him, and at last he halted before a large, and singularly constructed house, the various storeys of which seemed to overlap each other.

The exterior of it was dirty in the extreme, indeed it looked as though the proprietor absolutely scorned the idea of soap and water.

"This," said Robin, pausing on the threshold, "is a house known as the 'Toad in the Hole,' but, heaven's mercy! if a toad got into such a dirty hole as this, and was compelled to stay long, he would surely be suffocated. It is filled from cellar to roof with big cobwebs, and the spiders belonging to them are of such a size that they have been known to carry off whole bottles of wine, and to run away with the hats and boots of the guests, and—"

"The Virgin have mercy upon thee for a liar!" exclaimed Pipkin. "Of a surety the gentleman with the cloven hoof will oblige thee ere long!"

"And," continued Robin, "it abounds with trap-doors and flaps of strange workmanship. But if there be time I will show thee."

Thereupon he entered the house, followed by Harold and Pipkin.

Truly the place was more filthy inside than out.

Along the centre ran a long, narrow table or counter, from behind which the landlord of the place—who was so big that he could scarce walk—was serving liquors of all descriptions to as motley a collection as could have been anywhere found.

Barrels of various sizes, and which were covered with huge cobwebs, were placed in all parts of the room, and upon many of them, in the worst stages of intoxication, were seated men and women.

Let our readers conjure up Hogarth's picture of "Gin Lane," and they will have before them the attitudes of the persons assembled.

It at once reminded Harold of his visit to Alsatia.

Robin was immediately recognised by several of the more respectable persons, and he was about to order a cask of ale, when suddenly he drew Harold and Pipkin back.

"Hist!" he said, "look ahead. As I live, there are Titus Oates and Hugh Jeffries! 'Fore heaven, we must not let them see us. We will go to the back, where is a comfortable room."

"And who is that lank fellow laughing so loudly?" asked Pipkin.

"Eh—the lank fellow? Oh, that is one of their Alsatian rascals, called Varney."

Harold started and turned slightly pale.

Leaning forward, he looked hard at the man indicated, then, to Robin's amazement, he hurriedly drew his sword.

"Heaven's mercy!" cried Robin, "what would you do?"

"Interfere not with me, good Robin," said Harold. "Behold one of the assassins of my father. This night he or I will fall."

"I pray you be not rash, Harold," said Robin. "An thou didst make an attack on that man, he could call to his aid a dozen of his associates. Look around you, and behold some of the greatest swindlers who ever soiled London's ground with their footsteps. Most of them are intoxicated, and are ripe for a quarrel. With so many I could not assist thee. Sheathe thy sword, for thou art attracting attention."

Yes, it was a fact that Harold was attracting attention, but Pipkin was certainly commanding more.

Many were the glances cast at him by the assembled women, and many of the men laughed outright at him, which caused Pipkin to feel highly annoyed and indignant; and he was glad when he saw Harold persuaded to return his sword to its scabbard and follow Robin to the back part of the house.

It was quite evident that Robin was well acquainted with every inch of the place, as also with the host, who, as he handed Robin the cask of ale, nodded and grinned profusely, and was most anxious in his inquiries after Mistress Renard's health.

Through several rooms Robin led them, and at last he entered one with a beautifully modelled doorway, the top of which was adorned with the heads of animals, carved out of the solid oak.

The walls and ceiling of this room were likewise beautifully decorated;

so much so that Pipkin expressed his astonishment that such a foul den should possess so grand a room, and, moreover, he expressed his intense astonishment that the crevices were not covered with cobwebs.

"Express no wonder, good Pipkin," said Robin, as he lifted the little gentleman from the floor and placed him on the lofty mantelpiece. "The host, who is a man delighting in dirt, is bound to keep this room tidy. For why? Well, I have seen it crammed with Court nobles and their favourites, and," he whispered, "I have seen that chair," pointing to the head of the table, "occupied by none other than his Majesty. See the fire-irons? These hands made them. See how they are twisted? These hands twisted them. And I will wager my soul that there is not another man in all London who would do the like."

"On my soul, I believe thee, good Robin," said Pipkin. "And when I lead a noble damsel to the altar, as the astronomer of Whitefriars predicted I should, I shall be pleased to order my fire-irons of thee."

"I thank thee," replied Robin, bowing low, "and thy orders shall be promptly obeyed, providing thou dost pay the agreed sum before thou hast them delivered. 'Sdeath, I will wield thee such a pair of fire-irons that the simple sight of them should assuredly frighten thee. But fear not. They shall be strong and tough, so that they will not break on thy back when thy good wife—if thou dost ever have one—may think fit to whollop thee."

Despite the fierce thoughts in his mind—the one desire of his life; the desire which every day became more and more intense; the desire to avenge his father's foul murder—Harold could not resist a smile at Pipkin's wry face as Robin said this.

"But come," continued Robin, "let us drink this ale. But stay, Pipkin, hast thou any money?"

"Plenty, friend giant," replied Pipkin, as he plunged his little hand into his pocket.

"Then thou shalt treat thyself and Master Harold to sack."

"I have already ordered it, and see, here is the attendant with the tray."

The attendant having placed the wine upon the table, Robin broke the necks off the bottles, and filling the glasses, handed them to Harold and Pipkin, after which he took the head off the cask, and placing it to his lips, completely drained it, and before the amazed attendant could recover from his astonishment, Robin placed the cask upon his head, to the infinite amusement of Pipkin, who, being convulsed with laughter, dropped his glass and rolled off the mantelpiece on to the fireplace, thereby nearly smashing himself.

Robin picked him up, and having carefully dusted him, replaced him on his perch.

"Robin," said Harold, "it is true that I came here to amuse myself, but in the face of the fact that under this roof is one of the murderers of my father, it is impossible. I must and will stand face to face with this man."

"But—" commenced Robin.

"Listen," interrupted Harold. "You may have heard something of my father's murder, but I will tell you all, and then you will be able to understand my desire to be face to face with this man."

"I have heard it, Harold, and know right well that thou art the true son of Sir Harold Harcourt; yet take my advice, for I am older than thou art, and have seen more of the world. I will send for this man. He will come here, no doubt—that is if he is not too much intoxicated—then—well, then I will leave the rest to you."

"Good—I thank thee. It will be the best plan, no doubt."

"Hast thou ever spoken to this man?"

"But once, and that was at Whitefriars. But then he knew me not."

"Did he get a good view of thee?"

"Nay, for it was too dark."

"'Tis well. Master Roebuck did tell me that thy features were the exact counterpart of thy father's. Who knows? This Varney may also see the likeness."

"It is likely. Well, cause him to enter, good Robin."

Robin left the room, and returned after an absence of about two minutes.

"I have sent for him," he said, "and

he will be here in a moment. And now listen, Harold. Stand thou there by the fireplace, and I will place this lamp on the table—thus, so that the light may fall only upon thee. Now, Pipkin, come with me to the door."

Pipkin accordingly obeyed. He and Robin stood by the door, while Harold stood erect by the fireplace.

In a few moments a heavy yet unsteady footstep was heard, accompanied by the clanking of spurs and a scabbard on the stone flags, and Varney, his broad-brimmed hat pulled low down over his brows, entered.

He was partially intoxicated, and in that state certainly looked a terrible ruffian.

"What ho! my bold Robin," he cried. "Hast thou sent for me to join thee in a bottle of sack? Zooks! thou wert ever of a generous disposition, despite thy size. Where art thou, eh? Hullo!" he added, stopping suddenly as he beheld Harold before him, "who art thou?"

"Look well at me," replied Harold, in stern tones. "Dost thou recognise me?"

Varney came to the table, and leaning across it, scanned Harold's features closely.

"By the soul of the Virgin!" he said, "I have seen thy face somewhere—and yet— Well, but who art thou?"

"I am the son of he whom you, years ago, foully murdered. I am the son of Sir Harold Harcourt, and I am here to avenge my father's death. I see thou art not so far intoxicated but that thou dost know well what thou art about; and I can see by the paleness of thy face and the working of thy hands that thou canst well remember all about that fearful crime. Draw, therefore, for I swear that either you or I do not leave this place alive."

Yes, there was no doubt about it. Varney had turned deadly pale.

He stood looking at Harold as if fascinated.

But no sooner did Harold draw his sword than, uttering a wild scream of terror, Varney rushed to the door.

It was fast locked.

Robin had locked it, and with Pipkin was standing behind the heavy curtains.

Another howl of terror left Varney's lips as he saw this.

He concluded that he had been led into a trap.

Harold, sword in hand, advanced towards him.

"I tell thee to draw, thou murderer," said Harold. "I would not kill thee in cold blood—draw!"

Suddenly a thought seemed to strike Varney.

Slowly drawing his sword, which was of enormous length, and plainly stained with blood, he said—

"Since I must fight, I must. Thy blood be on thine own head. Yet thou must stand on this side, for I cannot fight with my face to the lamp."

"Fight in any fashion thou mayest see fit," replied Harold, at once changing places with him.

Varney was therefore close by the fireplace.

Raising his sword, Harold prepared to attack him.

But suddenly arose a great cry.

Like a flash of lightning the lamp was seized.

There was a sudden crash, and then was heard Robin's voice—

"Fool that I was! I ought to have seen what he was about to do when he wanted to change places with you, but I forgot in the excitement of the moment. 'Sdeath, he has beaten us. By the side of the fireplace is a secret door, and by the crash of it he hath turned the lever which securely fastens it. But fear not. I know whither it leads. Follow me."

Thereupon Robin hastily unlocked the door and turned to the right.

Very soon Harold found himself in a narrow, stone passage.

Along this they went as fast as possible, for it was somewhat dark, and at last Robin arrived before a small door.

This he opened.

"All is dark here," said Robin; "but keep close, and there will be no danger to either of you. 'Fore heaven, this Varney cannot escape us."

Up a narrow flight of stone steps went Robin, followed closely by Harold and Pipkin, who was becoming somewhat nervous.

At last Robin again paused.

"This door," he said, as he felt about for the lock, "leads to the roof. This is a sort of double house, and a wooden bridge crosses the courtyard. The secret door through which Varney went leads to the other roof, and to get away he must cross over to this and so descend. So now prepare, Harold, for there is no doubt he is opposite us by this time."

Once more Harold drew his sword, and Robin opened the door, admitting a flood of moonlight.

In another moment the three stepped on to the roof.

At their feet was a long narrow wooden bridge, across which Robin swore he would not go for any amount of money, and which led to the opposite roof, but no living soul was to be seen.

"It is strange indeed," said Robin, as he shaded his face with his hands, and looked across; "where can he be?"

Suddenly there burst upon their ears a series of unearthly shrieks, and these after a moment were followed by loud shouts below, and then a crowd of persons flocked into the courtyard.

At the same moment a loud voice cried out—

"Fly—fly for your lives!"

Before our hero or his companions could understand what all this was about, a volume of smoke burst from a window just under the bridge on the opposite side, and this was instantly followed by tongues of flame.

"Great heaven!" cried Robin, "he hath set the place on fire. As I live he will be burnt alive! But where can he be?"

Again came the cries from below.

The landlord of the house was frantic, and was vainly imploring his customers to assist him in checking the flames

But as they saw volume after volume of smoke and flame issue from various parts of the place, their answer was to hurry away as fast as their legs would carry them.

Both Robin and Harold were beginning to think that Varney had met with his death, but suddenly he appeared at one of the windows.

Truly and indeed he was in a fearful state.

The whole of his hair was burnt off and so was a portion of his clothes.

The rolling of his eyes showed his awful terror and anguish.

"Save me, save me!" he shrieked.

"The bridge—the bridge!" cried Robin. "Take to the bridge! 'Fore heaven, Harold! there is a vast difference in seeing a man killed in fair fight to being burnt alive."

"True," replied Harold. "See! he understands you and is about to try it, but I fear it is rotten, for see, the fire is directly under it."

In another moment Varney, almost nude, rushed frantically on to the roof, which in many parts was burning fiercely, and staggered to the bridge.

All held their breath.

It was a moment of awful suspense.

Despite the fact that the fire was burning fiercely in the courtyard, the landlord and many of the guests watched Varney as he placed his feet on the bridge.

The bridge shook and swayed, yet Varney managed to reach the middle, but there the frail structure, made rotten by the fire, felt his full weight.

There was an ominous crackling, then with a loud hissing noise the bridge parted at the end, and Varney was precipitated headlong into the courtyard, amid shouts of horror and a great rush for the street.

It is needless to say that he was smashed to pieces.

"It is a terrible death," said Robin, "but it was his fate. Come, or the fire will reach this part and our escape will be cut off."

As it was they had much difficulty in reaching the street.

When they gained it, they saw a crowd of persons assembled on the opposite side, and in front of them Titus Oates and Hugh Jeffries, who were laughing loudly as they saw the flames rise higher and higher.

The sight of this put Robin in a terrible rage.

"Friends!" he cried, "behold the incendiaries!" and he pointed to Titus Oates and Hugh.

There was a dead silence for a moment, the laugh died away on the lips of Oates and Jeffries.

They knew well enough that if the

crowd believed it they might be torn to pieces.

"Did these people really set fire to my place?" asked the host of the ill-fated "Toad in the Hole," as he came forward, tears streaming down his bloated face.

"Well, if they didn't really fire it," replied Robin, "they are laughing at it, and that is almost as bad."

Suddenly Hugh caught sight of Harold, and drawing his sword, he rushed forward.

Harold had no time to protect himself, and had it not been for Robin it is a certainty that his life would have been forfeited.

Robin caught Hugh by the throat with one hand, while with the other he snatched away his sword.

"Friends," cried Robin, who was now thoroughly aroused, "that is his friend —seize him. They like fire, let us see how they like water."

In an instant Oates was seized, and despite his struggles was held firmly.

Nearly every one present knew Robin, and was quite willing to do as he asked them.

Robin led the way, dragging Hugh like a dog after him, amid the shouts of the now excited multitude.

Not far from where the fire was raging was a horse-trough, and up to this went Robin.

Hugh struggled violently, but he was like a child in the arms of a grown person.

As easily as a man would lift a straw did Robin raise Hugh, and the next moment he was wallowing in the water.

When nearly half drowned he was lifted out, and Oates was brought forward.

It was in vain he howled to Robin to show him a little mercy.

"No," replied Robin; "no mercy to the man who can laugh at the destruction of another's property. In with him!"

The next instant Oates was immersed and thoroughly ducked.

"Now, companions," said Robin, "yonder is friend Compton's oil store! Go there, and say Robin Renard wants a barrel of tar, a brush, and a bag of feathers, and say I will pay him anon."

The crowd knew for what purpose these articles were required, and forgetting all about the fire, they rushed over to the shop and soon procured them.

Then Oates and Hugh were thrown on the ground, where they cursed and swore in a fearful manner.

"List to them," said Robin; "know that this one is Titus Oates, the 'king's own clergyman.' Didst thou ever hear the like of his infamous tongue? And this is Hugh Jeffries, the son of the sanguinary judge. 'Sdeath! we will send him to his father in a right worthy condition."

And while the mob, laughing loudly, held them, Robin smothered them in tar, and then shook the feathers over them.

Truly they were in a sad plight!

When Robin raised them, they were greeted with a loud shout of derisive laughter.

"Go to!" cried the crowd, "go to, for dirty beasts! Away with thee, or we will throw thee into yonder fire, for of a truth ye would make good fuel for it."

Neither Hugh nor Oates required to be told twice to go.

No sooner did the crowd open a passage for them than they hurried off as fast as they could, and in different directions.

"Now," said Robin, "come, Harold, and let us partake of supper; and, Pipkin, you little— Hallo! why where on earth is Pipkin?"

"I have not seen him for some moments," replied Harold.

"Gad's life! Why he will be crushed to death. Yet stay, stay, he is all right, good Harold. He is given to strange tricks, I think, and he has suddenly bethought himself of the fact that he was here without the consent of his master. He will reach home safe enough. Come along."

"Nay; I intend to stay here until the fire hath burnt itself out," replied Harold, firmly.

"Eh! what?" cried Robin, much astonished. "For what purpose?"

Harold drew him on one side and whispered in his ear.

What he said caused Robin to start and turn pale.

"Great heavens, Harold!" he cried ; "you surely cannot mean it ?"

"I do, Robin, I swear it."

"Heaven's mercy! It is a terrible thing to think of, but still, if you are determined to do it, of course I cannot refuse to assist you, so I will stay with you."

CHAPTER XVII.

HAROLD'S INTERVIEW WITH THE KING—HIS APPOINTMENT— THE TERRIBLE CONTENTS OF A PARCEL WHICH REACHED SIR JOHN HUMPHREYS, AND WHAT COLONEL BLOOD THOUGHT OF IT—BLOOD ACCEPTS AN OFFER OF ONE THOUSAND CROWNS TO DESTROY HAROLD—THE VISION OF SIR HAROLD.

ON the following morning when Harold made his appearance in the sitting-room he was somewhat startled to observe, lying upon the table, a magnificent outfit.

It was most beautifully made, every portion of it being of the finest texture, and lavishly embroidered with lace.

There were also a jewelled sword and dagger of exquisite workmanship, shoes ornamented with silver buckles, and a superb hat.

Mechanically he turned over these things, wondering much to whom they could belong.

"Of a truth," he muttered, "I do believe they would fit me."

Forthwith he donned the hat, and looking in the glass admired it immensely.

At this moment nurse Alice entered.

She smiled as she saw Harold viewing the hat.

"Whose are these, Alice ?" asked Harold.

"They are thine, dear Harold, and I trust they will fit, for they have been made from my measurements."

"Who, then, gave instructions for their manufacture ?"

"Master Roebuck."

"Hem! I thank him, and will at once don them. My visit to the king is important, and it is but right that I should go there well attired."

"That is true, dear Harold. Pray retire and don them."

Harold did so, and soon reappeared equipped from head to foot. And truly he looked splendid.

"Thou art now the image of thy father," said nurse Alice, looking at him admiringly ; "thou dost look right well in them. Alas! If thou dost receive an appointment in the King's Guard thy clothes will not be quite so grand."

"I care not for that, Alice," replied Harold, "so that I gain the appointment. And now I must set out for Whitehall. I have the ring with me. For the time, farewell."

"Farewell, dear Harold, and Providence watch over thee!"

*   *   *   *

King Charles was in one of the anterooms of the court, surrounded by many of his nobles.

He was in a very good humour, for on a sideboard was a great array of wines, which had been sent to gain his approval, as also numerous dishes of fruit of all descriptions, and with the wine he was making somewhat free.

Presently a page entered and whispered to young Lord Travers, who at once advanced to the king.

"Sire," he said, "a young gentleman, who says thou didst make an appointment for his appearance here to-day, and who—"

"Eh, what dost thou say, my lord? We made an appointment? Tut, tut! no such thing. We have made—"

"But, sire," interrupted Lord Travers, "he hath sent this as a token."

And Travers handed the king a signet ring.

The king turned pale, and looking round to see that he was not observed, he said, hurriedly—

"We do now recollect, Travers. On our lives, but we had forgotten. And what is his name ?"

"Harold Harcourt, may it please your Majesty."

The king uttered a cry of astonishment.

Travers and several more started forward, but Charles waved them back.

"It was but a slight pain in my side," he said ; "it is of no moment. Let us see—what were we saying, Travers? Oh, we were talking of this youth. Pray desire him to attend us."

And his Majesty, placing the ring upon his finger, pretended to be indifferent, but it was a failure, and it was observed by a certain person who entered the room at this moment—namely, Sir John Humphreys.

He was still deathly pale, and the nervous twitching of his mouth had not deserted him.

He was wearing a long, dark wig. Advancing up the room, the king beckoned to him.

The king whispered in his ear for some few moments, during which Sir John's hands trembled violently.

"But, sire," he said, "I told thee in our conversation of yesterday that the child was positively dead."

"Odd's fish, man, I know it," replied the king. "You said that Master Roebuck, or his companion, or someone, accidentally killed the child. But here we have a paper from this man, in which he says that the child is under his protection, and that anyone who attempts to injure him is a dead man."

"Idle threats, your Majesty."

"Eh—idle ? By heaven's gracious mercy, Sir John Humphreys, I do not think so ; and the experience thou hast had at the hands of this extraordinary dare-devil of a man ought at least to have taught thee different. But list to me, Sir John. Thou wilt swear that thou didst not have a hand in the murder of Sir Harold Harcourt ? "

"I will, sire."

"Well, well, but Blood did——"

"I think he knows something of it. But your Majesty knows that if he does a deed of this description, he does it for the sake of plunder."

"No doubt, no doubt. Hem ! Well, Sir John, I pray you stand aside. The youth, whom this Master Roebuck says is the son of Sir Harold, is here, and about to attend on us."

"Here, your Majesty ?" gasped Sir John.

"Aye ; but stand aside, and I will explain his appearance here anon."

Sir John Humphreys thereupon drew back, but he placed himself in a position to see Harold plainly.

In a few moments Harold entered the room with a firm tread, and was introduced to the king by Travers.

The Court nobles were engaged in conversation among themselves, but as Harold entered they ceased as if by magic.

Harold's beauty was of such an uncommon character that they looked at him in great amazement, wondering who on earth he could be.

The king was also astonished, and he looked so hard at Harold, that our hero fairly blushed.

"Zooks ! " thought his Majesty, "the likeness between him and Sir Harold Harcourt is truly marvellous, and I can see that Sir John Humphreys is of my opinion. Hem ! there is certainly some mystery here, but, as Sir John says, the youth may be an adventurer, acting under the orders of Master Roebuck. But I must keep my promise."

Aloud he said—

"Come here, young sir."

Harold approached nearer to the king, who said—

"My lords, I pray you withdraw a moment, for I would converse privately with this youth."

The nobles drew back, wondering greatly.

Sir John, it is needless to say, was on thorns.

"Thy name was announced as Harold Harcourt," said the king.

"That is right, your Majesty," replied Harold, proudly.

"But is not thy father one Roebuck ?"

"Nay, sire," said Harold, "but he is my protector."

"Hum ! we did but inquire, that was all. Well, well—er—we— Listen to me. Thou dost want a commission in our Guards ? "

"May it please your Majesty," replied Harold, with a low bow.

"'Tis well. We will grant thee a captaincy in our Guards on condition that thou dost not use the name of Harcourt.

Harold opened wide his eyes.

"But, sire," he said, "that is my name."

"We are not so sure of that. We cannot be supposed to believe the word of every adventurer. We are acquainted with many particulars relating to thee, but there is much to be proved. At present we are bound to rely upon the word of Sir John Humphreys. Wilt thou accept these terms?"

"I am bound to do as my king directs me," replied Harold, "but I can assure your Majesty that my name is Harcourt; that I am the son of the murdered Sir Harold, and that one Humphreys — falsely calling himself Sir John—holds my fortune and estates."

"Well, well, we will talk of that anon. Thou art a youth who, besides being most handsome, is possessed of common sense. In our Guards—the warrant of your appointment to which shall at once be made out—thy name will be Harold de Witt. Guard well our person, and thy advancement shall be rapid. My lords, this is our new captain. He is but young, yet from what I have heard he is brave."

"By our Lady, my lords," said Buckingham, "there is a strange likeness between him and—and—let me see—who?"

"He is the very image of poor Sir Harold Harcourt, who was murdered many years ago," replied Clifford. "Odd's life, I never saw the like."

"Tush, tush! my lords," said the king, impatiently. "It is but your imagination."

"I crave your Majesty's pardon," replied Buckingham. "It is true that sometimes the imagination misleads one, but in this particular I know I am right, and—"

Suddenly Buckingham paused, and drawing another noble to his side, he said—

"Lauderdale, dost thou not recognise in that youth one thou hast seen before?"

Lauderdale looked hard at Harold, who would have departed had he received the king's orders.

"By heavens, yes," said Lauderdale, in low tones. "That is the very youth who wished to kill Blood at the 'Silver Flagon.'"

"Aye, and who then declared himself to be the son of Sir Harold Harcourt. Sir John Humphreys," added Buckingham aloud, "dost thou see the likeness between this youth and thy unfortunate kinsman?"

Room was made for Sir John, but he did not move.

Harold, however, at once took two or three paces forward, and for the first time in his life he stood before the man who had ordered his father's murder.

"Stay!" thundered the king. "My lords, we command you to cease this absurd conversation. Sir John Humphreys may not be of your imagination. Sir John, dost thou see any likeness?"

There was an awkward pause for a moment. Sir John Humphreys tried hard to look into our hero's face, but it was a dismal failure.

Suddenly he gasped out—

"Nay, your Majesty, I fail to trace the slightest resemblance!"

Harold's breast rose and fell rapidly, and more than once his hand glided to his sword-hilt.

"'Tis well," said the king. "Harold de Witt"—laying great emphasis on the "de Witt"—"we now dismiss thee. In the blue-room thou wilt find Sir Frederick Hilcombe, who will take down thy residence. In a few days thou wilt receive thy appointment."

Harold bowed and kissed the royal hand. Then he bowed to the assembled nobles, and bestowed upon Sir John Humphreys such a look that he trembled and turned away his head.

Then he turned and strode off.

But when he reached the door, he found a hand laid upon his arm, and a voice said—

"I like thee well, friend Harold. I am also in the Guards. My name is Lord Eustace Trevor. I will be thy companion and friend if thou wilt permit me."

"I thank thee, my lord," replied Harold, in a voice full of emotion. "I thank thee right heartily, for heaven knows I want a true friend badly enough."

"'Tis well," replied Trevor. "Rely upon me."

Lord Trevor accompanied Harold to the blue-room.

There they found assembled about a score of officers, young and old.

"Gentlemen," said Trevor, "let me introduce to you a new officer, Harold de Witt. He joins our ranks BY COMMAND OF THE KING!"

Instantaneously, and much to Harold's astonishment, every man drew his sword, and raising it over Harold's head, declared in loud ringing tones—

"BY COMMAND OF THE KING! Hurrah! Right welcome, Harold de Witt!"

"From this time forth," continued Trevor, "if he remain true to us, we remain true to him, and swear to protect him."

"We swear!" answered the men.

"And now let us retire below and try the strength of his Majesty's fresh wine."

* * * *

It was a positive fact that for many months Sir John Humphreys was getting gloomier and gloomier than ever.

Our readers know little or nothing of his history between the years of the murder of Sir Harold and when we introduced him.

Well, he had been singularly unfortunate.

His ill-gotten wealth had been a curse to him.

He was in very truth a haunted man.

Day after day, night after night, would the grave and reproachful face of Sir Harold Harcourt appear before him.

Yet this fact he kept securely locked in his own breast.

Three years after he came into possession of the fortune and estates, he married a beautiful lady of the Court, of the name of Lady Beatrice Barlow.

She bore him two children, a son and daughter, and beautiful children they were.

But as they grew up the demeanour of their father altered towards them.

They saw also that their mother became graver and graver, and one night they were awakened by loud screams of terror, which proceeded from an upstairs room—a room the interior of which they had never seen, for it was always fast locked.

They ran up the stairs, followed by Sir John.

A terrible sight met their eyes.

Across the threshold of the door of this secret room (our readers have guessed that it was the bedroom of poor Sir Harold Harcourt) lay their mother, and near her stood the shadowy outline of Sir Harold.

Of course they knew not who this vision could be, but Sir John Humphreys did.

A scream of terror escaped his lips, and turning, he fled down the stairs, followed by his two children, whose screams of affright were dreadful to hear.

It must be borne in mind that superstition was rife in those days.

The poor children ran to their room and cowered down in a corner as if afraid that the vision, or whatever it was they had seen, would follow them, and not even the entreaties of the servants, men or women, could move them.

In a few moments Sir John somewhat recovered himself, and, lighting a torch, and taking a naked sword in his hand, he again mounted the stairs, followed by many of the men-servants, some of them armed like their master, for they began to think thieves were in the house.

Raising the torch aloft and brandishing his sword, Sir John shouted—

"Away, thou visitant from the other world, away, away, away! I know thou art dead and cannot harm me. Away, I say, I fear thee not!"

At these strange words the servants paused and looked at each other significantly, but seeing nothing to alarm them they did not attempt to run.

Yet for all his high words, Sir John cast many glances of fear towards the door of the room before he ventured anywhere near it.

At last he approached, as also the servants, and looked upon his wife, who slowly raised her eyes to his.

"Unhappy woman," said Sir John, sternly, "how many times have I forbidden thee to enter that room? The blow thou hast received will cause thee in future to mark well what I say."

"Nay," replied Lady Humphreys, as

she shaded her eyes with her hands, "there will be no future for me. I have wrested thy secret from thee, but at the cost of my life! Start not—I am dying. See."

And she drew from her mouth a handkerchief.

Sir John and the servants uttered a cry of horror, for as Sir John raised his torch further over his wife's body, he and they saw that a stream of blood had poured from her mouth and had saturated her dress.

Handing the torch to an attendant, Sir John stooped to raise his wife, but she cried out—

"Stand back, Sir John Humphreys. Thy hands are stained with blood. I heard thy cry of terror, and know well the cause of it. Thou didst recognise in that vision he of whom for long past thou hast spoken of in thy dreams—the man who—"

"Stay!" thundered Sir John, "on thy life let not that name pass thy lips."

"I will not—not that I fear thee, for I am fast passing away—but for my children whom may heaven protect —for no protection or affection will they get from the man who has upon his soul a foul and—"

"Silence!" again cried Sir John, stamping his foot in fearful rage.

Then turning to his servants he directed them to call his lady's maids, and went below to attend his children.

They could not be found!

With frantic haste, and nearly maddened with despair, Sir John directed his now terror-stricken servants to bring lights and search the whole place, which was of vast extent and strange construction.

Every room, every passage was searched except one, and that was a room or cell at the top, used as a store-place for arms and so on.

But the servants had always regarded this place as haunted, and none would venture near it.

In vain did Sir John rave and swear, his servants would not budge an inch.

Seizing a torch from one of them he started up the narrow and intricate stairs at a good pace, alone.

Half-way up, the torch, being caught by a sudden gust of wind, was extinguished.

For an instant Sir John hesitated, deliberating whether he should proceed, or return for another light.

But the moon, streaming through a small aperture in the massive walls, and illuminating the stairs with a small ray, decided him, and he cautiously proceeded, still bearing in his right hand his drawn sword.

In a few moments he arrived in front of the door.

It was closed, but knowing there was no key belonging to it, and that it was therefore always unlocked, he gave it a violent push, and it flew open.

As it did so, such a cry of terror escaped his lips that it was heard by the servants below, who, at the bottom of the stairs, were anxiously awaiting the result of his search.

Before him, the moon causing the outline to stand out in bold relief, stood the figure of Sir Harold Harcourt.

His right hand pointed to one corner of the room, and the left to his breast, whence, as it appeared, a stream of blood was slowly flowing.

But directly Sir John uttered the scream the figure vanished.

For some few seconds Sir John stood on the threshold, trembling in every limb.

At last, however, he ventured to cast his eyes in the direction in which the terrible figure had pointed.

He saw what appeared to be two bundles of white.

A great and awful fear took possession of him.

Sir John shouted aloud the names of his son and daughter.

But no answer was returned.

Nothing was heard save the melancholy echo of his own voice.

He advanced further into the room.

With a sudden snatch, he pulled forth the bundles. Horror!

He saw before him, clasped in each other's arms, the dead bodies of his children.

They had died of fright.

For but a few seconds Sir John gazed upon them, then, with a low moan, he fell upon his knees and clasped them in his arms, and it was thus that, a little later, the servants, made bolder by the continued absence of their master, found him.

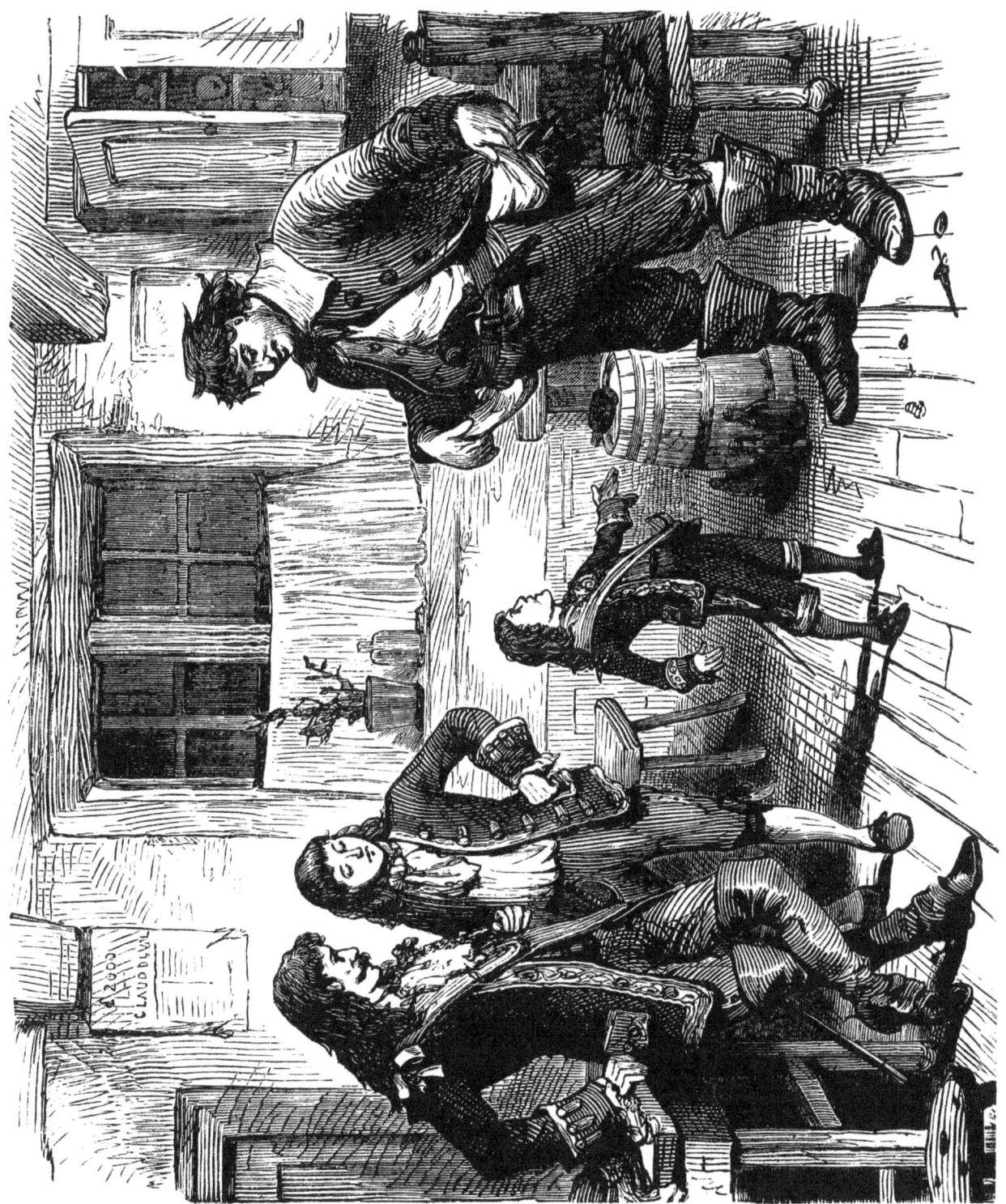

"'LOOK THEE, SIRRAH, THOU DIDST NOT PAY FOR THY SUPPER?' CRIED PIPKIN."

No. 6

That same night Lady Humphreys died, and once more Sir John was alone in the world.

Alone with his terrible thoughts, and with the vision of Sir Harold continually haunting him.

And there was something else which sorely troubled him.

Colonel Blood was always at his heels for money, and every time he visited the house he seemed to take greater liberties.

It will thus be easily seen that his life was a misery and a burden to him.

Yet, if anyone had said to him, "Will you renounce all this fortune—the estates at Bloomsbury, the grand pile at Epping, the favour of the king, and the smiles of his depraved Court—in return for peace," his answer would have been—

"No—a thousand times no! Better misery and wealth than peace and poverty."

When Harold left with Lord Trevor after his interview with the king, Sir John Humphreys had a brief conversation with his Majesty, and at once returned to Bloomsbury.

By the way he dismounted, and by the fierce manner he pulled the great bell, the servants knew that Sir John was in a terrible rage, and they therefore made haste to attend his commands.

The butler ventured to say that dinner was waiting to be served, but Sir John, with a fearful curse, told him to eat it himself.

One of the maids—and as pretty a wench as ever man saw—with a low curtsey, stammered out that she wished to ask him a favour, and was told, with a terrible scowl, that no favours could be asked that day, and nothing but curses granted ; and this rebuff caused the pretty maid to run off and hide her face on the breast of one of the serving-men—to his satisfaction.

Sir John retired to the study, and for hours and hours he paced it with rapid strides, pausing occasionally, however, to heap bitter curses on his ill-luck, and also on the head of Colonel Blood.

When darkness came on, he rang the bell and directed the butler to bring lights.

This having been done, he sat down and penned a few words to Blood.

This note he ordered to be taken to Blood's house in Whitefriars at once.

"And," he added, "let the footman take a spare horse in case Colonel Blood has not one handy."

Then he again commenced to pace the room, his mutterings being strange in the extreme.

The hour of midnight struck, but no Colonel Blood had arrived, and Sir John was beginning to fancy that he would not come, when there came a terrific ringing at the bell.

The door was instantly answered by one of the men-servants, who had been specially told off to wait at the door.

Imagine his astonishment when he saw before him a man of eight feet in height, with a box on his shoulder.

It was none other than our gigantic friend Robin Renard, but he was not known at Bloomsbury.

"Don't open thy mouth like a street-drain, friend of the livery," said Robin. "Dost think thou couldst swallow me —eh? Now here, friend of the livery, is a box, on which, if thou canst read, thou wilt see the name of Sir John Humphreys. Canst thou read?"

"Nay, friend giant, my mother had plenty to do without knocking letters and words into my skull."

"Thy thick skull, thou shouldst have said," replied Robin in disgust. "Thou wilt ne'er reach heaven if thou canst not read thy Bible. But there, there. Here is the box—take it."

"Who is it from, friend giant?"

"It matters not to thee who it is from—eh? Thou surely dost not wish to know thy master's private business? But," he added, confidentially, "of course I see thou art curious. Well," he whispered, "that box contains important documents, but I cannot tell thee where 'tis from."

"Very good. It shall be at once delivered, for Sir John hath not yet retired, and—ha! here is his guest. Stand aside, good giant!"

Robin, looking ahead, saw two horsemen coming along at a good round pace, and he slipped behind one of the pillars.

In a few seconds Colonel Blood

dashed up to the door, followed by the footman.

Dismounting, he at once entered the house, but anyone could see at a glance that he was the worse for strong drink.

When the door had closed, the footman left for the stables with the horses, and Robin came forth.

"Hum!" he muttered, "so Blood and Sir John are still friends? I will report that to Master Roebuck—but there, no doubt he knows all about it. There are few things he does not know. By the soul of the Virgin, if that box is opened in his presence, what will he say? Oh, oh, Colonel Blood! I wish I had a fair chance at thy ugly carcase. I would not leave a drop of blood in it!"

* * * *

Without knocking, Colonel Blood flung open the study door and walked —or rather staggered in.

Bringing his riding-whip with a crash upon the table, he said—

"Well, my right worthy companion and good friend, and—and banker, and how dost thou do? By the right hoof of the Evil One, thou dost look pale and troubled!"

Sir John sternly pointed to a seat, into which Blood dropped, and placing his spurred boots upon the table, prepared to listen.

"Colonel Blood," said Sir John, "I want none of thy insolent remarks."

"Eh? insolent? Ha, ha!"

"Colonel Blood," continued Sir John, "thou art an infamous liar!"

"Eh? Liar? Well, I know it. Liars, thieves, and murderers can live right well, but truthful and honest men starve."

"Well, I know thy experience as to the former is somewhat extensive, and—"

"And so is thine, Sir John Humphreys—eh? Yes; ha, ha! But conversation is always dry work, so prithee order a bottle of thy best, Sir John, and I will drink to thy good health and prosperity."

"Thou art already under the influence of wine or something stronger, and as I want to speak seriously with thee, I decline to give thee any more."

"'Tis well, then. Pray proceed."

"Colonel Blood," said Sir John, leaning half-way across the table, "I tell thee that thou art an infamous liar!"

And Sir John struck the table with his clenched fist with such force that Blood's boots fairly clattered.

"By the soul of the Virgin!" cried Blood, "that is the second time thou hast said the same thing! I *know* that I am an infamous liar, and a liar will I remain until the end of my days! But hast thou found me out in any *new* lies? That is the question."

"I have found you out in an *old* one."

"An *old* one!"

"Ay."

"Hum! What then is it? For thou canst not imagine I can recollect all the lies I have told in my life."

"Listen, then," said Sir John, who was now so excited that he could barely fetch his breath.

"I listen," replied Blood, calmly taking a huge pipe from his pocket.

"Thou didst swear that that child was killed. You know who?"

"I know it well enough. He *was* killed, certainly, and thrown down a well."

"Then how comes it that he is now alive and well? How is it he is growing a man—that he is under the protection of this fiend in human form, Master Roebuck?"

Blood laughed quietly.

"What are you grinning at, fool?" asked Sir John.

"Why, can't you see?" replied Blood.

"No, I cannot."

"Why, this is only another of Master Roebuck's tricks. He can put forward a claimant to vast estates as well as any other adventurer if he has the full particulars."

"Then you expect me to believe that this youth is simply one he has put forward?"

"That is precisely what—"

"But I have *seen* him!"

There was an awkward pause, during which the two scoundrels looked hard at each other as much as to say—

"Which of us two is the biggest liar?"

"Where?" asked Blood.

"At the Court of King Charles the Second, Colonel Blood."

"Well, what of that, Sir John Humphreys?"

"Simply that he is the very image of the late Sir Harold."

"Hem!"

"Hast *thou* seen him?"

"Never."

"Never?"

"Why certainly not, and don't want to, unless—"

"Go on."

"Unless I am paid to put him out of the way. That would quiet thee at all events, although as to his being the son of the late Sir Harold—pshaw! it is all nonsense. I tell thee what. This Roderick Roebuck—whom may perdition seize ere long, say I, for I am compelled to be civil to him—"

"For fear of thy life, yes," said Sir John.

"No, not for fear of my throat, but for many reasons. Well, this Roebuck has evidently a grudge against thee. It has reached my ears how thou didst arrive at the Court. Odd's life! I never *did* hear of such a strange way to pack up a baronet!"

And Blood laughed loudly.

"Laugh not," said Sir John, with a savage scowl. "It may be thy turn yet. But are you ready to accept terms for putting this youth out of the way?"

"I am."

"What amount would you expect?"

"What would you be prepared to give?"

"I always pay you liberally for what you do, do I not?"

"Ay, ay, you do. But name a price."

"I will give thee one thousand crowns on the day thou dost take me to look upon his dead body."

"Agreed. The day will not be far distant."

"I can give you his address, for I have made it my business to find it out."

"Oh, I will not trouble thee. I will lay in wait, trap him, and a fiend will do the rest, I'll warrant me."

"Who is this fiend?"

"A swashbuckler of the true sort. He would do anything for a gold piece, from the murder of his mother to the slaying of an infant."

And the cold-blooded scoundrel again laughed loudly and kicked his heels upon the table.

"I care not by whose hand he dies, so that he does die," said Sir John. "After all these years it would be hard to be ousted."

"Pshaw!" cried Blood, "who would believe what Roebuck or he said? No one."

"Do not be too sanguine. I told thee he had been to the Court."

"Thou didst. But on what business?"

"An interview with the king. Someone hath evidently placed him under the notice of his Majesty, and only this morning he appointed him one of his captains."

Blood turned pale.

"Of a surety," he thought, "there is some truth in what the boy said at the 'Silver Flagon.' And, moreover, he has a powerful friend in Roderick Roebuck. Odd's life, I am turning hot all over. I will question Varney more closely concerning this matter, and if I find that the child was not killed and thrown into the well, by the soul of the Virgin, I'll slit his ugly carcase in two! To think of him outwitting Colonel Blood! Well, well, well! But let him wait. Yes, child or no child of Sir Harold, he must be put out of the way, or my influence over Sir John will cease."

Aloud he said—

"Captain, eh? Hum! all the better for my plans."

"How can that be?"

"Why, wherever he may be quartered, I will send for him, organise a riot, and then, of course, he will be killed in fair fight, and no inquiries will be made."

"I see, I see. Well, at once arrange thy plans. I shall find out where he is to be quartered, and will at once communicate with thee. I will give thee a portion of the money on— Come in!"

The man-servant entered.

"What dost thou want?" asked Sir John, eyeing him with displeasure.

"May it please thee, Sir John, but a little while ago a man left a box for thee."

" What are its contents ? "

" He said deeds, Sir John."

" Deeds ? We expect no deeds. What sort of a box is it ? "

" About two feet by three."

" Well, and where did he say he came from ? "

" He would give no information ; he said thou wouldst know where he came from right well."

" I know nothing of it. This is somewhat strange."

" It may not contain deeds at all," laughed Blood. " It may contain another baronet."

The servant omitted to mention the height and bulk of the man who brought it, for had he done so, it is certain that Blood would have known who it was.

" Well, bring it in," said Sir John, " and let us examine these deeds. On my life, I know not what deeds they be."

" They may be dark deeds," suggested Blood.

But his untimely wit—if wit it was —only called forth a scowl from Sir John.

The box was brought in, and when the servant had retired, Sir John and Blood examined it.

" I see no opening to it," said Sir John.

" Nor I," replied Blood, examining it curiously.

" And yet, of a truth, it would appear to be from one of those thieves called lawyers, for see—the handwriting here is very bold, every letter being neatly turned."

" True, true. Well, here," and Sir John opened a drawer in the table and brought forth an instrument, " here is the thing with which to open it."

Blood inserted the end of it all round the box, and the lid easily came off.

" 'Sdeath ! " cried Blood, " of what a foul smell are these deeds, if deeds they be."

He took off the paper at the top, and instantaneously a fearful scream left his lips, and it was echoed by Sir John, who drew back appalled.

The box contained the body of a man !

All except the face was terribly burnt, and looked perfectly horrible.

It was the body of Varney.

" The holy saints protect us," moaned Blood, wringing his hands, " what a terrible deed has been done ! "

" But what is the object of sending this to me ? " said Sir John, in a hoarse whisper. " Whose body is it ? "

" It is the body of the man Varney, of whom I have but just spoken. He it was who assisted me in the murder of Sir Harold, for, of a truth, it was murder, although appearing fair fight. Varney it was who knocked his sword aside, while I ran mine through his body."

" Contrary to what I told thee, for I told thee to kill him in his bed, as also the child."

" True, true. But here, look, is a paper attached to it."

" Is there any writing upon it ? "

" Ay."

" Read it then, for I would not touch it for a thousand crowns."

Blood, who had somewhat recovered his composure, took up the paper and read—

" JOHN HUMPHREYS—Behold the foul corpse of one of my father's murderers. He was called Varney. The other of my dear father's murderers was one Blood—his body ere long shall reach thee. Beware, Sir John Humphreys ! thy time grows short. By my hand shalt thou fall. The fortune and estates that thou dost hold, and which are mine by virtue of rightful descent, are nothing in my eyes. My father's voice calls to me from his grave. I shall obey it, and it shall be blood for blood.—Signed,

" HAROLD HARCOURT."

When Blood came to the words, " one Blood—his body ere long shall reach thee," his hands trembled so violently that he could scarce hold the paper, and when he read the signature, he dropped it like a red-hot coal, and fixed his eyes upon Sir John, down whose face the perspiration was pouring in torrents.

Blood had entered the house partially intoxicated, but he was perfectly sober now.

For some moments the two men gazed into each other's faces.

No sound was heard save their heavy breathing.

At last Sir John pointed to the box.

"Take it away," he said, in husky tones.

Blood slowly shook his head.

He opened his mouth as if to speak, but no sound issued from his parched lips.

Sir John walked to a cabinet, which he unlocked, and taking out a flagon of brandy, he poured out a good draught of the liquor and handed it to Blood, who swallowed it at a gulp.

Sir John then placed the flagon to his own lips, and drained it.

"Now," he said, "let us sit down and discuss this document. But first remove that foul thing to the sideboard."

"Nay, nay," replied Blood, fearfully; "rather let us sit at the sideboard, and call the servant anon to remove it."

There was no doubt in the world that Blood was a frightful coward.

He would not mind stabbing a man in the dark, but he would not meet him in fair fight.

And he had an awful horror of anything which had the slightest suspicion of the supernatural or mysterious about it.

Sir John would not have touched the box for all the wealth of which he was then in possession—albeit not rightly.

"Very good," he said, "then we will sit here at this sideboard. But first the paper."

Blood picked it up and offered it to him.

"Burn it," said Sir John.

Blood placed it over the lamp, and in a moment it was consumed.

Sir John then seemed to be easier in his mind, and he motioned Blood to take a seat by his side.

"Thou seest," said Sir John, "that while this youth lives, and is supported by this man Roebuck, we are doomed men."

"I have seen it more plainly within the last hour," replied Blood, who could not sit still in his chair.

"Then thou wilt see that it is as much to thy advantage as to mine that he should be destroyed."

"I agree with thee, and by heaven! I will leave no stone unturned to accomplish his destruction. Fear not; he shall not long be alive."

"As for this Roebuck, I will persuade the king to send a troop of horsemen after him. If his capture is not effected then, it will not be my fault."

"I should be glad to assist thee if—"

Blood suddenly started to his feet.

"By the blessed Virgin!" he said, "I could have sworn I heard a voice! Ring the bell, Sir John, and have that box removed, for, while it is here, I cannot remain."

Sir John rang the bell, and the butler appeared.

"Take away that box," said Sir John, "and place it in the lower vault."

The man approached the box, but no sooner did he see the contents than, with a howl of horror, he took to his heels, and in his flight overturned and extinguished the lamp.

At the same moment came the words, slowly yet distinctly—

"Blood for blood!"

Both Colonel Blood and Sir John turned to rush from the room, but suddenly they stopped and clasped each other.

They were transfixed to the spot.

Their eyes seemed starting from their sockets.

Before them, with one hand pointing to his breast, stood the outline of Sir Harold Harcourt.

The outline was perfect, and so wonderfully distinct, that it seemed human.

"Mercy," gasped Sir John, "mercy!"

"Sir Harold Harcourt!" shrieked Blood, in horror-stricken tones.

The vision slowly raised its right arm and pointed to its breast.

Blood watched it, and another terrible cry escaped him.

As we have before said, he was a fearful coward.

Suddenly Sir John released himself from Blood's undesirable embrace, and rushed to the door.

It is needless to say that Blood followed him with the rapidity of lightning.

At that moment several of the servants appeared with lights, and no sooner did Sir John find himself safe, and in their presence, than he tried to laugh.

Blood followed his example, but the laugh died away on his lips, and left them paler than ever.

The two scoundrels held no further conversation that night.

Before another ten minutes Blood had mounted his horse, and was speeding along, *en route* for his house in Whitefriars.

He had received a terrible scare, from which there was no doubt he would not recover for some time to come.

CHAPTER XVIII.

SHOWS HOW BLOOD ENTERTAINS TITUS OATES, HUGH JEFFRIES, AND A NUMBER OF "ALSATIANS"—THE PLOT, AND IN WHICH IT IS SEEN HOW HAROLD RECEIVES A MESSAGE—HOW HE OBEYED IT AND FINDS HIMSELF ENTRAPPED—THE TERRIBLE FIGHT ON THE BALCONY OF BLOOD'S HOUSE —HAROLD'S DESPERATE LEAP INTO THE THAMES, AND HIS TIMELY RESCUE BY LORD TREVOR.

FOR two weeks after the extraordinary incidents we have described in the previous chapter, Blood disappeared from the neighbourhood of Whitefriars.

His house was fast closed.

Not a living soul was to be seen anywhere about it.

This was a matter of great wonder and speculation on the part of many people, especially numberless drunken court gallants who admired Blood's strange company and his smuggled wines and brandies, and also the denizens of Alsatia who frequently met and conversed over the strange matter.

They were beginning to think that Blood had met with his deserts somewhere, when one night he drew up at the "Silver Flagon," hot, dusty, and, no doubt, thirsty.

The place happened to be full of the noble swashbucklers, and the women who seemed to cling to them, and they welcomed the "right worthy captain" with a howl of joy.

They crowded round and fawned upon him, for a glance showed them that he was more handsomely dressed than was usual with him.

They concluded that he had a large amount of money about him, and was ready to spend some of it.

"Well, my brawlers!" cried Blood, as he cracked his riding whip, "and how are you all—eh? You look glum! Who cries drink?"

At this question a regular roar went up.

Everyone cried drink.

Every man and woman present was always ready to drink whatever came in their way.

Blood smiled grimly.

"Now, good host," he said, "a keg of thy best brandy, and a full glass to each in turn; and see that it is *full*, mark ye, or thou wilt have to sing for thy money."

The brandy was produced, and a full glass of the fiery compound having been swallowed by every man and woman present, Blood said—

"List ye, companions. Thou hast not seen me for a long time past because I have been on an expedition, which has produced me a pile of gold, and now that I have returned, I ask ye all to join me to-night in a right royal carouse—"

Another loud shout went up.

"At my noble residence," continued Blood. "Everything is ready, and waiting, and no doubt by this time the place is well lit up, for I brought servants with me especially to attend to it. And thou wilt see two well-known characters, who will join us in our carouse. They are Hugh Jeffries, the son of the Judge—"

Blood was stopped this time by loud groans.

"Hist!" he shouted. "This son is not like his father, for he can enjoy himself right well, as thou wilt see. Then the other one is Titus Oates—"

A loud roar of laughter here interrupted him.

"Yes, Titus Oates," said Blood; " and all of ye know that he is as well with a carouse as with his piety. Odd's life! but he is a most blasphemous wretch, yet for that reason he is all the more welcome. What say ye all?"

It is needless to say there were no dissentients.

All were quite ready to partake of the hospitality Blood offered.

The majority of them—principally the women—knew that the good things Blood kept in his house were not to be sneezed at.

They would probably not have cared half so much for it had they known it was honestly come by.

But there were very few men or women, who knew Blood, who were not aware of the fact that every keg of brandy he had, as well as every bottle of wine, was smuggled.

Blood now left the "Silver Flagon." One of the men took his horse by the bridle and led him along, while the other men and women followed in twos and threes.

Blood's house—he had called it his for some few years, yet he had no deeds in his possession to show that it belonged to him—was once the property of a Jew of the name of Izehoff.

This Izehoff was for many years a well-known character about the neighbourhood of Whitefriars, and it was stated that he was possessed of great wealth.

Suddenly he disappeared, and was never again seen or heard of.

Blood had several times been accused of his murder, until at last he was arrested for it; but at the trial no evidence was forthcoming against him, and so he was discharged, Judge Jeffries and Councillor Bates, before whom he was arraigned, intimating that "grave suspicions" rested upon his head.

Blood's reply to them was to laugh in their faces, and to impudently tell them that if they disappeared at any time he hoped their disappearance would not be laid upon his shoulders, and to this the judges, knowing his terrible reputation, had not the heart to make a reply.

The house stood at the end of a narrow alley, and at the very edge of the Thames.

It was very old, and of most peculiar construction; each storey—and there were four—seeming as though a good push would send them headlong into the river.

The lower part of this house had been used at one time as kitchens, for at low water the sideboards, the shelves, the niches, the huge fireplace, the spit hanging from beneath the mantel-piece, all could be plainly seen.

It was evident that the river and the rats had undermined the foundations of the house, and had caused it gradually to sink.

The consequence was that at high water the kitchens were flooded, for the water reached to the top of the bars of the front door which led to them, and a boat could come right under the balcony of the first storey.

Arriving at the house, Blood took a whistle from his pocket and blew it loudly.

It was immediately answered by a man who, holding a lighted torch over his head, stepped on the balcony which looked into the alley.

At Blood's request the man threw the torch down. Blood picked it up and directed the men and women to follow him.

It being low water, and having many behind him, Blood decided to enter by way of the kitchens.

Alone, he would not have ventured through the place for a hatful of diamonds.

Pushing the door open, he entered, followed by the Alsatians, much to the consternation and terror of hundreds of rats, who were heard scampering off in all directions.

Through the kitchens, which were smothered in filth, they went; up one narrow flight of steps and then another, until at last they arrived at the first floor.

Here a wonderful transformation met their eyes.

The whole place was illuminated with oil lamps and torches, which were either stuck in the iron rings in the walls, or hung on rusty chains dangling from the ceiling.

This combination produced a most peculiar and extraordinary effect, which was heightened considerably when the men and women, dressed, as they were, in the most extraordinary dresses it is possible to imagine, stood under the glare.

Opposite was a lofty arched doorway—the door, however, stood on one side on the landing, instead of upon its hinges—which led to what, Blood said, was his "banqueting room."

Through this they went, and found themselves in a fine, large room, adorned with various devices, in oak and Spanish mahogany.

Besides heads of martyrs—kings, queens, and celebrated nobles of past ages—there was more than one model of the Virgin Mary ; and at the farther end, and exactly at the back of the principal chair, was a finely executed painting of our Saviour carrying the Cross. *Ecce Homo.*

The table, which reached almost from one end of the room to the other, fairly groaned beneath the weight of wines, spirits, and viands of every imaginable description.

So well laid and furnished was it that the Alsatians could not suppress an exclamation of astonishment.

"Ha, ha!" cried Blood, " ye can now see the princely way which Colonel Blood can entertain whenever he thinks fit. What ho!" he cried, "serve up the hot joints ; yet, stay! Where are my other guests ? "

"Upstairs," replied one of the servants, with a grin. " They are speaking with—"

"Silence !" yelled Blood. "What matters it to thee with whom they are speaking ? "

The man was about to say—

"With Sir John Humphreys," for, disguised, he was there.

The Alsatians took their seats at the table, where they were soon joined by Blood, Sir John, and Hugh.

Titus Oates also came in.

He was attired in a semi-clerical habit, and looked more bloated and repulsive than ever.

"I greet you kindly, friends," he said, " and trust, ere you depart, that you will fill your empty stomachs with good things. Yet it is but fitting that you should say just one prayer—"

"Silence, thou fool !" cried Blood ; " dost thou not know that this house is not of great strength ? "

"Eh ? what, I pray thee, good Blood, has that to do with it ? "

"To do with it ? If thou didst say but one prayer in this house, it would surely fall ! Sit thee down, and eat and drink good things."

Thus called to order, Oates sat down and commenced to eat like a savage.

And as the wine went down his short, thick throat, his tongue was loosened, and the blasphemy of the Alsatians' conversation was nothing in comparison with his.

When the men and women had finished eating, they drank, and deeply too, not wines but spirits.

And, of course, as they got more and more intoxicated, their riotousness became greater, until at last the place became a perfect pandemonium.

And all this, mark you, in the room where stood the beautiful and angelic face of the Virgin Mary, and the noble form and sad face of our Saviour !

Truly the scene was indescribably horrible and repulsive.

"Now is the time," whispered Blood, who then, unobserved, slipped out, followed by Sir John, Oates, and Hugh.

The next floor consisted of several rooms of various sizes, but the principal one, having a balcony in front, looked on to the river.

Into this went the four, and took their seats at the table.

"Now," said Sir John, "thy plans, Colonel Blood, and at once ! "

"Be not impatient," replied Blood, as he reached a huge pipe from the mantel-piece, before taking his seat ; "calmness is everything."

" Yet thou must remember the words of the Latin poet," said Oates, as sinking into a chair he crossed his hands on his chest, "for verily they are true, *tempus fugit*, which means 'time flies.' And no time hast thou to lose, good Blood. Of a truth, I am getting impatient, for I long to see the young scoundrel spitted upon—"

"Quiet !" cried Hugh, " for see, Blood is about to open his mouth."

"My plan is this," said Blood. " In a few moments—hist ! "

Every man started to his feet as, from beneath the balcony, there came a prolonged shrill whistle.

"They must have anticipated me," said Blood, with a grim look from the window.

All looked in the same direction.

They saw beneath the first balcony a boat manned by four watermen.

"Well, what are these men?" asked Sir John.

"My servants," grinned Blood, as opening the window he stepped upon the balcony.

"All ready?" he cried.

"Aye," replied the man at the stern; "and where is thy note?"

"It is here," replied Blood.

"Good," said the man; "lower it, for no time is to be lost."

Blood took a packet from his pocket, then a piece of string.

Having tied the packet to the string he lowered it to the man, who, unfastening it, seated himself, and, waving his hand, called upon the rowers to pull away.

In less than ten minutes they were out of sight.

"I see that everything is properly prepared," said Sir John; "yet I cannot understand the nature of the plot."

"Let us again be seated," said Blood, "and I will tell you. Of a truth," he cried, "my thousand crowns are in sight this night."

"Proceed," said Sir John, who was, beyond doubt, becoming impatient.

"Listen," said Blood; "we don't want murder."

"I know it," growled Sir John.

"Of course you do," continued Blood; "and I know it too. I have watched his movements for a long time past, and know exactly where he is to be found, and also at what time. He relieves guard to-night, and just after that the note thou didst see me lower will be placed in his hands. The contents I will not tell thee, but it is such as will fetch him here as rapidly as possible. When he comes he will be conducted to this room by the front so as to avoid the lot in the banqueting-room. Then I will raise a cry that the King's Guard are upon the Alsatians, and will tell them that the captain is upstairs. What will be the result? They will fall upon him, kill him, and hurl his body into the Thames.

Neither Colonel Blood nor anyone else will therefore be responsible for his death."

"Of a truth," exclaimed Sir John, "his death this night is certain."

"Verily, verily," cried Oates, stroking his stomach.

"By my soul," cried Hugh Jeffries, "I will at least have one stroke at him. He shall pay for his defiance of me."

"Let us join the men below," said Blood. "I shall leave you with them, and slip away to watch."

"One moment," said Sir John: "how dost thou know that this youth is not acquainted with this house?"

"Bah!" replied Blood, "do you think that I have not taken care—but there! wait and see, wait and see."

"Oh, that he died to-night," said Sir John, "then I should feel safe."

"He will die to-night," replied Blood, fiercely; "thou canst rely upon that."

* * * *

Harold Harcourt had duly received the necessary papers appointing him to a captaincy in the King's Guard, and besides that he was appointed to one of the principal positions, namely, Whitehall.

On the night that Sir John Humphreys received the terrible box, he was joined at nurse Alice's house by Robin, and soon after by Master Roebuck, who listened eagerly to Harold's recital as to all that had passed.

He then gave Harold some excellent advice, and with Robin departed.

Since that time, strange to say, Harold had neither seen nor heard anything of him.

This made him exceedingly miserable, for he felt sure that something had happened to him.

He had paid several visits to Robin, whom he always found busily hammering away at his anvil and singing merrily, but he had not heard of him, neither had he seen aught of Pipkin, which, he said, grieved him sorely, for he had begun to look upon him as a little brother.

Then Harold despatched messenger after messenger to Plumstead, directing his letters to "Master Roebuck," but it appeared that he had not been seen there for some time.

Just after the boat had shot off from

Blood's house, Harold had relieved the guard, and returning to the guard-house, sat himself down to think.

The thoughts uppermost in his mind were, of course, his lamented father, of Sir John Humphreys, and of Colonel Blood.

For over an hour he sat, deep in thought, but at last he was aroused by the challenge of the guard, and a few moments after a man entered, doffed his hat, and bowed respectfully.

He was one of the men we have seen in the boat under the balcony of Blood's house.

"Thy business?" asked Harold.

"I have the honour to stand before Harold de Witt, captain of his Majesty's third division," said the man.

Harold bowed.

The man looked round the apartment curiously, pretending to be afraid.

"What art thou peering about for?" asked Harold, not curious as to the man's business.

"Are we alone?" whispered the man.

"Quite," replied Harold.

"I have a lettter for thee. See, here it is; thou wilt find thy name plainly written on the outside."

Harold took it, and having glanced at the name, which he found correct, he tore off the tape, and opening it, read as follows—

"DEAR HAROLD,—First let me entreat thee to express no surprise, or my capture is certain. Thou hast not seen me for some time, for I have been far away in the country; but returning last night, I was pursued and nearly captured. It was a narrow escape, but, alas! I am sorely wounded. Come to me at once. The bearer is one of my most trusted men, and will conduct thee to where I am lying—at the house of a Jew in Whitefriars. He brings a boat, so that thou canst enter the house by the river, and so be unobserved. Make no remarks, for the rowers know nothing.—Thine as ever,
                          "ROEBUCK."

"Where is thy boat, companion?" asked Harold.

"At Whitehall Stairs," replied the man in a whisper.

"Good," said Harold, as he seized and buckled on his sword. "Haste thee there; I will join thee in a moment."

The man departed, and Harold fastened his cloak about him, first, however, placing a couple of pistols in his sword-belt.

He thought that though, of course, they might not be required, they made him feel safer.

He was just about to cross the threshold, when suddenly Lord Trevor appeared before him.

"Hallo, Harold!" he said. "Whither bound, and why so fast?"

"I am just about to visit a sick friend," replied Harold.

"Ho, ho! of a truth, I am sorry, for I came to ask thee to come for a row on the river. See, it is a beautiful moonlight night."

"Another time, Trevor, and I am at thy service. Yet, I shall go to my friend's house by water, and may meet thee somewhere on my return."

"Good; I will look out for thee. Farewell for the present."

"Farewell."

Harold, gathering his cloak about him, hurried off to Whitehall Stairs, where the boat awaited him.

Jumping in, he took his seat at the stern, and instantly the boat pushed off, and Harold soon found himself being hurried down the river at a good pace.

Not a word was spoken, for Harold was lost in thought. He was wondering to what extent Master Roebuck was injured.

He was suddenly aroused by one of the men crying out, "Whoa! gently!" and by the bump of the boat against a pillar.

Standing up, he saw he was under the balcony of a house.

"Odd's life!" he said; "this is truly a strange-looking place."

"Ay, ay," replied the man who had delivered the note to him; "and it is a strange person who has it. It is the house of a Jew—a miser; but his name I forget. Thy visit is to be kept secret; so, sir, get ready."

Thereupon the man whistled thrice.

In a few seconds, a little grey-haired old man peered forth, and in a cracked, whining voice, said—

"Who goes there?"

"See, Jew," said the man, "I have brought the gentleman."

"Oh, yes, yes! Prithee, good sir, clamber up the balcony, and mind thy footing."

This, as we have before said, was no difficult task, as the boat touched the railings of the balcony.

Harold was on the balcony in an instant.

"Follow, good sir," said the supposed Jew, as he went through the window.

Harold followed, not dreaming of the slightest danger.

Directly he passed through the window, the man in the boat gave the word, and the rowers pulled away with all their might.

Through the first-floor room, which was illuminated only with a small oil-lamp, went Harold.

Under the table in this room, were Blood, Sir John, and Hugh.

By some means they had silenced the row in the banqueting-room opposite, and had placed the door in front of it.

As Harold passed, the place was as silent as the grave.

Up the stairs went the Jew, followed closely by Harold, who marvelled much at the strange appearance of the place; and at last they stopped and entered the room on the second-floor.

"If thou wilt wait here but a moment," whined the Jew, as he washed his hands in imaginary soap, "my wife will conduct thee to the unfortunate Master Roebuck."

Harold bowed politely, and walked to the window, whence a fine view of the river was obtained, while the Jew hurried downstairs with silent dread.

When in the first-floor room, he threw off a false wig, beard, and gown, and stood erect, Jew no longer, but the blasphemous Titus Oates!

Blood, Sir John, and Hugh were awaiting him, each with a drawn sword.

"My task is done," said Oates. "Now for thine, good Blood."

"Mine will soon be accomplished," said Blood, who thereupon walked to the door of the banqueting-room, flung it aside, and cried out—

"Quick, men, for your lives! The King's Guard are upon us. They have stolen into the house. Quick! Draw your swords and cut down the first man who attempts to bar your passage!"

For, as it seemed, the space of two seconds, the men appeared stupefied.

Nearly every one was intoxicated.

Then with a fearful yell of rage they started up, drew their swords and rushed to the door, the women seizing the decanters or whatever came to their hands and urging them to hack the guards down.

All occurred just as Blood wanted it.

Harold heard these cries and involuntarily the word escaped his lips—

"Entrapped! For I swear I heard the voice of the murderer Blood! Entrapped! Ay, it is so! That cry came not from the throat of one man, but many. Yet, I will sell my life dearly, albeit I see there is no escape for me."

Unsheathing his sword and drawing one of his pistols, he commenced to descend the stairs.

"See!" exclaimed Hugh, pointing out Harold to the now excited, nay, frenzied men, "there is the captain, cut him down! No mercy for the man who dares to penetrate into the private houses of Alsatians."

"Cut him down!" echoed Blood.

"Ay, ay!" cried Oates, as he produced a cross and held it aloft, "cut him down, and by this cross I absolve ye!"

"In the king's name I command ye to pause!" shouted Harold. "I mean that I came not here of my own free will; I have been entrapped by the murderer Blood. I call upon you—"

"List to him!" shouted Blood. "See, men, he but parleys with you to allow of his men coming up. Hark! do you not hear them? They are in the kitchens."

Had the Alsatians thought a moment they would have known that no one could have been in the kitchens, it being high-water now.

But they were too maddened by drink and rage to pause.

One of them with a terrible oath rushed towards Harold who stood in about the middle of the stairs.

Harold, of course, saw there was no

hope of arguing with them, and that the only thing left to him was to defend himself as long as he was able.

As the man rushed towards him, he raised his pistol and fired.

The ball struck the man in the region of the heart, and with a terrible cry and a most appalling curse, he dropped dead across the stairs.

As soon as Harold fired, he raised the pistol aloft and sent it flying in the direction in which Blood stood.

It missed Blood, but fell with a terrific crash fair on Oates' cheek, causing the blood to rush forth in torrents.

Another loud shout went up, and the men with a mighty rush were upon Harold.

But Harold never moved.

The stairs were too narrow to admit of his being surrounded.

He met the points of half-a-dozen swords with a firm hand, backing slightly as he did so.

For some few moments the place fairly rang with the clash of steel. So loud indeed was it, that one was reminded of the anvil in a blacksmith's shop.

Suddenly, Harold drew his other pistol and fired point blank at the infuriated men, then turning, he ran back up the stairs.

Rushing into the room, he slammed the door to, and bolted it. Then he rushed to the door and tried to open it.

It was fast locked.

Seizing hold of a stout oak stool, he raised it over his head, and brought it down again and again on the window-frames, which flew about in all directions.

Harold's blows were echoed by the hammering of the men on the door of the room, and above the din he could hear the loud voice of Blood calling upon the men to burst it open, and offering a hundred crowns to the man who first struck Harold down.

Yet it must be borne in mind that Blood was perfectly certain there was no chance of his escape.

"If he throw himself into the river," he said to Sir John, "he will assuredly be drowned. Still, I would rather see him killed first, and then hurled into the river."

Presently, with a loud shout, the men burst the door open, and rushed pell-mell into the room.

They were again upon Harold before he could reach the balcony, albeit he he had smashed the window to atoms.

Raising the stool high above his head, Harold turned it round and round for a moment and flung it at the foremost men.

It crashed among them with fearful force, knocking several of them down senseless.

Now Harold backed on to the balcony, for he thought that he should be safer there, and stand less chance of being surrounded.

As he backed he snatched off his cloak and wound it as best he could round his left arm.

This acted as a capital shield for his breast, for now he was being hard pressed indeed.

How he wished for the assistance of gigantic Robin Renard!

Suddenly, amid the shouts of the maddened men, the voice of Hugh Jeffries was heard urging them on.

Harold at once recognised it, and he cried out—

"Beware, Hugh Jeffries! Thy time will yet come—and soon."

"Have at thee!" shrieked Jeffries, as he struggled to the front, "have at thee!"

And raising his right hand, which held a large decanter, he hurled it with all his force at Harold, who avoided it only by a hair, before it smashed to pieces on the balcony railings.

It was fortunate for Harold that, besides being possessed of great courage, he was, when in danger, calm and collected, for had he been otherwise, his life would certainly have been brought to a sudden termination.

Blood now pressed forward, armed with a gigantic horse-pistol.

He had determined not to slay Harold himself; but he saw that something must be done at once to put a stop to the fight, or it was likely enough the watch would become aware of what was going on.

He advanced as close to Harold as was possible, having regard to his own safety, and fired.

The shot took effect, for it struck Harold on the left shoulder.

Yet only a deep groan escaped his parched lips.

He knew now that he could not hold out much longer, yet he saw that to endeavour to push through the intoxicated, maddened men in order to reach Blood or Jeffries would be useless.

Again and again did Blood call upon the men to rush upon Harold and cut him down.

But it was all very well to cry out to them.

They were getting quite disheartened, for several of them lay dead or dying in the room, or on the balcony, which latter was quite slippery from the blood which almost covered it.

Making a sudden dash at the foremost ruffian, Harold dealt him a fearful stroke on the skull, causing him to fall backwards.

Then drawing back, Harold placed his sword between his teeth, and clutching the railings with both hands, vaulted over into the river, into which he fell with a loud splash.

By this time Blood had again loaded his pistol, and, hearing the shouts as Harold went over, he rushed upon the balcony.

A cry of rage escaped him.

Suddenly Harold rose upon the surface of the water, and Blood, kneeling upon the balcony, took steady aim at him and fired.

The shot was watched with breathless interest by all. With the report Harold dived under the water, and Blood made certain that Harold was hit.

Imagine his astonishment then, when, after a few seconds, Harold re-appeared on the surface of the water some yards further on !

Blood fairly howled and stamped with rage.

"A boat!" he roared. "A boat! Fifty crowns for a boat!"

But he was not answered unless it was by the echo of his own voice.

The boat he had hired, as our readers will remember, he had ordered to be taken away directly Harold reached the balcony.

Down the stairs to the next balcony ran Blood at break-neck speed, followed by the Alsatians, both men and women, who now began to think that Harold was possessed of as many lives as a cat.

"A boat, a boat !" shrieked Blood, still keeping his eyes fixed upon Harold, who was making great efforts to escape.

Unfortunately he made but little progress, for the wound in his shoulder began to tell upon him.

"Fear not," said Oates ; "he cannot escape. See how he struggles. There is no one near to pick him up, and he cannot remain long on the surface of the water. He will sink presently, depend upon it."

"But cannot a boat be anywhere obtained ? " asked Sir John.

"Nay," replied Blood ; "the hour is too late for the watermen to be— Ho ! look ahead ! A boat, a boat ! A hundred crowns for a boat ! " he shrieked, as, not twenty yards off, but yet nearly in the centre of the river, a boat suddenly appeared.

It being a splendid moonlight night, they were able to see the boat distinctly, as also the occupants, of which there were five.

The sound of Blood's voice was heard by them, and one—a man in the stern—turned.

At that instant Blood and his confederates were startled by Harold's voice.

"Help !" cried Harold, "help ! I am sinking ! help !"

Instantly the boat stopped.

The man at the stern stood up, and in another instant the boat put about, and the rowers pulled towards Harold.

Blood, who made certain that the occupants of the boat were watermen, shouted—

"Seize him—seize him, in the king's name ! A hundred crowns for him ! "

The boat stopped, and they saw Harold lifted in.

There was a pause, during which Blood, Oates, and Hugh rent the air with shouts of "A hundred crowns ! "

To their rage and mortification, the boat again turned and went off at a terrific pace in the direction of Whitehall. The boat belonged to Lord Eustace Trevor, and he it was who sat in the stern.

"By the soul of the Virgin!" cried Blood, fairly dancing with rage, "he hath escaped us after all!"

"Better have done what I advised thee," replied Sir John, "and have despatched him thyself."

"And have been haunted by him as thou art by the father. Nay, nay; yet had I shot him it would have been called fair fight."

"Look," said Oates, "the boat is still; and see, a man rises in the stern. He is richly dressed, thou seest, so he cannot be a waterman. I wonder much who he can be."

The man in the stern—Lord Trevor —held up his hand for an instant, and then over the water came these words, slowly and distinctly—

"Beware, Colonel Blood! This deed of to-night shall be well repaid!"

Blood's answer was another howl of rage.

"Odd's life!" cried Oates, "who can the man be, Sir John?"

"Eh? How should I know!" replied Sir John, pretending to wipe his face.

But he knew the voice well.

"Of a truth," he muttered, "it is Trevor. Thank goodness, I was not seen!"

"Yes, he hath escaped," said Blood, as he suddenly plucked the sword from his scabbard and raised the hilt before his eyes; "but by this cross I swear that I will leave no stone unturned to compass his death. By my hand he shall die!"

"Well said!" cried Sir John, warmly; "and on this spot I swear that thy reward shall not be one, but five thousand crowns."

"Agreed," replied Blood; "but yet hadst thou not increased the reward, I would have his life. I hate and curse him!"

"I believe you," said Oates, "but you do not hate him more cordially than I do."

"Nor worse than I," put in Hugh; "but now let us order these men to remove their dead and leave the house. We will then see whether we can draw up another plot for him. And this time let us hope it will be successful; and thus we shall have removed one whom I fear is dangerous."

CHAPTER XIX.

GIVES THE READER SOME IDEA OF THE MANNER IN WHICH KING CHARLES WAS IN THE HABIT OF AMUSING HIMSELF—POLL LYNDON'S HOME—THE CRY FOR HELP—HAROLD TO THE RESCUE—SHOWS ALSO HOW NEAR ENGLAND CAME TO LOSING HER SOVEREIGN.

SOME four days after the incidents recorded in the preceding chapter, Harold, as he sat meditating in the guard-room, was startled by the entrance into the courtyard of a man attired in a long black cloak, and a low slouched hat pulled over his brows so as to conceal his features.

It was evident that he had passed the guard at the gates unseen, for Harold had heard no challenge.

It was, however, a very dark night, and easy to slip past the guard unobserved.

The man entered the courtyard with a martial and commanding tread, and it was evident that he knew every inch of the ground.

Harold was still very weak and not able to walk very fast, yet he hurried up to the strange-looking individual, and placing his hand upon his shoulder, cried—

"Halt!"

The man turned swiftly.

"The password?" asked Harold.

"Eh? The password!" replied the stranger. "The password is, To the deuce with thee!"

"There I differ from thee," replied Harold, calmly, "for it is nothing of the kind. I repeat—the password?"

"I refuse to give it thee."

"Then I command thee instantly to leave the precincts of his Majesty's palace, or I shall place thee under arrest."

The man uttered a defiant laugh.

BY COMMAND OF THE KING ; OR, THE DAYS OF THE MERRIE MONARCH.

"'MERCY! WHO CAN HAVE DONE THIS DEED?' CRIED THE KING."

No. 7

"*Thou* place me under arrest?" he said. "Thou art a fool. Nay, nay," he added, as he saw Harold place his hand upon his sword, "I was but jesting, Harold de Witt. Thou seest I know thy name. Ha, ha! And no doubt thou knowest mine."

He raised his hat, and Harold started back in astonishment.

It was the Duke of Buckingham.

"I crave thy pardon, my lord," he said; "I did not recognise thee or thy voice, and, therefore, I did what was only my duty."

"True, true. Well, then, let me tell thee that I wanted to be unobserved. Go to thy room, De Witt, and shouldst thou see any other gentlemen pass, take no notice."

Harold bowed, and returned to his room.

He did not sit down, but stood at the door.

In a few moments he observed a gentleman attired like Buckingham enter.

Presently another followed, and then another, until there were six.

"Strange proceeding," muttered Harold, "and I presume they are all nobles. Hem! I wonder much whether his Majesty is aware of this secret meeting, for so I take it, it is."

In a few minutes they came from the courtyard and passed the guard-house.

Now Harold had distinctly counted six enter, but as they passed him he counted seven.

"On my life," he thought, "this is strange indeed. Where did the other spring from? Well, well, this is beyond comprehension. Yet in the morning I will not fail to report the circumstance to his Majesty. But," he added, as he watched the gentlemen out of sight, "all seems well now, so once again I will go and search for Master Roebuck."

* * * *

The seven individuals who had emerged from the courtyard proceeded to the house of the Duke of Buckingham in the Strand.

The seventh man, whom Harold had not seen enter the courtyard, was addressed as Master Rowley, and his wit was more prominent and his laughter far louder than that of his companions.

He seemed to be under the influence of strong liquor.

His attire was much after the style of the others, but a close observer could have seen that the scabbard of his sword and his spurs were of gold, and that nearly all his fingers were ornamented with costly rings.

"This way," said the duke to his companions, "and pray thee be quick, or our supper will be cold."

"I trust not," said Master Rowley, "for before I proceed on this night's business I must eat and drink, for then I get bold and courageous—ha, ha!"

"True, true," replied Buckingham, "and so do we all. What say ye, gentlemen?"

"Ay, ay," they replied, "nothing like Dutch courage—so runs the proverb."

Buckingham led the way up the broad and noble marble staircase, the niches of which held statues and paintings of a most costly and elaborate description.

On the landing stood several handsomely-attired lacqueys, who bowed almost to the ground as the gentlemen appeared.

A bell was rung by invisible hands, and the massive doors on the right immediately opened, revealing an enormous and sumptuously-furnished room, to describe which would almost take up the space of an ordinary volume.

This was the duke's "study," but in which he never studied.

Master Rowley entered first and Buckingham last.

"See that the supper is immediately served," he said to the butler, who, bowing, was about to retire, when the duke recalled him.

"Has anyone been here?" he asked.

"Yes, your grace," replied the butler; "the person you expected, and she awaits your pleasure in the anteroom."

"'Tis well. After supper show her in."

And the duke entered the study and closed the door after him.

"It is now some time since I was last here," said Master Rowley, as he took his seat in a raised chair at the head of the table.

"It is," replied Buckingham, "and I am right glad to be able once more to entertain you."

"I presume we are as free from observation as ever?"

"Oh yes. No one will venture here without giving notice."

"Then I will slip off this obstruction," said Master Rowley, who then slipped off his hat and false beard, and was revealed in his true character.

And who was that?

No less a personage than "his Most Gracious Majesty King Charles the Second."

Yes, it was the king, sure enough. There was no mistaking that face, which would have been handsome had it not borne such unmistakable traces of dissipation.

"The person is here," said Buckingham.

"Oh, here, is she? I am glad of it."

At this moment a bell rang.

It was answered by Buckingham ringing another, and before many minutes had elapsed a splendid supper was placed upon the table.

The discussion of it lasted for fully an hour and a half. The remains were then cleared away, and a fresh supply of wine placed upon the table.

Buckingham then ordered the butler to show up the "person who had called."

"Be careful, Buckingham, what you say," said Master Rowley, as we will here call him.

The door opened, and a woman, attired in a long black robe, and wearing a hood, entered the room.

She was a woman of about the middle height, but terribly thin.

Approaching the table, she bowed low and then stood erect.

"Take off that covering," said Master Rowley, "and let us gaze upon thy lovely features."

At this the gentlemen burst into a loud roar of laughter.

The woman took off her hood and revealed a face of horrible ugliness.

Her skin was of the colour of parchment, and her features sharp and prominent.

Surely in all London a more dreadful-looking creature could not have been found.

This was Polly Lyndon, one of the most notorious women in London, and as well known to his Majesty as she was to every dissipated Court gallant.

"Well," said Master Rowley, "I hope you have some good news for me."

"Yes, sire; I—"

"Silence!" roared Buckingham. "It is not 'sire,' but Master Rowley."

"I crave thy pardon," replied the woman, humbly. "I had forgotten. Yes, Master Rowley, I have some good news."

"Is the lady beautiful?"

"As handsome a one as your Maj—as you ever beheld."

"Of what age?"

"Eighteen, or thereabouts."

"Her name?"

"Nelly."

"Nelly what?"

"That she refuses to say."

"Hem! Well, that is of no moment. She is handsome, you say. That is enough. Is she dark or fair?"

"Fair, and she is the loveliest creature you ever beheld."

"I am anxious to see her. Where is she?"

"At my house."

"Good. What say you, gentlemen—shall we go together?"

"Nay, nay," cried the woman, as she hastily took a step forward and raised her hands; "that would never do."

"And, pray, why not?" asked Lauderdale, in sneering tones.

"Because she would feel that all was not right. If Master Rowley goes by himself it will be best."

There was a pause for a moment.

Those present—the body-guard of the king *pro tem.*—were considering the advisability of allowing his Majesty to go by himself.

"Rather than that," said Clifford, "I would suggest that the lady be brought here."

"Nay," said Master Rowley; "on second thoughts, I think it better that I should go alone. No one can recognise me."

"Very well," replied the gentlemen.

"I will order the coach to be got ready," said Buckingham, as he rang the bell, "and you will be able to return with her in it."

In a few moments the coach was

announced, and the king, again assuming his disguise, and seeing that his sword was handy, left, being preceded by the cunning old hag.

As the pair were about entering the coach, a tall man mounted on a superb horse rode slowly by.

His broad-brimmed hat was pulled well down, rendering it difficult for anyone to see his face.

He was apparently lost in thought, but as he came opposite the coach he started violently and muttered—

"Lyndon and—and—hem! More villainy! What unfortunate creature have they in their clutches now, I wonder?"

With this he passed on, and the next moment the coach, to which three splendid horses were attached, went off at a spanking pace.

Lyndon's house was situated near Bloomsbury, and not very far from that in the occupation of nurse Alice.

It was one of the finest houses to be found in Bloomsbury, and furnished sumptuously.

There the coach soon arrived. The door of the house was instantly opened, and Master Rowley entered, followed by the woman, and there for a short time we will leave them.

*　　*　　*　　*

Harold wended his way to Little Britain, but Robin had heard nothing of Roebuck.

From Little Britain he went to a Jew clothier's, where, having donned a disguise, he set out for Alsatia.

Here he pursued his inquiries among those whom he knew were Roebuck's staunch friends, but all were sorry to say that they had heard no tidings of him.

Sad and sorrowful in the extreme Harold returned to the Jew, exchanged his clothes, and set out for nurse Alice's.

She had retired, but she at once arose when she knew Harold was present, and sat with him for some time discussing the strange disappearance of Roebuck.

At length Harold rose, and announced his intention to continue the search, and, if necessary, to go himself to Plumstead.

He walked thoughtlessly through St. Giles' and into Bloomsbury.

By this time it was early morning, and although the heavens were crowded with stars, it was very dark, and the silence of the dead reigned everywhere.

Suddenly a prolonged and piercing shriek burst upon his ears, then another, and another, and then the cries of "Help, help! Mercy! Help!"

Instantly Harold drew his sword, and started off in the direction of the sound.

"By heaven!" he muttered, "that voice is the voice of a woman."

In a few seconds he came up to the house of Polly Lyndon, although he did not know it was hers; indeed, it was doubtful whether he had heard of the woman.

A strange sight met his eyes.

Before the door a handsomely dressed man was struggling with a young and beautiful girl, whom it was evident he was trying to get into a coach, the door of which stood open.

The man was being assisted by two or three females, who were trying as hard as they were able to cover the poor girl's mouth with a gag.

The sight made Harold's blood boil.

Rushing forward he seized the man by his neck, and hurling him backwards, so that he nearly fell, he cried—

"Stand back, thou coward!"

The girl uttered a stifled sob, and sinking upon her knees, buried her face in her hands.

"Dastard!" cried the man, whom our readers know to be Master Rowley. "Thou shalt answer for this outrage with thy life!"

And his sword flashed from its scabbard.

"Dastard to thy teeth!" shouted Harold. "Who, think you, is the greater dastard? The man who attacks a defenceless woman, or the man who protects her? My life shall answer? Take care, dastard; take care that thy life doth not answer. Advance, sir. I await thee."

And throwing back his cloak, Harold awaited his opponent's attack.

Suddenly Polly Lyndon darted from the house, and raising her hands, cried—

"No, no! Fight not, I implore thee. Good sir"—this to Harold—"thou dost not know—"

"Silence, fool!" cried Master Rowley; "keep thy tongue still. I am well able to chastise this idiot for his impudence. Stand aside!"

Lyndon reluctantly withdrew.

"I will give thee five minutes in which to say thy prayers," said Master Rowley; "for of a surety thy life is now not worth so much as a straw."

Harold answered him with a loud laugh.

"I fear me, sir," he said, "thou dost overrate thine own abilities."

No further words were spoken, for Master Rowley immediately attacked Harold with terrific fury.

He was beyond question a fine swordsman, and so he should be, for he had been under many masters of the art.

But he lacked one great thing, namely, experience, and besides that he had been partaking of wine much too freely.

This Harold knew not, and he met the attack of Master Rowley with complete self-possession.

As he warmed to the work, he, in his turn, attacked his opponent, and with such fury and with such judgment that it was certain at that rate the fight would not last long.

Polly Lyndon was ringing her hands in despair, and moaning and bewailing in the most awful manner.

The two women who had been helping Master Rowley to get the poor girl in the coach, watched the fight with stupid fascination.

They were both too dumfounded to speak. The unfortunate girl whom so far Harold had rescued, now lay upon the ground totally insensible.

Harold noticed her precarious state, and wishing to terminate the fight as soon as possible, he increased his movements, compelling his opponent to fall back many paces.

Watching his opportunity, Harold got his blade at the hilt of his opponent's sword, and by a swift and extraordinarily clever movement, he caused it to snap off short, much to Master Rowley's astonishment.

Then Harold rushed at him, amid the shrieks of the women, and clutching him by the throat drew his sword's point back on a level with his heart.

"Dastard!" he cried; "thy life, as thou seest, pays the penalty."

"Mercy!" gasped Master Rowley.

But Harold's eyes showed no trace of mercy. Another moment and his opponent's life would certainly have been forfeited; but even as he was about to give the fatal stroke, the sudden sound of a horse's hoofs was heard, and then a tall, dark figure seized Harold's sword, and a voice—a voice he recognised only too well, cried out—

"Hold, for the love of heaven! It is the king!"

Harold's sword fell to the ground, and he drew back in horror, for even as the words "It is the king!" had fallen from the newcomer's lips, Master Rowley's disguise fell off, and Harold saw that his opponent was indeed Charles the Second.

There was an awkward, and we may say, terrible pause for a few moments, during which Harold looked sternly into the king's face, and the king in his.

The thoughts that ran swiftly through Harold's mind were—

"What am I to do? Fall on my knees and beg his forgiveness? No. I found him, as I thought, a stranger, attempting to carry off and no doubt insult a young girl; he was ashamed to reveal himself, and, as a stranger, I fought with him, he, all the time, knowing that I was not a stranger. It is but right that he should apologise to me."

The king's thoughts were—

"How am I to get out of this scrape? It is most unfortunate, and I don't know how to get out of it or what to say. If I say, I am not King Charles, no doubt this youth—one of the captains of my own guard, too, heaven wot!—will pick up his sword and again attack me. Hem! when I granted this youth a commission, I little thought when our next meeting would be."

Aloud, he said—

"I thank thee, good sir, for thy timely intervention, and I am forced to say that what thou hast said is correct. Thou hast rendered me a service by saving my life, and have done me a lasting injury. First, by shouting out 'It is the king!' and secondly, by accidentally striking off my disguise. And now, before I speak further, pray tell me how thou didst know me? From thy dress I should have taken thee to belong to our Court, but I know thee not, yet—yet," he added slowly, " methinks I have seen thy face before. Have I, and where was it?"

"At Hounslow."

"What is thy name?"

"Master Roebuck, at thy service?"

And the man bowed in the politest manner in the world.

The king started and turned pale, but he at once recovered himself.

There was no mistake about it; King Charles the Second was certainly a remarkable man. His talents were numerous, but strange to say he put them always in the wrong channel.

"Oh, Master Roebuck—eh? Odds life! The politest scoundrel in the world stands before me! I again thank thee for saving my life, Master Roebuck—to which I call the Virgin to bear witness; but mark thee, thou hast committed so many daring robberies, that the saving of our life will have no effect upon thee when the day comes for thee to be taken to Tyburn."

Roebuck again bowed politely.

"I am pleased to hear thee speak the truth," he said, with a smile. " I only do my business. You do more than yours. Dost thou not know I only relieve those who have too much, so that I may give a portion to the poor?"

"Such intelligence hath passed mine ears."

"Dost thou not believe it?"

"I know not what to believe."

"Have I ever relieved thee?"

"Nay."

"Then I will do so now. Sire, thy purse!"

The king hesitated.

Was this a joke? Surely it must be. His Majesty smiled.

"I assure thee," said Roebuck, sternly, "that I am not joking. Thou sayest I am, if caught, to go to the scaffold. 'Tis well. When I am on the road the knowledge that I took at least one pound from thee will be a source of much comfort and gratification to me. Sire, thy purse!"

And drawing a pistol suddenly, he with all the coolness in the world, presented it within a yard of the king's head.

The king snatched his purse from his doublet, and in a great rage flung it upon the ground, where it fell with a loud thud, showing that it was well filled.

"Take it," he said, "and beware!"

"Pah!" replied Roebuck, "I am to be hung if caught, and I can be only hung once. Sire, I repeat, thy purse!"

"Odd's life, man!" cried the king, pointing to the ground, "dost thou not see it?"

"Ay, ay, sire. But I did not say, 'Put thy purse on the ground;' I said, 'Thy purse,' which means, 'Place thy purse in my hands.' Sire, thy purse!"

Harold could not resist a smile at his cool impudence.

But he did not attempt to pick the purse up.

The king turned paler than ever, and glanced enquiringly at Roebuck.

He saw that he was undoubtedly in earnest, and so, without further ceremony, he stooped, picked up the purse, and placed it in his hands.

"Now, sire," said Roebuck, "I would recommend thee to be gone at once, or harm may befall thee from other hands."

Without another word the king was about to enter his coach when Master Roebuck stopped him.

"Stay, sire," he said. "Look at that young girl. She is in a dreadful state. Surely you will lend her your coach so that she may go to her home."

His Majesty could say nothing to this, and he reluctantly consented.

Harold in vain tried to get the poor girl to speak.

She was far too much exhausted.

"Take her to nurse Alice," whispered Roebuck "I will ride by thy side."

He assisted Harold to place the girl in the coach, and then, telling the king it should return in a short time, he sprang upon his horse, and giving the word, he and the coach moved on.

"Farewell, sire!" he said, raising his hat and waving his hand to the king, who stood upon the threshold of Polly Lyndon's house. "I will not fail to drink thy good health anon."

CHAPTER XX.

IN WHICH IT IS SEEN HOW ROEBUCK AND COLONEL BLOOD COME FACE TO FACE IN ST. JAMES'S PARK—"BRANDED FOR LIFE!"

ARRIVING at nurse Alice's house, and the unfortunate girl having been carefully carried into the principal room and laid before the astonished eyes of Alice, who, after Harold's unexpected visit, found sleep entirely out of the question, Roebuck beckoned to Harold to follow him.

"Harold," he said, in a voice of emotion, as he clasped both Harold's hands, "I thank heaven that I have found thee well! I have now no time to converse with thee on the matters nearest my heart. But I may tell thee that not many hours ago I met Lord Eustace Trevor.

"He knew me not, but as I knew he was in the guard, I was sure he could tell me about you. He told me all about Blood, Oates, and Hugh Jeffries, although the particulars were not so minute as if you had told me.

"But that matters not. When I fortunately discovered you to-night I was on my way to meet a person in St. James's Park.

"I must at once begone there or my appointment will fail. I shall not be absent long, and when I return I have much to talk about. Take great care of the girl, Harold."

"I have been very, very anxious about thee," said Harold, as he returned the pressure of Roebuck's hands. "And I have caused inquiries to be made, and searched high and low for thee.

"Thank heaven thou art safe! And that thou didst arrive in time to avert the stroke which would have deprived England of her king. But tell me, Roebuck, canst thou not put off thy appointment for a future time?"

Roebuck started and trembled violently, and Harold saw that a tear was stealing down his cheek.

"Nay, nay," he said. "My appointment must be kept. It is on family matters, Harold; family matters which concern thee not. They are relating to—"

Here with a sob, which seemed to come from his very heart, he stopped, and dashing the tears from his eyes, cried—

"Good-bye, my boy, good-bye! I shall return soon."

The next moment he had mounted his noble and singularly patient animal, and had disappeared.

"A strange man!" muttered Harold, as he returned to the room in which was the girl. "I fail—utterly fail to make him out!"

*   *   *   *

Roebuck put spurs to his horse, and went along at a good round pace until he reached the Mall in St. James's Park.

Here he drew rein, and looked about him.

Not a soul was in sight. The whole place was as silent as the grave, save for the slight rustling of the leaves, disturbed by a gentle westerly breeze.

He took off his hat so as to allow the wind to cool his heated brow.

"How quiet everything is here!" he muttered. "Even the sheep are silent —locked in sleep! I would to heaven *I* could throw myself on the green sward there and sleep and forget all my—Ah!"

His meditations were broken off by the sound of horse's footsteps advancing at a swift pace.

Was it the one he had come to meet?

Surely not; for the horseman made no attempt to draw up.

When within a dozen yards Roebuck suddenly placed his horse in the centre of the road, and then, raising his hand, cried—

"Halt!"

The horseman paused in astonishment, and his sudden pause caused his hat to fall off.

Roebuck uttered a loud cry.

So did the horseman.

Master Roebuck and Colonel Blood were face to face!

For, it might be, the space of twenty seconds, neither spoke.

They sat firm in their saddles surveying each other steadily.

Even the horses seemed to share the astonishment of their masters, for they stood as still as if carved out of the solid marble.

What were the thoughts of these two men at this moment?

Colonel Blood's thoughts ran thus—

"At last then I have met the very man whom I would have given any amount to have avoided. It is, of course, just my accursed luck! What will he say? And what will he do? Dost he know of the last attempt on the life of the confounded youth whom he has thought it worth while to take under his protection?"

Master Roebuck's thoughts ran—

"At last! At last I have the man before me, who in conjunction with Sir John Humphreys has been trying to destroy the links which I have been at so much trouble to put together.

"Here, above all places in the world, I meet the blackguard and murderer Blood. 'Fore heaven! it must have been the hand of Providence which caused me to keep an appointment in St. James's Park.

"And what is this man here for? I neither know nor care. All that concerns me is that he is here, and that, consequently, he has saved me the trouble of seeking him out in Alsatia."

Aloud, he said, in low, stern tones, which resembled the muttered thunder announcing the coming storm—

"So, Colonel Blood, we at last meet face to face!"

Blood tried to smile, but failed miserably as he said—

"At last, thou sayest. Hast thou been searching for me then?"

"No, but I should have done so ere long."

"I feel honoured, Master Roebuck," said Blood. "May I ask why thou wouldst have sought me out?"

"Thou dost already know. Colonel Blood, thou hast known me long as a man who, when he speaks, means what he says."

"I know nobody's business but mine own, Master Roebuck, whatever thou mayest think of it."

"Well, I see that it is useless to bandy words with such an abandoned scoundrel as thyself. Here we are, Colonel Blood—here in one of the most secluded spots in all London. Dismount, please."

And as the last word left his lips, Master Roebuck leapt from his saddle.

Instantly Blood's hand was upon his holster, but Roebuck saw the movement.

"Cowardly as usual," he said, as he placed his left hand under his cloak. "Attempt any foul play, Colonel Blood, and thou knowest what will follow."

"But if I refuse to dismount?" replied Blood.

"Then thou wilt go on without thy hat," replied Roebuck, satirically, as he pointed to the hat lying upon the ground. "Pray dismount, Colonel Blood."

"I have no time to stay talking with thee," cried Blood, impatiently. "I have important business that——"

"Tush, tush!" interrupted Roebuck, with a grim smile. "I presume thy important business is thy usual business—that is to say, the slaying of some unfortunate devil. My interruption, therefore, as thou wilt admit, allows thy victim a longer grace than thou wouldst have allowed him. Dismount," he thundered.

Our readers have had plenty of opportunities of judging of Blood's character.

But of all the men he stood in awe of, it was beyond question Roderick Roebuck whom he feared most. To him, as to everyone else, Roebuck seemed a strange, mysterious and awful being.

Indeed, there were many people who believed him to be possessed of supernatural gifts, and possessed of the power to appear and vanish as it pleased him.

"But what have I to fear?" thought Blood, as the word "Dismount," uttered in such commanding tones, left Roebuck's lips. "I have more chance of running my sword through his body than he has through mine, for I fancy that I am the most skilful, although I have never yet crossed swords with him—yet there is no doubt that he is the strongest."

Blood dismounted.

"Draw!" cried Roebuck, sternly, as he calmly drew his sword and, throwing his cloak over his shoulder, stood erect.

"But why do you wish to force me to fight?" asked Blood, who reluctantly drew his sword from its sheath. "I have not quarrelled with you."

"Listen," replied Roebuck. "It is true you have not actually quarrelled with me, but you have done worse."

"Worse?"

"Ay, worse, worse, worse!" and with each word Master Roebuck became more excited. By a great effort, however, he calmed himself. "Listen," he said. "Yet why I should delay I know not. Colonel Blood, you, Hugh Jeffries, Sir John Humphreys—whom may heaven confound is my most devout wish!—and the blasphemous, depraved and drunken Titus Oates, who for so long has cheated Tyburn, have sworn that you would not leave a stone unturned to take the life of Harold Harcourt, falsely called Harold de Witt."

Roebuck paused, evidently to watch the effect of his speech.

Blood started violently.

"How does he know this?" he thought. "One of the Alsatians turned traitor, I'll be bound. But there! I was a fool to invite them. It was the action of a madman, for I ought to have recollected how they hold this strange, devilish, mysterious man in their estimation."

"It is a lie!" he said, aloud.

Roebuck smiled ironically.

"Nay," he said, "it is no lie. I am well acquainted with thy actions, Colonel Blood, there is not much doubt of that, and with them I should not interfere, but when thou dost meddle with mine, then thou must answer for it."

"I have meddled with naught of thine, and to that I swear."

"Naught of mine? Naught of mine? There thou liest. For a long time thou hast meddled with Harold Harcourt, whose father thou didst foully murder. I know all now—all. But to proceed. Time after time hast thou plotted to take the life of Harold Harcourt, the youth whom I value more than my own life. I have clung to the lad all through the years of his life, ever since he was a child," and here his voice wavered slightly.

"I—but there, thou hast meddled with my affairs, and for that thou must answer. If I fall, I shall die with the knowledge that at least I did what I could to punish the man who plotted against one I value more than everything I possess—more, as I have said, than my life."

Blood saw that Roebuck was resolute. He knew he must fight.

Another instant, and the swords of the two men crossed with a clash, which caused the horses, who were quietly grazing with their heads close to each other, to look up in wonder.

It would be absurd to give a minute description of the fight between them.

Our readers, knowing the characters of both, can imagine with what determination this duel was fought.

Many times the combatants paused, and their heavy breathing showed how each had exerted himself.

Both were bathed in sweat, Blood more so, however, than Roebuck.

In one of their pauses Blood said—

"Roebuck, I know thy love for money. Cease, I pray thee, this fight, and I swear that to-morrow I will place in thy hands a thousand crowns."

Again the low, ironical, smothered laugh left Roebuck's lips.

Blood fairly shuddered at it, blackguard and depraved wretch though he was.

"My love for money?" said Roebuck. "Thou art strangely mistaken, Blood. I have no love whatever for money. I hate and curse the sight of it. And thou wilt give me a thousand crowns if this fight is stayed? Truly, truly thou dost not know me even yet. But mark thee—if thou didst have the power to open the heavens and rain gold and diamonds at my feet until they formed a barrier between me and thee, I would carve a way to get at thee and renew the fight. Colonel Blood, I await thy pleasure. I beg thee not to distress thyself, but my time is getting somewhat short."

With a groan—a groan that sounded like a groan of despair—Blood once more stood ready.

At last the slow, hollow tones of the

clock at Whitehall Palace chimed the hour of Roebuck's appointment.

Roebuck pressed forward with re-doubled energy.

Suddenly Blood stumbled and fell.

His sword dropped from his hand, and a cry of agony and terror combined escaped his lips.

Roebuck stood over him, his sword poised to give the fatal stroke.

Blood would have shrieked for mercy, but terror held him speechless.

He could only *look* what he would have said.

Roebuck lowered his sword.

"Craven heart!" he said, bitterly, "I would thou couldst see thyself now, for thy character is written on thy face as plainly as yon moon shines in the heavens. I cannot feel it in my heart to strike thee dead thus, yet did I do so, of what a load of misery, of what a hound should I not rid London?"

"Mercy!" gasped Blood at last.

"Aye, mercy I will show thee," replied Roebuck, "to this extent. I will allow thee to rise, pick up thy sword and defend thyself. To thy feet—quick!"

Blood rose with alacrity, but trembling violently.

"Pick up thy weapon," said Roebuck.

Blood essayed to pick it up, but it was a failure. Terror was in his face; it ran through his blood and paralysed him.

"I cannot," he gasped.

"I will be thy servant then," said Roebuck.

And picking up Blood's weapon, he handed it to him.

"It is not damaged," he said. "Now, quick!"

Blood raised his sword.

It trembled violently, and the next instant fell to the ground.

"Thy craven heart will not allow thee to fight," said Roebuck, sternly, and in tones which seemed chilled with ice, "but I cannot take advantage of thy cowardice and slay thee. Nay, nay; Roebuck has done many wrong things in his time, maybe, but he never killed a man in cold blood. My mind is uncertain. *I* would spare thee, but a voice whispers in mine ears, 'Slay him, slay him!' But no, no, that I

cannot do—not yet, not yet! Colonel Blood, stand erect."

Blood tried to do so.

He knew well enough that his life hung upon a thread.

"Mark well what I say, Colonel Blood," continued Roebuck. "Are you listening?"

"Yes, yes," murmured Blood.

"'Tis well, then. I say, Colonel Blood, that thou art a *coward!* Dost hear that?"

"Aye, aye. I do—I do."

"And thou dost agree with it?"

No answer.

"I say dost thou agree with it?" thundered Roebuck. "Speak!"

"I do—I do," said Blood.

"Good!" cried Roebuck. "And since thou dost agree with it, bear the mark of a coward through thy life."

Roebuck raised his sword: there was, as it seemed, several brilliant flashes, and in another moment a shower of blood poured down the colonel's face until it seemed as if he were blinded.

Master Roebuck, with extraordinary dexterity, had marked upon Blood's forehead with his sword the sign of an arrow.

Three deep gashes they were, which, when healed up, would leave the arrow in white lines till his dying day.

It was the fearful sign of cowardice, and, although practised in other countries, well known in England.

Blood knew it immediately.

"Oh!" he cried, "kill me. Kill me at once!"

"Nay, nay," replied Roebuck, as he deliberately sheathed his sword; "I never slay a man in cold blood. Bind up thy wound, colonel, and go thy way. And mark thee well—beware how thou dost plot against Harold Harcourt, for, remember, I watch over him. Farewell for the present, and forget not that by the hand of Roderick Roebuck thou wast *branded for life!*"

Blood had fallen upon his knees, almost insensible.

When he recovered and looked around, Roebuck and his horse had vanished.

Uttering a loud and bitter cry, Blood rose and proceeded to bind up his terrible wound.

CHAPTER XXI.

"NELLY"—A STRANGE HISTORY.

OUR young and intelligent readers have been hurried pell-mell, and without being allowed to get breath, through so many exciting scenes, that we are assured they require a rest, or, if not exactly a rest, a "brief pause," as the stage instructor would be pleased to term it.

We will therefore place before their notice, in a more prominent manner than we had space for in the last chapter but one, an account of the girl whom Harold had rescued.

It was not until the afternoon of the second day after Harold had so courageously rescued this unfortunate girl, who had got into the clutches of the infamous Mistress Lyndon, that she recovered her senses sufficiently to be able to thoroughly comprehend the awful danger through which she had passed.

For many hours nurse Alice was afraid that her symptoms would develop into brain fever, but happily, owing to her summoning two or three eminent physicians, this was averted.

Nurse Alice saw that Harold, usually so reserved when in the society of strange females, took a great interest in the girl.

She noted his impatient pacing to and fro through the long hours of the day and night, and his constant and eager enquiries.

She was a woman of the world, and it did not take her so very long to ascertain that Harold was actually in love with the girl.

Well, she was pleased at this.

She knew that Harold's surroundings, taking them all in all, were not exactly suited to a youth of his age.

She felt assured that a young man like him, fighting as he was for his own rights, should have one or two gentle influences to bear upon him.

For some time she had noted with regret and much alarm, that he was becoming indifferent to all home influences, and many and many a night, when she had stolen to his bedroom,

she had watched the fierce look upon his handsome features, sighed at the difficult, as it seemed to her, breathing, and shuddered at his muttered curses upon the heads of the men who so continually rose up to bar his passage to his rights.

She seemed to feel that, with all her and Roebuck's guidance, Harold would one day burst through the bonds of love and respect, and that some dreadful crime would be committed.

Well, on the evening of the second day, to Harold's intense delight, the girl entered the sitting-room, escorted by nurse Alice.

She looked very pale and weak truly, but her eyes spoke her gratitude to the youth who had so gallantly rescued her.

She advanced to Harold, and placed her little white hand in his, blushing beautifully as she did so.

"Sir," she said, in a soft, and as it seemed, sad voice, "how can I thank you for your noble conduct?"

"By not mentioning the matter, fair lady," said Harold, as he bowed politely; "I did only my duty."

"True, true; and yet—but no matter. Sir, wilt thou be pleased to tell me the name of the man who was about to forcibly carry me away?"

Harold started and looked enquiringly at nurse Alice.

He recollected that he had told her who it was.

A glance between them was enough.

Harold saw that Alice had not mentioned the name of the man.

"Alas!" said Harold, "that I did not ascertain. But thou canst rely upon it, fair lady, that the man was some drunken Court gallant."

"I am sorry thou didst not ascertain his name. And yet—and yet," she added, mournfully, "even if I did know, I should be powerless to bring upon him the punishment he so richly deserves. But, sir," here she paused a moment, "dost know the name of the house or the owner of it?"

"I do that," replied Harold, gravely; "but I will not insult thine ears with the name of it!"

"I understand you, sir, perfectly; although I must confess that my knowledge of London and its ways is more than limited. But now you, sir, and you"—to nurse Alice—"must, perforce, be wondering as to who I am. Alas!" she said, as she covered her face with her hands, and something like a sob escaped her lips, "I know not myself!"

Harold started, and nurse Alice looked grave.

"Pity me!" cried the girl; "pity me!"

"Heaven knows I pity you," said Harold, in kind tones, as he led her to a couch; "but thy words sound strangely in mine ears."

Nurse Alice turned sharply upon her.

"Girl," she said, severely; "how came thee to be in that house?"

The girl instantly saw the change in Alice's demeanour, and her sobs broke out afresh.

Before she could reply, nurse Alice said—

"Dost thou not know thy name?"

"My name is Nelly, madam."

"Nelly what?"

"Alas! I have no other name," sobbed the girl.

"Truly, girl, thou dost speak strangely. Harold, from what I can see, thine aid was misplaced. Thou dost know the class of house from which she came, and—"

Like a flash of lightning the girl started up.

Her eyes blazed furiously, and her little hands clenched themselves until the nails were embedded in the flesh.

She drew herself erect and said—

"What dost thou mean, madam? Ah, I see it only too well!

"Oh, heavenly Father!" she gasped in tones of fearful anguish, "look upon one of thy daughters and pity and have mercy upon her!

"Oh, madam! thou who hast been so kind to me—do not misjudge me! No, no, no! You will not — you will not! For I swear—I swear on this cross!"—and she took a small silver cross from her breast, and held it to her lips — "that I am honest as a baby!

"Madam! look in my face—look, and say—say thou dost believe me!"

Then, with another cry, a cry which seemed to come straight from her very heart, the poor girl fell on her knees before Alice.

"I *do* believe thee," replied Alice, in softened tones, as she stooped and, raising the girl, clasped her to her breast; "I believe thee. I crave thy pardon for doubting thee, and thine, Harold, for daring to say what I did. But thy welfare is ever uppermost in my thoughts, and that must be my excuse."

"I know it, Alice," replied Harold, "and my pardon is not necessary. But no doubt the fair lady hath some history which it may interest us to hear."

"Yes, yes," cried the girl, eagerly, "I have a history, a strange history, attaching to me. If thou wilt hear me, I will endeavour to relate it."

"Do, I pray thee," said Alice, once more leading her to a couch; "relate it in thine own way, and we promise not to interrupt thee."

"My name, as I have said," commenced the girl, "is Nelly. I know no other, for so many years have passed that I have forgotten it. My age is now eighteen. I can call to mind the time when, as a very little child, I used to live in a very large and grand house. Not in London, for I remember that on all sides woods and lovely fields abounded; and that the house was surrounded with lovely grounds, such as cannot exist in this city. My parents—"

"Stay but a moment," said Alice, "and pardon, I pray you, this unseemly interruption. Dost thou remember thy parents?"

"But slightly. My father, I remember, was a tall, grave man, who was dotingly fond of me. My mother was handsome—for I have heard people say so—but she, on the contrary, was not fond of me.

"Why, I know not; I was too young to understand. I remember, however, that my parents were continually quarrelling, and that often my nurse would seize me and take me away out of the reach of, as she said, the violence of my mother.

"I can recollect that the house used to be frequented by numerous gentlemen, and that there were many quarrels, but what about, of course, I do not know.

"But one night there was an awful quarrel, and I heard the clash of weapons and the cries and groans of people in pain.

"I was much frightened, but in the midst of it my nurse rushed into my room, wrapped me in some warm clothing, and ran down the stairs.

"As she was about to open the door at the back, a man with a gleaming sword in his hand, and whose face was covered with blood, seized my nurse and cried—

"'Hold!'

"I shrieked with terror, but the next instant I saw who it was. It was my father. He looked at me and said to the nurse—

"'Thank God she is safe. Don't shudder at me, Nelly—don't shudder—don't shrink from me. I am guarding thine interests. But there, poor child, what does she understand by interests?' Then he said: 'Kiss me, my child.'

"How I did it I know not, but he was my father, and I kissed his face over and over again. Then he seized my nurse's hand and said, 'Kneel!' The woman knelt.

"'Swear,' cried my father, 'that thou wilt guard her with thy life, and convey her to where I told thee.'

"'I swear before heaven I will!' replied the woman. Another moment, and she was flying along the dark road —where, I know not. I fell asleep, and when I awoke I found myself in the house in which I have remained ever since. It is no wonder I have forgotten my father's name. I seldom heard it spoken, and I was called nothing but Nelly."

"And the house in which you have been staying all these years?"

"Is in Smithfield."

"And the name of your guardian?"

"Is a Jew, whose real name is Phillips, but he is called by many the Maniac Jew. The house is of peculiar construction, looking more like a round-house than anything else, but—"

Harold interrupted her by darting forward towards nurse Alice, who had dropped into the nearest chair.

She seemed about to faint.

"What ails thee, Alice?" cried Harold in alarm.

"Nothing—nothing, dear Harold. A slight faintness, that is all."

Then she said, in a rapid undertone—

"Mind me not—mind me not. Let her proceed."

"A slight faintness, fair lady," said Harold, "nothing more. She wishes you to proceed."

"The Jew treats me kindly," continued the girl, "and so does his wife. I am supposed to be his daughter. And now I come to the strangest part of my history.

"Every month, or thereabouts," said Nelly, "a strange gentleman calls at the house. He is very tall and of commanding presence, and is always attired in the richest apparel. He has dark eyes, with heavy lashes, and a heavy pointed moustache. I think he must be someone of importance, for I once observed that under his cloak and upon his breast was a large silver star, and—"

"Ha!" cried Harold, excitedly, "it is—"

"Silence for thy life!" shrieked Alice, as, starting from her seat, she placed her hand over Harold's mouth.

Again she turned swiftly to Nelly.

"I crave thy pardon," she said, hurriedly; "he is thinking it is a man who has done him a great injury, and upon whom he has sworn to be avenged. I never allow him to mention his name, and in this case I am sure he is mistaken."

"Of that also I am certain," continued Nelly; "the gentleman I mean has in his face the gentleness of a woman, and more than once I have noticed that as he looked upon me his lips have trembled and a tear has fallen down his cheeks."

"What does he say to thee?" asked Alice.

"He says 'Art thou well?' I reply, 'Yes, I thank thee, kind sir.' Then he says, 'Heaven bless thee, my pretty Nelly;' and I reply, 'Heaven bless thee, sir.' That is all."

"Wonderful!" muttered Harold.

"Truly, truly, this Master Roebuck is more, far more than a mystery."

"Sometimes he brings me a present," continued Nelly, "and it is always costly. I have many of them in my box at home. And now I will tell you how I came to be in that house."

And Nelly told them how she got into the clutches of Mistress Lyndon (but she knew not her name).

"And now," said Alice, "what I propose is, that you return immediately to Smithfield."

"Oh, yes, yes," cried Nelly, eagerly; "I am sure Master Phillips will be distracted. But I cannot go alone."

"Fear not," said Alice; "Harold and I will go with thee, and explain all to thy guardian. I will at once get you and myself ready."

As she left the room, Harold ran after her.

"Alice," he said, "the man who visits her is Master Roebuck, is it not?"

"It is; but mention not his name to her."

"Dost thou know who the parents of this girl are?"

"I know nothing."

This she said firmly.

"Well, it is strange indeed; that is all I can say. But Roebuck must have seen who the girl was."

"I do not doubt he did, but he knew she was safe in our hands. Question me no further, dear Harold, for my lips are sealed. Master Roebuck was ever a man of mystery, as thou dost know. He respects those who obey him, and love him, and keep his secrets, but he is terrible to those who endeavour to penetrate them. I shall join you in a moment."

With this Alice ascended to her room to attire herself for the journey to Smithfield.

* * * *

It is needless to say with what delight the Jew, Phillips, welcomed Nelly. He fairly danced for joy, and returned thanks for her safety in several different languages, so confused was he.

He did not want to be told the names of her abductors.

She was safe, and he was satisfied.

Leaving Alice in conversation with the Jew's wife, Harold left and went off to Robin.

He felt that the presence of the happy giant would dispel many sad thoughts which crowded his brain.

He found Robin, as usual, at his work, and as black as a negro.

No sooner did he set eyes upon Harold, than he dropped his hammer, and advancing, seized hold of and shook Harold's hands with such heartiness, that it made him wince.

"By my father's soul!" he cried, "I am right glad to see thee."

"I have seen him," said Harold.

"What, Roebuck? Ay, I know he is safe, although I have not seen him."

"How canst thou tell then?"

"Whenever I see my brother I know he is safe."

"I knew not that thou didst have a brother," replied Harold, somewhat amazed. "Is he of thy stature?"

"Gad's life! no. Behold him!" cried the smith.

And he pointed to the bellows.

Harold looked, and there, perched fair in the centre of the bellows, and looking, in the glare of the forge, like some goblin, sat—who?

Pipkin!

Yes; there was no doubt about it, it was Pipkin, sure enough.

He was all there—what there was of him.

Harold burst into a loud laugh.

"Laugh not, good Harold," said Pipkin, shaking his head like a Methodist parson. "What Robin says is correct. We are brothers now—brothers for evermore. We swear it! If any man dare to insult Robin, I'll knock him down—on my soul, I'll knock him down! Aye, aye, fear not, Robin, I'll protect thee."

As he said this, he cocked his little legs in such an attitude, and folded his arms with such action, that Harold again laughed.

"I doubt thee not, Pipkin," said Robin, assuming much gravity. "If any man should attempt to strike me, fear not but that I will get behind thee, and so shall be safe. But now, Harold, wilt thou be pleased to seat thyself? Excuse the seat, for I fear me it is not very clean, but it will do this once. And now tell me what has befallen thee since I saw thee last."

Pipkin, anxious to learn what he could, slid down the bellows with the rapidity and dexterity of a monkey, and took his seat between Harold's legs, while Robin, shutting the door, seated himself upon his anvil.

CHAPTER XXII.

SHOWS HOW MASTER ROEBUCK SUDDENLY APPEARS BEFORE KING CHARLES IN HIS OWN BEDROOM—THE SIGNATURE, "WALLS HAVE EARS!"—SHOWS ALSO HOW SIR JOHN HUMPHREYS WAS WARNED TO FLY FROM LONDON.

HIS Most Gracious Majesty King Charles the Second was in what is known as a "beastly temper."

Many things had gone wrong lately at the Court, and he had on more than one occasion got into hot water, when, disguised, he had "taken his walks abroad."

A week had passed since the girl he had thought was in his clutches had been snatched from him by Harold, who, although as usual on duty, had not seen the king.

He had been thinking that he should be sent for; perhaps placed under arrest by the king.

But, no; not one word was mentioned.

It was evident, therefore, that all that had passed the king had kept—and wisely too—locked in his own breast.

Strange to say, Roebuck had not kept to his word.

He had never returned to nurse Alice's.

Now, it follows as a matter of course that the king was terribly annoyed at being stopped by Harold, and by being worsted in the fight.

But this was not what annoyed him most.

It was the sudden appearance of Master Roebuck. He wondered how it was he came to recognise him.

Although in his own mind he blessed him for being the means of saving his life, which but for Roebuck's timely appearance would undoubtedly have been sacrificed, he cursed him for crying out, "It is the king!"

When we now introduce his Majesty to our readers, he is seated in a gigantic and magnificently constructed armchair in his own bedroom.

The chair being of great size he was completely lost in it.

This royal chamber almost defies description as to its costly surroundings.

It was the most beautiful in Whitehall Palace, and some chroniclers have said that no room like it could have been found in the world, with the exception, possibly, of one or two to be found in an Oriental palace.

The chamber was fitted with more than one secret door, through which the king passed when he wished to be unobserved.

They led to various parts of the palace.

The time was near midnight, and the majority of the inmates having retired, profound silence reigned, but for the steady tramp, tramp of the guard pacing the passages.

The palace clock chimed the hour of midnight, and at the same moment a voice spoke a few words of command.

There was a pause, then the rattling of arms, the voice spoke again, and once more the tramping commenced.

The king started from his chair.

"It is Harold de Witt changing the guard," he muttered. "I had better summon him, and question him concerning the matter which is uppermost in my mind. I pray heaven he has spoken to no one on the matter."

He was about to pull the bell by his side, when a second thought struck him.

"No, that will never do," he considered. "If I summon him it may be remarked, or I may be overheard. Nay, I will await a more fitting opportunity."

So saying he again sank into his chair.

BY COMMAND OF THE KING; OR, THE DAYS OF THE MERRIE MONARCH.

"'BY COMMAND OF THE KING! HURRAH!' CRIED THE OFFICERS."

No. 8

But he was still thinking of the matter, and his thoughts found vent in indistinct mutterings.

Presently he said, half aloud—

"But this mysterious fellow Roebuck puzzles me. Either there must be a dozen Roebucks or else he is possessed of— Bah! I shouldn't be surprised if he were to—"

He paused and turned deathly pale.

Then he slowly rose to his feet, and gazed horror-stricken at the door in front of him.

A secret door he alone used.

It moved slowly back, and the next instant a tall, cloaked, and masked figure glided into the room, paused, bowed low, advanced again, and then stood motionless.

"Great heaven!" gasped the king, "who art thou? Speak!"

The figure raised its hat, removed its mask, and again bowed slowly. Then it said—

"Roderick Roebuck, sire, at thy service!"

So thunderstruck was the king that for some few moments he was powerless to speak.

He seemed to be asking himself whether he was awake or dreaming.

But suddenly, advancing a few paces, he said—

"Heaven's death! I see it all. This is all through Harold de Witt, who shall suffer for it, I swear! For this insult he shall lose his life! And as for thee, sirrah, beware! Thou dost not leave this palace alive! The King of England to be insulted in his own bedroom! By the blessed Virgin! I—"

He was about to seize the bell-rope, but Roebuck placed his back against it.

"But one moment," he said, "then thou canst ring the bell and have me arrested if thou dost think fit. It was not by the aid of Harold de Witt, as he is wrongfully called, that I was enabled to enter here. He knows not that I am in the palace. How I managed to get here I will leave for awhile, but I am not here to assassinate thee. I advise thee to summon no one to thee, and after I have concluded my mission I will depart as I came, and no one will be the wiser."

Roebuck said this so calmly, so collectedly, and so seriously, that the king was startled.

He was so enraged, however, that he could not find words in which to vent his wrath.

Roebuck took from under his cloak a small ebony box bound with gold.

This he handed to the king.

His Majesty, instead of taking it, started back in alarm.

"What is it?" he asked.

"A present for thee, sire."

"A present for us? Eh? Ah! Dost thou think King Charles is a fool? Thou wilt find it is not so, I—"

"Sire, it is a present for thee, and a most valuable present, too," interrupted Roebuck.

"Or an infernal machine?" said his Majesty, looking upon the box as he would have looked upon some deadly reptile.

Roebuck smiled, then taking a pace forward he opened the box, and poured the contents upon the table.

Wonderful! Marvellous! Exquisite!

It looked, as the light from the lamps in the room fell upon it, like a quantity of glittering water, but as it rested upon the table, there was no mistaking what it was.

The king uttered a low exclamation of astonishment and rapture.

He seemed for a moment riveted to the floor, and his eyes looked as if about to start from their sockets.

The contents of the box were a large number of lustrous diamonds.

There they were, of all shapes and sizes.

"Diamonds!" cried the king.

"Right, sire. They are yours."

"Eh? Mine? I know thou art a daring fellow, but these—these are not from the Tower—eh? Odd's life! Since that assassin Blood attempted to steal our crown, we have taken more care of it."

Roebuck saw the king was pleased.

"They were mine," he said, "they are now thine, if—"

"Yes, yes, if? See, I try to be patient with thee, Master Roebuck," said the king, as he took up a handful of the diamonds and let them fall again in a glittering shower upon the table.

"If," said Roebuck boldly, "thou wilt sign this paper."

And taking a parchment from his pocket, he handed it to the king.

His Majesty took it, slowly opened it, and as slowly perused it, then it dropped from his hands.

"By heaven's gracious mercy!" he said, "thou art indeed a very fiend. It is impossible! By heaven, it is impossible!" and he stamped fiercely upon the parchment.

Roebuck picked it up calmly enough.

"Then, sire," he said, "since thou dost refuse to sign it, I will replace the diamonds."

"Wait! wait!" cried the king. "Give me a moment."

"Dost thou thoroughly understand the nature of this parchment?" asked Roebuck.

"Ay, right well!" replied the king; "it is a warrant for the arrest of Sir John Humphreys, and requiring only our signature."

Roebuck bowed.

"Thou art right, sire," he said.

"Delay it for a day—eh, Roebuck? and then I will see what—"

"There must be no delay, sire," said Roebuck firmly.

"But if brought to trial, how canst thou prove that he did the deed? How canst thou prove that this Harold de Witt, as we have been pleased to call him, is the rightful heir to the Harcourt estates?"

"Leave that to me. I—"

"Nay, if I sign this thou must not be seen in connection with this matter."

"Good. I have witnesses."

"Well, well. I believe it will all fall to the ground; still that will not be our fault. These diamonds are very valuable—eh, Roebuck?"

"Of enormous value, sire."

"Hum," muttered the king, who then, taking the parchment from Roebuck, took a pen, and at the bottom of the document, under the words, "Given under our hand and seal," &c., he wrote in a bold hand the name—

"Charles Rer."

"And now, sire, if you will be pleased to summon Harold de Witt, and will place this in his hands for immediate execution, all will be done."

"Well, well, it shall be as you wish. Vanish!" Roebuck returned to the secret door, while the king rang the bell.

An usher entering, the king directed him to send Harold to him at once.

This order was overheard by one of the men on guard. Nor was this all, for almost every word that had passed between the king and Roebuck he had heard.

Yet he seemed from his appearance more like a statue than anything else.

Harold soon appeared.

He was ushered at once into the king's presence, and the door secured.

When Roebuck suddenly appeared before him he almost fell to the ground in astonishment.

He could hardly credit his own eyes.

What passed in that room, and what orders Harold had, will be seen in a moment.

*   *   *   *

The man on guard listened eagerly to all that passed, but when he heard footsteps approaching the door, he resumed his position with marvellous rapidity.

As Harold crossed the threshold the king said—

"Yes, yes, at daybreak—at daybreak."

And thereupon the door closed.

Without a moment's delay Harold ran off to Lord Trevor's quarters.

The man on guard watched him out of sight, and then he set off down the corridors at a quick pace.

*   *   *   *

"Now, Master Roebuck, vanish, and trouble me no more. But first tell me how you managed to reach this door."

"I would rather not tell thee, sire. I have only to say that what I have been long trying to effect is near consummation. I bid thee farewell."

And Roebuck, bowing lowly, stepped to the secret door.

"Wait, wait!" cried the king, excitedly. "There is something I had forgotten. Thou hast not returned my purse, which thou didst steal the other night."

His Majesty was so serious as he said this, that Roebuck felt inclined to laugh in his face.

"Thy purse, sire," he said, "and the

contents also have long since gone to put a few loaves on the tables of the poorer classes of thy subjects."

Again Roebuck turned to go.

"Stay, stay!" said the king. "Not a word of what has passed—on thy life, not a word."

"Fear not, sire. With me a secret is a secret."

"'Tis well. But I tell thee, Master Roebuck, if thou art caught, the tree at Tyburn shall assuredly finish thee."

Roebuck bowed. Another instant, and he was gone.

The king paced the apartment after his departure for some considerable time.

More than once he started, with a muttered exclamation, to the bell-rope, but a glance at the glittering diamonds upon the table caused him to stop abruptly, and eventually he threw himself into his chair, but, becoming restless, he flung himself, dressed as he was, upon the bed.

"Alas!" he murmured, "how strangely true are most of Will Shakespeare's lines! But there is no truer line than 'Uneasy lies the head that wears a crown!' And, by our good Lady, I am continually being troubled."

*　　*　　*　　*

Sir John Humphreys was in a terrible state.

In the short time that had elapsed since we last saw him he had aged considerably.

His form was bowed, and his hair was fast turning white.

Added to this, there was a continual nervous twitching of his mouth and eyes.

His hands trembled at times so violently that he could scarce hold a pen to paper.

During the interview between Roebuck and his Majesty at Whitehall Palace, Sir John Humphreys was seated in the study of his house at Bloomsbury in company with Titus Oates and Hugh Jeffries.

It is needless for us to tell our readers what they were plotting. Suffice it to say that it was nothing for the benefit of Harold Harcourt.

Suddenly Sir John said—

"This is indeed passing strange. For days have I sent for Blood, but he is nowhere to be found. I much fear me that some harm hath befallen him."

"Fear not," said Oates; "he hath as many lives as a cat. Kill him one day, and he will turn up alive the next."

"Who knows?" said Hugh. "He may already have accomplished the destruction of this imp."

Sir John shook his head.

"Nay," he said, "my information is accurate, and I know that the youth still continues his duties. I pay one of his guards to keep me well informed of all that passes."

A knock came upon the door, or, we should say, a loud banging.

Each started to his feet.

"Come in, there!" cried Sir John.

The door was flung open, and a tall man, attired in a long cloak, entered.

His head was swathed in surgical bandages, and he looked as pale as death itself.

"Mercy!" cried the three, "Blood!"

"Ay," said Blood, "it is. I am altered, you think, eh?"

And he flung himself into the nearest chair.

"What has happened?" asked Sir John, in low tones.

"No matter now. I am here to take thy orders, if thou hast any. I pray thee proceed at once."

The three thereupon seated themselves, and the interrupted conversation was resumed, and carried on with much vigour for over two hours.

They were in the midst of an animated discussion, when another thundering knock came upon the door.

In reply to the order to enter, the butler appeared.

"A man desires instant audience with thee," he said.

"His name?" asked Sir John.

"He gave none," replied the butler, "but he desired me to say 'Forewarned is forearmed.'"

Sir John started violently, and in hoarse tones directed the butler to show the man in.

In a few seconds the man entered.

It was the man who had been listening outside the door of the king's bedchamber.

In hurried words he told Sir John all that had passed; but when he came to say that a warrant for Sir John's arrest had been issued, Sir John turned paler than ever.

"Alas!" he muttered, "all is over, then."

"Not so," cried Blood. "Dost thou mean to say that thou wilt allow this boy to gain the upper-hand of thee?"

"Nay; but I am powerless to prevent the due execution of the king's warrant."

"Then I will assist thee to defy the king!" cried Blood, rising.

"And I," said Hugh. "Didst thou say that thou didst hear his Majesty say that the warrant was to be executed by Harold de Witt?"

"I did," replied the guard.

"'Fore heaven, then," cried Hugh, as he flashed his sword from its scabbard, "I shall then have another chance with him, and this time I swear that I will never leave until life hath left his body! May I meet him face to face, and may the blessed Virgin paralyze his arm!"

"Amen," said Oates.

Blood sneered at these words.

"Listen," he said. "Do thou take my advice, Sir John. This house is too near Whitehall. Dost thou understand? It will take but a short time for the guards to reach here, and thou wilt have no time for defence—"

"What dost thou advise?"

"Order thy horses to be saddled—thou hast four of them—and let us mount and speed away to thy residence at Epping. There thou wilt be safe from the king's warrant until thou dost gain time to fly the country, and let time prove that this Harold Harcourt, as he calls himself, is naught but an adventurer, as I have told thee."

"Thy advice is good. What ho!" cried Sir John to his butler, who waited without. "Order the grooms to saddle the horses at once."

"I trust thy castle at Epping contains sufficient arms?" said Hugh.

"Yes," replied Sir John, "and many strong men who can use them."

"'Tis well. The warrant will never be executed."

"And," muttered Blood, "should this Harold fall, all will be at an end, except, I suppose, except with Roebuck, curse him!"

The horses were speedily brought round, and the party having mounted, they set off at full gallop for Epping Forest.

The guard who had warned Sir John had received a handsome sum as his reward.

He waited until the party had gone, and then he started to return to Whitehall.

As he turned the corner of the house to cross St. Giles's, a tall man darted out from the shadow of a huge oak, seized the guard by the throat, and brought him with a crash to the ground, almost rendering him insensible.

Looking up, the guard saw a pair of fierce eyes bent upon him, and beheld a gleaming sword poised on a level with his breast.

He made sure his life was forfeited, but for what?

He had not the slightest idea that he had been followed.

"Mercy!" he gasped.

"No mercy to a traitor," replied the man who held him. "I see thou art one of the king's guards, and a prying, infamous knave to boot. A traitor to his Majesty deserves death. I know all, so lie not to me. Thou hast warned Sir John Humphreys that a warrant was issued for his arrest?"

"I did," choked the man.

"Where is he gone?"

No answer.

"Where is he gone? Speak! Or I swear I will run this sword through thy carcase!"

"To Epping Forest."

"Hum! I thought so! What reward did he give thee for thy information?"

"A hundred crowns."

"Where are they?"

"In my doublet."

"Out with them!"

And placing his hand in the man's doublet, the speaker drew out a bag of money.

Then he started up.

"On thy feet quick!" he shouted, as sheathing his sword he drew a pistol and levelled it at the guard's head. "Go! Run, run! Or I will show thee no mercy!"

The man required no second bidding.

Jumping up, he took to his heels and ran like a deer.

The man who had taken his money from him returned his pistol to his belt, and with a quiet grin pocketed the money, walked off some distance, and looked carefully about him.

Then he muttered—

"It is useless, Sir John Humphreys! Epping Forest will not long shield thee. Now for Robin. We shall have thee, Sir John, or my name is not Roderick Roebuck!"

Placing a whistle to his lips, a beautiful horse led by our little friend Pipkin trotted up.

"All's well, Pip!" said Master Roebuck, as he vaulted into the saddle. "We are now for Whitehall and then for Robin. Give me thy hands."

Pipkin held out his hands, and Roebuck raised him up and seated him in front of him on the saddle, saying—

"Hold fast, for we shall ride quickly."

"Fear not," said Pipkin, in consequential tones; "I shall be all right, and so will Robin if he sees me by his side."

CHAPTER XXIII.

"BY COMMAND OF THE KING!"—THE BATTLE AT HARCOURT CASTLE—THE HORRIBLE DEATH OF SIR JOHN HUMPHREYS AND HUGH JEFFRIES.

ARRIVING at Whitehall, Roebuck scribbled out a hurried note to Harold, telling him to go direct to Epping, on which road he would meet him.

This note Pipkin delivered, much to the astonishment of the men on guard, who laughed immoderately at his small stature, and his swaggering gait. Then having once more placed Pipkin on the saddle, Roebuck dashed off for Little Britain.

* * * *

Was there ever a more magnificent residence in all England than that which had belonged to Sir Harold Harcourt, but which now, by foul means, was in the possession of Sir John Humphreys?

No! Emphatically, no!

Harcourt Castle stood near the borders of Epping Forest, and was surrounded by a splendid park, "well and plentifully supplied with good red deer and stocked with game, of a kind which we English gentlemen do well like to capture, either by bow, spear, or the gun," as Sir Harold Harcourt had written to some friends he had invited.

The castle was built in the reign of Elizabeth, and she on many occasions rested there during her journeys.

The moat which surrounded the castle, and which was crossed by four drawbridges, had been filled in by the late Sir Harold, who was of opinion that they were not necessary for a peaceful citizen.

The interior of the castle was certainly very grand, containing as it did magnificent rooms furnished with the finest articles of workmanship, and adorned with paintings and sculpture by the most eminent masters, collected at enormous expense by the late Sir Harold and his forefathers.

In less than two hours from leaving Bloomsbury, Sir John Humphreys and his companions reached the castle, and hastily entered, much to the astonishment and consternation of the retainers, who wondered what on earth had happened.

They wondered still more, however, when Sir John, calling them together, instructed them to immediately put the castle in a state of defence.

His orders were sharp and decisive, and the servants saw, from the agitated movements of his lips and hands, that something very unusual was about to occur.

Blood's orders, however, were more easily understood than were Sir John's, and before an hour had passed the loopholes of the castle, the battlements, and the walls of the courtyards were lined with men.

Upon the first battlement stood Hugh Jeffries; upon the second Blood, who, having flung off his hat, looked horribly ghastly with his bandages about his head; and upon the third Sir John, terribly agitated and deathly white.

"Now then," cried Blood, "we shall see whether the king's warrant will be executed! What ho! Sir John, what wilt thou give each of thy men if they stand to their posts?"

"A hundred crowns each," replied Sir John, whose voice could scarcely be heard above the murmurings of the men, "and a thousand to thyself and Hugh."

"'Tis well. Wait and watch!"

*   *   *   *

"Dost thou see aught of them now, Pip? Thy eyesight is better than mine."

"Nay, not yet."

"Dost thou, Robin?"

"Nay, on my faith, not a sign of them."

The speakers were, as our readers have guessed, Master Roebuck, Robin, and Pipkin.

They were on the Epping Road, and within a mile of the castle, the preparations in which they had noted.

"Strange," said Roebuck, "and it is broad daylight, too."

"I pray I came not here for nothing," said Robin, who armed from "head to foot," as the saying is, and bearing on his shoulder an enormous hammer, stood by the side of his gigantic horse.

"Nay, fear not, Robin," replied Roebuck, with a grim smile; "there will be work for thee, or I am mistaken— and sanguinary work, too."

"Fear not, though," said Pipkin, waving his hand majestically aloft; "I shall be with thee, and where I am, there wilt thou be safe."

"True," replied Robin, doffing his cap and bowing gravely. "May thy shadow never grow less, my brother. Thy presence is sufficient to charm away all harm. Pray heaven we are spared, dear little Pip, and as sure as my name is Robin, I will secure thee a good and true wife, and one of whom thou wilt not be afraid, and—"

"Hark!" cried Roebuck, rising in his stirrups so suddenly that Pipkin tumbled off the saddle in the road, but, fortunately, without injury, "hark, that sound! List! the tramp of horsemen, I'll be sworn. Look ahead, Robin."

Robin vaulted into his saddle, and, standing in his stirrups, looked ahead.

Suddenly, round a bend in the road, came vast volumes of dust, and in another instant a troop of cavalry swept round at a tremendous pace.

They looked a splendid sight, their helmets and naked swords flashing in the rising sun.

There were at least fifty of them, and they were headed by a tall young fellow, whose red sash across his breastplate denoted him to be a captain.

It was our hero, Harold Harcourt.

At the rear of the horsemen rode another officer. This was Lord Eustace Trevor.

As they came into full view, Robin and Roebuck set up a loud shout.

Harold raised his sword aloft in acknowledgment, and his men cheered lustily.

Very few words were spoken as Harold reined up and introduced Trevor to Master Roebuck and Robin, but when near the castle, they drew up and held a consultation.

Hardly a dozen words had passed before, on the second turret of the castle, a puff of white smoke appeared, then a rapid flash, a dull, sullen roar, and a round shot struck Robin's horse between the shoulders, killing him on the spot.

A terrible look rested upon Robin's face as he disengaged himself from the saddle, but he made no remark.

"They mean fighting," said Trevor, "that is plain enough, so let us lose no time in consultation."

"Let us attack the main entrance," said Harold, "and if we make a bold dash, their guns will be useless."

Placing himself at the head of his men, he cried out—

"Forward! and remember that you are the king's soldiers."

One after another the guns on the battlements were fired, but with no effect.

When they reached the principal gate, Master Roebuck's face fell.

It was a very massive structure, and bound with large iron shafts.

Harold raised himself in his stirrups, and, producing the warrant, cried—

"Sir John Humphreys, I call upon thee to surrender!"

"Away, fool!" answered a voice, and the evil face of Hugh Jeffries peered over the battlements. "Away, lest I send thee the contents of this gun."

And forthwith he fired, fortunately with no result.

"By whose command art thou here?" cried Blood, pretending to be ignorant of the whole affair.

"BY COMMAND OF THE KING!" returned Harold.

"Hast thou a warrant?" queried Hugh.

"Ay, it is here, in my hands."

"Then serve it," replied Blood, with a hoarse laugh, which, however, died away when he saw Roebuck ride up by Harold's side.

He trembled violently in every limb, and, strangely enough, from the half-healed, terrible wound on his forehead the blood slowly trickled down his face.

"Robin," said Roebuck, who did not forget how Robin opened the door of Master Croft's stable, "I pray thee open that gate."

"How can he do so," said Trevor, "when he hath not the key?"

"It is upon his shoulder," said Harold.

Robin advanced closer to the door, amid a volley from the retainers, which laid low three troopers, and, taking his huge hammer in his brawny arms, he swung it round his head a few seconds, and then brought it down upon the wicket in the gate.

Crash!

The ironwork of the wicket was crushed to atoms. Surely the men in the courtyard must have fancied that the troopers had a piece of cannon with them.

Crash!

The door quivered violently.

Crash!

"Good heaven!" muttered Trevor, "didst thou ever see such strength?"

Crash!

A loud cheer from the troopers, answered by another volley from the retainers.

A large piece of the oaken door, of immense thickness, was smashed to matchwood.

Robin's blood was up.

The loss of his horse maddened him.

He looked like a gigantic fiend.

Crash, crash, crash!

The blows descended like rain.

As the piece of the door fell into the courtyard, a retainer, armed with an axe, looked through.

His daring cost him his life.

With startling rapidity Robin seized him by the hair of his head, and dragging him through the aperture, raised him over his shoulders, and hurled him with terrific violence against the stone walls of the castle.

He was almost smashed to pieces.

"Bravo, Robin!" cried Pipkin, who had crept up, sword in hand ("his toothpick," Robin called it). "Thou wilt be rewarded, Robin, and I will be a better brother to thee than ever. Go on, good Robin, tap at the door again."

And folding his little arms, Pipkin stood erect, eyeing Robin's work with much satisfaction.

The fire from the retainers increased, but the troopers were now well under the walls of the castle, and so the fire was harmless.

Again Robin, down whose face the perspiration was pouring in torrents, commenced his work.

The door groaned and cracked beneath his ponderous blows, and the iron rods twisted themselves into all manner of shapes.

Suddenly, amid a tremendous shout, the battered door flew open, and the troopers, headed by Harold, Roebuck, Trevor, and Robin, poured in.

The troopers dismounted, and a terrible fight commenced.

Robin's towering form was well in view.

He did not wait to draw his sword, his hammer was quite sufficient, and the men upon whom it descended fell to rise no more.

The troopers could now use their firearms, and use them they did, and with awful effect, and with such rapidity that very soon the battlements and staircases were full of dense smoke, in the midst of which flashing swords and struggling men could be seen, and nothing heard but shrieks, groans, and bitter oaths and curses.

Harold was foremost in the fight, and step by step he fought his way from the courtyard to the first battlement.

On the top of the stone stairs, now reeking with blood, he came face to face with Hugh Jeffries.

Hugh certainly looked a very fiend incarnate.

In the course of the battle he had received more than one terrible wound, and the front of him was saturated in blood.

No sooner did he set eyes upon Harold than a fearful cry of rage escaped his lips—a cry which resembled the howl of a wild beast more than anything else.

Each looked at the other for, it may be, two or three seconds, and then Hugh screamed—

"Have at thee, thou villain ! Have at thee ! Have at thee, thou base pretender ! I will pluck out thy heart, and hurl it to yonder birds of prey. Have at thee ! and perdition seize thee ! "

"Thy tongue is like thy heart, Master Jeffries," replied Harold, as he calmly warded off the furious attack. " Death will certainly be thy portion, for thou art even now as good as a dead man ! "

At this instant Robin pushed forward, whirling round his head his ponderous hammer, and dealing death and destruction on all sides.

On his left shoulder sat Pipkin, with folded arms, calmly surveying a scene which every moment became more and more horrible.

Robin caught sight of Hugh, and raising his hammer aloft, he was about to bring it down upon Hugh's head, when Harold cried—

" Hold ! hold ! let me deal with him, I pray thee, Robin. Do thou seek Colonel Blood ! "

Robin made no reply but rushed onward like the wind, Pipkin's little voice urging him to " batter down the traitors of the king ! "

And now the fight between Harold and Hugh waxed fast and furious—even the men as they pushed onward, pausing a moment to view it.

Suddenly Harold with a swift downward cut broke Hugh's sword off at the hilt, and the next instant his own was buried to the haft in his body.

With a horrible curse and gurgling cry he staggered backward, clutching frantically at the cannon in one of the embrasures, but his hands had hardly grasped it before a long sword wielded by a strong arm almost cleft his skull in twain, and he fell over with a crash. The sword that had struck him was wielded by Roderick Roebuck !

" I have sought Blood," said Roebuck, " but can find him nowhere, neither do I find the blasphemous scoundrel, Titus Oates. I wish to heaven I could. But mark thee, Harold, I have left thee a prize. Upon the top battlement is Sir John Humphreys. There he has been all through the fight, and he and two or three of his men have contented themselves with hurling huge stones and round shot on thy troopers. He will fight, I am assured, for he will never be taken alive. Go, therefore, at once and meet him. And mark thee ! Avenge thy father's death, or thou art no true son of Sir Harold Harcourt. Go—and heaven be with thee ! "

" Amen ! " muttered a voice, and turning, Harold saw Lord Trevor standing close by his side.

The resistance of the retainers was drawing to a close. The clash of weapons was growing less and less, and the majority of the troopers, weary and sorely wounded, were leaning against the walls or sitting upon the blood-stained steps.

There was only one restless spirit, and that was Robin, who, hammer in hand, ran from passage to passage, vault to vault, in the hope of meeting Blood or Titus Oates ; but by some miraculous means they had escaped, at any rate they were nowhere to be found.

Up the stairs ran Harold, followed at a respectful distance by Roebuck and Lord Trevor.

In the centre of the battlement, hatless and breathless with the exertions he had made in hurling on the troopers huge stones and shot, stood Sir John Humphreys.

On all sides were men, dead and dying—horrible, horrible sights !

Sir John held his sword in his hand, but from the appearance of the blade it was evident that it had not been used.

No sooner did Harold appear before him than Sir John, with a loud cry, retreated a few paces.

"Away, away!" he cried. "Thou art not the son of Sir Harold Harcourt. He died—he was killed—he was—"

"No," replied Harold, calmly, "he was not killed: he was spared to avenge his father's death. He stands before thee now. Defend thyself, for I swear that one of us falls! I shall show thee no mercy, neither will I ask it of thee."

"I surrender myself," whined Sir John.

"It is too late. Yet here is the warrant for thy arrest," throwing it at his feet. "And now I have obeyed the king's command, I must obey my father's will. His voice hath cried aloud to me from the grave for years. Defend thyself, I tell thee, or I will strike thee dead as thou standest there!"

Sir John saw that what Harold said he meant, and in a state of frenzy he advanced and commenced the fight.

It was watched with breathless interest by those principally concerned, as well as the remaining troopers and his own retainers.

Robin, too, was there, and he watched the fight as eagerly as did Pipkin, who was still seated upon his shoulder.

It would be uninteresting to give a minute account of this awful duel.

Suffice it to say that it lasted for fully half-an-hour.

Harold could easily have taken Sir John's life more than once, but he would not take any undue advantage of him.

Suddenly Sir John paused, the sword fell from his hand, and his eyes fixed themselves on the entrance to the low-arched doorway leading to the battlement.

What he saw was known only to himself, but that pause cost him his life.

Harold took two steps forward, drew his arm back, and the next instant Sir John was transfixed upon his sword.

"Father," cried Harold, raising his hand aloft, "thou art avenged!"

"And Sir Harold Harcourt claims his rights," cried Roebuck. "A Harcourt —a Harcourt!"

The men, led by Robin, took up the cry, and "A Harcourt—a Harcourt!" rang in Sir John's ears as he sank dying amid the men by his side.

Sir John opened his mouth, evidently to speak, but no sound issued from his lips, and with his eyes fixed upon our hero's face, he died.

"Let us get hence," said Roebuck. "All is over now, and my mission is accomplished. Come."

Two hours later on, Harold, Trevor, Roebuck, Robin, and Pipkin, and ten troopers left the castle and took the road to London.

It was all that was left of them.

Not much was said during that journey.

Harold and Lord Trevor looked sorrowful indeed.

The loss of so many men deeply affected them.

As for Robin, he was loud in his exclamations of wonder as to what had become of Blood and Titus Oates, and he swore that he would willingly lose his left arm if he could reach them with his right.

"It is likely enough they are both slain, Robin," said Harold, "but among the many thou hast failed to find them."

CHAPTER XXIV.

THE DEPARTURE OF MASTER ROEBUCK—HIS VISIT TO ROCK HOUSE, AND WHAT TRANSPIRED THERE.

WHEN the particulars of the terrible fight were laid before the king, he became frantic with rage, and at once sent off a large troop of horse to search the castle and endeavour to find the bodies of Blood (whom he declared must have been the leading spirit in the affair) and Titus Oates, but no bodies were found.

The captain of the troop, interested

as to the manner in which they could have escaped, searched high and low, and soon it became as plain as the sun at noonday.

From one of the underground vaults a passage led to the high road. It was so narrow that in order to get through it a man would have to crawl upon his belly.

It must have taken them a long time to get through it, but certain it was that that was the only way they could have escaped.

The house at Bloomsbury was searched under Harold's supervision, and the documents which left Harold the estates found, and there was a large quantity of manuscript which set forth the late Sir Harold's fears that Sir John would endeavour to do away with our hero.

These were laid before the king.

Nurse Alice was summoned, and by the king's command she related all that had taken place on the awful night which opened our story.

The king was satisfied, and more than satisfied, when our hero—now Sir Harold—assured him that the money Sir John Humphreys had lent him (Harold's by right) would never be claimed.

It was with a happy heart that Harold, with Roebuck, went off, after his interview with the king, to Smithfield.

Not many words passed before Master Roebuck saw that with Harold and pretty Nelly it was a case of love at first sight.

"It is more than I could have hoped for," he said to Phillips. "I thank heaven for it."

"Aye, aye," said Phillips, "he is a right worthy youth. But wilt thou not now reveal the secret of her birth?"

"Nay," replied Roebuck, "not yet—not yet. Time enough—time enough!"

He sank into a chair, and covered his face with his hands.

Harold and Nelly were by his side in a moment.

"Master Roebuck," cried Harold, "What ails thee? Speak, Roebuck! Dear Roebuck, tell me, I pray thee."

"It is nothing, Harold, my boy—nothing. See, I am well now. It was a passing thought. And now—and now listen. Oh, it nigh breaks my poor heart. But now that I see thee so near thy happiness I must bid thee farewell."

There was a terrible pause.

"Farewell?" cried Harold. "No, no, do not say that—do not say that, I pray thee. Roebuck," he whispered, "give up the mysterious life thou art leading, and live with us. Nelly will be my wife. Live with us, and let the remainder of thy life be passed in peace."

"I have already given up the life I was leading, Harold," replied Roebuck, with a far away look; "but I must leave at once. I have many matters to settle."

"Roebuck," said Harold, "dost thou know the secret of Nelly's birth?"

Master Roebuck started.

After a pause, he said—

"I do."

"I pray thee reveal it, then."

"Nay, at present it is impossible."

"Dost thou, then, really mean to leave us?"

"I do."

"At once?"

"Yes," replied Roebuck, rising.

Giving his hand to Harold, he said solemnly—

"Good-bye, my boy, good-bye; and may heaven watch over thee. In thy happiness, do not forget the outlaw, but thy firm friend, Roderick Roebuck."

Seizing Nelly by the waist, he pressed a dozen burning kisses upon her lips, pressed the hand of Phillips, and rushing from the house, vaulted into his saddle, and soon had vanished.

For at least half-an-hour Roebuck rode on at a great pace, looking neither to the right nor the left; nor did he draw rein until he reached the then unsavoury neighbourhood of Wapping.

Wending his way through many of the narrow and filthy streets, he at last reached a tumble-down hostelry called the "Blue Anchor."

And here it was certain he was recognised, for many a man gave him a nod of recognition, though not a word was uttered.

He was well known to the host, who certainly did not treat him as a guest, for while the ostler took charge of his horse, he led him upstairs to a small but comfortable chamber, and quickly refreshments were set before him.

Of these he partook sparingly, for he was in no mood to eat.

Having written three or four letters, he told the host that he was about to try and get a few hours' rest, and desired to be called by eight of the clock.

Accordingly, at eight he was called, and he awoke refreshed and ready for anything.

Descending, he found his beautiful horse ready for him.

It had had a good feed, a long rest, and excellent grooming, so that now, like its fond master, it was ready to proceed anywhere.

Roebuck vaulted into the saddle and made his way to Craigs Lane, then a sort of market very much like Cloth Fair.

At one of the little wooden houses he stopped, and tying his horse to a ring, knocked for admittance.

Quickly the door was opened by a young girl, who, recognising him, at once admitted him.

The shop was in the occupation of a costumier—a Frenchman of the name of Latèlle and he and Roebuck, who spoke the French language perfectly, were old associates.

We need not inform the reader of what passed between them, but in less than half-an-hour Roebuck came out, disguised as a French officer, and really the disguise suited him to perfection.

Remounting, he set off at a sharp pace towards Camberwell, which was reached just after half-past nine.

Camberwell then was not the thickly populated, busy neighbourhood it is now.

At the time of our story, it was a pretty country spot, with market gardens and magnificent fields and meadows, which assisted, to a great extent, in supplying London with its vegetables and flowers.

Close by what is now "The Green," stood a large mansion called "Rock House," and which stood in its own grounds of many acres.

For years and years—how many the inhabitants of Camberwell could not exactly remember—it had been closed.

One person had charge of it, a man of the name of Glendore.

He resided in the lodge beside the great gates, and there the keys of the huge mansion were kept.

But, at last—to the astonishment of the Camberwellites—all within the grounds and the house changed like magic.

Workmen to the number of nearly a hundred were brought from the City, and the interior and exterior of the mansion began to show decided signs of vast improvements.

Gardeners, too, set to work upon the grounds.

Trees were felled, others planted in their places, while flower-beds were arranged and graceful walks planned out.

All this, of course, meant enormous expense, and the neighbours watched the operations in wonder.

Then some of them ventured to make enquiries of Glendore.

Point blank he refused to answer any questions.

It was of no use asking the workmen, they really knew nothing at all.

When all was finished, a coach, one day, drove up to the mansion, and Glendore, with uncovered head, opened the gates.

There was a rush of several of the more curious to obtain a glimpse of the occupants.

They were disappointed, for the blinds were down.

It was just a month from this that Master Roebuck paid a visit to the mansion.

All was very silent and dark when he arrived, and not a soul was anywhere visible.

But a dim light burned in the lodge, and Roebuck knocked upon the window with his riding whip.

The summons was soon answered.

Glendore, lantern in hand, came slowly out.

"Well, sir," he said, in harsh, grating tones, "what is it? I am lodge-keeper here, and am aware that no visitors are expected. No doubt you have made a mistake. This, sir, is Rock House."

"I am aware of it, my friend," replied Roebuck, "and there is no mistake. I am here on a visit to—"

"Yes, yes, to whom ? "

"The mistress of the house."

"Hem ! are you *sure ?*"

"Quite."

"Her name ? "

"Mistress Dorothy Darmley."

"Humph," said Glendore slowly and thoughtfully, as he surveyed the brilliant uniform of the rider, "I've heard nought of this."

"No doubt. And the reason is simply that I am not expected. Here, take this note to your mistress. But open the gate and I will ride up to the front."

"Nay, nay ; that cannot be. If you wait, you must wait here."

"So be it then ; I wait here. Go, my man, and be as quick as you can, for my time is valuable."

"Pardon me, sir ; are you a Frenchman ? "

"Ay, an officer in the Guards."

"Then you speak English remarkably well."

"True, I was partially trained in England."

Glendore shuffled off towards the chief entrance.

He was provided with a key, and therefore it was not necessary to summon either of the three servants—and there were *only* three in this great wilderness of a mansion.

On he went to the first landing.

Here he knocked upon one of three doors, all of which were concealed by heavy and costly curtains.

"Who is it ? " asked a woman's voice in low tones.

"I—Glendore," was the reply.

"What do you want ? "

"A gentleman has called, my lady, and has sent a note to you."

The door was at once opened, and a lady of about forty stood upon the threshold.

She was indeed a most beautiful woman ; tall, dark, with great black eyes, and as graceful as a gazelle.

But there were hard lines about the small mouth, and many an indication that she was a woman of fierce passions.

She was attired in a rich dress of black silk, while her well-dressed hair gleamed with many a costly brilliant.

"A note ? " she said.

"Here 'tis, my lady."

"A gentleman ? What sort of gentleman ? Young, middle-aged—"

"Middle-aged, I should say. He is a French officer."

Instantaneously the lady turned pale. Her trembling little white hand took the note and examined the name written upon it—

'TO MISTRESS DOROTHY DARMLEY.'

Tearing it open, she read the few words written.

Then, in low, tremulous tones, she said—

"I will see him—here—at once. Go, Glendore ; escort him here, and do not arouse the servants."

Glendore nodded and returned to Roebuck.

He then opened the gates and told him to follow.

A peculiar smile rested upon Roebuck's face as he walked his beautiful horse after the lodge-keeper.

"I must be wonderfully altered," he thought, "or that man would have recognised me."

Dismounting, he followed Glendore up the richly-carpeted stairs, and the next moment was within the room.

Glendore closed the door, and descended, muttering something about gentlemen paying visits at most unreasonable hours.

Roebuck looked around the room, noting the magnificent furniture, the beautiful ornaments, and the gorgeous mirrors and candelabra.

And a deep sigh left his lips as he muttered—

"Reminiscences of the past ! But shall I find her much altered ? "

In a minute the rustle of silk was heard, and Mistress Dorothy entered from an inner room.

She bowed gracefully, but her bow was replied to only by a nod.

"You are the gentleman mentioned in this despatch ? " asked Mistress Dorothy ; "a Monsieur Louis Lampré ? And you come from—'

She glanced up as she said this, and for the first time looked fully into the face of the supposed French officer.

Then she started, and again looked at the note.

"No, madam," said Roebuck, calmly. "That letter is a *forgery*."

"A forgery?"

"Exactly. I desired an interview with you, and, as I was well aware that a note from a certain French nobleman would at once procure what I desired, I had no hesitation in forging that signature."

"How *dare* you? How—"

She paused abruptly; her eyes opened to their fullest extent; she leaned partially forward, as if to convince herself of something, and then, in a hoarse whisper, she said—

"Claude—"

"Hist!" interrupted Roebuck, "do not let that name pass your lips. Not that I care, but for your *own* sake. For years I have been known as Master Roebuck—such will be my name while I choose to honour you with my presence."

With a low, moaning cry Mistress Darmley shrank back—back until she rested herself against the huge, carved mantel.

"Here? *You* here after all these years?" she gasped.

"Ay, why not? I could not come here before, because for years this house has been closed. You have been abroad."

"Yes, yes; I have been in several religious houses in France, and—"

"Lie not to me, madam," interrupted Roebuck, sternly. "Of what use would it be? I am well acquainted with your movements for years past."

"Impossible!"

"Impossible? Why impossible? Why, you have forgotten one most important thing."

"That is?"

"That is that the note which I sent up was addressed to Mistress Dorothy Darmley instead of Alderson."

Again did Mistress Darmley start, but she made no reply to this.

"Listen to me, madam," said Roebuck, in the same calm, measured tones. "I am going to tell you a story. Be seated; I would not ask a lady to listen standing to a story."

"No, no; I—"

"Be *seated*, I say!"

Tremblingly Mistress Darmley advanced to one of the carved chairs.

But before she seated herself, she said—

"One moment. A little wine—"

Roebuck smiled grimly.

"Wine?" he said. "Nay, not for me. I am in the habit of speaking without wine. I *do* take wine, it is true, but then it is always at a *friend's* house. I have to be careful when I visit the house of an enemy.

"For, on one occasion, I found a person I visited kept a bottle for those he liked and a bottle for those he *dis*liked.

"I assure you, Mistress Darmley, that the difference in the two wines was absolutely wonderful.

"It was, however, a pity the person I refer to kept these two sorts of wines, because, having found him out, I compelled him to fight in his own garden.

"The result was that he lost his life."

Mistress Darmley shuddered visibly as she sank into the chair.

Roebuck advanced to the polished table, over which he leaned.

"I will not ask you whether we can be overheard," he said, "because it is a matter of little importance to *me*."

"No," said Mistress Darmley, averting her head from his steady gaze, "we are alone. No one is in the house with the exception of the servants, and they are a long way below."

"Ha! your *husband* is not likely to appear suddenly?"

Mistress Darmley groaned audibly.

"Insult upon insult!" she said.

"Insult? I am surprised at your saying so."

"If, as you say, you know all, you must be aware of the fact that he is dead. His death took place in France, and the news, no doubt, swiftly travelled to England. Poor man! the disease of which he died—"

As she spoke, she chanced to look up, and her eyes met Roebuck's.

They dropped at once.

"There does not breathe on the earth a more monstrous liar or a greater impostor than *you*," he said, fiercely. "Darmley died of disease? No, no. My information is more correct than that: he fell by the hand of an assassin —just as your two *previous* husbands had fallen—and the assassin who slew Darmley was the French nobleman whose name I forged to gain admittance here."

"No, no ; it is false—false."

"It is *true*, madam, as true as that the canopy of heaven is above this house—this house, where fell one of the truest and best men ever born. But I will tell my story, because it will open up pages in our lives which have long been closed.

"Madam, years and years ago—it must be at least sixteen — Master Herbert Saville resided in this mansion, of which he was master, just as he was the master of great wealth and of estates in the country.

"His wife died after but a few years of married life, and left Master Saville with one child, a girl, a sweet little angel called Nelly.

"Master Saville was broken-hearted, for the affection between him and his wife had been most sincere.

"Time, however, partly healed the wound, and he resolved that, if he could meet with a lady who would be a mother to his child, he would marry her.

"At last he met with a young lady, who, with some truth, was said to be one of the most beautiful women in the world. Her name was Miriam Stormont. Who she was, what she was, was not known to many; but there was one person who knew her past history but too well.

"His name was Claude Duval—for the name must here be mentioned.

"Unfortunately, he was abroad at the time Master Saville proposed marriage to Miriam Stormont, or most assuredly he would have furnished him with such particulars that Master Saville, honest, upright, and true to the backbone, would have turned from her with scorn and loathing.

"Too late he heard that Master Saville had married Miriam Stormont.

"Too late ?—yes ! When I heard that news my heart sank like lead within me, for I felt certain what would follow.

"What could I do ? Nothing— nothing but wait. I did not have to wait very long before I learned that the woman, who had sworn before heaven that she would treat little Nelly as if she were her own flesh and blood,

had turned out a demon—that, in fact, she treated the poor child like dirt.

"But this was by no means all. Master Saville received an anonymous letter which caused him to be restless and uneasy. I met him, and he placed that letter in my hands.

"What was said in it I will not say, but it warned Master Saville to be on his guard.

"Master Saville had been a firm friend to me—indeed, he saved my life. He nursed me when suffering from a fever from which I thought I should never recover.

"Even then I hesitated to say what I wanted to. I left him, telling him to take little heed of anonymous communications, but, nevertheless, to be on his guard.

"No doubt he was, as he thought, *always* on his guard, but that did not prevent him from being assassinated by orders of his wife."

"False, false ! " gasped Mistress Darmley. "No one can prove it."

"Most true," continued Roebuck, dryly. "You took precious good care of that. He was suddenly attacked by certain men, and though he fought desperately for his life, he was killed ; but not before he had placed his child in the hands of her nurse, and made her swear solemnly that she would guard her with her life.

"Miriam got to know that the nurse, with the child, had left the house, and she at once despatched a couple of ruffians after them.

"They returned after the death of Master Saville, and said that they had come up with the nurse.

"She, they said, defended herself and the child—that one of them fired at the nurse, and that the bullet struck the child and killed it, whereupon they allowed the nurse to take it away.

"That was a lie—the child was not hurt. It lives ! That child is now a woman—a woman, madam, with friends who will demand what was taken from her.

"You do not speak. You do not say whether you believe what I have said or not ; but that is of no import- ance. Up to the hilt I can prove what I say.

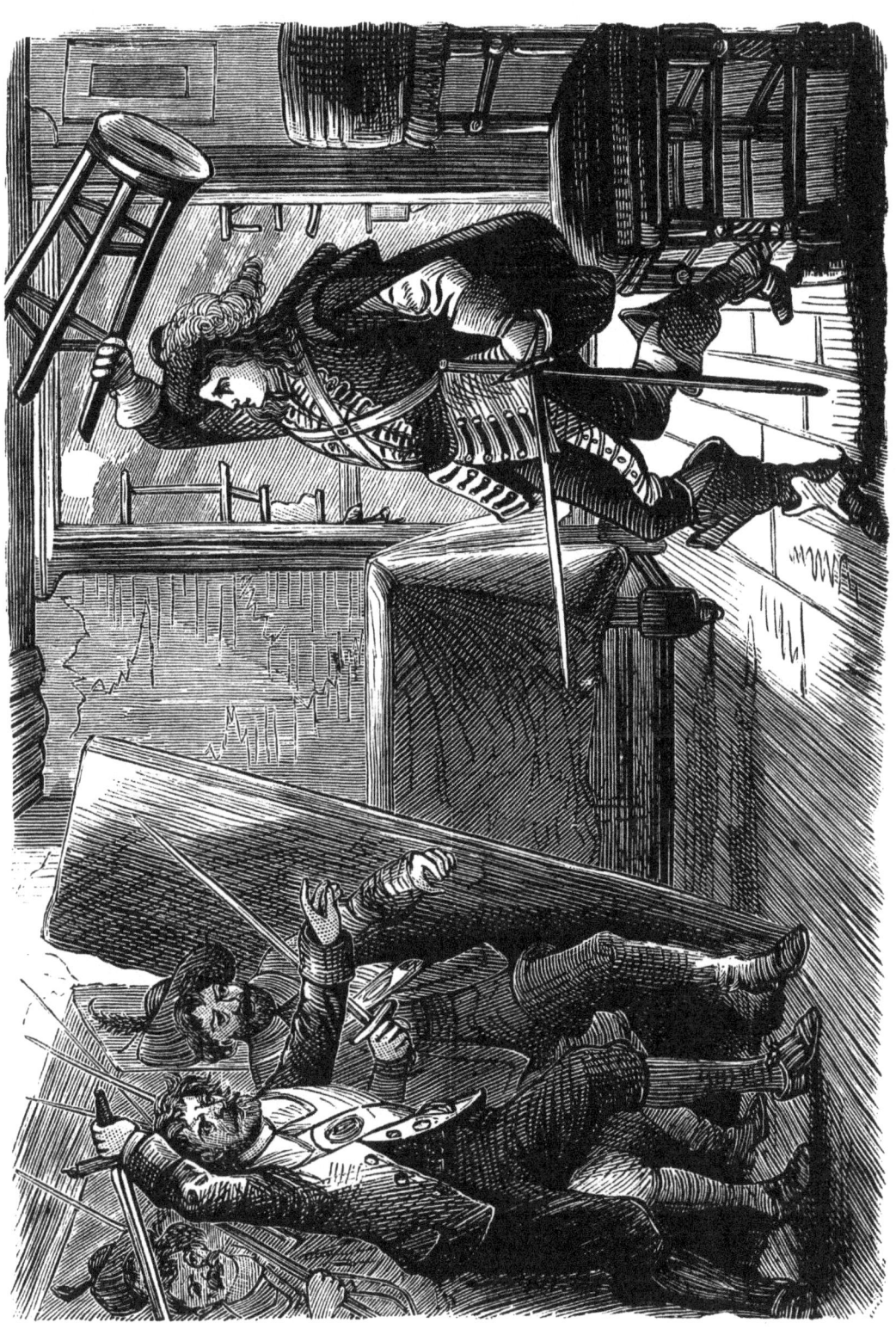

"HAROLD RAISED THE STOOL ABOVE HIS HEAD."

No. 9

" A month after this you left England for Geneva. There you met with a wealthy Englishman of the name of Alderson.

" After but a very short courtship, he married you, and you persuaded him to settle upon you a certain sum.

" Poor man! he knew nothing of what had occurred in England. He was intoxicated with your beauty, and believed you to be as pure as gold.

" He settled upon you the sum you asked.

" In three months from that he was a dead man.

" Then, in a few months from that, you—still mad with the desire for wealth—married Master Darmley.

" From what I can gather I believe you had more love for him than either of the others, and all might have gone well had you not met a certain French nobleman.

" As it was you lived with Darmley for some years.

" Infatuated with the nobleman—and filled with the desire to possess a title, you set your wits to work once more, and Darmley was assassinated.

" He left you all his wealth, and you—you lent it to this French nobleman, and perhaps it is scarcely necessary for me to say that you will never see it again."

Ghastly pale, and trembling from head to foot, Mistress Darmley started up.

" Listen," she said, "ten thousand pounds shall be yours—now—if you will but tell me how you obtained this —as no doubt you call it—information."

Roebuck smiled.

" One *hundred thousand* would not tempt me, madam," he said, scornfully —" I do not take bribes. But you are well aware that my information is nearly accurate.

" But I will tell you one thing. When Master Alderson died in Geneva —stabbed to death—it was necessary to obtain a doctor's certificate before he could be buried.

" You consulted a servant, and she fetched Doctor Capron and an assistant. Do you remember ? "

No reply.

" Do you not remember that the assistant was a Swiss, attired more like a herdsman than a surgeon's assistant ? Ay, I see you do. Well, that Swiss was—Claude Duval."

" No ! "

" Such, I assure you, was the case, and I can, if necessary, produce undeniable proofs. More, I can at any time produce the identical doctor, for he still lives, though not at Geneva."

" Tell me—tell me quickly—what is the real object of this visit ? Is it simply to torture me, and—"

" Torture you ? No. Think, madam, think, and you will assuredly guess what I am here for. But first let me tell you that for years *I* have watched over the interests of Nelly Saville."

" I cannot guess the object of your visit, unless it be to rake up the past."

" The object of my visit, madam, is to call upon you to at once set about drawing up a document, in which you hand over to Mistress Saville this mansion, the large amount of money left by her murdered father, and the estates in the country. You are perfectly aware that all this is hers by right."

" Master Saville left no will."

" He *did* leave a will. But you alone can tell what became of it."

" I never saw it."

" We will not talk of it now. The mystery relating to that may yet be cleared up. What principally occupies my attention now is the great wealth belonging to Nelly Saville. She is about to be married—"

" Married ? "

" Ay."

" To whom ? "

" To one who is in every respect her equal—to one who has proved his rights to title and property. I don't know why I need keep back the name —it is young Sir Harold Harcourt."

" I can give you no reply at this present moment," said Mistress Darmley, uneasily, " but, in a few days' time, I will communicate with you. I have to consult others."

" Others ? What have others to do with Mistress Saville's property ? "

" I cannot tell you now."

" There is something at the bottom of this. But I warn you—if I discover that what was Nelly Saville's has been squandered — nothing on earth can save you."

"What would you do? Would you, or those who call you captain, slay me?"

"Slay you? Think you we devote our time to the slaying of women? No! But I will tell you what will happen—the law will be put in motion, and you will be placed upon your trial. Witnesses I can produce in plenty."

"But what of yourself?"

"Myself?"

"What of *your* safety?"

"I am well able to take care of myself. That *you* well know. The law would be put in motion by me, but I should not be seen. Money would be required, of course, and I can procure it."

"I swear that you shall hear from me in a few days. Where shall I send a messenger or a letter?"

Roebuck considered.

Then he said—

"Send a letter to Master Roebuck, in the care of Master Phillips, of Smithfield."

Mistress Darmley took a pen and wrote down this name and address.

But it was with a terribly shaky hand.

"I will say no more now," said Roebuck, whose expressive face clearly showed the disappointment under which he suffered, "but I will remain in London and await your communication. I need scarcely warn you what will happen if you fail me."

"I will not fail you."

"That is all I have to say now. I go, madam. I can find my way out without the assistance of a servant."

Thereupon he turned, left the room, and strode down the stairs.

Mistress Darmley stood perfectly motionless beside the table, until her ears caught the sound of horse's hoofs.

Then, with a smothered cry, she sank into a seat, and buried her face in her hands.

"He will hunt me down!" she muttered. "Yes, he is *certain* to hunt me down, unless—unless I can enlist in my service someone who will undertake to do whatever I command.

"Money—estates? They have gone —gone! The gaming tables have long since swallowed them up. Heavens!

what can I do! What can I do! Ah! if Stephen Howard were alive, I—"

"When you have done dreaming, madam, may I request you to give me a little of your kind attention?"

Mistress Darmley started up.

On the opposite side of the table stood a man whose mud-stained cloak and boots seemed to show that he had been travelling for many miles.

He threw off his hat, and Mistress Darmley saw, marked upon his forehead, the shape of an arrow.

She well knew its meaning.

She had frequently heard of it, but this was the first time she had seen it.

"Man," she said, "who allowed you to enter this house?"

"No one. Fact is, madam, I had travelled many miles to see you. When I reached the house I saw that the gates were guarded by a lodge-keeper.

"Knowing that I was beastly shabby, I considered it quite unlikely that he would allow me to enter; so I went to a certain part of the grounds and entered by simply standing upon my horse's back, and leaping the palings.

"I made my way to the front, but, seeing a horse, I concealed myself.

"Just now the owner came out and rode away.

"By Satan's own, madam! when I caught sight of the face of the gentleman who has just left this house I nearly dropped in astonishment. Are you aware, madam, of the real name of the man who honoured you with a visit?"

"I am," replied madam Darmley, coldly, "but I am not acquainted with *your* name. And I may at once tell you that you have taken a most unwarrantable liberty in—"

"Wait a moment—wait a moment! What? is this the way then you treat old friends?"

"Old friends?"

"Er—well—acquaintances."

"I do not recognise you."

"No? Am I so *much* altered?"

Here the unexpected visitor marched deliberately up to one of the mirrors and carefully surveyed himself for some few moments.

"The arrow!" he muttered. "By

heaven! my blood turns to ice as I look at it."

Turning, he said—

"Lady, there can be no doubt I have *much* altered. So, too, have you, but not for the worse. You are quite as beautiful—pardon me!—as when, years ago, I took your instructions."

Mistress Darmley suddenly clasped her hands.

"What!" she said hoarsely, "can it be that Stephen Howard stands before me?"

"Ay, Stephen Howard does indeed stand before you."

Mistress Darmley did not endeavour to stifle a cry of joy.

"You are welcome a thousand times," she cried.

"Indeed? Am I? Well, I am indeed overjoyed. But first tell me, is Claude Duval a friend or an enemy?"

"A deadly enemy!"

"So well; as long as we understand one another. You see, if Claude Duval were a friend of yours, it would be impossible for me to stay another moment."

"Then he is an enemy of yours?" asked Mistress Darmley, eagerly.

"An enemy is scarcely the word for it. Look at my forehead."

"I have already observed the marks upon it."

"Do you know their meaning?"

"I do."

"Well, well, we will not speak of it. You can, no doubt, well understand that, every time I *think* of it, my blood turns cold."

"What had this man to do with the marks?"

"He inflicted them."

"Ha! But with what!"

"The sword. He came upon me suddenly, and, before I could defend myself, he cut me as you see."

"Were I in your place I would have a terrible revenge."

"Wait—wait. He shall be well repaid."

"So Stephen Howard is alive. I had heard of your death."

"So had every one else. I took care of that. So many warrants were out for Stephen Howard, so many bloodhounds of the law were upon his track,

that it was necessary that he should hide his identity for ever.

"Therefore, ever since, he has been working under his *own* name. Though you have been out of the country for so many years, you have heard of it, not once, but a thousand times."

"Indeed! What name is it?"

"Colonel Blood."

"What!" cried Mistress Darmley, as she started forward, "Is it really possible that Stephen Howard is the great Colonel Blood?"

Blood placed his hand on his breast and bowed.

"Such is the case," he said, "and I am entirely at your service. If you desire a man of my capabilities, you have but to command me. As to terms—well, we shall not quarrel.

"We may indeed come to some arrangement which would be entirely suitable to both of us."

"I don't quite understand."

"May I speak freely?"

"It would be as well if you did."

"Mistress Darmley, er—I am—er—unmarried."

Mistress Darmley's beautiful face remained devoid of expression.

She either did not, or pretended not to understand the hint.

"I am well aware that I am acting in a most audacious way in so speaking," continued Blood, "but I am a man who is in the habit of coming to the point at once.

"I say, madam, that I am unmarried, and I am well aware that your late husband is dead. Is that not so?"

"You are right."

"Well, is it not possible that us two, working hand-in-hand, may understand each other — I mean presently, of course."

"I think I now understand what you mean. Yes, it *is* possible that we may come to an understanding in the direction you refer to. I am now a widow, and entirely unfettered by any lover.

"But, supposing it to be probable that in the course of time we learned to like each other, marriage could never be possible until—"

She paused, as if for breath.

"Proceed, madam," said Blood, calmly. "Until what?"

"Until the man who has just quitted me is dead."

"Ay, ay."

"And also until a certain *girl* lies dead."

"A girl?"

"Ay, a young girl. You remember the night of the attack on Master Saville?"

"Considering that he nearly killed me, it is scarcely likely that I should forget. Considering also that three men I had with me were slain outright—"

"We will not enter into that now. It was a dreadful night, and, though so many years have passed, I still retain a vivid remembrance of it."

"Yes, it was a night of slaughter. I never saw a man defend himself to such purpose in all my life."

"Perhaps you may remember that the nurse ran away with the child; that your men pursued her, and that they returned and said that the child had been shot dead, and that the nurse had taken the body with her?"

"I have no distinct recollection of that, but no doubt what you say is correct."

"Quite. Well, I have just learned that the child was *not* killed."

"Not?"

"No; she was taken to the City and placed in the care of a man of the name of Phillips."

"Ah! Surely not the Jew Phillips who lives at Smithfield?"

"The same. So you know him then?"

"A little," smiled Blood.

"Tell me," cried Madam Darmley, as she excitedly clutched Blood's arm, "have you ever been within his house?"

"Disguised, yes, many a time."

"Then you must have seen the very girl."

"I *have* seen a girl there, it is true, and I must say I admired her, and frequently tried to get a word with her."

"What is she like?"

"Shall I tell you the truth or a lie?"

"The truth."

"She is one of the loveliest creatures I ever set eyes upon. And now that I come to remember— Why, by Satan, *here you are!*"

Blood suddenly turned and pointed to a picture.

It was the half-length portrait of a lady.

"Is that not a portrait of the first Mistress Saville?" he asked.

"It is."

"Well, the likeness to this girl at Smithfield is marvellous."

"Marvellous?"

"It is indeed."

"You are certain?"

"Perfectly."

Mistress Darmley's face instantly became livid with rage.

From her bosom she snatched a small, jewelled dagger, and, rushing to the portrait, she slashed the canvas right and left.

In a few seconds it was destroyed.

Nothing remained but the richly carved and gilt frame.

Blood smiled.

"She has a temper after my own heart," he thought. "We should get on admirably together."

"*That* proof is destroyed," said Mistress Darmley.

"Ay; and it was just as well to destroy it. Likenesses are dangerous things: that I have frequently proved. So, then, Mistress Saville is under the protection of the Jew Phillips? Strange—very strange."

"Not at *all* strange when you consider that he receives instructions from Claude Duval."

"Ha! is that indeed so? What is she to him?"

"Her father was Duval's firm friend."

"Indeed!" sneered Blood.

"But he knew Duval under another name, at least, such is my impression."

"It is probable. However, the principal thing to be discussed is the destruction of Master Roebuck, as Duval calls himself, and this girl. If Roebuck had not been concerned in the protection of the girl, the task as to her would have been easy.

"But, you see, he is able at any moment to summon a number of men who obey him in every particular.

"In my time I have had to employ scores of men, but I never found one to equal his."

"But can you not employ men now?"

"Any number, provided I can supply them with money."

"Can you not?"

Blood shrugged his shoulders.

"Things have gone badly with me of late," he said. "Not so very long ago I could have placed my hands upon thousands—now—well, now I am nearly penniless."

"Do not let that trouble you," said Mistress Darmley. "I will furnish you with what money you require, always providing that your demands are reasonable."

"I promise you they shall be."

"Have you time now to discuss the matter?"

"I am now and always at your service."

"There are many vacant beds in the house, and, if you choose to stay until the morning, one shall be placed at your service."

"I accept with thanks. But I will now go and get my horse. Perhaps you will instruct your man to attend to him?"

"Yes, I will accompany you for that purpose. On your return you will find ample refreshments provided."

Glendore, of course, was astounded when his mistress, accompanied by *another* "gentleman," made her appearance.

How on earth had *he* obtained admission?

"Glendore," said Mistress Darmley, "this is a very old friend of mine. He is about to stay the night. Remember that you are to give him admittance at any time."

Glendore bowed.

Blood told him to follow and he would get his horse.

They had scarcely reached the gate when Glendore said quietly—

"And what does Colonel Blood do here?"

Blood started, turned, and stared in the man's face.

"What!" he said, "you know me?"

"Of course. You must remember that, though my mistress has been out of the country, I have *not*."

"Well, and what use do you intend to make of your knowledge?"

"Oh, I can keep my mouth shut as well as the best of them. My terms are never *too* high."

"Listen to me, my young friend. Your estimable mistress is well *aware* of the fact that I am Colonel Blood?"

"She is?"

"Ay; *now* what terms do you demand?" he sneered.

"I will make no demand until to-morrow. You will sleep it over."

"*Think* it over, you mean?"

"Ay, and dream of the warrants out for Colonel Blood."

"I now begin to understand. I will tell your mistress what you say."

Glendore smiled.

"Aye, do," he said, "and she will advise you on the matter."

"Suppose I advise her to discharge you immediately?"

"She would not."

"Why?"

"Because she *could* not."

By this time they had reached the horse, which they found contentedly pulling the grass from beside the ditch.

Blood, after a short pause, said—

"I see that it will be as well if we steer along together. Here are ten guineas. Take them as an earnest of what is to come."

Glendore took them with a chuckle. "I *thought* Colonel Blood was not yet a fool," he said. "Oh, yes, we shall understand each other."

Blood requested Glendore to see that his horse was kept well supplied with food, and then he took one of the pistols from the holsters and placed his hand therein.

"Confound it!" he muttered, "I made certain that I had placed that paper there. Well, I suppose I made a mistake. No matter, I remember all that was on it."

* * * *

Meanwhile Mistress Darmley, after giving her instructions to Glendore with respect to Blood, returned to the room above and closed the door.

"Impudent fool!" she muttered, fiercely, "the ugly scoundrel—with the brand of a coward upon his brow! To dare to think that I—a woman loved by the highest—would condescend to think of him otherwise than as an assassin.

"Stephen Howard was bad enough ; but, when I find he has blossomed into Colonel Blood—by the Virgin, he must be mad.

"He is smitten with me, indeed ! How highly *honoured* I ought to feel. What would the haughty Comte de Seine think if he knew what Blood had said ? Ha ! ha ! it is most ridiculous ! But I must be careful to conceal my contempt lest he refuse to assist me.

"I will use Colonel Blood as I may think proper, and then, when I no longer require him, the Comte de Seine —who is one of the most expert swordsmen in the world—must pick a quarrel with him.

"Or, if he refuse, Blood must partake *of a special bottle of wine.*"

CHAPTER XXV.

OF THE FASHION IN WHICH ROBIN EXCHANGES A BARREL OF WATER FOR A BARREL OF WINE—MASTER ROEBUCK'S UNEXPECTED VISIT.

WHEN Master Roebuck passed out of the great gates he rode thoughtfully to the left.

But, quickly perceiving that he was taking the wrong road, he turned and rode to the right.

Thus, in a few moments, he came upon Blood's horse.

He paused in astonishment, for there was no rider to be seen anywhere.

Thinking it possible that the rider had perhaps been thrown into the ditch and required assistance, he dismounted.

No, no one was to be seen.

"Strange indeed, this," muttered Roebuck, "where can the rider be ? Can it be possible that someone pays madam a visit and avoids the gates ? Verily it looks as if someone has vaulted over this paling.

"This horse looks like a trooper's mount. And here—heavily mounted pistols in the holsters ?

"*Par Dieu !* a man must be a fool to leave his pistols at the mercy of passers-by ; for he may, perchance, receive one of his own bullets."

He examined the saddle, and then the interior of the holsters.

In one of them his fingers came in contact with a piece of paper.

He pulled this out, and, having satisfied himself that no one was about, took out a flint and steel and struck a light.

Then, from his saddle, he took a small box.

This he opened.

It contained a small piece of taper, and by its aid he was enabled to read the contents of the paper.

It was as follows—

"At the sign of the 'Three Crows,' at Vauxhall.

"I am here all safe, but neither sound in my body nor easy in my mind. And what is more, I am here with no money.

"You will, of course, be surprised to receive this, considering that it was agreed that we should not communicate with each other for a week.

"But the fact is that I have obtained information of a kind that should prove valuable to both of us.

"I will not pause to tell you how I got this information. That will do when I see you, but here it is—

"As you are probably aware, Mistress Gwynne is at Clapham. To-morrow night she sets out to pay a visit to a gentleman who is at present staying at Lambeth Palace, which, as you are well aware, is close here.

"She will come in a coach by way of the Kennington Road, and will travel *incog.*

"As to the gentleman she intends to visit I made enquiries and found that he is a person who has made Mistress Gwynne large advances. There can be no doubt that she is about to repay some of it, and, if we are careful, and arrange matters properly, we shall not want for some few thousands.

"You must join me at the hour of nine at the latest. As soon as you receive this, despatch a trusty messenger to Alsatia : you will find a few ready to rally round you.

"As ever,

"T. O."

"T. O.," muttered Roebuck. "By heavens, that is Titus Oates. Soh! here, indeed, we have valuable information. Good! I will pocket this and consider the matter."

Having placed the precious missive in his pocket, he vaulted into the saddle and rode away.

"Blood has paid Mistress Darmley a visit," he thought, and, apparently, an unexpected one. Now, what can be between them ?

"She has been abroad for years, while Blood has been in England. This is most— But let me wait. Who were the men who slew Master Saville ?

"Ha ! I think I begin to see daylight through the dark clouds. Is it not possible that Blood was the chief ?

"If he were, of course, he was well paid, but now that his finances are low, is it not more than likely that he has paid this visit to demand more, or, in other words, to levy blackmail ?

"Ay, I think I have hit the right nail on the head.

"It is likely that she may engage him to do some more dirty work. I must keep my eyes open, or it is more than likely that some unforeseen accident may happen.

"Blood knows the house at Smithfield, and he may undertake to see that Nelly troubles Mistress Darmley no more.

"Truly these are weighty matters, and I must devote hours to the study of them.

"It was not my intention to return to Smithfield for many a long day, but now—since, as I consider it, my errand to that vile murderess has proved abortive—I must go there.

"If aught should happen to that girl, I should be so distracted with grief that my brain would be useless."

* * * *

"Ding, ding, dong !
   The hammers merrily ring,
And the smithy strong,
The whole day long,
   Toils for his lord the king."

A deep, powerful voice sang this chorus, and it was echoed by a shrill, piping treble.

Many persons paused outside the smithy, as they passed up Bartholomew Close, to listen.

The men and the apprentices cried—

"Well done, little Robin !"

The women smiled and said—

"Robin is hard at it again. We can always tell when he is busy."

Aye, it was Robin's deep voice that was heard, and Pipkin's voice was assisting him.

Robin was certainly busy, and his fire was being blown by Pipkin.

"Well, I don't know, my little bantam cock," said Robin, as he picked up a cloth and wiped the perspiration from his forehead ; "we sing, ' The whole day long, toils for his lord the king.' That is not exactly correct, Pipkin, eh ?

"Very far from correct, good Robin, and a good job, too."

"Why ?"

"Because if you worked for Master Charles, and if, having completed the work, you requested payment, the king would tell you to go to the devil."

"Ay, ay, I don't think you are far wrong there. Poor Charley !"

"Eh ?"

"Poor Charley !"

"Why do you say so ?"

"Because he is poor."

"Yet, with all his poorness, he continues his pleasures."

"It is true. He still continues to throw the dice and to swim in strong wine. And that reminds me—this is dry work, Pip, eh ? Suppose we drink ?"

"With all my heart. What shall it be ?"

"Well, you see, not having yet contrived, with all my cleverness as a blacksmith, to forge an order for good wine, we must drink beer."

"Assuredly ; and a good drink, too. But where is it ?"

Robin marched to the further end of the smithy, and throwing aside a canvas, revealed a somewhat large barrel, which contained neither tap nor plug.

"Here we have it, and, by the marks, I reckon it is fit for us to drink."

"When did you purchase it ?"

"Purchase it? On my soul, I never purchased it. You see, a tradesman I know, who thinks a great deal of himself—too much indeed—placed several of these barrels outside his door."

"For what purpose?"

"Why, it seems that someone stole his stools, and, as his customers had nothing on which to sit, he placed these barrels for their convenience.

"I was one of his customers, and, when I had finished my mug of ale, I remembered that I required another seat in the smithy, and so I took this barrel."

Pipkin laughed so heartily at this, that he rolled clean off the bellows to the ground.

Robin took a hammer and smashed in the head of the barrel.

"Now for it," he said. "For what we are about to receive—"

He paused abruptly.

"What is it?" asked Pipkin.

"Well, verily I cannot smell beer. Do you come here and sniff it."

Pipkin did as desired, and at once began to laugh more heartily than ever.

But Robin was very grave.

"What is it, Pip," he asked—"white wine?"

"White wine? Ho, ho! why, it's white *water*."

Robin took some in the hollow of his hand and examined it.

"Yes," he said, "you are correct."

"You must admit," said Pipkin, "that you have been bitten *this* time."

"Yes, yes," replied Robin, slowly and thoughtfully. "What a fool I must have been to carry home a barrel of water!"

"And how the host must have laughed!"

"Indeed he must—I admit it—for, you see, when I had placed the barrel on my shoulder, he appeared at the door, and I asked him if he had any objection to my taking it. He said that he had not, and I replied that it would be all the same if he had.

"But I know what to do. Do you come with me, Pip."

"Where are you going?"

"I am going to the hostelry—the 'Seven Bells'—close here."

Robin thereupon threw off his apron and put on his hat.

Then, with great care, he refitted the head upon the barrel, placed a preparation round so that there was no chance of the water falling out, and then lifted it upon his shoulder.

Pipkin clambered on top, and thus they left the smithy.

The reader can easily imagine that, as they traversed the various thoroughfares, they were greeted with shouts of laughter.

Many, for the first time, saw Pipkin, and the women and girls especially were loud in their expressions of astonishment and delight, while nearly all heartily wished that they could have a few words with him.

The "Seven Bells" was soon reached.

It was a small hostelry, but with a very large front, and fitted with "arbours," for the comfort and convenience of customers.

Of these, however, Master Kempton, the host, had but few.

The reason was that the majority of people considered that he was too big for his shoes.

He was a haughty, domineering man—a man everlastingly talking of the "Corporation of London" (he was a member of one of the councils), and of what he should do in the future, "when Charles had settled down and the Government of London had enough dust taken out of its eyes to secure the services of its 'worthiest' citizens."

Robin often told him that he had quite enough to do to look after his *own* "corporation," which, certainly, was a most extensive one.

Robin deliberately marched into the hostelry—Pipkin still perched on the barrel—and knocked upon the counter.

Verily, the knock was like a peal of thunder.

The host, pretending not to be startled, came leisurely out.

"Your business?" he asked Robin.

"Why, you see," said Robin—whose head nearly touched the roof of the hostelry—"on opening this barrel I discovered that it did not contain beer."

"Who said it did?"

"It is so marked on the barrel."

"Probably."

"Well, on opening it, I found that it contained water."

"What of it?"

"I am not in the habit of drinking water."

"That is not my fault. You, with your usual insolence, took the barrel."

"With your permission."

"I did not interfere because I had no desire to quarrel."

"Ha, I see. Well, the water is of no use to *me*."

So saying he lifted Pipkin down and placed the barrel with a number of others.

The host smiled triumphantly.

"The next time, Sir Robin," he said, "you will, no doubt, enquire what the barrel contains."

"To be sure. And you, Master Kempton, before you levy a certain toll on a certain poor widow who can't afford it, will pause and consider."

"Consider what?"

"Whether Master Robin will be anywhere handy. But, now that I think of it, I have no money with me, and therefore can't pay for beer. Under the circumstances I will take back the water."

So he placed the barrel again on his shoulder, swung Pipkin on top and marched off, taking no notice of the host's loud chuckle.

"Well, Robin," said Pipkin, "you have done little good in going there."

"Eh? You make a mistake."

"Well, what have you done?"

"What? Where are your little eyes, eh? Did you not notice anything?"

"Nothing."

"Well, my little bantam cock, I pretended to take the barrel containing water, but instead *I took the next*."

"Ho! ho! But that, too, may contain water."

"I swear it does not. I well know the marks upon it, and can tell that it contains red wine."

"Good! good! If it does, Robin, I will drink to your health."

"Well, here we are. You will soon see that I am correct."

Entering the smithy he placed the barrel upon the ground, and, with his ponderous fist, at once knocked in the head.

Pipkin seized a horn and took out some of the contents.

"Hurrah!" he cried, "you are right, Robin. Bright red wine! Here's to you!"

Robin required no horn.

He seized upon a bowl, and having filled it, placed it to his lips.

It is scarcely necessary to say that he did not take it away until every drop had gone.

So busy was Robin and Pipkin, that they did not observe the door open, nor did they see a person enter the smithy.

Therefore it was no wonder that Robin dropped the bowl into the barrel of wine, as a voice cried—

"A goblet of wine, Sir Blacksmith, and I will drink to thy health."

So close was the speaker that, when Robin wheeled round he found himself touching him.

"Eh?" he said. "Who the devil—What! can it be possible? Master Roebuck—here?"

"It is—here safe and sound."

"Give me your wing," cried Robin, seizing Roebuck's hand, which he wrung so heartily that the tears stood in Roebuck's eyes. "Here, Pip! look you *here*, you silly little brat. Here's Master Roebuck, and be hanged to you!"

"Ay, ay," replied Pipkin, as he rushed towards, and was embraced by, Master Roebuck.

Robin darted out of the door and led in Roebuck's horse.

Then he carefully closed the smithy door.

Roebuck was well aware that these arrangements were unusual, and he looked anxiously into Robin's face, which had become unusually grave.

"What is it, Robin?" asked Roebuck.

"Have you not *seen*?" whispered Robin.

"Nay."

"Nor heard?"

"Nay, nor heard."

"Pip, fetch it out."

"It" was a little box concealed behind the bellows.

Pip opened it, and took out a large sheet of paper, which he spread open.

Roebuck at once saw what it was.

It was a fresh proclamation for him,

but differently worded to the others, and the reward was increased by two hundred pounds.

Roebuck took it and threw it on the furnace.

"Trouble not about that," he said, with a smile. "It would take many a score of them to frighten me."

"But that, I am sorry to say, is not all," said Robin.

"Not all."

"By no means. You have heard of that tall skeleton of a villain called Dominic Evans?"

"What, the informer?"

"Exactly."

"Residing at the old Round House at Aldgate?"

"The very man. Well, I am told, on the best authority, that he has undertaken to track you down."

"Indeed! It is very kind of him."

"I know he is a despicable villain, but when he undertakes business of this description, he is *not* to be despised! You see, he has always a lot of spies at his beck and call ; he has had extensive experience as a Newgate warrant officer, and he is ever ready to go to any extent to earn a big reward."

"Like many another I know, Robin —men who fawn upon you one moment and betray you the next. Now, what would you do with this man if you saw him prying about?"

Robin seized his ponderous hammer, and dealt the anvil a mighty blow.

"He would either have one like that," he said, "or I would put him on the furnace."

"Well, keep your eyes open, Robin ; you may be able to do him a good turn yet. I know the man well, and if I see him prying about, I shall know what to do."

"Ay, ay ; but what is it brings you here so quickly? I thought you said it was likely that we should not see you for a long time?"

"I *did* say so, but something, or, I should say, many things, have occurred which have caused me to change all my plans. But are you very busy?"

"Up to my eyes in work. Pipkin!"

"Ay."

"You ought to be ashamed of yourself. Here you are, standing beside a barrel of wine with a drinking horn in your hand, and yet you do not offer a drop to Master Roebuck."

"Trouble not," smiled Roebuck. "I have a deal of business to transact, and, for the present, must abstain from wine."

"What a pity," sighed Robin, "when it was so very *cheap !* But you asked if I was busy. Have you anything for me to do?"

"I should be thankful for your services to-night."

"I am your man."

"You will require your horse."

"He, too, is ready."

"I will not conceal from you, Robin, the fact that the errand upon which I am bent to-night is likely to prove dangerous."

"All the better."

"Am I to go?" asked Pipkin.

"To be sure you shall," said Robin. "You shall ride with me, Pip."

"I have something for Pipkin to do," said Roebuck. "Here are four letters, Pip. You will see that you have been to these gentlemen before. As soon as ever it is dusk, set out and deliver them ; you will not have to await answers. You might set out at once and deliver them, but I am afraid you would attract too much attention."

"So he would," said Robin. "He shall set off at dusk."

"Now," continued Roebuck, seating himself on the anvil, "listen, and I will tell you what has transpired since I last saw you."

Thereupon he told him all, and then read the letter with which the reader is acquainted.

"You see," he concluded, "I have so many matters of the very greatest importance to attend to that I should not interfere in this matter—since I feel certain that the lady will not be injured—only I may be able to turn this adventure to my own advantage. You do not see that?"

"I have not your brains," sighed Robin, as he fished up the bowl and swallowed another lot of wine.

"From what I have told you, can you not see that it is likely that Nelly will not be safe at Smithfield?"

"Ay, ay ; by heavens, I see *that.*"

"Well, if all goes well, this advantage will cause her safety to be secured. But more of that anon.

Now Robin, here is a little present for you."

"Eh? What is it?"

Roebuck handed him a small black leathern box.

Opening it Robin found it full of gold pieces.

"Nay, nay," he said, "I require it not. Why should I take it?"

"Because I ask you. If you do not, you will offend me."

"Well, well, I will have it and thank you. But money is of little use to me, you see; as soon as ever I get it, lo! 'tis gone."

"What odds, if there is more to follow? Now remember, Robin, you will meet me at the back of Kennington Church at the hour of eight."

"I will, without fail."

After some little more conversation Roebuck departed.

He was still attired as a French officer, and his handsome dress and gallant bearing attracted much attention as he proceeded slowly through the crowded thoroughfares.

* * * *

It was a strange thing, but nevertheless a fact, that Lambeth Palace, at the period of our romance, was surrounded by a crowd of small wooden houses, wherein resided some of the biggest rogues in London.

Indeed, it was a common thing for them to boast that they were, in every respect, more clever than their neighbours on the "other side."

By that, of course, they meant the scum in Alsatia.

Nestling amid a swarm of these houses was the hostelry at which Titus Oates had "put up," and a more dirty, foul-smelling place could not have been found in all London.

On the first floor was the room in which Oates was accommodated, and the hour of eight saw him impatiently pacing the bare boards.

Blood had not come, nor had he given any sign that he was about to put in an appearance.

"But I am sure he will be here," Oates muttered for the twentieth time. "He has now but little money, and, if he thinks he can well line his pockets without much difficulty, he will not hesitate. By Satan! I hope and trust he will come, for I am completely cleaned out."

A very short time had wrought a wondrous change in Titus Oates.

He presented the appearance of a hunted hound more than anything else, while his clothes were fearfully shabby, and his face and hands were utterly neglected.

Again and again the lying hypocrite and impostor paused, opened the door, and listened.

The only sound which reached him was the rattling of the metal measures and glasses, and loud voices.

But at last the clatter of horse's hoofs was heard.

Then came a heavy tramping up the stairs.

Oates seized a taper and opened the door.

Before him stood Blood.

For a moment Oates surveyed him in silent astonishment.

Well he might.

Blood was more superbly attired than he had ever seen him.

"Right welcome," he said, at last. "Enter my chamber, and take notice that you do not hurt the costly and artistic furniture."

"No jesting," said Blood; "this is not the time for it."

"You are correct. But—er—you have been in luck's way."

"What makes you say so?"

"Your handsome costume."

"Does it become me, think you?"

Well; but it would become you much better if— But that matters not."

"If what? Out with it."

"It it were not for that ugly mark on your forehead."

Blood frowned fiercely.

"Ay," he said, "you speak the truth, or I would knock you down in an instant. But do not fear—I will have my revenge for it."

"I would leave no stone unturned to obtain it."

"I will not. But you said that I have been in luck's way. Well, I have; I have found a lady who, in defiance of this wound, has taken a fancy to me."

"Indeed! I am pleased to hear it. I wonder if it is likely that any lady will take a fancy to *me*?"

Blood burst into a hoarse laugh.

"Look at yourself in the glass and see," he said.

"There is no necessity," replied Oates, trying to force a grin; "I am very well acquainted with my personal appearance. But the lady who has taken a fancy to you—may I ask who she is?"

"You *may* until domesday, but hang me if I should answer. You cannot expect me to open my heart to you, Titus Oates, eh?"

"Not exactly; but I thought it possible I might know the lady."

"No; and it is not likely you ever will. But now to business. You are well aware of the fact that I said it would be better if there was no communication between us for some considerable time?"

"I *am* well aware of it, and there would have been no communication so far as I am concerned, had it not been for the fact that the information I sent you fell into my hands, and that by the merest accident."

"You would have done wrong had you not sent to me, for, by Satan's own! I am sadly in want of money."

"Your lady friend, then, is not a rich woman?"

"Did I say so?"

"You did not, but I infer—"

"Infer nothing. I repeat that I am sadly in want of money."

"So am I, and I am the worse off of the two. Look at the table."

"I see it. There are plenty of bottles upon it."

"All are empty."

"What! have you no money for a bottle of wine?"

"None. I was about to ask you to pay for one."

"By all means—a dozen if you like," said Blood, throwing down a guinea with a swagger.

"I can now quench my thirst," said Oates, pouncing upon the coin, "and I can assure you that for hours it has been intolerable."

"Do you mean to tell me that the host would not trust you?"

"Trust?—not he Go and look at his clock behind the counter."

"His clock? What has that to do with it?"

"*All* to do with it. It conveys an unmistakable intimation."

"To what effect?"

"The hands are taken away, and in their place are these words: 'No tick here,' and 'tick,' as you are probably aware, is a vulgar phrase for credit."

"Humph!" grunted Blood, "no doubt he thinks himself very clever. But shout out for the wine."

The wine having been brought up and partaken of, Oates said—

"What of the men?"

"They are within a hundred yards of this house."

Oates rubbed his hands joyfully together.

"You are prompt," he said. "Are the men mounted?"

"Ay."

"And the number?"

"Six."

"Quite sufficient."

"Now, are you perfectly certain that it is Nell Gwynne who is about to travel, or is it only one of her maids? It sounds strange to talk of Nell Gwynne's maids, eh?"

"Very, very, indeed. Her sudden prosperity sounds like a fairy tale."

"Well, like others, no doubt, she will blaze for awhile, and then die out."

"Probably; and a lot it will trouble us, eh? But there is no maid in the matter. True, a maid, or even two maids, may travel with her, but Nell herself will ride in the coach."

"From whom did you obtain the information?"

"From one of the servants at the Palace. I met him not far from here, and recognised him as a man I had known years ago. He tried to avoid me, but I forced myself upon him, and he, seeing that it was impossible to get away, was wise enough to be civil."

"*Wise* enough?"

"Ay, for he knew that, if I chose, I had but to say a dozen words, and he would be shown the door at the Palace."

"I understand. Good!"

"What a thing it is to have a good memory!" said the old scoundrel, as he twiddled his dirty thumbs and grinned.

"Not *always*," answered Blood, in significant tones. "But go on."

"Well, I persuaded him to drink, and at last he consented—"

"And so you treated him to wine when you had no money," interrupted Blood. "*Very* good."

"Wait, wait. When he consented to drink I borrowed of him. Ho, ho! it was an excellent idea. So he drank and drank, and at last he got into that state when a man tells either the most monstrous lies or the truth. This, of course, I know from experience; and I wormed out of him the information with which I supplied you. Nell Gwynne sets out from Clapham at the hour of ten."

"But why so late?"

"Well, it appears that she will be entertaining friends until nine. But come to the Palace she must."

"She has borrowed from the gentleman you refer to without the knowledge of the king, eh?"

"No doubt of it; nay, I am *sure* of it; for the man said the money-lender, he had heard, had threatened to communicate with the king in the event of Nell Gwynne failing to keep her appointment."

"That I don't believe, or, if he said so, he didn't mean it. It is more than he dare do."

"Why?"

"Because the king would not believe him. And what do you think the amount will be?"

"Some thousands."

"Let me see," said Blood, "she sets out at ten. Then we had better be off at once. But how will you get a horse?"

"If a deposit is paid, the host will lend one. But it is not so much how I will *get* a horse as how I will *ride* him."

"You will have to do the best you can. Get yourself ready; I will pay the deposit. And you are certain as to the way Nell Gwynne is about to travel?"

"Ay, along the Kennington Road."

"But are you sure that she will come by coach? I'll swear that none of the king's coaches are at Clapham."

"Is it likely that they *would* be? If Nell was driven by the king's servants, she would probably be betrayed. No; she is about to ride in a coach hired from Master Allmack, a builder close here. It will be drawn by six horses, and—"

"Fool!" said Blood, "why did you not say that at once?"

Oates stared.

"What for?" he asked.

"I will show you—that is if it is not too late. Come; let us first of all go to this man Allmack. Is it far from here?"

"No," answered Oates, wondering what on earth Blood was about to do, "it is within a stone's throw."

He led the way out of the hostelry, and Blood, leaving his horse in charge of an ostler, accompanied Oates to Allmack's.

His two shops were about a couple of hundred yards off, and on approaching the gateway which divided the two and led to the yard containing coach-houses and stables, they saw the horses being put to a somewhat elaborately painted, but lumbering coach.

"Good!" chuckled Blood. "Apparently it is *not* too late."

Oates, even now, could not understand what he was about to do.

Blood inquired of one of the men for the master.

"There's three, your worship," replied the man, "three brothers. Which do you want?"

"The chief of the three."

"That's Master Arnold. There he be, in yon office."

Blood stalked into the little office opposite, where sat a little elderly man, with sharp, Jewish features.

As soon as he saw a "gentleman" with an elaborate costume enter, he jumped up like a Jack-in-the-box and bowed profoundly.

Blood saw at once what sort of a man he had to deal with, and he noticed that he bore a striking resemblance to two men about the coach.

"My friend," said Blood, "may I ask you the name of the person for whom you are preparing the coach?"

Allmack shook his head.

"Can't give it," he said.

"And why?"

"We have been paid not to reveal it."

"Indeed! Well, I am prepared to *pay* you to reveal it. If it is not for the person I think it is, you shall keep the money all the same."

At once Allmack consented.

It was, of course, a rascally proceeding, being a scandalous breach of trust.

"It is for Mistress Ducrow," he said.

Oates was about to say something, but Blood trod on his foot.

"Good," said Blood, "the very person. She is now staying at Clapham."

"Correct," replied Allmack.

At once Oates saw the drift of all this, and he chuckled with delight.

"Listen to me," continued Blood, with his usual astounding impudence. "I am Sir Francis Ducrow, and the husband of the lady who is coming from Clapham and about to stay, I fancy, at the Palace. I have no doubt you will not be surprised to know that it is my wife's intention to elope."

"I had no idea of all this. I—"

"No, no ; I will not accuse you, but, having told you which way the wind blows, I must call upon you to assist me in putting a stop to my wife's intentions. But I do not expect you to do this for nothing. Certainly not. Name your own terms."

"With all respect to you, sir, this would be impossible."

"And why, pray ?"

"The law compels me to make inquiries in such a matter."

"Then you think inquiries would be necessary in a case like this ?"

"I must say I do."

"Hark you. I will give you a hundred guineas to do as I may direct, and I will pay you the sum of twenty guineas in advance."

Allmack, senior, who was a most avaricious man, immediately snapped at the offer.

Blood handed him a goldsmith's note for the amount, whereupon Allmack left his office to call his brothers.

"Excellent !" chuckled Oates. "On my soul, I did not think of such a thing. The money is certain to drop into our hands."

"Of course it is—thanks to my brains."

"Exactly. Truly, you ought to have made a vast fortune long ago."

"It is not too late to make one. But, hist ! they come."

The three brothers now entered, and it was then seen that the resemblance between them was most extraordinary.

Allmack the elder explained what had transpired, whereupon his brothers became grave.

Blood and Oates were fearful at first, for there was, of course, a chance that one of the brothers might recognise at least one of them.

But they did not.

Almost the whole of their business was on the Surrey side of the Thames, whereas Blood's operations had been nearly all on the other side.

"You see how it is," said one. "If what you have said turns out to be not correct, we are liable to be called before a judge."

"Pah ! " said Blood, haughtily, "there is no fear of that. But come, decide at once, for time presses."

The brothers consulted, and finally they accepted.

"My instructions are exceedingly brief," said Blood, "and you will see that you will have scarcely any trouble. Instead of proceeding along the main road, you will turn off at Kennington Common, and go at a rapid pace to the left. There—"

"One moment," interrupted Allmack. "If my brothers take that direction, they will find themselves on the chalk path which crosses the Marshes."

"Exactly. That is what I want, for, while I talk to my lady, we are certain not to be interfered with. But you said your brothers. Do they conduct the coach ?"

"Ay ; it is our best, and worth a very large sum of money, therefore we do not trust it to our men."

"I see. Well, you know exactly what to do. I shall have, perhaps, half-a-dozen of my retainers with me, as well as this gentleman, who joined my wife and I in holy matrimony."

Oates turned up his eyes and assumed a sanctified air.

"At what time do you expect to reach this part of the road ?" asked Blood.

"At about half-past ten."

"Good. So then, for the time, adieu. The amount agreed upon shall be faithfully paid in less than twelve hours."

BY COMMAND OF THE KING; OR, THE DAYS OF THE MERRIE MONARCH.

"BEFORE THE DOOR A HANDSOMELY DRESSED MAN WAS STRUGGLING WITH A YOUNG AND BEAUTIFUL GIRL."

No. 10

Blood, followed by Oates, left the yard and returned to the hostelry.

"What say you now?" queried Blood.

"I believe you are more clever than ever. Verily, it was a masterful stroke of business."

In consideration of a small amount deposited, the host lent Oates a horse, and in less than ten minutes the pair set out.

Half-a-dozen men were impatiently awaiting them at a little distance, and Blood, having given them certain instructions, and assured them that a handful of money awaited each, and that there would be nothing to do for it, the whole party rode away in the direction of Kennington.

As they turned into the Kennington Road they saw the coach, drawn by six very fine horses, proceeding at a sharp trot in the direction of Clapham.

But the brothers Allmack, who were attired as postillions, took no notice of them.

They were too far off to recognise Blood or Oates, or the six drunken-looking ruffians, or they might have considered that all was not exactly right.

But, in any case, for their rascally betrayal of a secret, and for their consenting to betray the person who, in the first place, had employed them, they deserved severe punishment.

And they were destined to get it, though it was not to be physical punishment.

Blood and his companions proceeded leisurely to Kennington, and, when they reached the Common, they went straight to the back of a belt of huge trees which skirted it, and which were close to the Marshes, about which thousands of treacherous "will-o'-the-wisps" were disporting themselves.

The night was profoundly dark, so that it was impossible to see across the Common.

But, even had the moon been shining, it is questionable whether they would have noticed a tiny figure which, as they placed themselves in position, seemed to rise out of the earth and run in the opposite direction with extraordinary speed.

It was Pipkin.

Straight away he went, and did not pause until he reached a blacksmith's shed half-a-mile distant.

Knocking upon the door, he was at once admitted by the owner, who was a friend of Roebuck.

Within the smithy, which was a very large one, was Master Roebuck, Robin, and four friends.

Each was mounted and well armed; Robin, in addition to his mighty sword and a pair of pistols, having an enormous hammer slung at his saddle-bow.

"Sword and pistols may fail at any moment," was Robin's opinion; "but a good, honest English hammer—never!"

"Well, Pip," said Roebuck, "what news?"

"Good—very good. You could not have placed me in a better position, for of course I could see who came along the road as well as the Common. Blood, Oates, and six men have arrived."

"Ha! You are sure you are not mistaken?"

"Mistaken? Nay, that would be impossible. And Blood is arrayed in a most gorgeous costume."

"What are his companions like?"

"Alsatians, I fancy. They have hidden themselves behind some trees on the left."

"Seven men, my friends," Roebuck said, "for that impostor, Oates, will not fight."

"May I get hold of him," said Robin. "By the Virgin, I'll make his bones ache to some tune. The wretched rat deserves a shaking. Why not secure him, and let him dangle at the end of a rope, Master Roebuck?"

"That will probably be his end, but we will not anticipate the common hangman. Now, listen. We will leave the smithy and proceed along the road towards London for a distance of half-a-mile or so. Then we'll turn off to the left, ride across Snow's Fields, and so reach the Common that way. What say you, Master Hillyer?"

This was to the blacksmith, who replied—

"You could not select a better way, for you will be almost opposite to those you are after, and yet not be seen."

"Come, then," continued Roebuck.

The blacksmith holding wide the gates, the horsemen passed out.

Roebuck, as well as his companions, were all attired as ordinary civilians.

The latter were fine men, and had taken part with Roebuck in many a dangerous enterprise.

The adventure upon which they were now engaged suited them admirably.

Robin, too, was delighted to take part in it, and so was Pipkin.

Heartily indeed did the blacksmith laugh as Robin Renard, stooping in his saddle, lifted little Pip upon his broad shoulder.

"Keep there, Pip," said Robin, "and I pray you interfere not with my right arm if I have to use it."

"Fear it not, good Robin," replied Pip. "Use your arm freely; and, depend upon it, I will guard you from all danger."

CHAPTER XXVI.

HOW BLOOD WAS FOILED, AND WHAT HAPPENED TO TITUS OATES.

THE house at which Nell Gwynne had been staying at Clapham was in the occupation of the beautiful Mistress Elenor Marleigh, the unfortunate lady who afterwards met her death at the hands of an enraged lover, and who, at the time of our story, was a constant attendant at Court, where, it may be said, she was much more respected than the majority of ladies.

In addition to her great beauty, she was highly accomplished, and, what is more, strictly honourable.

She had taken a very great interest in Nell Gwynne, and the latter, confiding to her the fact that she was indebted to a money-lender to a very large amount, Mistress Marleigh had agreed to advance the money, and this was the real reason that Nell was at Clapham.

Mistress Marleigh kept a large staff of servants and a stud of good horses; but there was one thing she did not possess, and that was a coach.

The fact was that she had a horror of the huge, cumbersome vehicles.

Nell Gwynne, therefore, was compelled to order one from Allmack's, for had she sent to the royal stables, the king would quickly have known that she was about to travel, and, with his usual jealousy, he would have endeavoured to find out where.

With her, at Mistress Marleigh's, Nell had a couple of maids; but even these she would not take with her.

At half-past nine the coach arrived, and the two postillions, having partaken of the refreshments provided for them, and the horses having been watered, they awaited the coming of the lady whom they had betrayed.

Just before ten, Nell, accompanied by her beautiful hostess, made her appearance, and, after a few hurried words, entered the coach.

Then one of the men-servants placed a box beside her, the door was closed, and, in another few minutes, the coach rolled off in the direction of Lambeth.

The servant whom Oates had nearly made drunk at his own expense was correct.

Nell was certainly travelling with the money she was about to refund— with the exorbitant interest charged.

But though she had so much money with her, she was not at all alarmed for her own safety or for the safety of the large amount of money she had with her.

The road from Clapham to Lambeth was supposed to be one of the best, and travellers were very rarely interfered with.

The horses travelled splendidly, and went on without a halt until Kennington was reached.

Nell was leaning back amid the luxurious cushions, lost in thought, when the coach suddenly swung round to the left; so suddenly indeed that it was a wonder the vehicle was not overturned.

Nell started up in alarm, and looked out of the window.

"Hold!" she cried, in the commanding tones she so well knew how to use when she thought proper. "Hold!

You are off the right road.   Hold, I say!"

The postillions heeded her not.

Mercilessly thrashing their now frightened horses, they tore along the chalk path which crossed the Marshes.

Then, suddenly, they came to a halt.

Before Nell could again open her lips, the coach was surrounded by half-a-dozen men.

For a moment Nell was speechless with astonishment, though decidedly not with terror.

But in that moment she guessed that the postillions were confederates of the men who had thus surrounded her, or, if not confederates, they had been bribed.

"What is the meaning of this disgraceful trick?" cried Nell, indignantly.

The man nearest the door took off his hat and bowed.

"Pray excuse us," he said, "but there are times when we like to see *old acquaintances.*"

"Great heavens!" cried Nell, "Colonel Blood."

"Correct," said Blood, with a grin, "and I trust I see Mistress Gwynne quite well?"

"Colonel Blood," said Nell, quietly, the while her lovely eyes flashed fire, "you will suffer for this.   I will inform the king—"

"Pardon me," interrupted Blood, with a sneer, "you will do nothing of the sort.   This journey, at any rate, will be kept from the king's ears.   But I have no desire to detain you, Mistress Gwynne."

"Why stop me at all?"

"Well, you see, times have been bad with me—"

"*And* with me," interrupted Oates, uplifting his eyes.

Blood scowled, and continued—

"And knowing that you are in possession of a certain sum of money, which will be of great service to me—"

"*And* me," again interrupted Oates, who seemed determined not to let Blood have all the talking.

Nell answered Oates — whom, of course, she had recognised—this time.

"Hence, horrible impostor and lying hypocrite!" she said in disgust. "Away, lest the very air about me becomes tainted!'

Oates tried to force a grin, but it would not come.

There was no doubt that he felt exceedingly small at that moment.

"You desire the money I carry?" said Nell.

"That is all," replied Blood.   "I assure you that I have no desire to injure you."

"Injure me! I dare you to attempt it. But if you have no desire to injure me, why do you have all those men at your back?"

"Oh! I invariably travel with an *escort.*"

"You will travel with a *special* escort one of these days, Colonel Blood."

"A special escort?"

"Ay."

"I am sorry that I fail to understand you."

"I mean to the gallows."

Blood forced a laugh as he asked—

"By whose orders, think you, shall I go to the gallows, madam?"

"By the orders of a judge, who will be supported by an outraged public."

"What! are you *already* assuming the *rôle* of dictator, Nell?   But no, you are mistaken.   If a judge ordered my execution, you are well aware who would countermand it."

"*I* am?"

"*You* are, Mistress Gwynne."

"*Who*, think you, would countermand it?"

"The king."

"Nay, 'tis *you* who are mistaken. Once let a judge pass an order for your execution, and *I* will see that the king does not countermand it."

"Thanks," sneered Blood.   "But we are wasting time.   Hand over the money, and you may depart."

To this Nell made no reply for some few minutes.

She was considering.

And when she remembered that her friend, Mistress Marleigh, had been so kind to her, and at what great trouble she had been put to to collect the money, she nearly burst into tears.

But what was she to do?

Was she not at the mercy of the ruffian Blood and his associates?

But at last she said—

"Suppose I refuse to hand you the money?"

"I should be sorry, because force would have to be used."

"Well, I will not hand you the money, Colonel Blood. If you must have it, you will take it."

"Certainly," replied Blood, who then directed two of the men to dismount and secure the prize.

They opened the door, quickly found the box, and handed it to Blood, who in turn passed it to Oates.

The reader can imagine how the old false swearer grasped the box, and what a series of joyous chuckles left his lips.

Blood directed one of the men to reclose the coach door.

When this was done he raised his hat, but ere he could utter a word, several shots rang out, and three of the men, including the one who had just closed the coach door, fell.

Blood, with a yell of terror, stood bolt upright in his stirrups, the while he placed his hands upon his pistols, but the next instant he dropped into his saddle again.

"Master Roebuck, by all that's infernal!" he muttered, "and well supported. To fight would be useless. Let every man look to himself!"

Turning, he thought to snatch the box from Oates, but that scoundrel was now at some distance away.

Blood did not wait.

Putting spurs to his horse, he rode away like the wind.

The three mounted Alsatians fired one or two random shots, but that was all.

They were not effective, for they were too terrified to take a steady aim.

Meantime, while Roebuck was calmly directing his friends, Oates, with the box clasped close to his breast, crept cautiously away.

But suddenly he saw before him a monstrous horse, with what looked like a small tower upon it.

It was Robin.

Wide indeed did Oates open his mouth as his horse abruptly stopped.

"Well met, Master Oates, on my soul," said Robin.

"Well met, thou prince of liars!" cried Pip, who was still perched on Robin's shoulder.

"Jest not," said Oates. "I pray you let me proceed."

"If you attempt to pass *me*," said Robin, "I will pound your rascally carcase into a jelly."

"I should like to thrash him with a thonged whip at the cart's tail," said Pipkin.

Robin dismounted, and seizing Oates, despite his weight, lifted him clean out of the saddle and threw him upon the ground.

Then he snatched the box away and handed it to Pipkin.

"What?" cried Robin. "Did you think to so easily supply yourself with money, eh? Wait but a little while, and, by the blessed Virgin, we'll supply you with something."

"Ay, ay," said Pip; "there is a rod in pickle for you, Master Ananias. But here is Master Roebuck."

Oates groaned.

Roebuck! Truly he had fallen into a mighty fire.

"Keep him safe, Robin," said Master Roebuck. "Blood has escaped, or I would have made short work of him. Hand me the box, Pip."

With the box beneath his arm, Roebuck went to the carriage and opened the door.

"Mistress Gwynne," he said, "I trust that you are not much frightened at what has occurred?"

Nell uttered a cry of astonishment, but it was not unmingled with joy.

"Master Roebuck!" she said, "*here?*"

"Ay, here to restore to you that which you have just lost. See, here is the box, and the contents is untouched."

"By heaven, your appearance here was most timely! And the box is safe?"

"It is, together with the contents, which, of course, these ruffians had no time to abstract."

"You have rendered me a very great service, Master Roebuck, and I cannot too warmly thank you. How came you to be here at this—"

"Have you thought how Blood and his rascally associates came to be here?" interrupted Roebuck.

"Nay, how did *you* know?"

"Through the black impostor, Master Oates. Accidentally I found a letter from him in one of Blood's holsters. As to how Oates obtained the information contained in the letter I cannot say. It would be a mistake to inquire, for nothing but lies would be forthcoming. Oates and Blood, Mistress Gwynne, are the principals in this. Blood has escaped, but Oates remains and should be punished. It is my intention to punish him. I trust you have no objection ? "

" Objection ? Not the faintest. For *many* reasons I should be glad indeed to see the wretch well punished."

" Then there are the postillions. I suppose you have no sort of doubt but that they were in league with Blood ? "

" I have now no doubt but that they accepted money from him to act as they did. They deliberately turned here, and did not pause, in defiance of my calls."

" I know it. One moment."

Roebuck then called to the two postillions, who very reluctantly came forward.

" Your names ? " asked Roebuck.

" Allmack," replied one.

" Are you both named Allmack ? "

" Ay."

" That is the name of the man from whom the coach was hired," said Nell.

" Are you partners," asked Roebuck, " or simply postillions ? "

" We are brothers and partners, and, having given you this information, no doubt you will allow us to resume our journey."

" A very reasonable request, on my soul ! Resume the journey with this lady as a passenger ? It is very likely, certainly. Now, sirs, give an explanation of your conduct—if you can."

The brothers, after some hesitation, told Roebuck what had passed between them and " the gentleman who had ridden away."

" Supposing what you say is correct," said Roebuck, " you have most grossly betrayed the confidence reposed in you by this lady, and deserve the most severe punishment ; and it is my intention to punish you."

" If you attempt to touch us—"

" Be silent ; I have not finished yet. Having committed an outrage, you will immediately apologise to this lady."

The men made no attempt to do so,

and Roebuck, drawing his sword, said, in tones there was no mistaking—

" Apologise, I say, or, as sure as you stand there, I will make short work of you ! "

With great haste the men humbly apologised.

But Nell made no reply, nor could they expect it.

They had led her into a danger which might have cost her her life.

" Now," continued Roebuck, " what do you reckon is the value of your coach ? "

" Fifteen hundred crowns."

" So much, eh ? Well I should not have thought it was worth it."

" It is a new coach."

" So it seems. Well, I will attend to it in a moment."

" Are we not at liberty to go ? "

" By no means ! I have not done with you yet. On another occasion, before you enter into a matter of this description, think it well over, for there is no telling how much it is likely to cost you."

The men went to their horses' heads. They expected they would be told they could go in a few moments.

" Mistress Gwynne," said Roebuck, " there is an excellent way of punishing men such as these, and that is through their pockets. You will see presently that it will be impossible you can proceed further in this coach, but I will see you safely to your destination. Will you object to ride before me ? "

" Not at all. I will willingly ride before you, for I know I shall be perfectly safe."

" Thank you."

" Shall I descend from the coach ? "

" Do."

Mistress Gwynne accordingly stepped from the coach.

" Dismount, Robin," cried Roebuck.

Robin was out of the saddle in an instant, and he placed Pip on the ground.

Roebuck then directed the postillions to take the horses out, and this, after but a brief pause they did.

" Robin," continued Roebuck, " get your hammer."

Robin at once procured his ponderous hammer, and brought it forward.

The postillions shuddered as Robin passed them.

Never in all their lives had they beheld such a mountain of muscle and bone.

"What was about to be done?" they asked themselves.

They were soon to learn.

"My friends," said Roebuck, once more addressing them, "when you made your statement, you omitted to mention how much you received for your breach of faith. But we do not desire to know. I feel perfectly certain that you did not receive as much as fifteen hundred crowns, and, therefore, you will see that you are woefully out of pocket. Robin, see how long it will take you to demolish that coach."

The postillions, with wild, frantic cries, rushed forward, imploring Roebuck to spare the coach.

But they were not heeded.

At a signal from Roebuck, Robin raised his hammer, swung it over his head, and brought it down.

Crash! it went against the panel, smashing it clean in, and causing the whole of the lumbering coach to tremble violently.

Again and again was the ponderous hammer brought down, and each time the richly ornamented wood was splintered in all directions.

In less than ten minutes nothing remained of the vehicle but part of the body and the wheels.

"You may depart now," Roebuck said to the Allmacks, who were now in tears, "and I am sure that this lesson will teach you to pause before you again betray a customer."

The two men made no reply.

No doubt they considered it would be a wise plan to keep a still tongue.

Mounting their horses, they rode away.

Titus Oates, now in a state of the greatest terror, was then dragged forward.

"What can I say to you, you load of iniquity?" said Roebuck. "What can I say to you, who would betray your own mother if you thought you could put a few gold pieces in your pocket?"

"Did he ever *have* a mother?" said Robin, eyeing him with unutterable disgust. "I don't believe it. He may have had a father, and he still lives."

"Who is he?" cried Pip.

"The devil."

"Spare me," cried Oates, "spare me, I entreat, good Master Roebuck."

And he fell upon his knees.

"Do not fancy that you will make any impression upon me," Roebuck said. "You are one of the chiefs in this outrage."

"No, no; you have been wrongly informed, you have indeed. It was Blood. Mistress Gwynne, intercede for me, I beg. Until you descended from the coach, I knew not that you were in it. I thought it was a lady who—"

"Cease your lies!" Roebuck interrupted, as he drew forth a paper and held it before Oates' face. "What about this? This is your letter to Blood, which happened, in the strangest manner, to fall into my hands. No doubt you will swear that you never wrote it."

Oates made no reply to this, he was so astonished.

Roebuck conferred with his comrades, and then he said to Robin, who was most anxiously awaiting his orders—

"Robin, secure his hands behind his back."

This was done in a few seconds.

Then Roebuck called Robin to his side, and gave him further instructions.

Robin at once acted upon them.

In the first place he tore Oates' coat to shreds.

Then he pushed him to one of the numerous pools of filthy water, and, despite his bulk, hurled him in.

Pipkin was unable to contain himself; his laughter made the Marshes ring.

But only for a few moments, when it was drowned by Oates' yells.

From side to side he floundered, trying hard to regain his feet.

But the slippery state of the sides and his tied hands prevented him.

When he was wet to the skin, Robin lifted him out.

"Now," said Roebuck, "put all the wood of the coach together, Robin, and when it is flaring merrily, take Oates and throw him into the centre."

At this a fearful yell left Oates' lips, and he dropped helpless to the ground.

"You do not intend that that should be done?" whispered Nell.

"Nay; it is but to terrify him," answered Roebuck. "But, nevertheless, the wretch richly deserves it."

"Most true."

Robin soon collected a pile of wood, and, placing the whole of it between the wheels, set fire to it.

In a few moments great sheets of flame shot upwards and illuminated the Marshes from end to end, but so deserted was this part at night, that no one was attracted to the spot.

The anguish of Master Oates as he watched the flames may be imagined.

He certainly thought that presently Robin would take hold of him and throw him into the fire.

And he was allowed to think so for some considerable time.

That, indeed, was his worst punishment.

When the fire began to die down, Roebuck once more turned to him.

"We will spare you this time," he said, "but beware how you act in future, or a death as terrible as I threatened may speedily overtake you. Robin, assist Mistress Gwynne to my saddle, then take the box, mount, and follow."

In another five minutes the whole party were moving off in the direction of Lambeth.

Oates tried again and again to walk, but he could not.

At last he managed to crawl to the fire, and there he remained, alternately groaning and cursing.

In the morning some labourers found him fast asleep beside the embers of the coach.

They were about to render some assistance when they caught sight of the dead bodies of the men whom Blood had hired.

This so alarmed them that they sped away like the wind to inform the authorities.

CHAPTER XXVII.

THE JOURNEY TO LAMBETH—HOW ROBIN AND PIPKIN OBTAINED REFRESHMENTS GRATIS.

"MASTER ROEBUCK," said Mistress Gwynne, as they proceeded, "you may depend upon it that I will speak of this to the king."

"I advise you not to do so."

"And why?"

"Pardon me, this journey was undertaken unknown to the king?"

"It was."

"Then do not rouse his jealousy by speaking of it. It would not be made known to him by me, and, depend upon it, neither Blood nor Oates would mention it anywhere."

"But I was thinking of benefiting *you*."

"I thank you cordially, but you can benefit me in another way."

"You have but to name it."

"I will—at once. Is it your intention to return to Clapham after your visit to Lambeth?"

"Nay; the king, no doubt, thinks my stay already too prolonged."

"I admire his anxiety."

"You were *always* gallant, Master Roebuck."

"Ay, I am sometimes gallant when my heart is as heavy as lead."

"Is your heart heavy now?"

"It is."

"What makes it so?"

"Anxiety."

"Ah! you fear arrest?"

"Not at all. That does not trouble me in the least, I assure you. My anxiety is for the present safety and the future welfare of a young girl. She is betrothed to young Sir Harold Harcourt."

"Indeed! Then why be anxious?"

"I will tell you all. I know well that you can keep a secret."

"Ay; I have and *do* keep many."

"True—only *too* true. May neither of them be the means of destroying the position you have attained."

Nell laughed merrily.

She soon forgot a trouble or a danger.

"If ever my position is destroyed,

Master Roebuck," she said, " it will be found that, to some extent, I have provided for my future."

" Assuredly you would be very foolish if you did not."

Roebuck told her Nelly's history, and, indeed, all concerning her, to which Nell listened with profound attention.

"And," she said, you think her unsafe at Smithfield ? "

" I do. And you ? "

"Most decidedly she is unsafe there. Depend upon it that woman will go to any extreme to remove this poor girl. Roebuck—tell me candidly—do you wish me to advise you ? "

" Nay ; I request you to take charge of the girl for a short time. Will you do so ? "

" With all my heart. To-morrow I shall be at Soho, and you can bring her to me there."

"Impossible."

"Impossible ! How so ? "

" I would not trust the girl in *any house* which the king was likely to visit."

"Neither would I," said Nell, candidly, " but I do not mean Sion House. That is now mine, as, no doubt, you have heard."

"That I have not."

"Yes, it is mine ; Charles made it over to me."

"Well, I can't wonder at that. Women like you are dangerous."

" Are we ? "

"Yes, because in a few hours you can, as the saying goes, twist a man around your finger ; then, having got him completely in your power, you can persuade him into anything."

Nell laughed heartily.

"Yes," she said, " Sion House is mine, but, you know, the king might one day gamble to such an extent that he may desire to raise money on the lease. In that case I am no longer owner. Then, again, I have considered it possible that one of these fine days the king, when going about in disguise, may meet with a fatal accident, or he may be shot dead or run through the heart."

"More than likely. I wonder that he has not been killed long ago."

"Therefore," continued Nell, " I have provided for myself ; I have purchased a house and its contents in Soho, and put into it a person who is, in every respect, a lady. It is close to Sion House, and yet the king knows nothing of it."

"See that he does not," said Roebuck, earnestly.

"Nay, nor does anyone else. You are the only one who knows it."

" I will not betray your confidence."

"Well, now, if—but wait. Suppose you remain close to the Palace while I transact my little business ? Then I will rejoin you, and together we will ride to Soho. Then I will introduce you to the lady I speak of, and you can make whatever arrangements you think proper."

"Do you think it would be safe ? "

" What ? "

" If you rode with me to Soho ? "

" Perfectly. At any rate, I am pre- pared to risk it. Can you not borrow a cloak from one of your companions for me ? "

Roebuck smiled as he replied—

" If I told them that you required their cloaks, hats, doublets, and all the money in their pockets," he said, " they would hasten to see who would be the first to lay the articles at your feet."

Again Nell laughed heartily.

And her laughter appeared to be thoroughly enjoyed by Roebuck.

No wonder.

There was no woman in England who had a more musical, genuine laugh than beautiful Nell Gwynne.

Master Roebuck continued—

" I will get a cloak then, and when you again ride before me, I will cover you in such a way that no one will be able to tell whether you are a boy or a woman."

Lambeth being reached, the party paused in one of the silent roads, and Roebuck, on foot and carrying the box, escorted Mistress Gwynne to the Palace.

Then, when he had placed the box in the hands of a servant, and the door had closed, he returned to his companions.

Just within an hour, Nell, entirely alone, rejoined them, and she was quickly placed before Roebuck and enveloped in a cloak.

Then Roebuck gave certain orders to

his four companions, and they rode away.

Then he turned to Robin.

"Robin," he said, "return to the Close, and take Pipkin with you. Mistress Gwynne has consented to provide for Nelly's safety, and I am going with her to make the necessary arrangements. Then, when daylight comes, I must communicate with Sir Harold. After that I will join you."

"For heaven's sake, take care of yourself. Remember *the hound!*"

"The hound?"

"Ay, Dominic Evans."

Roebuck smiled as he replied—

"Fear not, my dear Robin; I shall have my eyes open. Adieu."

"Adieu," said Robin, sadly.

He was not at all easy in his mind.

He wished a thousand times that Master Roebuck had returned with him to the smithy.

"I know my belongings are not of much account," he thought, "but there's always a clean bed, and a barrel of ale or wine at the 'Silver Bells' for the carrying of it."

"Good-bye, Pip," said Roebuck, "you will soon see me again."

Pipkin made no reply; his little heart was too full.

He, like Robin, was thinking of danger.

Roebuck took his tiny hand and pressed it, then, with another adieu he rode away.

"Pip," said Robin, "I feel downhearted, low-spirited."

"Ay, and so do I. Danger's afloat."

"You are right, and a deal of it. And you see, that infernal Blood has escaped. On my soul, he has as many lives as a cat."

"Rather say he has the luck of the devil."

"I wonder how Oates feels, Pip?"

At this Pip could not restrain a loud laugh.

"I'll warrant he's drying his hide against the blazing coach," he said.

"No doubt. Well, there's one thing, he'll have nothing near to drink, and if he had he could not drink it, because his hands are tied. Talking of that reminds me that I am thirsty. And you, Pip?"

"Oh! don't trouble about me. A table-spoonful would be sufficient for me. And you? How much would *you* require?"

"Oh! very little, Pip, very little indeed. Say four quarts—that would be ample."

"Ha, ha! I should say so. Well, I am afraid that your four quarts and my spoonful will have to wait."

"Why?"

"Every hostelry is closed."

"No doubt," said Robin, ruefully, "they always *are* when a man is thirsty. But you have plenty of brains in that little noddle of yours, Pip. Now, tell me what to do."

"Ride to the smithy, where some wine remains."

"It can't be done," almost groaned Robin. "Even a horse wants refreshment."

"Yours has not yet asked for any."

"He's asking for it now."

"Ha, ha!"

"Don't laugh. I assure you he's asking."

"How?"

"Can't you hear his tail swishing against my back?"

"I can."

"Well, that's his signal. One swish means water, and two means corn."

"I heard him swish three times."

"That means both. But we will ride slowly along, Pip, and if by any chance we come upon a place where refreshments may be had—well, we'll have them."

On they went, Pip looking to the right and Robin to the left.

But no hostelry, open or shut, did they see for some time.

Then they came upon a large one, which was closed.

Robin drew up, and mournfully surveyed it.

"Ah!" he said, "if I had my way all would be different. If I were but a statesman!"

"What would you do?"

"I'll tell you. I would make an Act which would compel every host to keep his house open an hour after midnight."

"They do that now."

"Not they. If a host feels tired he closes his house and goes to bed. But let me continue. The rest of the Act would be to the effect that, before the host retired, he should put a certain quantity of his best refreshments outside the door for the benefit of thirsty travellers; and there should be a box, in which the travellers would pay the money."

"Ha, ha! ho, ho!"

"What are you laughing at now?"

"At your Act."

"Don't you think it would work?"

"Admirably, but not to the benefit of the host."

"Indeed! Why?"

"Suppose the first, the second and the third travellers were honest men, and put certain sums into the box?"

"Yes. Well?"

"Then, presently, along comes a thief. He swallows the remainder of the refreshments and walks off with the box under his arm."

"Ay, I had not thought of that. What a pity that a paltry thief should destroy the whole of a good Act!"

"If we reflect— But look yonder, Robin."

"On my soul, it is a hostelry, and open, too!"

"Yes, and unless I am much mistaken, they are transacting business."

"Truly, after, all, we must have been born beneath lucky stars. Let us get on to it."

"I have money if you have not, Robin."

"I have plenty now. We do not require fine things, Pip, *unless they are free!*"

The hostelry, the door of which they saw open, was called the "Seven Swans' Necks," a sign which caused Robin to say he wondered if the poor birds had been executed for any offence.

Dismounting, Robin and Pipkin looked in the doorway.

Both were pretty well astonished when they beheld in the room on the left three persons, attired as gentlemen, seated round a table, upon which were several bottles of wine.

At a side-table, on which a spotless white cloth was laid, the host was busying himself in preparing the various articles for supper.

"Well, on my soul, this is something," said Robin.

"They must be persons of large means."

"They may *look* it, but they are not. No; I recognise one."

"Do you? Which?"

"You see that one with the lantern jaws and big, sunken eyes at the head of the table?"

"Ay."

"Well, who do you think he is?"

"I haven't the faintest idea."

"You've heard me speak of that wretched informer — the man who fancies he is going to capture Master Roebuck?"

"What, Dominic Evans?"

"Yes, of Aldgate."

"Do you mean to tell me that that ugly villain is Evans?"

"It is. Now, you see, Pip, this Evans is not a man to spend any large sum in an entertainment unless he has been wonderfully successful in something, or unless he wishes to make himself look large in the eyes of someone who is about to employ him. Just look at the villain's airs and graces as he sits at the table. One would fancy that he was a judge at least, eh?"

"He may *think* he looks very fine, but my opinion of him is that he looks a fool."

"That is also my opinion, Pip. If he was to—"

"What is that smell?"

"Smell? What, do you mean to say that you can't recognise roast fowls? But there are other smells mixed in, so it is evident that they are going to have a fine spread. Ah, me?"

"What are you sighing about?"

"I was thinking how dreadful it is to be hungry and smell savoury things."

"Well, the effect is to make one feel more hungry than ever."

"To be sure. You, no doubt, could manage to pick a small leg?"

"Easily. And you?"

"Oh, I could manage two or three fowls, for, you see, I've had nothing since the last meal. Be patient, Pip, and we may get a very excellent supper."

As he spoke the host, having concluded laying the table, came out of the room.

Pipkin thought Robin was about to hail him; but no, he took care he should not be seen.

Presently the host and his wife, each

bearing a tray containing steaming hot fowls and other things, came out of the kitchen and passed into the room.

Having placed all the articles upon the table, both retired and closed the door behind them.

The host advanced to the door of the hostelry, and was evidently about to close it, when Robin said—

"Not so fast, my friend. Just wait a bit."

The host, with a low cry, started back in amazement.

He had heard of giants, it is true, but this was the first time he had ever beheld one.

But quickly recovering himself, he said—

"What seek you?"

"Refreshments."

"Can't supply you now. Come in the morning, and—"

"I'll see you in France!" interrupted Robin, angrily. "What! you can't supply us, when you have three persons in yonder room, guzzling fit to break their necks?"

"Their refreshments were ordered."

"Well, we'll order *ours*, and, what is more, we'll pay for them."

So saying, Robin turned, seized his enormous hammer, and thrust it into his belt.

Then, telling Pip—who was inclined to burst into a loud laugh—to follow him, he entered the hostelry.

The host very quickly retreated behind his counter.

"I trust you will not be long, Sir Giant?" he said, now very civilly.

"Nay, I shall *never be longer than I am already*, host, just as I pray heaven my friend here will never be *shorter*."

"Heaven help me," thought the host. "If this man starts he could, no doubt, drink every drain of liquor I possess."

"Listen to it," said Robin. "You, of course, well know your guests in yonder room?"

"Not at all."

"Well, I know *one* of them, and he is the most contemptible villain unhung. It is a sin and a shame for a man like him to sit down to such a supper as I see you have provided. Now, it is my intention to make him go without his supper; but do not think you will be blamed. You are nothing to do with

it, but I warn you not to interfere. And, mark you, whatever I call for, do you promptly supply, and here is a guinea in advance."

The host made no reply; he was too much astonished.

Telling Pipkin to follow him, Robin marched to the door and flung it open.

At once the three men, who had just sat down to the supper, started up.

"Robin Renard?" cried Dominic Evans.

"The same," said Robin.

"How dare you enter—"

"Hush, hush! Speak not so loud, for children may be asleep over our heads. You see, Master Evans, we have been seeking supper, and, for a long time, were unsuccessful. But fortune at last directed us hither. We are just in time."

"For what?"

"Supper."

"Host," yelled Evans, "come hither at once, and—"

"If you shout in my ear like that again," said Robin, "I will pound thy long carcase into a jelly. So now be cautious; I am hungry, and a hungry man is sometimes dangerous. Now, Master Evans, get out of that chair and stand beside the fireplace until I have had my supper."

Evans did not move, so Robin took him by the collar and, with one hand, raised him up and stood him beside the fireplace.

"If you move," he said, "it will be the worse for you. Now, gentlemen," he added, to the other two, "seat yourselves, and I will serve you well. Be *seated*, confound you!"

The two men, who were trembling like leaves, dropped as if shot into their chairs.

Having made a place for Pipkin, Robin picked up a bottle of wine.

This he demolished with remarkable speed, and pronounced it excellent.

Then he proceeded, in the gravest manner, to serve the plates.

For Pipkin he selected the choicest bits, and then he served the men.

Lastly he served himself, but, considering the plates too small, he used one of the largest dishes.

The way the fowl disappeared was nothing short of marvellous.

In but a little time he had finished one and begun another.

But the two men ate not a bit.

Fear had taken their appetites away, and they could only look on at Robin in silence.

Dominic Evans was frantic, but he dared not attempt to interfere.

Pipkin, as cool as a cucumber, went on and finished the meal with much relish.

Having finished the second fowl and half a large pasty, Robin called the host, and told him to bring in two or three quarts of good ale.

The host brought it in without a word.

Robin supplied Pipkin with wine, and then offered the two men a share of the ale.

They declined, and so Robin swallowed the whole.

The meal being over, Robin rose.

"I thank you for your hospitality, Master Evans," he said, "and you, too, gentlemen. I am sorry you did not think the fowls good enough to eat. I assure you they were excellent. I bid you good-night, Master Evans."

"*Wait!*" hissed Dominic Evans. "I will have my revenge for this gross insult."

"Insult! Is it, then, an insult to eat? Fie, Master Evans, I am ashamed of you. Come, Pipkin, time flies. We are well satisfied, and I am sure these *gentlemen* are."

With Pip at his side, he marched out of the room, took his change of the host, watered his horse, and then, with Pip before him, rode away.

And until the darkness hid him from sight, the host could hear his hearty laughter.

CHAPTER XXVIII.

BLOOD DETERMINES TO GET POSSESSION OF **NELLY**, AND ENGAGES FOUR MEN TO ASSIST HIM—HOW ADMISSION TO PHILLIPS' HOUSE WAS OBTAINED, AND WHAT THE RESULT WAS.

BLOOD, after acting in such a cowardly fashion, rode on at full speed until he had put two or three miles between himself and Kennington.

But, knowing what a splendid rider Roebuck was, and what a fine horse he rode, it is probable that he would have continued for two or three more miles.

But his horse showed signs of exhaustion, and he was compelled to walk him.

It was then that he began to think of what he had lost, and the time and trouble he had expended over the affair.

"I seem to be foiled at every turn by him," he muttered. "When I think that I have secured a prize, lo! he seems to start out of the very earth to check me. If I could but have—yet wait. I have thought of something. By Satan's own! I have a most brilliant idea.

"Roebuck is at Kennington, and he assuredly will not leave Mistress Gwynne until he has seen her safe to her destination. I know him too well

for that. This will occupy a long time, and, therefore, he cannot be at Smithfield.

"I will proceed there at once and—but no, it would be absurd to go alone. Whom can I get to render me assistance? Ay, that is a question, for I have been so unlucky of late that I have exhausted the patience of nearly all who formerly believed in me.

"Still, I have plenty of Mistress Darmley's money about me, and I can pay in advance. I will make the attempt, at any rate. What were her last words?

"'Kill her, understand. And on no account leave her until you are certain that she is dead.'

"But I am afraid that would be impossible. She is too lovely for that—unless, of course, circumstances compel it.

"If I proceeded cautiously to work, it is more than likely that I should *capture* her. What a mighty revenge that would be! Yes, I will go on to Smithfield."

He called at a hostelry, and having refreshed himself without dismounting, he resumed his journey and reached Smithfield just after midnight.

He made straight to a hostelry which was known as the " Glory of the Fair," and where, under the name of Captain Gletton, he was fairly well known.

No doubt the majority of men who frequented the place well knew him to be none other than Blood, but they did not openly say so.

It did not pay them.

The host and ostler were the only two persons visible.

Having given his horse into the care of the latter, he entered the house, ordered a bottle of wine, and requested the host to share it.

The host accepted the invitation with alacrity.

" I see," said Blood " that your house is destitute of customers to-night."

The host smiled as he replied—

" It is, apparently, but the fact is, I have some guests upstairs."

" Do I know them ? "

" I think not."

" Do you ? "

" Right well, but this is the first time I have seen them for two or three years. One is a very well-known person."

" Indeed ! Who is he ? "

" Philip Collins, the lion - tamer. Ever heard of him ? "

" Doesn't he come from Yorkshire ? "

" He comes from *many* places," grinned the host. " Sometimes he comes from Dover, and then he gives it out that he has come straight from Buckingham. Between you and me, captain, he is no more a lion-tamer than I am."

" And his companions ? How many are there ? "

" Three."

" What do they really do for a living ? "

" I could not tell you exactly. But look you, captain ; if you want three or four men to assist you in anything, they will just do for you. But I warn you that they will not move until they have money in advance."

" You can introduce me ? "

" Certainly. Drink up your wine and follow me."

In another moment Blood was in an upstairs room, where at the table sat four men.

The eldest, a short, stumpy man of about sixty, was known as Philip Collins, a lion-tamer.

As a matter of fact, he never tamed a lion in all his life.

He would not have gone near such an animal for any amount.

Blood was introduced as " Captain Gletton," and he quickly informed Collins what he desired to do.

But, until the offer was accepted, which it was at once, he mentioned no names.

But as soon as he uttered the name of Phillips, Collins burst into a hearty laugh.

" I know him well," he said. " Some few months ago I sold him what he thought was six boxes of wine. He paid me the money, but when he opened them—ho, ho ! "

" What did they contain ? "

" Water—ha, ha ! "

" Well, it is not often that you can take a Jew in," said Blood. " But that makes me think of an excellent idea."

" What is it ? "

" This. Could you not call upon Phillips, and say you regretted such a mistake had been made ; that you only recently found it out ; and that you had come to refund the money ? "

" The idea is certainly a good one, but look at the hour."

" He never retires until very late."

" Maybe ; but even if he is up, he would not admit me into the house."

" It is more than likely that he would. I never yet knew a Jew to refuse money."

" Phillips is a very sharp Jew."

" Well, you can try it. If you are successful, a lot of trouble will be saved."

" And if I am *un*successful ? "

" We will wait a short time, and then force our way in. But I don't think you will have the least difficulty."

The arrangements were soon made, for in another quarter of an hour Collins left the hostelry and proceeded to Phillips'.

He was followed at a distance by his three men, while Blood brought up the rear.

In more than one window of the Jew's house a light was burning, and this seemed to indicate that all the occupants had not retired.

"Once admission is gained," chuckled Blood, "I shall be able to have my own way. There is no one there who is able to offer the least resistance."

He was utterly mistaken.

Nelly was again for a brief space under Phillips' protection, and it was but natural that our hero should, on every possible occasion, pay her a visit.

But it so happened that, on this particular night, Harold had ridden to the City on some urgent business.

He transacted it much more quickly than he had expected, and so, instead of going West, he went straight to Smithfield, where, as on every occasion, he received the warmest of welcomes.

He was urged to stay until the morning, and to this he consented.

The result was that a very happy and pleasant evening was spent.

When Nelly retired, Harold and Phillips entered into conversation respecting the past and the future, and many another important matter.

They were conversing respecting Master Roebuck, when a knock came upon the door.

Phillips did not immediately rise.

"Roystering gallants often so amuse themselves," he said. "There can be no one for me at this hour."

But when the knock was repeated, he rose.

"I will go to the door," he said. "Yet I shall be careful to keep the chain on. One can never be too cautious in these days, Harold."

"Nay, indeed ; we can never tell where that villain Blood is. If he fancies that Master Roebuck has left the country, there is no telling what he will do."

Downstairs went Phillips, while Harold, turning down the light, looked cautiously from the window.

Of course, he could not see who was at the door, but his sharp eyes detected three or four men peering round the corner of an opposite house.

At once he crept to the head of the stairs to listen.

Almost as soon as Phillips opened the door he recognised his visitor.

"So, then, it is you, vagabond ?" he said. "What is the meaning of this? Is it your intention still further to insult me ?"

"On my soul, I deserve all the reproaches you can heap upon me," said Collins ; "but I am not here to insult you. Heaven forbid! You may not think it, Master Phillips, but it is only this day that I have discovered that what I sold you was not wine. And it might have remained undiscovered on my part until Domesday, only the man from whom I purchased it, when the worse for drink, confessed it. I am here to refund the money."

"Your honesty does you credit, Master Collins," said Phillips.

Collins did not notice the sneer.

"Whatever people may think of me," he said, "I always endeavour to do whatever business I undertake in a straightforward manner."

"Something is wrong here," thought the shrewd Phillips, "but I cannot understand what it can be."

Aloud he said—

"It is but right that you should refund the money, and it is but natural that I should accept it."

"To be sure. If you did not I should feel very uneasy in my mind."

"One moment. I will see if my wife has gone to bed, and then you can enter."

So saying, and seeing that the chain was all safe, Phillips ascended.

As he did so, Harold retired into the room.

"Have you heard what has passed?" asked Phillips.

"Every word. What *is* the man ?"

"The biggest villain unhung, or, perhaps I should say, one of them. There is some trick here, Harold, but at present I cannot understand what it can be. He sold me what I supposed was wine, but which turned out to be water. Now he pretends that he has only just learned the trick played, and wishes to refund the money.

"I know him too well to believe that. From what a friend has told me, the trick he played off on me is quite a common thing with him."

"Depend upon it, he has been sent here by someone, and the idea is to gain admission. He is not alone."

BY COMMAND OF THE KING; OR, THE DAYS OF THE MERRIE MONARCH.

"'DON'T SHUDDER AT ME, NELLY—DON'T SHRINK FROM ME,' HE CRIED."

No. 11

"I feel that it is possible he has friends not far off."

"I am sure of it, for chancing to look from the window, I saw three or four men lurking beside one of yonder houses. They are evidently on the watch to ascertain whether he succeeds in entering the house."

"Then there is no longer any doubt. What do you advise me to do?"

"Say your wife has gone to bed, and admit him, then leave the rest to me."

"But what are really your thoughts about the matter?"

"I will tell you plainly. They are that this trick is being played with Blood as the chief. It is probable that he intends to strike Roebuck and I through Nelly."

"Ay, ay, the double-dyed villain! But look you, Harold. This is a secret panel. Behold!"

As he spoke he touched a tiny spring in the woodwork just behind Harold, and a panel sprang upward.

"There is a small hole just here," said Phillips, "and through it you can see what is going on. Then, behind the panel, you will find a rather large knob. With your hand on that, you can have the panel open in an instant."

Harold, snatching his pistols from a sideboard, where he had placed them on his arrival at Phillips' house, darted through the panel, which at once descended.

The whole of the above conversation had been so rapid that but very little time was occupied.

Phillips descended.

"My wife has now retired," he said, "and you may enter. You see, she has a very great objection to visitors at such an hour, and rightly, too."

"I could not get here before," replied Collins. "As you are aware, I sometimes have to travel many long miles."

"True, true. Now follow me quietly, for more than one female sleeps here, and, as you are probably aware, females have sharp ears. There is another thing. Neither my wife nor anyone else knows how I was taken in, and I have no desire that they should."

As he spoke, Phillips unfastened the chain and admitted Collins, who was overjoyed at the easy way in which he was earning the promised reward.

Phillips conducted him to the room upstairs, and produced a bottle of wine.

Pouring out a small, silver gobletful, he handed it to Collins, who, wishing him health, drank the wine with much relish.

"Of course," said Phillips, "I will give you a receipt in full for the money."

"That is all I desire, and, as the hour is so late, if you will make it out at once I will pay you the amount."

Phillips went to a cabinet to get pens and paper.

While he was searching for them, Collins produced a short, heavy bludgeon, and crept towards him.

In a few seconds he had reached him, and he had raised the bludgeon to strike, when he was seized by a powerful pair of hands and flung violently to the floor.

With a furious yell he half-rose, to find his face within a couple of inches of a gleaming pistol-barrel.

Harold's quick action had certainly saved Phillips from receiving a fearful blow.

Collins was instantaneously cowed.

He made no further attempt to move or to speak.

And yet, concealed about him, were a couple of pistols.

The fact was that, like scores more of his class, he was a thorough coward.

"Put down that bludgeon, you brutal wretch," said Harold.

Collins threw it aside.

"You have been caught very nicely," continued Harold, "and, when you leave here, it will be in company of a few officers of the Fleet. You came here, no doubt, to commit a robbery, but I can prove that murder—"

"No, no," interrupted Collins, terrified at the idea of being arrested, for he well knew the sentence he would get if tried; "you are mistaken. I will turn king's evidence."

"Ah! you will, will you? Against whom?"

"Against the man who sent me here."

"Very well. That may do you some good, to be sure. But I warn you that you do not leave here until we have ascertained that what you tell us is correct. If it prove true, you shall go."

Collins thereupon told them of how he and his companions had been engaged by "Captain Gletton."

"Describe him," said Harold.

Collins did so.

"No doubt about it," said Harold. "it is the murderer, Blood   And he is close here?"

"He is."

"With your three companions?"

"Yes; within a pistol-shot of this house."

"Soh! I thought I was not mistaken," said Harold. "And you were to come here, obtain admission under false pretences, overpower Master Phillips, and then signal to your companions?"

Collins nodded.

"A very fine scheme indeed," continued Harold, "but, thank heaven, it has proved abortive. And what is the signal to your companions?"

"Two low whistles."

"Now, listen to what I say. Captain Gletton, as you call him, is, as I have said, Colonel Blood. He has offered you the sum of fifty guineas to assist in the carrying out of his scheme, Now, if you agree to do as I tell you. I will give you double that amount. I have not the money with me at this moment, but Master Phillips will pay for me."

"Certainly," said Phillips.

"I agree," said Collins, "on condition that nothing happens to me or my friends."

"That I promise. But I warn you that if there is any treachery, I will leave no stone unturned to hunt you down and bring you to justice."

"There will be no treachery. After all," he added, with a grin which made Harold shudder with disgust, "he is no friend of ours."

"Go to the door, give the signal, and, when Blood comes up, tell him that you are entirely successful, and that Phillips has been overpowered. Add that you dealt him such a heavy blow with your bludgeon that he is lying on the floor unconscious. That is how he will appear on your re-entering the room. You quite understand that?"

"I do."

"I shall not be seen on your entry, but I shall quickly appear."

Collins descended, and Harold instructed Phillips to lie upon the floor in such a way that it would appear as if he had been suddenly stricken down.

In a few seconds Collins' whistles were heard.

Then, before two minutes had passed, footsteps were heard ascending the stairs.

Blood was the first to enter the room, and Harold, who saw him distinctly through the little spy-hole, stared hard indeed as he saw how elaborately attired he was.

"Soh!" said Blood, "you have done well, Master Collins. And in consideration of the help thus afforded, I will not object to you and your comrades helping yourselves to whatever you please. Then we must see to the girl. Is the old man much injured, think you? Not that it is of any importance, of course."

He then approached and bent over Phillips.

At the same instant Harold crept from the panel, noiselessly approached him, and, suddenly throwing his arms about him, put his knee to his back and threw him.

Blood snatched a pistol from his belt, and with a terrible oath, fired at random.

The report of the shot was followed by a wild yell, and Collins, leaping high into the air, fell dead.

The three men, terror-stricken, turned and fled down the stairs like the wind.

Harold was too sharp to give Blood the chance of firing again.

Snatching his sword from its sheath, he held the point of it to Blood's throat.

"Take this pistol from his belt, Master Phillips," said Harold.

Phillips fearlessly did so.

As he placed it on the table, a woman's face peered in at the door.

It was Mistress Phillips.

"In heaven's name," she said, "what has happened?"

"Tell us quickly," said a low voice behind her.

It was Nelly.

The shot, of course, had alarmed both of them.

"All is well," said Phillips, hastily; "retire, I beg of you. An outrage has been attempted, but, thanks to Harold, it has been completely frustrated."

"Let Mistress Phillips dress herself," said Harold, without moving an inch or even lowering his weapon, "and let her immediately proceed to the Watch-house in Smithfield. Give the officers my name, and tell them to bring strong fetters."

"You hear?" said Phillips. "Be quick."

"Whom have you there?"

"The murderer, Blood."

"The Virgin guard us! is it possible? Come, Nelly, come. Assist me to dress—quick."

"So, Colonel Blood," said Harold, "we are once again face to face! Well, I will put you in safe hands this time, be assured of that."

"You had me at a disadvantage," growled Blood. "Let me get up, and you will see—"

"Dog! remain where you are, or I will instantly pinion you to the floor. You cowardly wretch! Well, I will now use my best endeavours to put an end to your career. There are plenty of witnesses against you, and I will be one of the principal. Would you like to know how the tables were turned on you?"

"I can guess, and, though I did not fire at him purposely, the man who betrayed me is dead."

"Had he lived, it is probable that the hangman would have claimed him."

"Look you," said Blood, after a brief pause, "let me rise, and I will fight you fairly."

"Liar! when *did* you ever fight fairly?"

"Well, if you will not give me the chance of fighting, will you allow me to go if I give you particulars as to why—"

"Silence! I do not desire to converse with you at all."

Blood, with a smothered curse, now remained silent.

But he had his sword beside him, and keenly did he watch for the chance to draw it.

But none came.

Harold never took his eyes off him once.

Mistress Phillips ran off to the Watch-house, and, in less than ten minutes, returned with four of the officers.

They were in a state of wild excitement.

To be able to say that they had arrested no less a person than Colonel Blood was something.

They had brought with them not only the strongest fetters they could find, but also rope.

Moreover, each was heavily armed.

"This man," said Harold, "is Colonel Blood. I command you to arrest him, convey him to the Watch-house, and see him placed in a strong cell by himself. On no account place anyone with him, and do not remove his fetters. I am Sir Harold Harcourt, and will be responsible for all that is done."

"Wait a moment," frowned Blood, as the men advanced. "Upon what charge am I to be arrested?"

"The present charge is breaking into a citizen's private house."

"That I did not do."

"What you did amounts to it. But many terrible charges will be preferred against you, monster, do not fear as to that."

The four men completely disarmed Blood, put him upon his feet, and, placing his arms behind his back, put the irons upon his wrists.

For still further security, they tied the rope round and round the upper part of his arms.

Had he been possessed of the strength of six men, he could not have broken his bonds.

It was fortunate for him that he was arrested at such an hour, when the streets were deserted.

Had he been taken through the streets in the daytime, when the apprentices were about, there is no telling what would have happened to him.

Knowing only too well the character of his associates, the officers made him proceed at a swift pace, and in a quarter of an hour he was secure in one of the cells.

CHAPTER XXIX.

HOW BLOOD GOT OUT OF THE WATCH-HOUSE AND PROCEEDED TO CAMBER-
WELL—OF WHAT OCCURRED AT "ROCK HOUSE," AND HOW, AT LAST,
VENGEANCE OVERTAKES MISTRESS DARMLEY.

ONCE again Colonel Blood was to be lucky.

Fettered though he was, and placed in the most secure cell—a very violent prisoner being taken out of it to accommodate Blood—the wretch did not despair of being able to strike a blow for liberty.

But he certainly little dreamt that the chance of freedom would absolutely be "flung in his teeth."

When Mistress Phillips went to the Watch-house, which was one of the largest in the City, and knocked upon the low, massive, nail-studded door, she was answered at the wicket by a man of the name of Foulchard, a tall, sullen-looking fellow of about fifty, whose scarred face told the tale of many a wound.

He, after a brief parley, admitted her and conducted her to the chief officer.

Being curious, he remained to listen to what was said, and he started when the name of Blood was mentioned.

Then, as he returned to the wicket, a peculiar grin spread over his face, and he muttered—

"Ho, ho! singular, to say the least of it. I made certain he was out of the country. Well, this is most excellent, or it *will* be, no doubt, if he is not searched, for I never yet knew Blood to be without money. If he should not have it in his pocket, it is concealed somewhere about him. I' faith! this is likely to prove a stroke of luck. We shall see."

He was at the door when Blood was brought in.

But, though Blood looked at him, he did not recognise him.

Yet they were old associates—very old associates indeed, as the reader will see.

When Blood had been safely lodged, the guard was changed, and one of the turnkeys and Foulchard were told to visit Blood at intervals.

This was exactly what Foulchard desired.

His turn came in less than a couple of hours.

A quiet chuckle left his lips as he threw open the door.

Blood sat in one corner of the cell, but he did not look up as the man entered.

"What ho, colonel!" said Foulchard. "What ho, my gallant Alsatian buck-hunter, how fares it?"

Blood looked up now, and Foulchard at once noticed the great alteration which had taken place in him.

"Are the turnkeys instructed to insult prisoners here?" asked Blood, with one of his black frowns.

"No, they are not *instructed*, but they can do very much as they like with a prisoner."

"Indeed! Well, you will find that you cannot do very much as you like with *me*."

"No! And why not? But we will not argue as to that. Do you *want* anything?"

"No, and be cursed to you!"

"Ho, ho! I know you *do*. You want to get out of *here*, Colonel Blood, eh?"

Blood's eyes flashed.

"Ah! times are altered with you, Blood, eh? So they have with me. I believe the world must have turned upside down lately, or I should not be here. I can remember the time when I and a man who was feared in every direction, even by the king, used to make a journey to various parts and well line our pockets. I can even remember the first time I joined him. We went to a certain house at Camberwell—"

Blood started up. He was pale to the very lips.

"Tell me," he whispered, "who are you?"

"Dick Cannon," grinned the man, "but I am known here as Foulchard."

Blood immediately remembered the man whom, years before, had been one of his leading assistants.

He was one of the very men who had assisted in the murder of Nelly's father—Master Saville.

"Cannon—here?" said Blood. "I should as soon have thought of meeting the devil himself. Cannon turned turnkey? Ho, ho! this is indeed a huge joke."

"Ay, you may laugh, but you must remember I am not so young as I used to be. All men do not carry their age like you."

"Why, it is years since I saw you."

"It is, and a good many, too. But perhaps you don't remember what happened to me?"

"I think I do. You were arrested when acting contrary to my orders, tried, and sentenced to be hung—"

"Hish, hish! not so loud."

"But," continued Blood, "you contrived to escape. "That is about all I can remember."

"Well, I went to France, and joined a number of individuals there; but I never made anything, and, somehow, I always got the worst in a fight. I got so battered that, when I returned to this country, no one knew me.

"Then I thought I would try a *quiet* life, and so I applied at the Fleet for a place at one of the Watch-houses. I was put here after awhile."

"Well, and how do you like it?"

"Not at all. There is too much work and very little pay."

"How would you like to go back to France?"

"Very well."

"Assist me to get out of here, and I will give you enough to take you to France and live well there. I have plenty of money upon me now."

Foulchard did not hesitate.

"How much will you give me?" he asked.

"Fifty guineas. But I will tell you what: you can come with me, and, in two or three days, we will go to France together."

"Good! the bargain is struck."

"Can you get a file for these fetters? It will have to be a sharp one."

"A file will not be necessary; I can get the key. The chief turnkey is asleep in his room. I can get in and procure the key easily enough."

"Do so, then, as quickly as you can, and at the same time get some arms. If also you can lay your hands upon some wine—"

"Leave it to me; I will return shortly."

Foulchard returned in less than a quarter of an hour.

He carried beneath his cloak a pair of pistols, a sword, and a small bottle of wine.

As soon as the fetters were unlocked, Blood swallowed the wine without asking the man whether he cared for any.

Then he buckled on the sword and thrust the pistols into his belt.

"Free once more," he said.

"Wait!" replied Foulchard, "we are not out of the place yet."

"If anyone attempts to stop me now that I am armed," said Blood, "it will be a bad job for him. Now lead the way."

Foulchard crept noiselessly to the door, followed closely by Blood, and opened it.

The latter's foot was on the threshold when a sudden rush was heard.

Turning, Blood saw a man running along the passage.

It was one of the turnkeys.

Without the least hesitation Blood drew one of the pistols, cocked it, and fired.

Whether the man fell or not he was unable to say, for, seizing the wicket, he closed the door with a crash.

"Follow me at full speed," said Foulchard, who, turning, ran like the wind in the direction of Holborn.

Blood kept close to him, though he had great difficulty in doing so, for he was not accustomed to run.

As he flew along the silent streets, he thought of his horse.

But he knew it would be madness to attempt to get him, for, in a few moments, Smithfield would be searched from end to end.

The pair scarcely paused until the "White Horse" at Fetter Lane was reached.

It was closed, but Foulchard quickly obtained admission, being acquainted with the ostler.

"Listen to me," said Blood, as he took a handful of money from an inner pocket and gave it to Foulchard. "It is of the highest importance that I at once make my way to Camberwell, for I must see a person who is indebted to me in a large sum of money. Now, if you remain here until—"

"No, captain," interrupted Foulchard, decisively, "that cannot be."

"Why not?"

"I should not be safe here. Besides, it is not *fair* to leave me behind. I am prepared to run any risk with you, but not to stay here."

Blood considered.

If he persisted in setting out alone, he thought, it was possible that the man might prove dangerous.

Besides, after all, Foulchard might be useful, and certainly there was plenty of room at Rock House.

"Well," he said, "you shall go with me. See if you can get the ostler to lend you a couple of horses. Here is a deposit—a goldsmith's note for ten guineas."

Foulchard succeeded in getting the two horses, and he and Blood mounted and set out.

"We will go towards Blackfriars," said the latter, "and get a ferry across the river. And now mark what I tell you. We are going to the very house where, years ago, a certain affair you remember took place."

Foulchard stared, but said nothing.

"I will introduce you to the lady of the house," continued Blood.

"Not at this hour," said Foulchard.

"I think so; it is more than likely that she is up. You see, the lady I speak of has such an *easy* conscience that, like me, she does not require sleep. But let me impress this upon you : you must well support me in anything I may say."

"Rest easy as to *that*."

"You see, I am commissioned by her to slay a certain girl, and it was while I was attempting to do that that I was pounced upon. Now you will support me when I inform her that the girl is killed. But as we proceed I will still further instruct you. Be careful how we go, for I wish to avoid the Alsatians."

*   *   *   *

Half-past three had struck, but Mistress Darmley had not retired.

It was very seldom that she went to bed until the morning was well advanced.

But. on this occasion, she was not alone.

Seated beside her was a man of about thirty.

It was the Comte de Seine, her lover—or, at least, so she believed.

The Comte, whom she had first met abroad, was unquestionably a very handsome man.

He was tall and of commanding presence—in fact, he was considered to be a prince among French aristocrats.

Mistress Darmley was under the impression that he was the possessor of great estates.

It was one of the greatest mistakes she ever made in her life, for he was only an adventurer.

So also was her idea that the Comte was infatuated with her.

The Comte fancied that Mistress Darmley was the possessor of vast wealth in hard cash.

Certainly he had reasons for thus believing.

He had frequently borrowed—under the pretence that he did not want to "trouble his stewards"—large amounts from Mistress Darmley, and the money was always at once forthcoming.

"And so," said the Comte, "you are expecting a visit from this villain, Colonel Blood?"

"Well, he may arrive at any moment. He is not particular as to hours."

"And he, you say, has the audacity to aspire to your hand?"

"Yes," laughed Mistress Darmley, "such, Comte, is the case."

The Comte frowned.

"You have no reason to be jealous of him," continued Mistress Darmley, "for his appearance is frightful."

"From what I understand, he is engaged in a certain task on your behalf?"

"Exactly; and he is under the impression that my hand will be the reward of success."

"Ah! I see."

"But, as I have hinted, Comte, you can, if you think proper, render me a vast service, and at the same time rid yourself of a rival, a *dangerous* rival."

" Dangerous ? "

" Ay. Have I not told you that he is a man who hesitates at nothing? He would as soon murder you in the dark as he would drink a bottle of wine."

" *Pardieu !* I have heard of him to that effect."

" Well, Comte, if he is successful in the task I set him, you will take the first opportunity of picking a quarrel with him. You are an expert swordsman, and are bound to slay him."

" But accidents happen even to the most expert swordsmen. Besides, I have a decided *objection* to fight such a man."

" I can well understand that, but then, you must remember, it is for *my* sake."

The Comte bowed.

" I am ready to obey any orders you may give me," he said, " but, before you command me to pick a quarrel and fight this notorious ruffian, listen to my suggestion."

" Proceed, Comte."

" The man arrives, we will say—"

He paused as a knock came upon the door.

But we must, for a moment, return to Blood.

When he and Foulchard reached the lodge, they found Glendore standing at the door.

This surprised Blood not a little, and he told him so.

" Ay," said Glendore, " I ought to have gone to bed long ago ; and I should have gone, only madam said something seemed to tell her that you would come. Well, she is right."

" This is a friend of mine."

" He can enter with you."

" One moment, Glendore. Has anyone visited the mistress during my absence ? "

" Not a soul."

Glendore replied thus, but he was well aware of the fact that the Comte was in the house.

The reader, therefore, fully understands that Glendore was a man who would sell himself to anyone.

When the knock came upon the door, Mistress Darmley started up.

" Blood *has* arrived," she said, with some excitement, " you may depend on that."

She opened the door.

" *He* is here," said Glendore.

" Show him up."

" He has a friend with him."

" A friend ? Male or female ? "

" Male."

" Show both up ; and remember, Glendore, *strict silence !* "

Glendore smiled and bowed.

" They will remain here," added Mistress Darmley, " so you can put their horses in the stable."

Another five minutes, and Blood and Foulchard entered the handsome room.

The Comte, of course, had disappeared.

" My friend," said Blood ; " a very *old* friend. He has seen you before."

" Indeed ! When and where ? "

" Some years ago—in this house. He was with me when— But we will not talk of that now."

" Nay ; it is not necessary. I perfectly understand. He is welcome."

Foulchard bowed awkwardly.

Mistress Darmley invited them to be seated.

Then she placed wines and goblets upon the table, and tasted the wine herself first.

" I am trying to restrain my impatience," she said.

" Well," said Blood, " success has been mine, or, perhaps I should say, ours."

" And the girl ? "

" Is dead."

" Dead ! Are—are you *certain* of this ? "

" I should say so," grinned Blood. " But it seemed a pity, for she was very handsome. Many gentlemen would have been glad to *adopt* her."

Of this Mistress Darmley took no notice.

" Dead ! " she said, " but tell me all."

" We obtained admission to the house at Smithfield—"

" When ? "

" Three or four hours ago only."

" Ah ! then you came straight here after carrying out my orders ? "

" Not exactly straight, or we should have been here long before. But, as I was saying, we obtained admission to the house. I disguised myself, and pretended that I was a person owing Phillips money. He answered the door, and suddenly I felled him with a blow with the butt-end of a pistol.

"Then we entered the house. We soon found the room in which the girl was sleeping. The door was locked, and so we had to force it. The girl sprang from the bed and seized upon a fire-iron. In self-defence I was compelled to hit her. As she fell, my friend here passed his sword through her."

Mistress Darmley did not even shudder at this.

Blood continued—

"In a few hours you will be able to ascertain whether what I have said is correct or not," he said, "for you can easily send someone to Smithfield."

"I shall never forget the girl's look as I drew my blade from her," said Foulchard.

As he spoke, he half drew his sword from its sheath.

Mistress Darmley noticed that the blade was covered with blood.

She thought it was the blood of the girl she had sentenced to death, but the fact was that, on the way to Camberwell, Blood, thinking that a gore-stained weapon would have some effect on Mistress Darmley, had told Foulchard to pass his sword through the body of a goat they came across.

"You have done well," said Mistress Darmley, "and are entitled to a handsome reward."

For some time they sat talking over the affair, and then Foulchard, much to Blood's satisfaction, was conducted to a bedchamber by Glendore.

"Now," said Mistress Darmley to Blood, "claim your reward."

"Was that not agreed upon ? What better reward could I have than your hand ?"

"It is yours as soon as your statement is verified."

"Good ; and I again say that we shall get on well together. Of that I am certain. But I now ask you to do me a favour."

"Name it, and if it be in my power I will grant it."

"I have, in the care of a well-known goldsmith, jewellery to the value of some thousands. I should like to obtain them from him on purpose to present them to you. For the sum of five hundred guineas I can redeem them."

"It is a large amount, but I think I have it. I will see. If I have, you are welcome to the money."

"And now for a little advice."

"Proceed."

"It is this : that you, as soon as possible, prepare to go abroad, for, as soon as Master Roebuck discovers what has been done, he will hunt you down. We can go abroad together, and I can take you to a place where Master Roebuck, with all his cleverness, will fail to find you."

"Your advice is good. Yes, I must go abroad. But I will see whether I have got the amount you require. I should much like to be the possessor of some valuable jewellery."

"So should I," thought Blood.

Mistress Darmley rose.

"I shall not be long," she said.

"Good !" chuckled Blood, as she swept from the room, "all goes well. Pah ! what a fool even the cleverest woman is ! How a man, good at hatching up a few lies, can deceive her ! Ha, ha ! a few hours' rest, and then, hey ! for Greenwich. On the road I can get rid of Foulchard, and then take a vessel to the coast of France. There I must remain some time."

Meanwhile Mistress Darmley, instead of proceeding to her private room, passed into a small room on the next landing.

There sat the Comte.

At once Mistress Darmley related all that Blood had said.

"Do you believe that he has killed the girl ?" asked Mistress Darmley.

"It is more than likely, of course ; but, on the other hand, it is probable that he has told a pack of lies. Still, in any case, there is no doubt that you would be much safer abroad than here."

"Yes, I think so."

"You possess this girl's fortune ?"

"Yes."

"Is it a very large one ?"

"Very large."

This was, of course, a deliberate falsehood.

It *was* a large one at one time.

but Mistress Darmley now possessed but little of it—it had been squandered.

"Realise as much as you can," said the Comte, thinking of himself, "and I will take you to one of my castles. There no one can molest you."

"You are *too* good, my dear Comte. I am sure it is not necessary for me to say how delighted I shall be to accept your offer. With you I would go to the end of the world."

"Very likely," thought the Comte, "and when I had pocketed all I could, I should be delighted to *leave* you there."

Aloud, he said—

"Now listen to the suggestion that I was about to make a little while back. But now that the man himself is here I can add to it. Let him have plenty of wine, and have him taken to a bedroom some distance away from his friend. When he has fallen off to sleep, I will enter the chamber. You understand that?"

"I do—at least, I think so."

"It is easy enough. He will trouble you no more. You will be near me, for your presence will nerve my arm."

"Comte, if you despatch that man, you will indeed be doing me a great service."

"You may depend upon it that I will despatch him. I prefer to do that than fight him."

"But his companion? What shall I say to him?"

"*Ma foi!* it is easy enough. You will say that Blood received five hundred pounds; that you thought he had retired to his room, but that, instead, he departed. In that your man can confirm you."

"Excellent! Comte, I did not think you were so clever."

"You will give Blood the five hundred, for we can take it away when he is dead. Now go at once to him, or he may leave the room to ascertain what has become of you."

Glendore, as we have seen, conducted Foulchard to a bedroom, and, having seen him within it, he at once left the house to go to the lodge.

The bedroom to which he had conducted Foulchard was at the top of the house, and therefore on the floor just above the room in which sat the Comte.

Foulchard was just about to retire, when he heard the rustle of a dress.

Creeping from the room, he saw Mistress Darmley.

Another few seconds, and he heard voices.

Thereupon he descended the stairs and listened at the door.

But only for a few moments.

What he heard caused him to descend to Blood.

He found that worthy—apparently very much satisfied with himself—in the act of drinking a goblet of wine.

But Blood quickly put it down when he saw Foulchard's scared face.

"What is it?" he asked, in hoarse tones, for it struck him that the wine might be poisoned.

"Hush!" said Foulchard. "Captain, she told a lie. There *is* someone else in the house. He is a foreigner, that I can tell, and he is planning with the lady to kill you in your sleep. Be cautious; drink no more wine, and above all, sleep not. If you do you are a dead man. And remember, captain, I shall recognise your whistle."

All this he said with the speed of lightning, and before Blood could recover himself sufficiently to ask him any questions, he was gone.

"Ha!" muttered Blood as he resumed his seat, "so *that* is it, eh? Good! I am on the watch. He can't be wrong? No, he is right. So no wonder her precious ladyship is so long. A foreigner is here, eh? Who the fiend can he be? No matter! I am on my guard."

When Mistress Darmley entered, she found him in the act of replacing a goblet upon the table.

But he had not drunk from it.

"After a long search," said Mistress Darmley, "I have found the amount, and here it is."

"Many thanks," said Blood, as he placed the money in his pocket. "In but a short time I shall have the pleasure of placing the jewellery in your hands. But now, as I am so tired, I will go to bed. A few hours' rest, and I shall be able to discuss anything."

"Shall I summon Glendore?"

"By no means. I can, with the aid

of yonder taper, find my way to my bedchamber. *Au revoir*, madam. Soon, doubt it not, we shall be working hand-in-hand."

"True ; and, to tell the truth, I shall be glad when the time comes."

"We will go abroad, and there, in some sunny clime, we shall be happy indeed. A good-night to you."

"Good-night ; and may sound sleep dispel all your weariness."

Blood took the taper and retired.

"The *fiend!*" he muttered, "the double-faced wretch! Yes, Foulchard is correct ; I can see murder in her eyes. But who can this foreigner be? A lover, I'll be sworn."

"The fool!" hissed Mistress Darmley, as Blood retired, "the idiotic hound! And what a fool he must take *me* for, when with scarce one question, I hand him over the sum of five hundred pounds. Little does he dream that, in but a short time, it will again be in my possession.

"And now to wait one hour. I would the Comte were with me, but, as he thinks it best we should be apart, in case Blood takes it into his head to promenade the house, why I must be alone."

For a little while she paced the richly-carpeted floor lost in thought, but at last she seated herself in one of the great armchairs, and in that, in a few minutes, she dropped off to sleep.

But suddenly, and before twenty minutes had passed, she started up.

The room was in darkness, and the peculiar smell which pervaded it told her that the lamp had burned itself out.

She felt her way to the table, where she knew she would find a flint and steel.

But scarcely had she reached it, when a bright light of a circular shape appeared on the opposite side of the room.

So startled and alarmed was Mistress Darmley, that she was unable to move or utter a sound.

Gradually the light became larger, until at last the frame of the picture she had cut to pieces with her dagger was distinctly visible.

Just as suddenly as the light, a figure appeared within the frame.

It was the outline of Master Saville.

The figure stretched out its hand towards Mistress Darmley, and these words fell upon her ears—

"*Vengeance at last!*"

Mistress Darmley, with a low cry, staggered back and fell insensible beside the chair from which she had just risen.

There she remained until the Comte, lantern in hand, stole into the room.

"*Pardieu!*" he muttered, "what means this? Dorothy, Dorothy—awake, awake—the hour has come! *Bon! Elle se frotte les yeux.* She wakes."

Mistress Darmley looked wildly around her.

"It was true!" she whispered.

"True! *What* was true?"

"The vision."

"*Diable!* You do not say this house is haunted?"

"No, no; but I—I—thought—"

"Think not. You fell asleep, and tumbled from the chair to the floor. See that you do not do it again, or you may injure your beautiful face. Come —stand—so. Now, when again you dream, let it not be of visions. A little spirits will do you good Have you such here?"

"On yonder sideboard."

The Comte procured brandy, and poured out a glass for Mistress Darmley.

Then, having swallowed some himself, he said—

"Let us no longer delay. Come—do you hold the lantern."

Mistress Darmley took the lantern, but the Comte did not notice that her hand trembled like a leaf.

"You will not use a pistol?" she asked.

"No ; it makes too much noise. I have my sword, and this."

And he took from its sheath a long, Spanish dagger.

"One blow," he added, "and he is a dead man Did he have plenty of wine?"

"Ay; he was partially intoxicated when he left me."

"That is good. We shall no doubt find him in a heavy slumber."

The pair left the room, the Comte being first, and they glided noiselessly towards the chamber occupied by Blood.

The only thing they thought of now was whether Blood had secured his door.

They little thought as they moved across the landing that a pair of eyes were watching them very closely.

Such, however, was the case, for Foulchard stood at the top of his staircase.

But he did not intend to move unless he heard Blood's whistle, for it had also struck him that Blood had secured his door.

But such was not the case.

When the Comte and his accomplice reached it, they found it ajar.

Gradually the Comte pushed it, until it stood nearly wide open.

Then Blood was seen.

There, only partially undressed, he lay on the bed, and, apparently, he was in a profound sleep.

He presented the appearance of a man who, while in the act of undressing, had been overpowered by the drink he had imbibed.

The Comte glanced significantly at Mistress Darmley, who smiled.

Then the Comte, drawing his long dagger, stole to the bedside.

His intention was to bury the weapon in Blood's heart.

He had raised it high over his head, the better to deal a blow which must instantaneously have proved fatal, when Blood, with extraordinary agility, jumped up.

He seized the Comte by the throat, and the next moment his sword, which had been concealed among the bed-clothes, had passed completely through his body.

At the same instant Blood's shrill whistle rang out.

Mistress Darmley, with a scream of terror, dropped the lantern and fled back.

Another moment, and a wild and fearful cry rang out ; then another and another ; and finally a heavy thud was heard.

Blood seized the lantern, which had not become extinguished, and ran along the passage.

He had not taken twenty paces when he came to a halt.

There, stretched upon the floor, a dagger buried deep in her body, lay Mistress Darmley.

She was dead, and Foulchard, pale and apparently terrified, stood over her.

"I made a mistake, captain," he said. "I heard your whistle, and ran down the stairs. Then I heard a rush along the passage, and thinking it was the man who intended to murder you, I, as I thought, pounced upon him. It was only when I heard her shriek, that I knew I had struck a woman."

" Don't alarm yourself," replied Blood, coolly ; " you have done well. She was quite as bad as the man I killed."

"What ! have you really killed the man ? "

" I have. I was all ready for him, and gave him a couple of feet of cold steel. But hark ! Here come the servants."

Yes ! the servants now made their appearance.

Each was only partially dressed, and their white faces and wild-looking eyes showed how terrified they were.

When they saw Blood and Foulchard, they were about to run back.

" Wait," said Blood, "and look here— at your mistress. She has beeen killed by mistake, it is true—but she deserved her death, for she was assisting a man, a foreigner, to murder me. But, being warned, I was prepared for them, and this is what followed."

The servants could only look at the speaker in amazement, and at the body of their mistress in horror.

They had never before seen Blood or Foulchard, and they did not know what he meant by a foreigner, the simple reason being that they had never seen the Comte.

" Come with me," continued Blood, "and I will show you the man who attempted to murder me."

But neither of the women moved or spoke until Blood, in a voice of thunder, repeated his request, accompanied by a threatening look.

Then they followed him, Foulchard bringing up the rear.

Blood requested the latter to search the Comte, but very little was found in his pockets.

There was, however, a letter from

Mistress Darmley, which convinced Blood that the man he had killed was Darmley's lover.

"Now," said Blood to the servants, "we are about to leave the house, and, as we do not wish an alarm to be raised, you will remain here for the present."

"In this room with a dead man?" cried one of the servants. "Oh! pray let us go. *Do* not be so inhuman."

"What I say I *mean*," scowled Blood.

Thereupon he locked the door upon them.

"Shall we wait to search the house?" asked Foulchard.

"Nay," replied Blood; "I am anxious to leave the house at once. Listen: it is quite evident that the man at the lodge was quite aware that this foreigher was here, eh?"

"No doubt about it."

"If he comes out, say nothing."

The pair then left the house, proceeded to the stables, and saddled and mounted their horses.

Foulchard was just about to dismount at the gate to unfasten it, when Glendore, who looked as if he had been asleep for some time, made his appearance.

"What, going, captain?" he said.

"Ay," replied Blood, in affable tones, "pray you open the gate."

"I thought you were about to stay the night?" said Glendore.

"I was—but—well, I've altered my mind. I shall be back soon, and then I shall not forget you. But I will give you now a few guineas, so that— But hark you—who is the foreign gentleman within?"

Glendore started.

Then he said—

"Foreign gentleman? I have not seen him."

"No? Well, I believe you. Here, take these."

Glendore came close to the saddle to take the money, when Blood, swift as the lightning's flash, snatched a pistol from its holster and dealt him a fearful blow on the head, felling him to the ground.

"Ho, ho!" he chuckled, "treachery must be well rewarded. He will have a singing in his head for years."

"I don't think so, captain," said Foulchard. "You've cracked his skull like an egg-shell."

"Served him right, eh?"

"Ay; he was too clever. But whither do we go now?"

"We will push on for a few miles, when, in the first place, we will seek some house where we can get a complete change of clothing, and burn what we have on now. Then we will find a hostelry, and, having rested a few hours, push on to Gravesend. Then, ho, for France! How does that suit?"

"Excellently well. And you *will* take me with you?"

"Assuredly."

"You will not, I am sure, captain, forget that, but for me, you would have been lying in yonder house with a dagger in your heart."

"Forget it? Never! You will soon see that I am not ungrateful."

Thus spoke the lying scoundrel, when all the time he was thinking how he could get rid of the man beside him.

CHAPTER XXX.

HOW TITUS OATES, BY HIS INGENIOUS LIES, OBTAINS ADMISSION TO A LADY'S HOUSE, AND HOW HE SWALLOWED WHAT HE PREPARED FOR ANOTHER.

To return to Titus Oates, for we shall now see what eventually befell him.

He remained beside the embers of the coach until morning was well advanced, when a horseman rode up to him.

Oates at once saw that he was some sort of servant, and, in the tones he knew so well how to assume, he begged him to cut his bonds.

The man at once dismounted, and did as desired.

"In heaven's name, sir," he said, "how did this dreadful calamity occur?

—for I see two or three dead men about."

"They were my servants," whined Oates. "Oh, that this *dreadful* affair should have happened! My men killed, my box of gold stolen, and my coach burned!"

"Tell me, sir, what occurred."

"I was attacked by robbers; my servants defended me, but were shot down. Then I was dragged from the coach, shamefully ill-treated, and my hands tied. Then they took my gold, and, as I have said, burned the coach. Lord! Lord!"

And Oates, pretending to weep violently, rocked himself to and fro.

"I sympathise with you most deeply," said the man. "Do you live far from here?"

"Ay, miles—near Epsom. Oh, that a minister of the Gospel should be thus shamefully treated!"

A minister! The man was most awe-stricken.

Oates, of course, fully expected the man to make him an offer of succour, and he was not mistaken.

"My mistress resides close here," he said, "and at present her son is with her. I will go and relate what you have told me, and I feel sure that they will offer you hospitality until you are able to communicate with your friends."

"I thank you sincerely. If you will do that you will confer a great favour upon me—a favour which I am not likely to forget."

"What name shall I say?"

"Parson Summers of Kingsbury, Epsom."

The man rode off, and was absent nearly half-an-hour.

When he returned, he was accompanied by another man and a spare horse.

"My mistress and young master," he said, "deeply regret what has befallen you, and offer you their house."

"I thank them from my heart," said the vile impostor and prince of liars.

"If," continued the man, "with our assistance you can mount this horse, he will carry you quietly to the house."

"Thanks, thanks. My blessing on you."

It was with difficulty Oates got into the saddle, for he was bruised from head to foot.

A quiet ride of a quarter of an hour brought them to a rather large house nestling in its own grounds, on the northern side of Kennington.

Oates was delighted with the prospect of remaining in such a place for a few days.

It was the residence of a widow lady of the name of Wendlow, who had been an invalid for many years.

With her was staying her son Charles, a youth of about eighteen; a smart, shrewd young fellow, who bade fair to be as accomplished as his late father, Maurice Wendlow, one of the most clever physicians who ever lived.

To him Oates was first of all conducted, and Charles, in a few words, bade him welcome.

Oates was profuse in his thanks, sending forth a perfect volume.

Charles took him and introduced him to his mother, who also bade him welcome, and told him to consider the house his home until he communicated with, and was relieved by, his friends.

The old butler then took him to a small ante-room, and provided him with refreshments.

He had received orders to supply the "reverend gentleman" with what he desired, and when Oates ordered wine, he placed it before him.

Never before, in all his born days, did that butler see a man eat and drink at such a rate.

It seemed as if he had not eaten a meal for a week.

The day passed away, but Oates saw nothing more of the son or the mother.

In the evening, when the butler came to light the room, he questioned him.

"Oh," said the butler, who was an exceedingly simple and unsuspicious man, "he is pursuing his studies in his room at the top of the house. To-night at ten he departs."

"Departs?"

"Ay; he goes to his college in London."

"Then he is a student?"

"Yes."

"Of what? The law, physic, or is he studying for the Church?"

"Physic. His father was a celebrated physician."

"Indeed! Well, I trust he will be entirely successful."

"He is already very clever, and his mother is justly proud of him He is particularly adept in the study of poisons, and in his room——"

Oates raised his hands in horror.

"For heaven's sake," he said, "don't talk to me of poisons. I cannot bear the sound of the word."

"You have, of course, heard of his father, Maurice Wendlow?"

"To be sure. He was a very wealthy man, was he not?"

"Wealthy? Very wealthy indeed, but he did not value it to any extent."

"Neither do I," sighed Oates.

"But his wife," continued the butler, "my mistress, is far wealthier than her husband. Why, you must know," he added, confidentially, "that my mistress purchased the whole of the costly jewellery which belonged to the Duchess of Dorset."

"Indeed!"

"Ay. She was pleased one day to show it to me, and my poor old eyes were dazzled indeed. Years ago, when quite a youth, I was connected with the Court, and it was there, and there only, that I saw anything like it—except, of course, in the Tower."

"Ay, ay."

"But my poor mistress will never wear it, for, as you have been told, she is a confirmed invalid."

"I should not have purchased it had I been her," said Oates.

The butler smiled.

Proudly, he said—

"Ah! you see, she had an object. She had her thoughts fixed on the future, when her son will marry his cousin."

"I see—I see. She intends, then, to make the young lady a present of these costly articles?"

"Exactly."

"Noble and generous lady! But I do sincerely hope, my friend, that she has placed them in the hands of a banker whose honesty is unquestioned. Latterly there have been rumours concerning many."

"She does not trouble a banker to take care of them," replied the butler; "she keeps them in her own room."

"Very wise—very wise. Hundreds of pounds' worth of valuables should be carefully guarded."

"Hundreds! Why, they are worth thousands."

Oates was pleased to hear this.

"How sad that your mistress should be an invalid. She can take no exercise?"

"None whatever."

"Alas, alas! Well, I trust she sleeps well, for to be denied that——"

"I am sorry to say that she does not sleep," interrupted the butler, with a grave shake of the head. "Half-an-hour at a time—that is all."

"Sorry indeed am I to hear it. But look you, my friend. Perhaps it may amuse your mistress if I converse with her for a time."

"I will tell her," replied the butler. "No doubt she will be very glad of your company, since Master Charles will be absent."

The butler withdrew.

Oates chuckled with delight.

"Good!" he muttered. "Poisons are upstairs, and the son will be gone. So be it. Titus Oates, you may yet enrich yourself before you set out for your *estate* in Buckingham. Ho, ho! here's to you.".

And the blackguard drank success to himself.

Not the faintest idea had he that anyone was watching him.

But a couple of pairs of eyes had been fixed on him for some little time.

On the left side of the room there was a secret passage.

At one time a door connected the passage with the room in which Oates was seated, but Doctor Wendlow, not liking the idea of such a thing, had it taken away and a panel inserted.

It was through an exceedingly narrow crack in that passage that the son and another gentleman had been observing Oates.

Charles had not been upstairs, as the butler had supposed; he had, for some considerable time, been in search of the gentleman beside him.

The fact was that, after some consideration, Charles thought that the "parson" bore a very strong resemblance to a description of the arch-hypocrite, Titus Oates.

BY COMMAND OF THE KING; OR, THE DAYS OF THE MERRIE MONARCH.

"GREAT HEAVEN, WHO ART THOU? SPEAK!' CRIED THE KING."

No. 12

The more he thought of it, the more the fact grew upon him, and at last he went off to find the gentleman who had furnished him with the description.

As soon as he saw him, he said—

"Yes, my young friend, you are quite right, much to my astonishment. It is certainly Titus Oates."

They listened to all Oates said to the butler, and understood perfectly his reasons for putting the various questions.

They also heard him muttering when the butler had withdrawn.

Then both crept from the passage.

"I do not advise you what to do, Charles," said the gentleman, "because you are clever enough to checkmate a man like that. But, for heaven's sake, keep your eyes wide open."

"I will tell you what I intend to do," said Charles, grimly. "I will give him rope enough, and probably he will hang himself."

In a few moments the butler returned, and informed Oates that his mistress would be very pleased with his company.

Oates nearly jumped for joy.

He was soon ready, and followed the butler to his mistress's room.

Soon afterwards Master Charles, cloaked, booted, and spurred, made his appearance, and took an affectionate leave of his mother.

Of course, he had not mentioned a word to a soul.

Mistress Wendlow was totally unconscious of the fact that she was in close proximity to one of the most dangerous men in London.

Then Charles took leave of Oates.

"I am exceedingly sorry you should have to take your departure," said Oates. "I would we could have had some conversation respecting your future. My advice is generally considered valuable, and I would willingly have given you all the advice I possibly could.

"But I wish you a safe and pleasant journey; and, above all, I trust that you will be very successful in the future."

Charles thanked him, and then set off.

The butler and other servants saw him come to the door.

Imagine their astonishment when he whispered—

"Listen to me. I am not going to London, and therefore my horse can be returned to the stable. I am about to remain here, because I have discovered that the man who calls himself a parson is none other than the notorious Titus Oates.

"Ay, you may well start and turn pale. Such is the case, and I am about to see what the villain intends to do. But not a word to your mistress; not a look, not a hint; and, above all, treat this scoundrel with apparently the greatest respect."

A couple of hours passed, and the servants, with the exception of the butler, had retired to their respective rooms.

But not to sleep.

Nay; they were anxiously waiting for what was to follow.

Oates had not once left Mistress Wendlow's chamber.

He "entertained" her with story after story.

At last Mistress Wendlow suggested that, since he had talked so much, a little wine would do him good.

"To be sure," said Oates. "I thank you very much indeed. But I cannot think of partaking of wine unless you share it with me. A little wine to a person in your health should be invaluable."

"Do you think so?"

"I do; and especially at this hour. When ill, I generally take a fair quantity of wine, and I find the effect beneficial, inasmuch as it sends me to sleep."

"Ah, if I could but sleep!"

"My dear lady, allow me to advise you. Try it by all means."

"I am afraid it would not send me to sleep. However, I will partake of a bottle of wine with you."

She stretched out her hand for the bell-rope, but Oates quickly hastened forward.

"I pray you do not disturb yourself," he said. "I will go below to the butler."

"Thank you—thank you. You are indeed very kind."

"By no means. It is a *duty*," replied Oates, quickly.

Thereupon he went out, quietly closing the door after him.

Instead of descending, he remained on the landing for some few moments, listening.

Not a sound was to be heard.

He came to the conclusion that the servants had all retired, so, taking off his shoes, he cautiously ascended the stairs.

Reaching the top, he saw a door opposite partly open.

Now, was this the son's studio, or was it simply a servant's bedroom ?

Having made up his mind what to say in the event of being confronted by anyone, he went to the door and peered in.

He saw at once that it was the son's study.

It was, in fact, a small laboratory, and a well-stocked one it was.

Ascertaining that no one was within, he entered, and rapidly ran his eye over the various bottles.

He knew quite enough Latin to make out the various inscriptions.

At last he placed his hand upon a small phial, and took it from its place.

Concealing this he left the room, and rapidly descended the stairs.

No sooner had he gone than one of the female servants came up from the next floor, proceeded to a huge chest, and unlocked it.

Charles Wendlow got out.

By means of a hole he had bored in the side of the chest, he had seen Oates' movements, and had watched him take the bottle.

A few words only passed between Charles and the servant.

There was no time for words.

Rapid action was what was wanted.

Charles took from the chest a long rope.

This he fastened to the window-sill, which, with the servant's assistance, he quickly mounted, and clambered down the rope to the ground.

He was too wise to go to the bottom of the house by the stairs.

Meanwhile Oates had entered the butler's room, and told him what Mistress Wendlow desired.

The butler, with much graciousness, produced his keys and went to the wine-cellar, from which he brought a bottle of the finest wine.

Then he brought out a silver tray, and a couple of small, silver goblets.

He offered to take the articles up, but Oates assured him that it was a pleasure to him to wait on a lady who had been so charitable.

Thereupon he ascended to Mistress Wendlow's chamber.

But, in the meantime, Charles had re-entered the house by a back door, and had made his way to his mother's room.

In defiance of his warning, the good lady uttered a cry of astonishment, and no wonder, but it was not heard below.

Charles rapidly told her all that had occurred.

On being informed that the supposed parson was none other than Titus Oates, Mistress Wendlow nearly fainted.

" Listen," said Charles, speaking rapidly. " From what I told you, you will understand that this wretch desires to possess himself of your jewellery, and he would drug you. Now, watch him closely, and, when he has poured out the wine, beg him, in your sweetest tones, to descend and ask the butler for a few cakes."

" I will do exactly as you ask me, my son. The vulgar impostor ! And to think that, but for you, I might have been dead within another hour ! You are indeed clever, Charles. But where will you be ? "

" Beneath the table here."

" Good ! I should be uneasy were you out of the room."

Against the wall was a long table, or, as we in these days would call it, a sideboard.

The front was fitted with sliding doors, so that any articles might be placed within it.

Charles got in and closed the doors.

He could see plainly enough all that took place in the room, although the keyhole was a very small one.

Oates, the tray in his hand, soon appeared, his bloated face wreathed in smiles.

" A task such as this, my dear lady, is a pleasure—a real pleasure," he said.

Mistress Wendlow smiled, nodded, and thanked him.

Oates placed the tray on the centre

table, and then drew a very small one close to Mistress Wendlow's couch.

Then he poured the wine in the goblets.

For a moment he had his back turned towards Mistress Wendlow, and, in that moment, he emptied part of the contents of the phial into one of the goblets.

This he placed on the little table.

"A thousand thanks," said Mistress Wendlow. "Did the butler give you some cakes?"

"Cakes?"

"Ay; I cannot drink wine very well without them. How foolish of him not to think of it."

"Don't mention it, my dear lady. I will fetch them."

"Why not ring the bell?"

"Nay, nay. I assure you it is not the least trouble."

He ran downstairs, and was back with the cakes in a couple of minutes.

But Charles had in that time *changed the goblets!*

"Mistress Wendlow," said Oates, who was dying to get at the wine, "I wish you every happiness."

And he drank off the contents of the goblet.

He turned to place the goblet down.

Then a great cry left his lips, for, standing calmly at the end of the table, was Charles Wendlow.

"Master Wendlow!" said Oates. "I thought you had gone?"

"I changed my mind, for I knew that no one would be safe in this house with the notorious ruffian, Titus Oates."

Oates slunk back.

It was of no use to deny that he was Titus Oates.

"Soh!" he said, "you have learned my real name?"

"Ay, and your intentions. But I have foiled you, Titus Oates. I changed the goblets, and you have partaken of the contents of the one you intended for my mother."

"No!" screamed Oates.

"I say yes. You have swallowed a drug that will make you insensible for hours and hours. In that state you will be taken from this house to the place where you were found, and there deposited."

Oates breathed more freely.

It was *not* a poison then—only a drug.

"Hand me the phial," said Charles, in stern tones.

As he spoke a deadly faintness seemed to seize upon Oates.

He staggered still further back until he reached a chair.

Into that he fell.

Charles came forward, and Oates handed him the phial.

The instant Charles looked at it his face became deathly pale.

"By heaven!" he cried, "I have made a mistake. This is not a simple drug, but a deadly poison, and you have taken enough of it to kill *three* men."

Oates leapt from the chair.

He opened his lips to speak, but no sound issued from them.

From side to side he staggered, and finally fell with a crash to the floor.

"The antidote, Charles," said Mistress Wendlow; "quick!"

"It is too late," replied Charles, gravely; "he is dead. I see now how the mistake came about. I changed the places of the phials, and, in the excitement consequent on the discovery that this villain was Titus Oates, I had forgotten it."

"He alone is to blame, my son."

"He has met a well-deserved end, mother, and his death, I know, will make the minds of many a man and woman easier."

"I cannot forget that, had it not been for you, I should certainly have been poisoned."

"Yes; there can be no doubt of that."

"What is now to be done?"

"We must remove the body below, and, as quickly as possible, inform the authorities of what has occurred."

The butler now made his appearance, followed by the female servants, and the body of Titus Oates was, with some difficulty, removed below.

We may here add that the authorities exonerated Charles from all blame in the affair.

Oates was buried at dead of night in an unconsecrated corner of Kennington Churchyard.

But his death, and the manner of it,

was kept a profound secret for many months.

When it became known, much satis- faction was expressed that at least one of London's greatest rogues would trouble peaceful citizens no more.

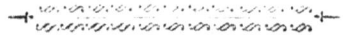

CHAPTER XXXI.

THE LAST ACT.

THE night after Roebuck saw Mistress Nell Gwynne safely to Lambeth, and then to Soho, he went to Smithfield, and there learned what had transpired.

"Thank heaven, Harold was here," he said, "for there is no telling what that villain would have done."

"He would have murdered the poor girl," said Phillips, "and afterwards, so that we could give no information, he would have murdered us. And to think that, so quickly after being taken to the Watch-house, he should have escaped."

"What! escaped? Do you mean to tell me that he has escaped?"

"Ay, sure enough."

"But in what way?"

"Bribing one of the turnkeys, who went off with him."

"Then he must have had plenty of money with him?"

"No doubt of it."

"Well, he is certain to meet with a terrible death, and probably before long. But I should like to see the villain hanged."

"I am no lover of such sights, but, on my soul, I would travel a long distance to see *him* hanged."

"From what has occurred, Master Phillips, you will see that Nelly is no longer safe here."

"You are correct. I am bound to say that you are *quite* correct. But Blood has never done this on his own account."

"Nay, it was on *hers*—the fiend in the shape of a woman, and of whom I have so often spoken."

Phillips held up his hands in horror.

"Is it possible?" he said. "I was not aware she was in England."

"Yes, she is. I paid her a visit, and you may guess what followed. She agreed to send me a certain message—instead she sends Blood. I pay her

another visit directly. If I— But see, who comes?"

A horseman was observed to be galloping towards the house.

The next moment he was recognised. It was Harold.

Roebuck rushed to meet him, and, with a joyous cry, the pair embraced.

"Something struck me you could not be far off," said Harold.

"Nay, but a short time ago I had no idea I should be here now."

"You are working on Nelly's behalf —of that I am sure."

"Correct. If I—"

"Pardon me, Master Roebuck," interrupted Phillips, "has not the time now come?"

Roebuck considered.

Then, after a few moments, he said—

"Yes; I will now tell them the story. Let Nelly come down."

Roebuck then told them the story concerning the murder of Nelly's father, and with which the reader is acquainted.

It is scarcely necessary to say that he was listened to with the greatest attention.

Nelly was profoundly affected, and sobbed bitterly.

As to Harold—he was loud in his expressions of admiration for Roebuck's conduct.

"You will see, Harold," said Roebuck, "that this is no longer a safe place for Nelly. But I have another for her. Here is the address of a lady in Soho; she is really in the employment of Nell Gwynne. She has consented to take charge of Nelly, and with her, until all arrangements are made for your marriage, she can remain in safety. As to the woman I have spoken of and Blood —leave them to me. I came here to-night intending to take Nelly to Soho, but now I shall leave that to you."

"And you? Whither do you go?"

"To Camberwell."

"I entreat of you be guarded. Blood may be there."

"No such luck."

"He *may* be there," said Phillips, "and half-a-dozen of his blackguards."

"I shall take someone with me," said Roebuck, "and then I should not care if the house swarmed with men."

"Who will you take?"

"Robin."

"Good!"

"And now I will bid you adieu for a short time. If I succeed in getting possession of Master Saville's will, I shall be satisfied."

"Roebuck, you will make me one promise?" said Harold.

"Name it."

"It is that you do not quit this country until we are married."

"Well, well—I will promise that."

"You must not forget, Harold," said Phillips, gravely, "that if Master Roebuck attends your wedding, he will place himself in great danger."

Roebuck smiled.

"I will risk all danger," he said, as he rose. "And now once more adieu."

Mounting his horse, he rode to Bartholomew Close.

He found the smithy door closed, but a light was burning within.

Standing in his stirrups, he looked through a little ventilator.

What did he see? This—

In one corner, seated upon a barrel, was Robin, fast asleep.

His huge arms were placed about Pipkin's little body, for the latter was also fast asleep in Robin's lap.

"It is a pity to disturb them," thought Roebuck, "but I must, for it certainly would not be safe for me to visit that house again alone."

Dismounting, he picked up a few stones, and then, getting into the stirrups again, he dropped one through the ventilator.

But it did not arouse either of the sleepers.

Nor did the second; but when the third was dropped, Robin slowly opened his eyes.

The next moment Pipkin awoke.

"Anything wrong, Robin Redbreast?" he asked.

"That's what I was asking myself," replied Robin.

"You have been dreaming, perhaps, eh?"

"Ay; I dreamt a number of things. And you?"

"Oh, I always dream."

"The *same* dream?"

"Nearly always. Shall I tell you what it is about?"

"Ay, do. Perhaps I can interpret it."

"I dream that I have grown to three times my present size, and that I am ruling a nation."

"Eh?" said Robin, opening wide his eyes.

"I say I dream that I am ruling a nation."

"Is that *all*?"

"That is all. Now, can you interpret it?"

"Easily."

"Well, do so."

"It means, first, that you will always remain at your present size; secondly, that it would be too much trouble for anyone to manufacture a nation small enough for you to rule."

"Pah! And now for your dream. Let me see whether I can interpret it."

"Ay, ay. Well, I dreamt that this smithy was turned into a dining-hall; that I was transformed into a baron—"

"A *baron*? Yes, go on."

"And that the place was filled with guests, all beautifully attired; and that servants were bringing up casks of ale, bottles of wine, and mountains of meat, and so on. Now interpret that."

"Easily. You dreamt that you were a baron?"

"Exactly."

"Well, the interpretation of the dream is that this smithy will be *barren* of everything of the sort."

"Too bad of you, Pip, on my soul! Now if you— Eh—what was that?"

"Somebody is throwing stones at us."

"They can't throw stones through the roof. If anyone— *Hillo!* Confound you! What's the meaning of it, eh?"

Another stone had fallen close to his feet.

Robin started up and threw back the door.

"What!" he cried, "Master Roebuck, safe and sound?"

"As sound as a bell, Robin."

"A bell is not always sound," cried Pip. "It is often like a human being."

"Oh! How is that?"

"A little cracked."

"Quite true," said Robin, with a sigh; "and I must have been a little cracked, or I should not have drunk all that red wine. Had I saved it, I should have had it to drink now. But enter, Master Roebuck. I need not tell you how welcome you are."

"I hope you are not very tired, Robin?"

"Tired! Nay; work is now somewhat slack."

"And the last he did," said Pip, "was never paid for."

"Not paid for?"

"Nay," said Robin. "When I took it home the man told me that he had no money. Yet he swore that, as soon as the work was done, he would pay. I soon saw that he wanted to get the work without payment at all."

"What, then, did you do?"

"Oh! I threw the work into the Fleet Ditch, and the man after it."

"It served him right; but it was a pity he did not guess what was likely to happen."

"That was, no doubt, because I trusted him before. But now, Master Roebuck, I see that you have need of my services. Tell me what it is I can do, and you may reckon upon me."

"And me," said Pip. "You may depend that Robin is not going without me."

"I would not *think* of such a thing," said Robin, and so seriously that Roebuck could not help laughing outright.

But his merriment quickly died out, and a serious expression took its place.

"I am glad indeed to find that you are such firm friends," he said. "I sincerely hope that you will ever remain so. Soon I shall leave you, and it is more than likely you will never see me more."

"Don't talk like that," said Robin, as he pressed Roebuck's hand. "Why go away, when, if you liked, you could be happy in England?"

"It must be so. Soon I shall be on the road to France. But do not fancy that I go abroad because I am afraid to remain in England. No; I have business of the greatest importance to attend to in France. It is business connected with my own life. But now, Robin, and you Pip, get ready. I am going to Camberwell, and, on the road, I will tell you a story, or, perhaps I should say, a series of stories, the principal of which will be concerning the house to which we are going."

"I must have my horse," said Robin Renard.

"Ay, and see that your pistols are all right. I do not know that they will be necessary, but it is as well to be prepared."

"I shall be ready in five minutes. Pip, don't stand staring there. Get ready, you imp!"

In a remarkably short space of time Robin was in the saddle, with Pip, as usual, before him.

The three then started for Camberwell, and, for the whole distance, Roebuck entertained Robin with the particulars now so well known to the reader.

"So, then," said Robin, as they reached the house, "you think it likely that Blood is here?"

"It is possible."

"Well, I trust he is. You will, of course, give me permission to do as I like with him?"

"Most certainly."

Robin picked up the hammer, which he had hung at his saddle, and significantly balanced it in his hand.

"His head may be as hard as a cannon-ball," he said, "but I'll swear I crack it with this."

Reaching the lodge, Master Roebuck shouted for admittance.

To his astonishment, a tall, dignified-looking man, clad in black, made his appearance.

"Whom do you seek?" he asked.

"First," said Roebuck, "tell me, who are you? Are you a new lodge-keeper?"

"I am lodge-keeper, sir," he said, "for just as long as the authorities desire me to stay here."

"Authorities! What authorities? Tell me what you mean. I am quite at a loss to understand you."

"Did you know the man who was lodge-keeper here?"

"Certainly. His name was Glendore."

"Good. I am glad we have found someone who knows him. Enter, gentlemen, and I will conduct you to him. Did you also know the lady of the house?"

"Yes; Mistress Darmley."

"You, then, are the very man the authorities have been waiting for."

"Don't enter," whispered Robin.

"There is nothing to be alarmed about," replied Roebuck.

Then he added to the man—

"Be good enough to tell me what has happened, for that something *has* happened I am certain."

"You are correct. Twenty-four hours ago or so a watchman, chancing to pass here, heard groans. Getting within the grounds, he found the lodge-keeper among the shrubs. He was in a terrible state from a wound on the head. The watchman asked him what had happened, but the only reply he got was 'Blood, Blood, Blood!' In a few moments he saw that the man was mad."

"Mad?"

"Ay, and there is no chance of his recovery. The watchman conveyed him to the house and put him in one of the rooms. Of course, he thought the house contained servants, and he shouted out; but getting no reply, he went over the house, and he came upon something which nearly robbed *him* of his senses.

"First he found a lady with a dagger buried deep in her body; next he came upon a gentleman, evidently a foreigner, who had been slain with a dagger or sword."

"Great heavens! At once conduct me to the place where—"

"But, sir, would it not be as well if you saw the bodies?"

"Are they still here?"

"Yes; the authorities decided to let them remain on the chance that someone would be able to recognise them."

"I will go with you," said Roebuck, in hollow tones. "Be quick!"

The man lit a lantern, and they ascended.

Upon the table in the beautiful sitting-room two bodies had been placed side by side.

Roebuck, forgetting what enemies he and Mistress Darmley had been, respectfully doffed his hat as he entered the chamber of death; so also did Robin, who would rather have walked a dozen miles than look upon a sight like this.

The man held the lantern over the bodies, while Roebuck examined them.

"Do you recognise them?" he asked.

"I do," was the reply. "This is Mistress Darmley, and this the Comte de Seine."

"A French count, eh?"

"Ay."

"Was he any relation to this lady?"

"I believe he was her lover. But were there no servants in the house when this discovery was made?"

"Not one. They had fled."

"That is indeed a pity, for they might have given valuable information. They fled, I suppose, because they thought it possible that they might be accused of this. Still they may be found. Was nothing found on the body of this man?"

"Nothing."

"And the lady?"

"Nothing was found on her, but in her bed-room, in a secret drawer of a *secretaire*, a number of papers were found, among them a will."

"A will?"

"Yes; the will of a Master Saville."

"Thank heaven for that. It was to obtain possession of that that I came here. But let me see the lodge-keeper. Maybe he will answer a question or two."

"I am afraid not. However, come to him."

They went below, and, in one of the kitchens, they saw the man Glendore.

He presented a shocking spectacle.

His head was heavily bandaged; his face was ghastly pale, while the upper part of his clothes were stained with blood.

Roebuck was shocked, while the sight so affected Pipkin that he was compelled to turn aside.

"Glendore," said Roebuck, in kindly tones, "do you not recognise me?"

The man stared hard at him for some

few moments, then his lips slowly parted, and he said, in hoarse tones—

"Blood, Blood, Blood!"

"There," said the man who had been placed in charge, "I told you so. That is all he says. He means, of course, his blood-stained clothes, but we—"

"Nothing of the sort," interrupted Roebuck. "I can tell you exactly what he means. He means that the *name* of the man who struck him what was evidently a fearful blow is Blood—Colonel Blood."

"Never!"

"Such is the case. Colonel Blood was in the habit of coming here to see Mistress Darmley."

"Do you think she knew who he really was?"

"No doubt of it."

"Then she cannot have been a woman of good character?"

"No, very far from it. But I can see I shall obtain no information from this man. Do you show me to Mistress Darmley's bedchamber."

Accordingly the man conducted them upstairs.

Carefully laid out upon the table in the bedroom were the articles belonging to Mistress Darmley.

But there was only one thing of any importance to Master Roebuck, and that was Master Saville's will.

It was an exceedingly simple one.

Save a by no means large sum of money to his wife, and a few legacies to servants, he had left the whole of his property to his daughter Nelly.

"I say again," said Master Roebuck, "that it was for this I came here."

"I am sorry that it is not in my power to allow you to take it away," said the man, "but if you will remain in the neighbourhood a day or two, and give evidence at the inquiry, no doubt the coroner will hand you the will."

"So be it," replied Roebuck; "I will remain in this house. It will be here that the inquiry will be held?"

"Certainly."

"If you stay here," said Robin, "I shall do the same."

"And I," said Pip.

"Until the morning you may remain," said Roebuck, "and then I shall want you to deliver several messages for me."

On the following morning several o the parish officials visited the house and it was arranged that the inquiry should be held on the following day.

One of the servants, it seemed, had come forward and volunteered to give evidence, and the excitement was intense in the neighbourhood.

Moreover, the news of the terrible tragedy had spread all over London, and many travelled from a distance to Camberwell merely to look at the house.

Master Roebuck had sent out his letters by Robin, while Pipkin remained with Roebuck.

On the following day—as was usual when a matter of public importance was being investigated—the doors of Rock House were thrown open, and the crowds battled with each other to be the first to obtain admission.

The first witness called was the servant, who told with remarkable clearness all she knew, and so minutely described Colonel Blood that there was no doubt as to the assassin.

Roebuck followed, and then, amid a deep silence, gave Mistress Darmley's history.

The result of the inquiry was that the jury returned a verdict of "Wilful murder against Colonel Blood and another," and expressed a hope that now, as there was so clear a case, Blood would be captured and put upon his trial.

Harold and Nelly, with Phillips, as well as a great many other friends, were present during the inquiry, and paid the greatest attention to all that took place.

When all was over, Harold and Nelly attempted to make their way through the crowd towards Roebuck.

But, suddenly, half-a-dozen men with drawn swords dashed into the crowded chamber, the first holding a paper in his hand.

"Hold!" he shouted, "do not let that man go."

And he pointed to Roebuck, who, with folded arms and entirely unmoved, stood against the table.

"Not let him go?" said the coroner. "Why?"

"What name has he given?"

"Roebuck."

"It is false. This man is Claude Duval, and I hold a warrant for his arrest."

"Dominic Evans, as I'm alive," muttered Robin. "I've a mind to wring his neck. But let him try to take him."

The coroner and the great crowd of persons present looked enquiringly at Roebuck, who, in a few moments, spoke.

"Yes," he said, "what this man says is correct. I *am* Claude Duval."

"I repeat," said Evans, "that I hold a warrant for your arrest. Have the goodness to peruse it."

At this Robin pushed his way through the crowd, seized the warrant, tore it in pieces, and flung them in Evans' face.

"Out on you for a paltry informer," he roared. "I have a mind to thrash you within an inch of your life."

"Peace, Robin," cried Roebuck; "this cannot be helped."

"What! you never mean to surrender?"

"It must be so."

Dominic Evans grinned.

He was thinking of the reward.

But his joy was short-lived.

Harold, at last, managed to make his way through the crowd.

Addressing Evans, he said—

"Do you hold the warrant?"

"I *did*, but that giant tore it up."

"Well, it was worthless."

"Worthless, sir? I beg your pardon, it was a genuine—"

"Read that," interrupted Harold, as he took a letter from his pocket and placed it in Evans' hands.

Dominic opened it, and his strange features underwent a very great change as he read the contents.

Having read it amid breathless silence, he doffed his hat, and, respectfully returning the letter to Harold, he said—

"Such authority cannot be disputed. Come, my men," he added, "let us begone."

"What!" cried Robin, "then you will not arrest him?"

"The letter produced shows that the warrants have been cancelled by the king."

At this there was a loud roar of applause.

"How is this, Harold?" whispered Roebuck, as he pressed our hero's hand.

"When your message reached Soho, I chanced to be at the house. When reading your letter, Mistress Gwynne herself came to the house, and I showed her the document.

"The instant she read it she became very grave, and expressed her belief that something was very likely to happen if you appeared at any public examination.

"You see how correct she was.

"After a little consideration she re-entered her coach and went direct to Whitehall.

"She returned in less than an hour, and handed me this letter. You will see that it is all in the king's own handwriting, and cancels the warrants for a period of three months.

"I thanked Mistress Gwynne, who merely said that one good turn deserves another."

Roebuck smiled.

"Mistress Nell never forgets a service," he said, "and for this I sincerely thank her. In three months from now many hundreds of miles will be between me and England."

"Mistress Gwynne," Harold continued, "requested me to invite you to her house in Soho, and she did not forget to mention that whatever friends you care to bring with you are right welcome."

"Good. I thank her, and will avail myself of the invitation. Robin, will you come with me?"

"With all my heart."

"I can promise you the best of wines, Robin," said Harold, "and the finest baron of beef you ever tasted."

"He will be all right with the *baron*," said Pip.

"Well, then," continued Harold, "let us at once leave this house. This is Nelly's property, it is true, but she can never live in it."

"Never," said Nelly, with a shudder.

The whole party left the house, and at once journeyed to Soho.

At the house there they received a hearty welcome from Nell Gwynne herself.

She requested all of them to remain as long as they thought proper, and the contents of a well-stocked wine-cellar were placed at their service.

* * * *

A month after this our hero and Nelly were married at the pretty church of St. Giles', when all our friends were present.

Immediately after the ceremony Master Roebuck bade them a final farewell, and, amid general regret, at once took his departure for Gravesend, *en route* for France.

At Gravesend he learned that Blood had been seen in the neighbourhood with a man whose dead body was afterwards found by the roadside.

He had received a bullet in the brain, and no doubt Blood was the assassin.

But Roebuck never again came face to face with him.

We may add that Roebuck never again returned to England. Nothing was heard of him for twelve months, when Harold received a letter from a French priest, saying that "Claude Duval" had succumbed to a fever contracted whilst nursing a friend.

But, a few months after this, it was said that Claude Duval had again visited England. Harold sought him out, and found that it was not his old friend, but a man who thought fit to assume the name of Duval. He was eventually hanged at Tyburn.

After the wedding, Harold and his beautiful wife went on a visit to a friend at Oxford. On their return to London, they proceeded to their own residence.

Our hero soon afterwards got Robin appointed to a position as one of the chief farriers to the Court.

It is needless to say that this suited Robin admirably, and that, in a short time, he made heaps of friends.

Pipkin became Harold's secretary, and right well did he fulfil his duties.

He was always beautifully dressed, and, consequently, as proud as a peacock.

But he never forgot "Big Robin."

Scarcely a day passed but what he paid him a visit, and much amusement did the two cause.

Harold rose high at Court and in the Army.

His opinions were highly valued by all, including some of the most skilful statesmen of the day.

He obtained the reward due to him at last, for he was made a peer of the realm

"By Command of the King!"

THE END.

NOTE.—For further particulars of the many extraordinary crimes committed by Colonel Blood, see "DARK DEEDS OF OLD LONDON," by the Author of " By Command of the King," " The Man of Mystery," &c., &c., which contains also full accounts of the Great Plague and Fire of London, including a graphic description of the burning of Old St. Paul's. The Work may be obtained of any Bookseller in the Kingdom, or direct from the Offices, 173, Fleet Street, London, E.C.